FRACTURED FREEDOM

FRACTURED FREEDOM

USA TODAY BESTSELLING AUTHOR

SHAIN ROSE

Page & Vine
An Imprint of Meredith Wild LLC

This is a work of fiction. Names, characters, places, and incidents either are the product of the author's imagination or are used fictitiously, and any resemblance to actual persons, living or dead, business establishments, events, or locales is entirely coincidental. The publisher does not assume any responsibility for third-party websites or their content.

The author acknowledges the trademarked status and trademark owners of various products referenced in this work, which have been used without permission. The publication/use of these trademarks is not authorized, associated with, or sponsored by the trademark owners.

Copyright © 2023 Shain Rose
Cover Design by Bitter Sage Designs
Editing: The Word Faery and KDProofreading

All Rights Reserved.
No part of this book may be reproduced, scanned, or distributed in any printed or electronic format without permission. Please do not participate in or encourage piracy of copyrighted materials in violation of the author's rights. Purchase only authorized editions.

Paperback ISBN: 979-8-9877583-8-0

Note on Content Warnings

As a reader who loves surprises, I enjoy going in blind with each book. Yet, I also want to give my readers the opportunity to know what sensitive content may be in my books. You will find the list of them here: www.shainrose.com/content-warnings

To all the good girls who know they're going to Heaven ...
But want to feel the heat of Hell first.

And to Krista who believed I could ... so I did.

TWO WEEKS BEFORE LOSING IT

From: Dante Reid <Dante.Reid1@us.mil.gov>

To: Delilah Hardy <Lilahsreading@gmail.com>

Lilah,

You wrote me all that ten minutes after I sent my email off to you. You must type a mile a minute now. Sorry I'm not responding faster. Missions here are in full swing lately. I've been going out at night and then sleeping all day. We only have a few computers, and people wait in line to use them. Tell the families I say hi, and when they bitch about me only emailing you, tell them you're the one who writes me most.

I hope you're doing well. The last time I heard from your brothers, they said you were named valedictorian. Those fuckers are so proud of you, even if they don't tell you. I know their asses are probably drinking away their lives in college. And probably TikToking or some shit. I don't get any social media here, so I don't know what's going on. Either way, take it from me, you're the best baby sister they could have.

Your sister has been writing me while she's in juvie. It's going to be all right for her. Time in juvie will get the drugs out of her system. She's strong like you. You're twins after all.

Come to think of it, you always had a little bit more fight in you. Remember the time you crashed your bike on the way down that massive hill? What the hell were you trying to prove again? We all knew that bike had no brakes. Your brothers probably set you up to get in trouble since they were always complaining you were too well-behaved for your own good. Damn, I was scared when I saw that car swerve and knew you couldn't brake. But you didn't cry when I carried you the whole way home. Makes you stronger than Izzy. Her ass would have been bawling.

Anyway, I don't type as fast as you. I'm getting hounded to get the fuck off here.

Tell everyone I love them, except that asshole brother of yours. You wondering which one of the four, aren't you? It's because every single one of them is an ass.

See you soon, Lilah.

Remember to breathe to seven, huh?

Dante

***

From: Delilah Hardy <Lilahsreading@gmail.com>

To: Dante Reid <Dante.Reid1@us.mil.gov>

Dante,

Well, now I'm taking it as a challenge to write you back quickly. I can't sleep anyway. My last final is tomorrow, then I'm freaking DONE with my senior year. And did I tell you I finally made my decision? UCLA it is.

It's far, and my mom is mad, but it feels right. I'm supposed to spread my wings and do something with my life, right? Why not fly across the country and do it myself? You're never in one place long. :-P

Things are still weird with Izzy gone. It's calmer, sure, but I miss her. And I feel her pain. I know it sounds dumb, but I do. She's struggling, but I know she'll get through it. She just needs our support. Mom and Dad telling her that I'm doing so well isn't helping, and my brothers are all gone, along with you. She was too close to you all, maybe, and fell into the wrong crowd after you guys graduated, since we were stuck still in high school. She needs people when I don't. So, I'm happy she can write you sometimes while she's in there.

Anyway, weird that you don't have any social media ... or maybe better. I can't be on it much with studying anyway.

That bike should have had brakes and I'll never forgive my brothers for that.

Get home soon!

I took seven breaths today and still miss you,

Lilah

CHAPTER 1: LOSING IT

Delilah

"What the ever-loving fuck, Delilah Hardy?"

I winced when he used my full name in that tone, but technically his dick was already all the way in. So, officially, I wasn't a virgin anymore, even if he decided to stop now.

"Just keep going." I wiggled, trying to adjust to the pain. I told myself I wouldn't gasp, but I'd ended up yelping when he'd thrust in. I mean, he was huge. Dante had been about two times the size of me when he'd moved in down the street ten years ago. I'd been eight, and he'd been thirteen. Now, he was twenty-three and had grown to maybe even triple my size.

I'd known his dick was going to be massive. Still, I couldn't trust anyone with my virginity but him.

Dante might have been my older brother's best friend and my twin sister's partner in crime, but he'd been my hero ever since I could remember. Over the years, he'd chased down guys who stole my bike, beaten up someone who made me cry, carried me home when I hurt my ankle, and most importantly, never overlooked me.

His eyes always found mine at family gatherings when he was home on leave. I got hugs from him and little animal carvings from around the world.

When he'd texted me that he was home and had a little present for me, I knew it was the only time I'd ever have to make something happen with him. I was going off to college, still firmly holding my v-card unless I gave it to him now.

And the timing was perfect.

All my brothers were off to college, raising hell on their own university campuses all summer. Izzy was still gone, and my parents had their annual two-week summer road trip.

I heard him breathing hard, felt the way his large hands gripped my hips to stop my wiggling beneath him. "Fuck. Fuck. Fuck." He let out a slow string of curses, and his forehead fell to mine. It was his only movement, like he was scared to shift us at all down below. "Shit, Lilah. Why didn't you tell me?"

"How exactly would that conversation have gone, Dante?" I opened my eyes just to narrow them at his piercing emerald ones. Jesus, he was so damn hot. That hard jawline was flexed to the point it would cut my skin if I rubbed my hand across it. I bit my lip before I continued. "'You want to come over and take my virginity? I'm about to go to college, and every guy has avoided me since I stepped foot in high school except you. You always know just how to make me feel special. So could you just do me a favor and take that pesky v-card of mine?'"

His neck strained, and I saw his pulse point going a million times a minute. A sheen of sweat coated his tanned skin. "Would have been a great introduction to what we were doing tonight."

"'K, well, sorry. Can you finish me off now or what?"

He shook his head over and over before he started to slide out of me, centimeter by centimeter. I squeezed my eyes shut. If he stopped now, this would be the most embarrassing experience of my life, and I'd had more than one. Most of them revolved around my four brothers picking on my twin sister and me. Dante was normally there alongside them, trying to rein in their asshole ways.

Still, this would be it. And wouldn't this be just a great way to remember my first time? I dug my nails into his firm ass. "We're already here, right? Can't we just try to enjoy it instead of stopping?"

"Just try to enjoy it?" His stare widened. "I'm going to hell for the fact that I drove here to hang out with my best friend's little sister. Instead of going home, I got seduced by her and didn't even take my time stealing her virginity." He proceeded to crawl off me and mumble to himself, "Should have used a condom."

"What for? I obviously don't have an STD and am on the pill. We went over this." I pushed myself up onto my elbows to glare at him.

God, he'd gotten ripped while overseas. Every muscle was defined, nooks and crannies of pure heaven covered in tattoos. The switch in his schedule had been just lucky enough for me to get him to myself instead of having my brothers fly home to see him. Military leave was only fourteen days long, so we all tried our best to be around when he came back.

This time, though, I hadn't alerted them that Dante had stopped emailing. It was normally an indication that he would be home soon, and Dante didn't call any of us beforehand either. His arrival times were classified and, quite frankly, getting in touch with my family was like playing a game of Whack-A-Mole.

When Dante texted me that he was home, my idea snowballed.

I was home alone.

And bored.

And horny.

When he showed up with my favorite steak tacos from the

food truck down the street and a tiny lamb the size of a quarter carved out of wood, I practically jumped him right there. He knew how much I loved those little animal statues. When he pulled me in for a hug, he whispered "Syria." He wasn't supposed to tell me where it was from, but he always did.

He'd brought me one every single time he came back to visit. And every time I squealed. My family thought it was just my innocent love for animals, but it was mostly my love for him.

I should have had those tacos with him and sent him right home. Instead, we watched *The Sound of Music*. It was a staple in our house. My mom played the movies she liked and that was a favorite. We all knew those songs by heart, and I think it was a sort of comfort for Dante. He sighed as the first song started and I smiled up at him on the worn leather couch of the family room.

This was where I normally felt most secure, sort of like when someone hands you an old blanket and you know exactly what it was going to smell like. Except my mind was racing with the ideas in my head, of how I would seduce him, of how his muscles already felt so good up against my arm.

When I laid my head on his shoulder, he petted my dark waves like it was nothing. Even then, my heart skittered around. When the sixteen-year-old in the movie sang about how innocent she was, I sang right along with her. He glanced down at me, his dimples showing with his smirk, and I was a goner.

I swear his eyes roved over my whole face and lingered on my lips.

It was then or never, so I did what I never would have before.

Our lips touched and it was like we both sighed into what we'd always wanted.

Or at least I think we did.

He didn't feel awkward or uncomfortable. It felt like my mouth belonged on his.

The kissing turned to making out and our cautious touches turned to heavy petting. He pulled away for a second to rearrange us on the couch, pulling me into his lap all while he murmured the reasons why he should leave.

"Shit, you're Dom's little sister," he said

"So? A lot of guys have little sisters. Is that all I am to you?"

"No, of course not—but you're too young."

"Eighteen's too young for you? I'm sure other guys wouldn't mind me being eighteen," I challenged.

"Jesus, what other guys?"

"The ones I'll call if you leave me like this?"

I loved how he seemed to get bigger then, more possessive, more territorial.

"Don't goad me, Lilah. You're too good for all of them ... and for me."

"Good? Does this seem good to you?"

I'd straddled him then and tried my best to lose my innocent act and embrace my vixen side.

He'd cursed himself over and over, but he hadn't stopped touching me.

His guilt only fueled my libido. He'd always wanted to be the definition of best friend to my brothers, but suddenly his desire to be with me was stronger than even that.

"When we were making out, I asked if you were on the pill. That would have been the perfect time to tell me you were a virgin," he pointed out as he stood there, his dick still glistening from being inside me. My core tightened just knowing he'd been the one to do that for me.

"Yes, there were like ten perfect times to offer up that

information. I could have told you when we were getting undressed, when I texted you, when I kissed you during the movie. I obviously didn't want to."

He shook his head, the angle of his jaw tighter now than it had been even a second ago. Dante had self-control that coiled around his anger in a way I'd never seen before. I'd only seen him lash out when he was in high school, and that was if someone was making fun of one of our families.

No one did that much. Dante made sure of that.

We came from a family of six, but it was just his mother and him. You'd think our backup was good enough and that Dante couldn't afford to alienate others by beating up a guy for telling my brothers our family should go back to Greece. He did, though. Dante always stuck up for what was right, and he charmed the town into believing him too.

Even now, when he was supposed to be pissed at me, I didn't really worry. Dante was that kind, immovable rock in my life.

He sat back to stare at me. His green eyes popped against his sun-kissed skin, inquisitive and searching like I had the answer to some problem he hadn't figured out yet. I didn't move as we assessed one another. I lay there open to him for what felt like a whole minute. I didn't close my legs. I didn't even lift the sheet over me.

It was my last-ditch effort and although I felt the blush rising over my whole body, I had to try. I knew he was about to walk away, to tell me this wasn't right. I was his friend's baby sister, and I'd been the good girl all my life.

Still, we'd ended up here, and his eyes appeared hungry.

Or maybe I was imagining it.

"Jesus." His voice was strained as his eyes stayed glued to my body. "I'm not going to forget how that feels for a very long time, Lilah."

"Oh, God." That sounded like he was going to leave. I'd rehearsed what I'd do if he let me down easy, but being open to him made it worse. We'd already started. He was basically turning down a virgin, which meant my good-girl personality really had made me that inaccessible. I shut my eyes and tried to will away the look on his face that I was sure would be full of pity. "This is going to be even more embarrassing to remember if you don't just go now." I tried to scoot away and grabbed for the sheet, but he ripped it from my hands.

"Go?" he growled. Then his eyes narrowed as he cranked his neck to the side like he was preparing for something huge. "I'm not going anywhere. We're starting over."

"What?" I tried to scramble up the bed, but his hand shot out and gripped my thigh. Then his other big hand was holding my opposite thigh down, leaving my slit open to him. His hands were so close to me that I hissed at the contact, knowing that I was getting wetter and wetter.

"I'm going to make you come this way first, Delilah. I should have slowed way down before. Shit, I was excited." He licked his lips as his eyes roved over me. "I've been deployed for three months, and it's not every day the girl of some of my hottest fantasies sticks her hands down my pants."

His hands started kneading my thighs as I lifted a brow and whispered, "Fantasies? About me?"

"Last time I was home, you wanted a ride to school, and the whole damn time, you chewed your lip while your sister asked me about my time overseas."

I rolled my eyes. I remembered that conversation. Izzy was always bolder than me and had shamelessly flirted by asking him if he was getting tail.

"And you got that look in your eye—the one you have

now—like you were jealous and ready to do it better than anyone I'd ever been with. Were you?"

I lifted my chin. "You know I like to be the best at everything. I was valedictorian for a reason. And, honestly, I have a jealous streak a mile long from hearing all the stories about the women you've been with."

His head lowered, and I felt the graze of his stubble on my inner thigh. "It was never a competition between you and other women, Lilah. You know that, right?"

"What do you mean?" I whispered, my heart starting to race.

"Half of this year has been me trying to stop picturing you every time I jack off, and I was on the verge of avoiding all family parties so I didn't have to see how hot you look every time I show up. I swear you imagine fucking me every time you look at me too, little girl. Do you? Tell me I'm not crazy."

I raked my teeth over my lips, thinking this had to be a dream. It was everything I'd ever wanted to hear. I panted out, "You're not crazy. I was always thinking of what you and I would feel like together."

His hand inched up my thigh, closer and closer to my center. His thumb skimmed close to my slit, and he rubbed up and down right next to it. It was delicious torture, purely evil foreplay, and he knew it. He smiled at me and whispered, "Were you imagining me sliding my cock into this pretty pink pussy, Lamb?"

"Jesus, you can't call me that anymore. I'm not so innocent now."

"You still are. You always will be to me. You want me to own your virginity because you know it's not just about getting rid of it, huh?"

I gripped the bedding, trying not to grind my mound into

the hand that was so close to getting me off. "I ... I ... Dante, I don't know what you're talking about."

"Your first time isn't about you getting rid of your v-card with me, Lilah. It's about you remembering every second of it." One finger slid inside me fast, and his thumb hit my clit at the same exact time. I nearly bucked off the bed as I gasped. "Excited tonight, aren't you? You've been waiting for this, picturing my hand getting coated in how wet you are, rubbing this perfect clit just right."

He said everything as slow as he moved his thumb and finger. Agonizingly slow, with the exact amount of pressure that made me want to beg. "Dante, please. Oh God, please."

"Mm. You seem to know how to be a good girl now." The way he said it washed over me. Lately, I hated being the one who was always listening, always doing the right thing. Here, though, I loved it. "Begging so nicely. Being so good. Didn't think that was necessary earlier when you should have shared with me what in the hell was going on, though?"

My breath hitched when he pinched my clit as if to punish me a little, but the act zinged through my whole body and came out of me in a guttural moan.

"I didn't think ... Oh, God." My head fell back as his thumb rolled over me faster, working me closer to an orgasm that I knew was going to be mind-blowing. I tried not to lose myself and shout. Wrangling myself into being the controlled person I'd always been was much harder than I had anticipated. "I just need ... I need ..."

I clamped my teeth over my bottom lip and hoped he could figure it out. I was riding his hand now, my body begging him to finger me faster, harder, with more vigor.

His straight teeth showed as he smiled like he knew he had me wrapped around his finger, right where he wanted me. He did, quite literally.

"Bite that lip all you want, baby, but when I fuck you later, I'm going to bruise it so everyone knows it's mine. Might as well give it a rest and just scream what you want me to do to you. Scream and beg me for what you want. Want me to work your pussy so my hand is drenched in you? You want to drip down my wrist as you come for me?"

I nodded vigorously.

He growled, "This is only the first high you're going to hit with me, Lilah. I intend to have you come all over my face tonight too."

Jesus, I knew Dante was going to be good in bed because women flocked to him. He looked like a freaking GQ model, but his dirty talk was something I wasn't expecting. Nor was I expecting my body to respond so quickly. I was wetter than I'd ever been, and I got myself off all the time. I practically heard him moving that finger in and out of me. "Please ... this isn't normal for me. No one has gotten me this close. Just ..."

Suddenly, his fingers stopped. "Another man touched you?"

I met his gaze, and there was green fire there, burning like it wanted to blaze down every man that might have touched me. My nipples puckered at the sight of him. "Well, a couple tried to do things with me, Dante. It just never progressed."

Jealousy and overprotectiveness looked good on him. He rubbed his thumb harshly over my bundle of nerves. "How many touched you here? All from school?" His gaze flicked down as my breathing quickened, and his jaw hardened.

"I ... only two."

"Names," He commanded.

"Seriously?" When he lifted a brow, I shrugged. "Garrett and David."

He'd started his slow pace again and slid another finger into me. I rocked at the extra pressure in my pussy, and my eyes rolled back as he curled them into my sex.

"They put their mouths on you?"

"Dante! No, okay? I really don't want to talk about this right now." My body was arching, trying to get more from him. "I just— Please let me come. Please. Please. Please."

At this point, I knew he was holding my orgasm hostage. I gripped his wrist with both hands and tried to bear down on his fingers, but each time I got where I needed to be, he reduced the pressure.

"You sure no one's tasted *my* pretty pink pussy, baby?"

"You're deranged right now," I ground out. I should have been mad, but the words sounded so good coming from his lips. "Yes, I'm fucking sure. I swear it."

I rode his hand as he slid another finger in, then moaned when he increased the pace. His fingers were thick and long and calloused in all the right places. I was so wet he'd probably have to soak his hands for days to get my smell off them, but I didn't care anymore.

I clawed at his arm as I chased the orgasm, and then he leaned over me and licked my nipple before sucking it into his mouth. I moaned and whispered, "I'm so close."

"Then you better come, baby, because I intend to have you ride my mouth next."

The orgasm that ripped through me wasn't even ecstasy. It bordered on pain, but still so pleasurable. My whole body seized as I convulsed around him, and my pussy must have done exactly what he wanted because he swore low and then his head was between my thighs.

"Shit, Lilah. You're everywhere. All for me. You smell that? Sweet, hot, wet. I'm going to drink you for days."

I couldn't focus on his words. My orgasm was still exploding through me, shattering something of the girl I was before this moment.

He massaged my thighs and let me slide down from my high. It was like he knew I needed a minute, like he wanted this to be perfect.

When his tongue started exploring every part of me softly again, though, I didn't stay relaxed for long. My hands were in his short dark hair, scraping against his skull and my body was heating up fast, blush covering every part of me.

He grabbed a pillow and tapped my hip. "Lift your hips."

"What do you mean?"

"I have to put this pussy on a pedestal so I can eat like it's on a platter, baby. Then I'm going to fuck you at just the right angle. Make sure you remember who makes you feel this way." He dragged his finger across my sex, and I hissed. Then he caught my gaze.

"Dante," I whispered, already on the brink of another orgasm just from his words. "This is too much."

"This is just enough. You feel this?" His fingers were back at my entrance, and I whimpered as he slid two in and rolled them around. "You need to be good and wet for me. I want you dripping enough that I slide home without pain this time."

"Please. I can take you now. Please let me feel you inside me." I would probably regret how much I begged for his cock later, but I was beyond embarrassment. I was on the verge of becoming a whore for him if he wanted that. I hadn't felt anywhere near this good ever before. Not even when I got named valedictorian after working toward that for four years. Nothing could compare to this, and it made me want to work that much harder to get it. "Your cock will fill me up just right, Dante. Please."

"Fuck, that sounds good on your lips." He slid his fingers from my core and dragged them up to my mouth. "Want to taste yourself, pretty girl?"

I didn't even hesitate. I needed to show him I could suck my juices off not only his fingers but other things too. I wrapped my tongue around him and sucked languidly, taking my time tasting the salty and sweet arousal of myself and his hand.

"How do you taste, Lilah? As good as you smell?"

I didn't stop licking and sucking as I nodded. I made sure both fingers were clean as I slid my tongue in between them.

"That's right. It's too sweet and addictive to go to waste. Remember that. You understand? Because, damn, I won't always be here. I can't give you this all the time. I'll deploy, and you'll go to college." His expression suddenly went far away; I lost him for a second before he said, "Just remember what I said, Delilah. If you let another man near you, you make them get on their knees and praise that sweet pussy, got it?"

I was whimpering around his fingers at this point. I couldn't answer him if I tried.

He took his fingers from my mouth. As he dragged them over my neck, hovering over me, he murmured, "Remember the way I feel."

Then his tongue was moving over my body. Sucking my nipples, licking down my stomach, dipping into my belly button. He didn't kiss my mound, he freaking smelled it. "I'm never going to forget this scent, Lilah."

His mouth descended on me then. And I was never the same.

Dante made me a woman. One who was addicted to the way his tongue fucked me. I became an animal, dying in heat to ride him into oblivion. I scratched at his head, trying to draw my orgasm, or maybe blood. I wasn't sure which. Maybe

I wanted to mark him as mine, or maybe I needed his tongue inside me, thrusting in and out over and over again, as much as I needed my next breath.

He gripped my hips on that pillow as he brought me to another mind-blowing climax, and he didn't let me buck off it. He held me there even as I tried to scramble away, the sensation too much as I flew over the edge into what felt like a black hole of bliss. I heard him lapping at my come, and I relished it. I realized I was chanting his name as he crawled up over me.

"You did so good letting me eat you out, baby." He rubbed a thumb over my cheek to wipe away the tears I didn't even know were falling. "So goddamn beautiful when you let go, Lilah. Don't share that animal in you with the world. Keep it only for someone special."

"You?" I choked out as his dick nestled between my legs. I was losing myself, slipping away from us just being friends and sliding into wanting more, needing more, dying for more. "Please, Dante, for the love of all that is holy, screw me now."

He shifted the pillow underneath my ass and grumbled, "Pussy on a pedestal, right where it belongs. Don't wiggle off here, got it? I want to hit every fucking wall of that cunt and make sure it's wet just for me."

I licked my lips. "I want that too. Now," I emphasized.

He smirked but didn't make me wait. His length was bare as he nestled right back in between my legs. So thick and hard, I wanted to get a mold of him somehow. He worked the tip around my entrance, coating it with my come, and then he pushed in inch by delicious inch.

I moaned so loud I should have been embarrassed, but the man was smiling down at me as he watched me take him in slowly. He dragged a finger over my cheek. "This is how it's supposed to feel. Like you were empty without me, like you were missing a piece of you and I just found the missing part."

I let out a string of curses as I dug my nails into his ass, wanting all of him, knowing he was still holding back. I was greedy now, ferocious in my need to feel whole. Dante's dick was my oxygen, and I couldn't live without it.

"Slow, Lilah. Slow. Revel in it," he murmured in my ear. Then his hands were tweaking my nipples, and his mouth was sucking my neck hard like he needed to leave his mark on me too.

Didn't he know he was already marking my pussy, branding it as his as he stretched it to fit his size? "I'm so screwed for other men."

"That's right, baby. You wanted me. You got me here and hooked on you. You'd better be hooked on me too. Take it all, Lilah."

He thrust the rest of the way in, and I gasped as I spread my legs fully and met his motion with mine. Something feral and deeply suppressed snapped inside me. I had always been the good one, never stepped out of line, never screamed, never stayed out past curfew. I knew where the line of bad or overindulgence was, and I never got close to it. I barely drank, didn't do drugs, and had gotten straight A's. Yet here, with Dante, I lost the chains on my indulgent soul, the one that was selfish and not trying to please anyone else. I scraped at the skin on his back, wrapped my legs around him, and rode his cock like I could catch another orgasm.

He was up on his elbows thrusting in and out of me as he watched my every facial expression. "This is how I always wanted to see you—perfect Lilah all fucked up ... and down."

I bit my lip because I wanted that for me too. I'd wanted to let go for one night, and he'd given me that. "God, this is too good. How am I going to—"

He dove down to kiss me then, cutting off any talk of us moving on from the moment. I took in his pillowy soft lips, how they somehow still dominated and crushed hard against mine. I took in how his hands gripped my hips harder and harder, how the muscles in his back rippled, and how he smelled like sandalwood. When his thumb ventured over to rub my clit again, my spirit might as well have left my body, because I was flying around the sun, and when he pinched me, I combusted, burst, and flew right into that blazing star. The orgasm seared through me, left me burned, blinded, and completely raw for him to see me at my most vulnerable.

I screamed his name over and over and over. Somewhere in my haze, he got off too, his hands latching on to my hair as he bore down and emptied himself inside me.

His forehead fell to mine, and we were left panting against each other's mouths, breathing one another in and breathing one another out.

With one long breath, he murmured, "Remember, when you come this hard and get this wet, it means you're getting fucked right. Remember not to ever settle, Lilah."

It shouldn't have felt so right and so wrong at the same time. I know that now. I was caught up in a man when I was just an immature new adult. I shouldn't have felt like he was part of me, but he was my missing piece all of a sudden. And I couldn't fathom him slipping away like he had a minute later.

He gathered up the pillow from under me before I could even look at the evidence of us, then he laid the sheet over my body. "You're beautiful, Lamb."

Why did I want to tell him to stay right then? My whole mind screamed at me to do it, to tell him he didn't have to go, that I hadn't texted him over simply to give me numerous orgasms. That we could be more than just neighborly friends.

We'd gone past that, right? At least, I had. I wanted more of this, more of him.

"Dante, I ... My parents aren't home for another week," I stammered out, suddenly not sure where all this was going but sure I wanted him to stay.

"Lilah," he warned.

"I'm just saying. We could ... you know ... for the week. Nothing longer or anything." I shrugged, trying to act nonchalant while my heart beat a million times a minute.

He rubbed his head. "You know, I kept telling myself through all this that even though it's going to be over after this one time, I'll still have that card you gave me, that I'll cherish it for a very long time, even if you tricked me into taking it. Now, I'm not sure I'm happy with just the taste of you."

His words sent shivers down my spine. "When do you deploy again?"

"I don't know yet. But I'm here for a week at least. Then I'll fly back to base."

I clutched at my sheet. "Maybe I can see you again tomorrow?"

His gaze ping-ponged around my room and then outside like he was debating everything. "You're the only damn person I would risk my friendship with your brothers for. You know that? We have to do this right if we want to go further. Got it?" he asked as he started to pull his jeans on. He tucked his cock back in them and pulled the gray T-shirt over his abs. I salivated the whole time. "Delilah, focus."

My eyes snapped to his as they sparkled at me with what I knew was humor. He liked that I couldn't stop staring. "Sorry. Um, right. Like I said, the family's out of town. I have to pack for the dorm, so I stayed home, but the house is empty. We can hang out here."

"I'm proud as hell that you're going to that college, by the way. It sounds big. Ma said it's hard to get in there. Make sure you're careful. Keep your grades up."

"Right." I rolled my eyes. Didn't anyone care about anything but my grades? "I'll do that while I remember exactly what you told me."

"What's that?"

"That when I come as hard as I do with you, I'm getting fucked right." I lifted a brow. I said it to shock him and piss him off, mostly for acting like he could give me big brother advice after having his dick up my pussy before any other man had.

Yet, he didn't take offense. He stalked forward and bent at the waist to grab my chin and have me look up at him. "You better make sure of it. No one deserves you if they can't fuck you like me."

"Really?" I quirked my head. "What if I can't find that?"

"I'm starting to think I don't want you to." The muscles in his jaw ticked. Something in him shifted, a weight came down on us that I wasn't ready for. His eyes grew dark, troubled, and cold. "Before, I would have told you I'm the only one who deserves you, Lilah. Now, I know that's not true. But I have a week to make you know what it is you deserve."

"Before what, Dante?"

He shook his head and then pulled my bottom lip from my teeth where I was worrying over his words all of a sudden. Then he kissed me slowly and deliberately. There was no hunger anymore. This kiss was a goodnight one. When he pulled back, his green eyes were warm and full of charm again. It was a mask to fend off anyone trying to get something more from him. "Hey, tomorrow, be ready for me, huh?"

I nodded. "Ready right now."

"Don't tempt me. I have to get back before my mom gets

suspicious."

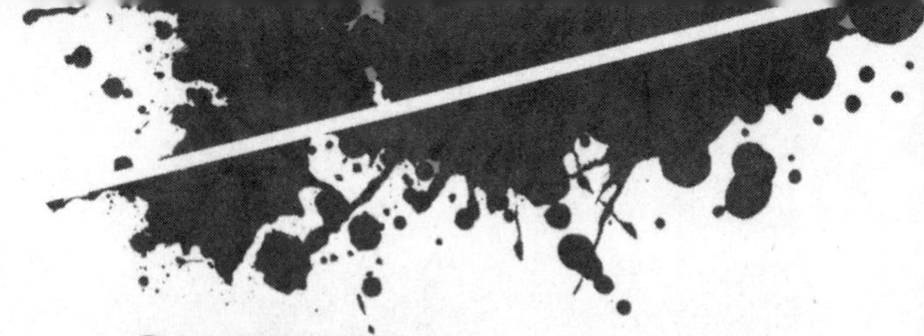

CHAPTER 2: TAKE BEST FRIEND'S SISTER'S V-CARD

Dante

It'd been a week.

One week of having her all to myself.

"Lilah," I whispered.

She murmured in her sleep and rolled over enough that the sheets lowered to expose her breasts to me. I'd marked them for probably the fifth time this week and didn't hesitate to run a finger over a bite mark.

I was going to hell. Not just the normal hell but the inferno. All the rings. Every fucking circle. My name was completely and utterly on point in this instance.

Dex, Dominic, Dimitri, and Declan were going to kill me. They'd fought off probably half the male population to protect their sisters over the years. I'd fought off the other half, and Garrett and David would be getting their ass beat by me, too.

Lilah was the town's angel. I'd told them time and time again. Those guys knew that.

Everyone did.

She was sweet and pretty in every way known to man. Her curls had been like Shirley Temple's until she was about twelve, and even then, her cheeks still got as rosy as the actress's when she was embarrassed. Her innocence shouldn't have been tainted by anything, ever. It was the one thing I'd looked forward to when I came home from leave, the way she'd blush when I gave her a trinket, or the way I'd get a shy smile when I said hello to her sitting quietly at a family birthday. Her only flaws were that her heart was too big, her fear too great, and her need to do right was too strong for us to be anything but friendly over the years.

Until we were more than friendly this week.

Damn, I didn't belong anywhere near her, but I'd been toeing that line for too long.

Our night together was probably bound to happen one way or the other.

I'd stared at Delilah for a whole fucking year in a way I shouldn't have. I swear, she turned seventeen and I saw her in a whole new light.

She'd always been an untouchable, beautiful girl, but I'd never considered anything more until she'd jumped in my car one day when I'd offered to drive her to school while on leave.

She'd turned seventeen that summer.

I'd been over in Afghanistan, graduated to Delta Force after being a Special Ops Ranger for three years. They'd psych-tested me, looked into my family history, and ran me through a physical that most rangers probably couldn't pass.

I'd aced everything.

Or their dicks were so hard after seeing my biological father's name on the file that they pushed me through. His mob connection and reputation as a sort of James Bond for the government twenty years ago made for a great story.

People didn't understand that the mob had been working with the government in some capacity for a long time.

No one had found my father since I was a baby. All we had

to show for him was a very nice farm and a small fortune in my mother's bank account. That and he left me DNA that gave me a knack for killing and having a precise shot. I didn't fold under pressure, I relished it. I didn't shrink from torture or pain, I inflicted it. But before all that, I'd lived a normal life. I grew up down the street from the big Hardy family, and I became best friends with Delilah's older brothers and her twin sister.

Then, I couldn't avoid the temptation of her, the lure of her soft smile, how she always smelled so sweet.

She'd enjoyed that way more than I anticipated. We'd been on orgasm three or four for her and still she'd come alive when I nipped that soft flesh.

She wasn't so innocent now. If the town knew, if her mother or her brothers or, God forbid, her fucking dad found out, they'd kill me.

I shouldn't have been proud of it. Yet, I relished this too.

Delilah Hardy had owned my heart, and now I owned taking her virginity.

She rustled in the bed where I watched her. I leaned in and gave her a soft kiss. "I think I love you, Lamb. I think you're the one thing I love too much to let go."

I wanted to think I had her heart too as I packed up to catch my flight.

We promised we'd write. I promised to find a way to tell her brothers and family. Just not now. It wasn't right to do it now when they'd flown home to see me, when I was flying out after just a week.

We promised we'd figure it out though.

We wanted to be together ... until I found out she didn't.

***

Two Weeks Later

From: Dante Reid <Dante.Reid1@us.mil.gov>

To: Delilah Hardy <Lilahsreading@gmail.com>

Lilah,

Sorry that I couldn't stay longer. I told you I would call, but I won't be able to for a while again. Missions got moved and I got moved up. I'm happy but pissed. I'm deployed again for a good while. You'll be at UCLA by the time I'm home.

I can still come visit, right? We won't have to sneak around there. I'd like to take you on a date or fuck you loud enough for the campus to hear.

You're going to tell the guys at that university that you have a boyfriend, right? Shit, I should have asked you while I was home. I didn't expect your brothers to fly in to see me. Everything happened so fast.

I have to tell them soon. Make it official.

Then, I'm thinking I need to send you a few shirts with my face on them, along with some pictures of me so that it's clear you're taken at that college of yours. I don't need some ripped surfer guy trying to steal my girl.

And you are mine.

That pretty pink pussy of yours belongs to me.

Forever and ever.

Count to seven over and over again if you're having a hard time catching your breath, Lilah.

Although, you breathing fast like I know you are now is one of the biggest turn-ons there is.

Write me back soon. I'm sick of missing you.

Dante.

* * *

From: Delilah Hardy <Lilahsreading@gmail.com>

To: Dante Reid <Dante.Reid1@us.mil.gov>

Dear Dirty Dante,

Jesus. It's what I have to call you now after that. Yeah, I'm moving to school in a couple weeks. I know you won't be able to email much, but I'll just reread your dirty emails.

They make me smile.

And breathe fast.

My brothers will freak out if you say a word and then they will hound me until you get back. Let's just tell them all when you're here. That way, they might be on their best behavior if we tell them in front of our parents or something. I don't know.

Or we don't have to tell anyone, because this doesn't

have to be what you want. It's okay that we had a fun couple weeks sneaking around, you know? I kind of tricked you into everything, and I don't want you to feel like ... I don't know. I'm just letting you know there's no obligations here. I appreciate you being amazing and don't want you to feel the need to keep this going just to save family dynamics or anything.

I'm not saying you're not being genuine, but you've never had a serious girlfriend, have you? Maybe you just never told me. Actually, don't tell me now. I'll get jealous. So many times while growing up I looked at you like you were freaking Superman, and every time I saw you with a Superwoman, I cried in my bed. I could get the best grades and do well in all my sports, but there was no way I was competing with some of the women you hooked up with.

I almost didn't come take care of the lambs and horses one summer because I knew you were going to have Willow over and she was freaking gorgeous. I'm pretty sure you taught her to ride one of your mom's horses that summer. I would cry in the stables about it.

How embarrassing. For her. Since I have you now.

Even so, I like to think I had a piece of you back then too. You still came to sit with me when a lamb needed a feeding and I loved that. Thanks for being there for me always. Thanks for being there for me now, even when you're not.

Let's see how it goes, but you can always come visit.

You know my number.

I breathed and counted to seven. Still miss you,

Lilah

* * *

Two Months Later

From: Dante Reid <Dante.Reid1@us.mil.gov>

To: Delilah Hardy <Lilahsreading@gmail.com>

I only got a second, Lilah.

Damn it's been a long time. I'm so sorry I haven't been able to write. I hope moving to UCLA went well.

You always had a piece of me, Lilah. You were my lamb, always will be. I'm sorry I can't write more, but you got all of me now.

Don't forget it.

Seven to heaven, baby.

Dante

* * *

From: Delilah Hardy <Lilahsreading@gmail.com>

To: Dante Reid <Dante.Reid1@us.mil.gov>

Moving in was great. UCLA is beautiful. I know you're

probably so busy. Don't worry about it. I've been busy too, and it's hard to get a moment to email. Let's just catch up when you get back. Hope you're well,

Lilah

* * *

From: Dante Reid <Dante.Reid1@us.mil.gov>

To: Delilah Hardy <Lilahsreading@gmail.com>

Lilah,

That email was short. And so sweet that it wasn't sweet at all. You're mad or hurt, and it's probably because of this damn place and the fact that I can't write to you. I gotta figure out something when I get back. It's been a shit deployment.

I'll make it up to you when I'm home.

* * *

However Many Months Later

Voicemail from Dante: I'm home. You didn't answer my call or my last emails. Guess that means we're done before we even got started. I have half a mind to go to UCLA and drag you out of that dorm room to ask you what's wrong. Your mom said you're fine though. So I hope UCLA is good to you. Seven to heaven, baby.

CHAPTER 3: GET ARRESTED

Delilah

"Don't say anything. I'm sorry, okay? Just don't say anything. I'll take the blame. It's my fault. It's all my fault," Izzy whispered.

When you see your own face mirrored back at you in complete fear, it's devastating. The hazel eyes that looked so much like mine were swimming with tears. My sister's dark wavy hair framed the frown on her heart shaped face, and then my heart dropped as they separated my twin sister from me. Tears sprang to my own eyes when she turned away.

We were on our own now and my brain wasn't processing what the TSA officer was saying. I saw his mouth moving, the way he took a breath and the gold badge on his shirt rose with his chest, and how he continued talking like he didn't really want an answer from me.

He'd made up his mind. I think I remember them telling us in Psych class that eight times out of ten, if someone comes to a conclusion or opinion about something, they'll find a way to justify it even when they know they're wrong.

This must have been how my sister felt every time she admitted she'd been to juvie. Or that she was a recovering addict.

My blood boiled for her. And then it felt like it stopped moving through my veins all together when my gaze darted around the room. Whatever she'd done, it was bad.

If she was going to jail, it wouldn't be like juvie. This would be worse.

This was real crime. At an airport, nonetheless.

I couldn't have her go alone. This was different than before. I saw her fear, I saw my baby twin sister try to take all the blame as they steered her away from me.

I glared over at the TSA officer. I made a decision right then and there. "Yes, it's my suitcase. And my sister doesn't know anything. I packed all of it."

If we both took the blame, maybe our sentences would be cut in half, right?

A better officer would have asked how many kilos, what drugs did you pack, and who asked you to do this. Right? They would have investigated further.

Did I know what it was that I packed? No. I knew my sister had a track record in our family of getting into trouble. She'd supposedly cleaned up. I'd backed her up over and over again, even when my mom called and said she didn't think it was a good idea for Izzy to visit me in Puerto Rico.

"Too many temptations and freedom when she's not home, Delilah." My mother's accent still carried through the phone after all these years. She'd slip back into Greek sometimes, and my father would chuckle because we all only understood about a third of what she was saying. We just knew we were in trouble when her native language flew out. "Haven't I taught you anything? You graduate from that university and you immediately start disobeying me. You should be in medical school, not traveling around nursing. You could be a doctor."

Reassuring my mother that I knew how to deal with my

twin sister would have fallen on deaf ears. I finally cut my mother off and told her this was my life. Plus I missed Izzy, and she was coming.

And now me taking the blame may have been my way of avoiding the truth, that mom was right and that my twin sister really did just screw us over.

She'd come for a weekend to visit me at my new nursing job. I'd only been there for two months, but I was trying my best to acclimate to a bilingual workplace and had just written up my ultimate bucket list. All on my own.

I was all on my own and embracing my very own life. Yet, she begged me to fly back to Springfield, our little town, with her for a couple days to visit family.

My baby twin sister had a knack for finding my weakness. "*The family misses you, Lilah. You went from UCLA straight off to nursing and you never visit. Mom cried the other night, I swear.*"

Was any of that even true?

"You want to admit to anything else?" He smiled wide, and I knew he'd probably pat himself on the back as he walked out of the interrogation room.

"I think I'll want to talk with a lawyer before I say anything else."

He sneered at me. "You're going to be in jail a long time, young lady."

I cleared my throat, trying not to panic. "I get to make a phone call, right?"

Like I had anyone to call other than my mom and dad. If I called them, they'd probably panic too. I needed a plan of action. My mom watched court TV and my dad worked most days marketing beer, but that was about all the knowledge I was going to get from them.

The TSA officer leaned forward and put his hands on the

table so he could look down at me sitting there, like I was the scum on the bottom of his shoe. "You're under arrest for the possession of cocaine and smuggling. It's a felony. You don't get your phone call yet. Now, hands behind your back."

Two other officers came in, like I was going to fight them.

Me. Delilah Hardy. Valedictorian of my high school class. I'd graduated *summa cum laude* from UCLA, for crying out loud. I'd never even so much as served a single detention in my entire academic career.

He read me my rights as I tried to suck in air and breathe it out slowly, methodically, and in the same rhythm.

The only person I knew to be calm in a terrible situation like this was a man I tried not to think about anymore. He was the reason I avoided going home. And yet every second I needed to take a relaxing breath, I thought of him. *Dante.*

He'd been sixteen when I was eleven and had locked myself in the dark basement of the neighbor's house.

"Let's count to seven, one breath out and one breath in, huh?" he'd said as he jiggled the lock. My brothers had left me, and Dante had found me ten minutes later, probably by hearing me hyperventilating.

We counted together. I heard the soft numbers rolling from his mouth, and by seven the door had opened for me to jump into his arms.

Seven was my number with him from then on. When they sent Izzy to juvenile hall for being high and stealing from a store while I was still in it, Dante and my brother Dom had been there to pick me up while my parents went to the station. We counted to seven. That time, I made him do it with me seven times.

I was probably going to have to count to seven about seven hundred times to feel better about this one.

Jesus. I was going to jail.

I wasn't ready for that. I'd taken this job after college that had delivered next to nothing of an experience. I found myself unfulfilled and completely scared that I would care about nothing my whole life, that I'd do nothing in it that would warrant someone looking twice at me.

I'll admit to having smoked weed once with my sister in the woods. And it had been through a freaking apple because we didn't have a pipe. We used a pencil to carve out a makeshift tube and bowl area to stuff the tiny bit of weed into. Honestly, my sister had done most of the work. I had sat there wide-eyed the whole time.

She'd graduated, obviously, to smuggling drugs and using me as a distraction since then. I'd graduated from nursing school. I was only trying to smuggle a good time out of my nurse gig.

I didn't know whether to feed my rage or my panic at that moment.

I was going to jail.

And I hadn't even done the goddamn crime.

* * *

"Bend over and cough."

Why did I want to cry right now? It wasn't like the woman was doing anything outside her job. Still, standing there naked and having to cough to see if I'd stuffed you-know-what you-know-where was degrading to say the least. I wanted to scream at the officer that this was a violation of my rights or my freedoms or my privacy or something.

I knew I'd be wrong, though. To them, I was a felon.

And they really believed I could have done it. I'd said as

much with my own mouth. I'd claimed the bags as mine, never denying the smuggled drugs shoved in shampoo bottles—lots of them. I wasn't sure what kind or exactly how much, but I was going to jail for it.

I didn't know when I would get to make a call or if I would find my sister in here with me. Had they let her go? Would she come for me?

My mind raced as I was handed a grayish-white sheet and a pillow. "Hold on to those if you want to keep them."

The clothing I put on was scratchy against my damp skin.

It was nothing like the movies. There were no calls allowed, no people I could talk to. I was sent to my cell, just given the number and pointed in that direction. A few women rolled their eyes at me and turned the other way when I nodded to them. Instead of engaging, I tried to keep calm and told myself, "One foot in front of the other."

I'd figure everything out once I knew where my new home would be. Tears sprang to my eyes at the thought. As I got to my cell, the white bars of the door were a stark indicator that this wasn't going to be a walk in the park.

To think I'd cried over things in my life before being here seemed trivial. All those tears seemed spoiled now. Is this how Izzy had felt all that time in juvie?

Helpless.

Alone.

Scared.

I was older, but the feelings were still there.

I sighed as I saw the empty mattress on the bottom of a bunk.

"If you're taking that bed, you better not snore," came a scratchy voice from above.

"I don't snore," I quietly replied, not sure if I should

introduce myself or just make clear what my cellmate wanted to know. I was a quiet sleeper. None of my siblings ever complained about sleepwalking or anything like that with me.

"Good." Her scrawny legs hung over the top bunk, and she swung them back and forth as she eyed me up. "Last girl here was loud as shit. Happy her boy got her out quickly. What you in for?"

I cleared my throat. "Um ... possession of drugs. I need to make a few phone calls."

"Good luck. Our bitch of an officer hasn't given us call time all day."

That's when I heard a laugh that sounded just like mine. I threw my stuff on the bunk and hauled ass out of my cell.

I rounded a corner and found her talking to another inmate. She laughed at a joke and seemed completely relaxed, her dark hair braided and hanging over her shoulder.

Izzy fit in everywhere, and here was no different. Somehow, she was gorgeous in the orange jumpsuit and happy to be the center of attention.

Her smile dropped off as soon as she saw me, though. "Delilah? What the fuck? Why are you in here?"

"What the fuck? What do you mean, *what the fuck*?!" My voice came out like a shrill bird squawking at something. She should have been happy to see me. I'd agonized over her being in here alone and probably sacrificed the next few years of my life for her. For family. And on the flip side, she'd put me here by her actions.

My turmoil whiplashed into anger fast. "Why am I here? How about why are we here?! Should we start with that?"

"I vouched for your innocence in the TSA office."

"Well." I cleared my throat. "I vouched for yours."

"You've got to be kidding me." She dragged a hand down

her face. "Oh my God."

"Um, you're welcome." My eyes bulged at her irritation.

"Welcome for what? I'm still here. What you said obviously didn't work," she scoffed.

"You!" I pointed a finger at her and took a step in her direction. A few women's eyebrows rose, and one even mumbled something about a catfight waiting to happen. I took a breath, trying to calm down. "You tricked me into coming back with you, and you were doing this."

"It's not a big deal. I'll get out in a few months. You need to get a lawyer to get you out sooner. Jesus, you won't last in here."

"Oh, this is a competition now? Who's the bigger and badder sister? You're so immature, Izzy. This isn't what life should look like." I sounded like my parents, but I didn't care.

She stared at me, her dark eyes hard. "I'm sorry I'm not good enough for you."

"This isn't 'good enough' for anybody. You smuggled drugs!"

"It was a one-time thing." She glanced around and then took my arm to hurry me into her cell across the way. "I'm done doing that stuff. I just got to get this one deal done. It's a long story, okay?"

"You said you'd cleaned yourself up," I whispered and shut my eyes in pain. She'd promised us all years ago. I thought she was doing better. Sure, she still hung out with people that weren't the greatest crowd, but who was I to judge?

"You don't understand. I'm clean. It's just—"

"You call this clean? You realize we all hurt when you do this, right? You realize Mom about died when you were sent to juvie. You couldn't stand, Izzy! You passed out on the damn sidewalk in broad daylight."

"That was years ago," she said quietly and looked away.

"And here we are today, smuggling drugs. Smuggling drugs, Izzy! You mean to tell me you're doing that clean?" I scoffed. "I vouched for you with the family. Mom even said she didn't want you to visit me here. You know that?"

"Well, Mom will never trust me."

"Rightfully so, I guess."

I saw the pain shine in her eyes, but then she covered it up with a couple blinks.

"I shouldn't have trusted you. I shouldn't have thought, 'Hey, we're sisters, we've been through it, and we got over it.' Screw that. You're an addict, and you've ruined this chance I got here. How am I going to fucking explain this to my boss? I'm going to be fired and ..."

The idea of it all was completely and utterly ridiculous, completely out of this world. I was in a jail cell, not even sure when I was going to be free again.

I leaned against a white brick wall for support and glanced around me. What if Mom and Dad couldn't get us out? We technically were guilty. I took another breath. No air came in.

Another.

No air.

I grabbed the metal railing of the bed to try to steady myself.

My sister jumped in front of me. "Breathe, Delilah. Breathe. In like this." She formed an O with her lips and sucked in, eyes wide on me like I should do the same.

I did.

Over and over again, we took one very big breath in and let it out as my heart and mind raced over every scenario. "I can't believe this."

"It's okay," Izzy murmured. "I have calls to make. Everything is going to be fine. Believe me. It's all going to be fine. Just go grab your pillow and stuff. Bring it to my cell. You can trade with my cellmate. She won't care."

I nodded and tried to will myself to move.

The tremor in my chin showed Izzy all she needed to know. "Okay, you know what? You stay here. Close the door behind me. I'll go get your stuff. What number are you?"

"Will that be what I'm reduced to here?"

"No. We're not going to be here long, okay? I just have to call Mom and Dad."

"Izzy, our bail hasn't been set. Our parents don't have money to fight this in court. You realize we could be here for years."

Yeah, she laughed like that would be insane.

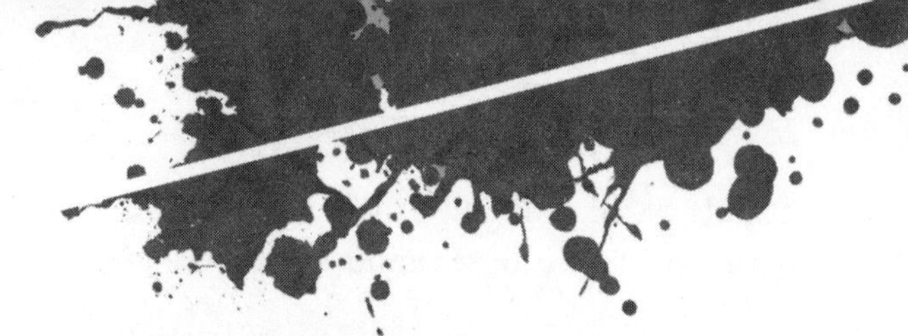

CHAPTER 4: GO TO PUERTO RICO

Dante

"So, we got a problem," Izzy grumbled, and her voice came out strained.

"No shit. You're calling me from jail." I chuckled and scratched my head, looking over another contract the government had sent that day.

"Right." I heard rustling and knew Izzy was probably trying to make sure no one was listening. "So, I can't go into detail, but ..." She cleared her throat. That was never good. Izzy and I had worked together long enough for me to know that when she hesitated, something was definitely off. "Delilah may be here with me."

"Delilah?" I whispered her name, confused. Yes, I worked with Izzy, and when I looked at her, I thought of her identical twin. But I'd learned not to dwell.

I'd *forced* myself not to dwell. She'd been the one that got away and the one I still considered dragging back to me.

When we sat in silence for another five seconds, the name bellowed out of me with rage. "Delilah? How the fuck does that happen, Izzy?"

"Well, you know I can't discuss that with you right now." She scoffed like I was an imbecile. Izzy didn't sugarcoat her attitude at all, and she really should have because this was beyond being the loose cannon that she sometimes was.

"You broke protocol."

"I didn't. Look, I can't talk about it. You know this." She sounded irritated.

I'd vouched for this girl time and time again. When those I worked with asked if I was sure she could do this job, I didn't hesitate. She was a part of my crew, always had been.

When she got out of juvie, her parents got her into a drug rehab program, and I'd talked to her about school. She pursued an associate's degree with the knowledge that I could get her a job if she held her grades. She worked hard, but everyone's trust had been broken. Her going undercover in the wrong crowds for me to sniff out drug operations was risky, but Izzy had a knack for it.

She'd made a name for herself, and we became a team.

"You got balls being condescending when you got your sister locked up with you," I growled. This was a big operation. Someone in Puerto Rico was moving masses of cocaine, and we needed to figure out how. She was just getting into the ring and now this.

"In my defense, I tried to take the blame. She took the blame too."

"She shouldn't even have been on the trip with you in the first place." I fisted the contract in my hand. Delilah Hardy was my little lamb. She was so damn innocent that there was no way she could survive a night in a facility. She wasn't equipped to deal with jail time.

"I know." She gulped audibly.

I turned to my cousin, twice removed, and held the phone away from my mouth. "Get to the airport."

"Yes, good. I was going to say I definitely need you to

handle that because I have to stay in for a few weeks," Izzy mumbled out.

Did she just say what I think she did? "I'm not leaving you in a damn jail cell, Izzy."

"You have to!" She sounded desperate. That was her real problem. Izzy wasn't addicted to drugs anymore. She was addicted to the job. "I'm this close."

"You fucked up." She'd fucked up royally, but I wasn't about to rub it in right now. "It's not safe for you in there."

"I can take care of myself. Just take care of Delilah, okay? She's— She won't last."

"No shit," I grumbled. Delilah was the opposite of Izzy. She was good and quiet like the lamb I called her.

Except for when I was fucking her.

Jesus. My dick was already responding to that thought and it made me want to punch something. She'd been sweet and innocent and had done everything right until me.

I should have felt guilty for that, but instead my cock grew by the second.

"You know what to do." Then Izzy hung up on me.

That girl was the biggest pain in my ass. Well, except for her sister, who I pretty much would have done anything for. Lilah brought me peace when everything else in my life was hell.

Until she ghosted me.

FUCK.

"So, guess we're going to Puerto Rico," Cade announced, his bright grin contrasted the darkness of his eyes, his neck full of tattoos, and his hair. Cade embodied a black hole except when he was grinning like a fool. Now, he just looked downright eerie.

"Why the hell are you smiling?"

"Well, I ain't got shit to do here for a while. My brother's holed up with his wife, and I need some fun in my life. You look like you're in literal pain, which means this is going to be fun."

"You shouldn't be enjoying this. You're supposed to enjoy the damn internet, not my demise."

Cade didn't interfere much with us in reality. He got lost in virtual worlds, codes, and algorithms most of the time. He was one of the best hackers in the world but, even so, kept a level head.

That alone proved to me that there was something completely off about him. Most people who spent that much time isolating themselves from the real world ended up in a mental fog or got depressed.

I'd seen men back in the military struggle with it. Their unhappiness with deployments, PTSD, and physical and mental illness led to them disappearing into a space that wasn't real. And we lost them, time and time again.

I'd been lost once too. That's what stopped me from backing away from Cade when others had.

"My fun can be telling Izzy she fucked up," he said.

"You won't be telling her anything, because she's staying in until someone else bails her out. We don't want to blow her cover."

He sighed like I was personally deflating his balloon. The dumbass had a hard-on for pissing that girl off.

"She was flying with her sister, and when they got separated and questioned, fucking Delilah took all the blame."

"'Fucking Delilah'?" he asked with an eyebrow raised. "Do you happen to know this Delilah?"

"I know Izzy's whole family. They grew up down the street." I remembered their family could be heard barreling up the block, screaming like a pack of banshees in the night, there were so many of them.

"But you know Delilah better than the rest, huh?"

I didn't answer his stupid question. But he was damn right I did.

CHAPTER 5: SURVIVE JAIL

Delilah

It'd been two days. And in that time, I found that most everyone left me alone. Mothers, sisters, daughters, and people in pain. There wasn't a difference between any of us at the end of the day.

Except the one girl who stabbed another with a whittled down piece of metal from someone's ceiling pipe. In her defense, the other girl had called her a terrible name.

Izzy caught me looking at her with pity. "Don't even think about walking over to console her, Delilah. The guards are coming, and you'll put a target on your back."

"She looked like they backed her into a corner."

"Yeah, well, we're all in corners, and we all have to deal with the consequences of what we do in them."

I sighed and walked away with her that day. Later, my sister swore at a woman who came near me asking to use my shampoo. Before I could give it to her, my sister snatched it away.

"Do we look like your fucking charity, Crenshaw? Get out of here."

"Izzy!" I hissed as the girl turned away, giving us the finger.

"Don't appear weak in here, Delilah, or they'll make you

weak."

"Sharing isn't weakness," I huffed. We were standing under lukewarm water, and it was a communal shower, a huge white tiled space with only a few shower heads. I really was in no position to argue when I felt completely exposed and outside of my element.

While I wanted to shake in fear and crumble in defeat, Izzy stood tall. "In here, it is. You need to be smart."

"Smart? *Smart*?" My voice was shrill as I turned off the shower and grabbed my tiny towel to dry off. I rubbed aggressively at my legs, leaving red marks on every inch. "How in the hell did we get in here, Izzy? *Smart* would have been never carrying drugs into an airport in the first place."

She rolled her eyes. She'd done the same thing when I told her she needed to call Mom and Dad. When I had, they'd both cried and said they would make calls. My mother was beside herself, and I almost cried with her.

Almost.

I couldn't, though. I didn't need her worrying, especially if I was going to be in here a while. I explained that it was comfortable enough and went into detail about how Izzy and I got to share bunks.

My mother didn't say much about Izzy. I knew she blamed her, and I couldn't stop myself from blaming her too.

Back in our cell that night, I lay in my bunk and stared up at hers. "How could we have been born from the same womb at the same time and have such different lives?"

"Well, technically, I was born three minutes after you. So, that's probably why."

I kicked her mattress as I chuckled. "I mean it. Where did it go wrong for you?"

"Wrong?" she asked like I'd insulted her again. "I don't

know that anything is wrong with how I turned out."

"Izzy." My tone was condescending, and I hated that I couldn't stop the word vomit, but my anger had it spewing out of me faster than I could control. "Your friends are pieces of shit. You don't come to family stuff. You went to juvenile hall when you were only seventeen, and your grades were shit. You told me you were going to school, but we never went to your college graduation, so I'm guessing that's a lie. You've been smuggling drugs for money, haven't you?"

"Well, if you have it all figured out ..." She trailed off, but I could hear the pain in her voice. I felt that same pain in my heart.

How could I change her when I could barely change myself? I'd always been the good one, and I never veered away from it even when I knew I wanted to take more risks and live my life. I couldn't fault her for not being able to change herself either.

Except my life didn't hurt others, and maybe that's why my resentment toward her pushed more hateful things from my mouth. "Figured out? I'm in jail because of you. I hope it was worth it. Did you get paid a lot, or was it just to keep up your status in whatever shitty group you've been hanging out with?"

"Lilah, go to sleep. You're being a bitch." She said it softly, but the words still stung.

"Do you even want to apologize for this?" I threw back. "I'm a bitch because I finally stopped being gullible after all this time. I'm finally siding with our family. You're the addict, and you've been dragging us down because you won't go out and get help. Grow up. Take accountability. Be sorry." I wasn't ever confrontational with her. Never had been really. Maybe the shock of it had her mad enough to respond.

"Fine!" she yelled, cutting me off as she whipped her head

over the side of the bed so I could see her glare at me.

I gasped when I saw tears streaming down her face. Izzy never cried. I did. And she was always there hugging me when it happened. We were allies even if we didn't hang out in the same crowds. I was the yin to her yang. Sweet to her spicy. Tame to her wild. Twin sisters against the world. I'd believed her for so long.

Maybe it was the heartbreak of her lying to me or that our bond was truly severed here and now, but tears slid down my cheeks too as she said, "I'm sorry for all of it, okay? What do you want me to say? That I'm a fuckup? Sure. I was always the black sheep. Mom didn't even think she was going to have me, Lilah. Five D names and a left over I, right?"

My mother only got one ultrasound without health insurance and Izzy had hidden behind me. When I was born, they'd quickly informed my mother of another child. She'd named her Isabel rather than another D name. I didn't think it bothered her, but I guess it had.

"I didn't care about school or my life like you did," she continued. "You had it all, and I had some friends, okay? People liked me just for my fun personality and it meant more than school, okay? I don't really know how that's possible, just that it is. I always felt beneath all of you, and somehow you always climbed up that happiness pole and found the freaking sun when I was left clawing through the darkness."

Her apology didn't appease me. It made me feel worse for what I'd said before, my words curdling in my stomach and souring like rotting milk.

I wasn't always happy, wasn't always perfect.

I just didn't share my sadness with any of them.

"That's not true," I whispered. She didn't know about the days in college where I couldn't see a thing because I'd been sucked into a black hole of pain that didn't seem to ever let up.

She didn't know I'd carried a baby. A baby that I'd lost.

Nobody did.

"Oh, whatever," she scoffed and flew back over the side of her mattress. "Don't try to paint me a picture of you not doing well, Delilah. You always have and you always will."

It wasn't the time to share my own demons. I needed to be strong for both of us, so I didn't respond to her.

I let her drift off to sleep while I cried silently below her that night, wasting my tears on a twin sister who I wasn't sure knew how to love me the same way I loved her.

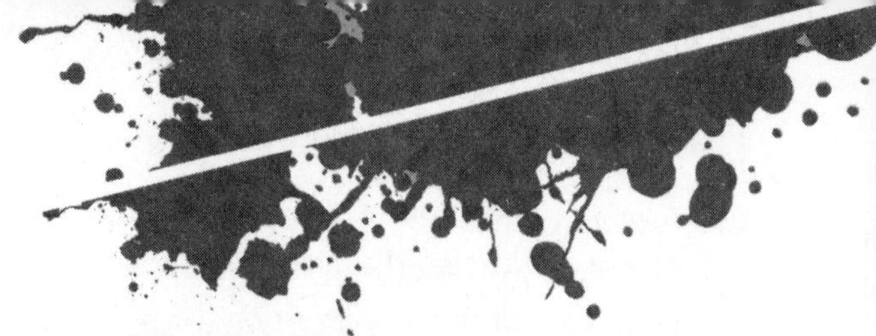

CHAPTER 6: PICK UP YOUR EX

Dante

I'd worked with the authorities to get Delilah out quickly. My clearance within the United States made them willing. Had they given me any trouble, I would have just called my family. They were the ones that really ran the United States, government be damned. Money was power, and the Armanellis had most of it.

Delilah didn't know that side of the family, though. To her, my name was Dante Reid.

Not Armanelli. Not the mob.

And she wouldn't be figuring it out today. I already knew our story was going to be too tough for her to handle. Anyone who learned their friend was working undercover with their sister was going to have a hard time.

Not that I'd call Delilah a friend at this point.

I don't know if it was ever right to call her a friend. She was too bright-eyed and bushy-tailed for hanging around Izzy, me, and her brothers.

And then I'd fallen for her.

Hard.

My squad told me it was because we didn't get enough pussy overseas and that I'd get over her Dear John-ing me when I got back. I knew it wasn't true, though. Getting over Delilah was something that took years. Hell, I'd been tortured, beaten, waterboarded. Still, nothing compared to her silence when I sent an email and she didn't respond.

And even after all that, I remembered how she smelled, how she felt, how she tasted. She'd infected me with a lifetime disease of my body responding to her, and when she walked out of that penitentiary building, the same thing happened.

"What the—" Those wide hazel eyes of hers grew when she saw me. The sun kissed her golden skin, and the dark waves of her hair blew around her face. "Where are my parents?"

Delilah Hardy, the girl who'd haunted every corner of my nightmares and dreams since the moment I'd met her years ago, was now a very hot, very fuckable, and very frustrated woman standing right in front of me.

I hated that I'd taken her virginity and hated even more that we'd swept the whole event under the rug like we could hide it forever, especially when my dick wanted to do nothing of the sort. I'd seen her only a handful of times after that week, and every time she'd practically run in the other direction. If I cornered her, she looked at me with embarrassment or sometimes even hurt. Like I'd defiled her that night.

I'd fucked that girl like it was the one job I had in the world to do right. I knew I hadn't hurt her. I'd worshipped her.

And we'd exchanged emails. We'd been fine. For a minute, I'd wanted to make Delilah Hardy my damn wife.

And then, over the years, I'd dreamt about doing it again, only to have a follow-up nightmare of her looking at me the way she was right this second.

With visceral pain. Her chin even trembled like she might cry at the sight of me.

I rubbed my buzz-cut head. "Your mom called mine, Lilah." It was an easy enough story that she'd believe.

She huffed and crossed her arms over her chest as she looked toward the sky and blinked rapidly. How had we gotten here? How had I lost even the cordial friendship we'd shared over the years in just one week?

"Okay," she breathed out.

"Sorry, Lilah. I'm just here to pick you up," I mumbled. I didn't know why I was apologizing. I'd spent years in the military making people apologize to me. I didn't say sorry. It wasn't in my vocabulary until right that second.

Time had left her short, but her curves had filled out in all the right places. I wanted to explore each curve and see if she liked me sliding around them fast or slow. They'd given her clothing back when she was released, and I saw that she'd abandoned the sweaters she used to wear for something much more revealing: a white tank that barely covered her ample cleavage.

I'd tried to forget all this about her: the way my heart beat out of my chest, the way my dick twitched immediately, and even when she blinked away the pain in her eyes and met me with a sudden glare. She had fire there now, like she was ready for me all of a sudden.

"You came all this way because our parents told you to? Are you out of your mind? And my mother even asking you to do this ..." She pressed the heels of her hands into her eyes hard before she sighed. "That's really ridiculous. You shouldn't have come."

She stomped past me toward the car and then stopped halfway there to turn and shut her eyes before she said, "Thank you. I'm really on edge right now. I've lost a lot of sleep, and I need to sit down or something while we wait for Izzy to get out."

I nodded slowly and took a wide path around her, eating up the cement to get to my car rental. I opened the sleek black door for her and waved her in. "Just sit and relax, Delilah. Everything is going to be okay now."

Running a hand through her chocolate-colored hair, she listened.

By the time I got to the driver's side, though, she'd already started to fall apart. "My sister is coming out of there, right? I mean"—her leg jumped up and down— "it's taking them a bit long to release her. They didn't call her name with mine. Why do you think that is?"

I cleared my throat, ready for shit to hit the fan when I told her.

She continued without letting me say a word. "I'm sorry, I don't know why I'm asking you that. I always envision you running around like James Bond doing whatever you want and knowing everything. My family paints that picture, you know? Like maybe you know everything that's going on right now when obviously you don't." She took a big breath that didn't really do much to calm her. "And I'm rambling when I shouldn't be."

"It's fine." Her rapid breathing was starting to stir something in me that I couldn't handle right now. I put my hand on my chest. "Delilah, seven breaths? Huh?"

She glanced at my hand, and her brow furrowed. Then she whispered, "Seven'll bring heaven?"

I nodded and smiled. We breathed together. Synced for just a second. It was enough time to calm us both, though, to get us on the same page.

After seeing color return to her cheeks and how her shoulders relaxed, I said, "It's good to see you, Lilah."

She pursed her plump lips and then she chuckled. It was huskier than I remembered. "Not under these circumstances, though."

"Still good to see you. You haven't been back over the last couple of years when I was home from leave."

"Yeah, life I guess." She shrugged while she stared out at that building.

Damn, this was going to hurt.

I knew avoiding the truth and pain it brought never helped. I only waited when it would prolong the torture for some enemy I was dealing with. Now, with her, I needed to be honest.

I dropped the bomb as I pushed the car ignition. "Your sister's staying in jail."

"What?" The screech that rang through the car was full of fear, anger, and shock. I didn't reply and started to shift into drive. But that little hand of hers, so small I could break it, went right on top of mine and shoved the gear back into park. "Dante! What the fuck? What do you mean?"

I lifted a brow at her swearing. "I mean what I said."

"You can't just leave." Her hand dug into mine harder, and I saw the pink on her cheeks deepen in anger rather than embarrassment. That pink was almost the same color as something else of hers I remembered, and fuck me, I did not need to be imagining it right now.

I had years of training. I went to great lengths to keep those around me calm, keep us focused on a mission, and complete objectives flawlessly.

Yet, most of those situations were life and death.

Here, I didn't know how to act. I'd been with women and made them comfortable, understood their emotions. They understood mine too. Delilah and I were different.

She was so good that her mom once told my mom that she'd forgotten Lilah somewhere because she was so quiet and well-behaved that there was no way of knowing whether she was there or not.

It wasn't like that for me. Today, and most every day, I knew when she was there.

Maybe I'd invested too much in hope, pictured our families merging with her taking my damn name. I realized I'd loved her for a long time. And when she didn't write, I still held on to hope.

I wanted her to see me, thought the holidays would be better.

Instead, Christmas had been a shit show.

***

"Man, what the fuck you dressed up for? We going out to the bar after dinner?" Dom asked me as I searched the room for her.

Telling my best friend that I'd put my damn cologne on for his kid sister was not something I was about to do. "Well, I'm not going out looking like your ass. You wearing sweats to pick up Susie tonight?"

"I don't need to wear anything to pick up Susie." He waggled his eyebrows at me, and Dex elbowed him with a glare, probably because he was sweet on Susie at this point.

This was the normal cycle of the small town: we all flew back in, enjoyed our family, then went to the little bar in the village. High school flames were rekindled for a night, along with drama and petty bullshit.

I loved it.

It was comfort; it was home.

It'd been only two weeks earlier that I'd been overseas, on top of a building that was on fire, trying to snipe a terrorist. That year, I'd become ruthless in my missions, and when Lilah didn't email me back, I'd pushed for more training within Special Ops. I'd taken contract work. I'd worked with the government, the mob, specific embassies. Hours of running, sleep deprivation, and fighting.

"What the hell are you trying so hard for anyway, Dante?" Dom asked. "You're making us all look like pansies. Delta Force and dressed in some expensive jeans. How much did those cost anyway? I could make millions in tech, and every girl is still going to only want you."

I chuckled. He wasn't lying.

I only wanted one girl, though, and when she came down the steps, I heard her immediately. Her voice was like sex on a stick that I wanted to lap up. When I turned to look at her, the punch to my gut hit much harder than men in the military when we were scrapping. In ripped jeans and a black sweater that didn't even do a mediocre job of hiding her curves, she looked more mature, like she'd grown up in only six months. Like I was missing moments with her. She went to hug my mom and let everyone fuss over her for a minute. She was the kid sister, and Izzy was out of juvie now but still hanging with the wrong crowd.

My mom immediately asked how school was going and if she'd made any good friends.

"School's good. I'm sure you've heard that I'm going into nursing. And I've made friends. It's been great." She drifted off, and her eyes searched the room. When they landed on me, they froze. Hazel and gorgeous. They were rainbows of green and gold twisted up with fear and pain. Then, her cheeks blushed that familiar rosy pink and she continued, "It's been busy, really busy."

"I bet. I know college is full of booze and boys. You make sure you have some fun with both." My mom nudged her and laughed. Delilah tore her stare from mine and giggled at my mother's joke too.

She murmured that she was going to help with food and then floated out of the room just like she'd floated in, without a hello or a how are you. Without so much as an I miss you.

It didn't take long for neighbors to stop by and for the Hardy Christmas to get into full swing. Alcohol was flowing, mistletoe was hung, and Mr. Hardy was at the piano trying his best to sing "Let it Snow" like he did every year. We ate ham and cheesy potatoes and probably a million different desserts, surrounded by family.

Izzy showed up with her crew. Mrs. Hardy rolled her eyes as they all beelined toward the punch bowl. "Izzy, don't drink too much now. You know alcohol can be a gateway—"

"Mrs. Hardy." I threw an arm over her shoulder and steered her away from Izzy, winking at her. "Let's see if you and my mom can out-sing that husband of yours, huh?"

Mrs. Hardy laughed, and Izzy mouthed thank you like she couldn't handle her family harping on her anymore.

I got it. She'd done her time in juvie. She'd gotten clean. Except her family seemed to think she wasn't really all that clean because of how she presented herself in front of them.

Still, my mother and Mrs. Hardy sang "White Christmas," and they harmonized so well together, you would think they had been going door to door caroling their whole lives.

Joy flowed through us all.

But the rage in me grew and grew.

Delilah wouldn't look at me.

When she did, it was like a storm of misery passed over her features. She combed her hands through her hair when I held her gaze at the end of the night, right before Dom told me to get ready to go to Ray's.

As she disappeared down the hall, I nodded to him. "Sure. Going to go to the bathroom and tell your mom thank you for the dinner. I'll meet you guys there."

He shrugged, not thinking anything of it, and filled his flask before Dex yelled at him to hurry up.

I was down the hall in half a second, following the girl of my dreams before anyone could see my real objective.

She turned and gasped when she saw me right behind her, but I didn't give her time to object. I yanked her into the bathroom and shut the door.

When I turned the lock, her eyes bulged, and she poked me in the chest. "What are you doing? Someone might find us in here!"

"Your brothers just left, and our parents are entertaining the neighbors. We're fine," I said, then leaned against the door to ensure she didn't try to make a run for it.

"Well, I ..." She twisted her dark curls, and then her hands were wringing themselves together. Her gaze jumped everywhere in that bathroom but never landed for one second on me. "I have to get back to my room."

"Lilah," I murmured while trying to get her attention, but she kept looking down. "Lilah. Look at me."

She took a breath, and this time it was shaky, like she was pulling in air she could barely hold. "I don't want to."

"Why?" I croaked out and hated that it sounded so full of my own anguish. "I wrote you. I know it wasn't much, but I was gone. I was doing a job. What happened between us?"

"What happened?" she whispered. "Nothing. Nothing happened. We slept together a few times, Dante. And then we were better off not together."

"Is that so?" I asked and saw her bite her lip. She was struggling with something, but I was struggling with losing her. My pain wanted revenge, and even though I knew I should have kept digging to figure out what the real problem was, I wanted her pain even more. "Better off how? Better off with me going to fuck some random woman in this town tonight because I can't have the one I want?"

She gasped, and then her eyes met mine with a fire that was bold, full of an emotion other than pain. "You don't mean that."

Finally, I saw life when she looked at me. I saw a reaction rather than regret. I pushed the envelope further. "Mean that I'll fuck someone else or mean that I still want you? I mean both of those things. The latter more than the former. I've always wanted you, and I probably always will. And it's your fault, Lilah. You dragged me down into that fucking hole, and now I can't climb out."

"It's just better this way, Dante. You have the military. You're doing so well. I heard you got into–"

"Don't," I cut her off. "Don't make me feel good, Lilah. Unless you intend to make me feel good everywhere."

My eyes raked over her body. Her breasts swelled as she breathed in, and then goosebumps popped up over her smooth skin. I couldn't stop myself from stepping toward her and pulling her bottom lip from her mouth. She let me, even licked her lips as I stared at them. "Jesus Christ, I know you're wet for me right now, pretty girl. I can practically smell it. I know the way it tastes too."

"I can't do this," she whispered.

"You can't or you don't want to?"

"You know I want to, but I'm not strong enough. You're gone and I'm here. It's too much."

"You knew I was in the military." I pushed her. Something was off.

"I knew a lot." She stepped back, and my hand fell from her chin. "I thought I knew so much. Until I didn't know anything."

"That doesn't make sense, Lilah."

"We don't make sense," she threw back. Then she shook her head. "I can't with you. I just can't. You're my brother's best friend, and I've already lost so much."

"So much what?" I practically bellowed. The woman didn't make any sense, and I'd been gone too long, away from civilian life, away from working through my emotions. She jumped back at my yelling, and I wanted to tell her that this wasn't me, that I didn't want to scream at her, but it was me.

I was trained in screaming at people now.

I was trained in assassination and torture and extracting information. Maybe that's what this was. Or maybe she couldn't handle the distance or the pressure.

It didn't matter.

"You know what? It doesn't matter." I rubbed my head and looked toward the ceiling. "You're right."

"I know I am." She nodded and stood tall like she was regaining confidence in her stupid argument. "We're better off letting what we had die."

I nodded. "Sure are." But I wasn't going to let her off that easy. She didn't get to have all the confidence that she was doing everything right here. "Except that mouth of yours that's spewing all this bullshit is going to miss mine. And you can deny that you want me all you want, but your pussy is going to regret that decision, Lilah."

"I don't think you're the guy I thought you were." She narrowed her eyes at me.

"No. I'm the guy you'll always remember, though." I took her mouth in mine. I bit down on the bottom lip that I wanted to brand as mine, and I pulled her thighs up around my waist before I shoved her ass back onto the counter. Her arm hooked around my neck, and she gave as good as she got.

I yanked at her hair and pulled it back so that her head tilted enough for me to gain extra leverage and exposure. Consuming Lilah was my mission right then, and I couldn't see past it. She tasted like the only thing I wanted, and that was love and lust for her.

She moaned loud when my hands slid up her skirt and my thumb brushed over her panties.

"Soaked like I thought they would be. Jesus, why play with me, huh?"

"I'm not," she whimpered, but now I was onto her games.

Still, I couldn't stop myself. I wanted her to remember what we had between us, even if this was all a game to her, even if she wasn't going to do anything past this night with me.

I told myself I didn't want anything past this night either at this point.

When I pushed her panties to the side and traced my middle finger over her slit, her hips thrust forward. I pulled back, though. "You're not getting off that quick, Little Lamb. You told me you don't even want this."

"I don't. We can't." Her brow was furrowed; a sheen of sweat made her skin look like it glowed. Her chest was up against mine, rising and falling quickly. Instead of pushing me away, her arm around my neck tightened and her other hand went to my wrist, trying to push my hand farther into her core as I worked her.

"I think we can. I think you'll beg me before we're done here."

"Dante, I can't get off, okay? I'm broken or something." She rolled her hips on my hand, but tears welled in her eyes as she said the words, like she knew she was chasing an unattainable dream.

"Lilah, what the fuck are you talking about?"

I started to pull my hand away, but her nails dug into my wrist. "Don't you dare stop. I haven't been able to get off since. Please." Tears streamed down her face now. "I'll beg, okay? Please. Please, please."

She pulled me close, and when she kissed me this time, her tongue moved with love and pain, fast then slow, with a purpose to taste every part of my mouth. Suddenly, the love for me was back in her, how she spread her legs, how her body clung to me.

I didn't stand a chance at denying her. Fuck, I'd been saving myself for her.

And her words cut pain and jealousy through me as my finger dove into her folds. Someone else must have touched her.

Someone else had tried to get her off while I'd waited for her.

I curled my finger inside her and hit the spot I knew she'd loved six months ago. She gasped, and both her hands flew to my shoulders like she needed to steady herself.

"You can always get off, Lilah," I growled in her ear.

She shivered, and I pushed my thumb into her clit. "Oh, God."

"Nope. God can't get you there. No one can but me. I'm the one who rules this pussy, baby. You gave it to me, remember? And I didn't give it back. I'm never going to."

I slid another finger into her, and her wetness dripped down my wrist as she moaned and rode my hand faster and faster.

"Dante, Jesus, I missed you. I'm sorry I didn't write you and I'm sorry I didn't call you back after you left that voicemail. I—"

A knock on the door had her hips freezing and her eyes flying to it. She tried to shove me away as someone wiggled the doorknob.

"I'm in here. Just give me a ..." She started, but her words tapered off as I kneeled down in front of her and sucked on the side of her thigh, my second finger sliding back and forth inside her with the first to the rhythm of my tongue on that plump thigh of hers. Maybe it was her trying to deny me now that someone was around, or maybe it was my need to be the only thing she remembered now that I was back in her life that night, but I wasn't stopping for anything.

"Lilah, are you in there?" Her mom's voice carried through

the door.

Her hazel eyes widened on me, and she tried to yank me up by pulling at the fabric of my shirt.

I mouthed, "Get rid of her," and then I pinched her clit as I removed my fingers to replace them with my mouth. Both of her hands hit the countertop, loud, and her mother must have heard her gasp.

"Lilah, is everything alright?"

"I ... Yes, yes. Good. Everything is perfect." She purred when she said it too, not pushing me away at all this time. Her legs wrapped around me and squeezed, like we were on the brink, like I was about to push her over the same edge that I was nearing.

"Well, I'm going outside by the fire if you need me. We should talk a bit more soon, Lilah. I want college to be good for you. I feel so far away, though, like maybe you should just move back home."

"Oh my God, Mother. Please." She moaned the word and smiled as my tongue lapped at her slit. "Please, I need a minute. We'll talk later."

As her mother's footsteps grew distant and quiet, the sounds between us got louder. I let her give in and ride my face the way she needed to. Delilah wanted this as much as I did, and when her head fell back, ready to release everything she was holding in, I knew exactly what I needed from her.

"Look at me, Lamb. If I don't see your pretty eyes, you don't see stars."

Her gaze snapped to mine, and I saw the vivid color before they dilated. We pushed the level we could be on in that moment; we moved the mountains of barriers, the silence over the last few months, and the pain that was somehow between us. The piece of my fucking heart that was missing was back in place for a second, and when she hit her high and convulsed around my tongue, I almost lost it right there.

She clawed at my head, and then her jaw dropped to let out a scream. My hand left her hair to muffle the sound as I milked the aftershocks from her.

As she breathed heavily into my hand and I licked up the last drops of her release, one of her hands went to my shoulders and the other to my wrist to pull it away from her mouth. "I'm sure everyone heard me."

"Then maybe we should let them know what I wanted to tell them the first time I tasted you."

"And what's that?" she asked, biting her lip as she glanced down at me rising up to stand over her.

"That you might be a sweet innocent lamb, but you're my lamb all the same."

She sighed and scooted back as I said the words.

When I said her name again in question, she winced without looking at me.

"Why won't you look at me, Lilah?"

"I can't," she whispered. The pain in her voice brought a storm of torture down upon my soul too. "If I do, I'll end up ruining everything for both of us."

"How can you say that?"

"We can't be together. I— I'm sorry." She combed her hands through her hair before glaring up at me. "You have to move on. I have to also. We should be friends like we were. We're better off that way. If we date ... Our families, Dante."

"You knew that before."

"It's still a good reason. It just wasn't one I made the right decision on in the past. And I'm sorry about that."

"So what? You want me to forget this happened?"

"Yes."

"Forget I took the most sacred thing from you?" I was

whisper-yelling at her.

She bit her lip. "It won't be that sacred once I'm with others, Dante. And you'll move on too. There's a line of women at the bar that'll be more than happy to make you forget."

I shook my head at her. "I don't think you'll forget. I won't either."

"We can try. Please. Let's just be friends."

Shit, a woman was begging me to forget her, but I was standing there like I couldn't let her go. It wasn't right. I'd tried. I'd near begged her on my knees to stay with me. "Fine, Lilah. Try. Try all you want. But if they can't make you feel like I make you feel, you've got the wrong one."

* * *

Her mother told mine that she thought Lilah was going through depression from being at college, that she'd get over it. She was the strongest of the bunch, plus they had to worry about Izzy.

Izzy, who'd been a little hellion growing up but had been right by Dom, Dex, Declan, and Dimitri when we ran amuck.

Izzy was close to death. Close enough that I feared for her life. Opioids could grab ahold of you like that, tear apart your life while destroying all the people in the way. And she was family. We were going to be in her way. We didn't leave family behind. I'd stuck by my mom and her mom to scoop up the pieces of that girl. I took her under my wing, even though I wanted to do something totally different to her twin sister.

And Izzy made it. She was one of the lucky ones even if she was undercover in jail at the moment.

"Lilah, I care about Izzy too. You know she's one of my best friends, okay? But you have to believe me when I say this is for the best."

Her eyebrows slammed down as she scoffed at me and tried to kill me with a glare. "Oh, I know how good of a friend she is to you, Dante. Which is why I'm disgusted that you would even try to leave her here."

Anger wasn't the norm for her. Sadness, pain, embarrassment—that's what I'd seen from her over the past five years. I'd never seen her this mad. I dealt with terrorists who were mad. I was fine handling that. I could waterboard a guy for so long he got over that anger real quick. I dealt with civilian women who were mad at me too, but normally I fucked their anger into submission.

I couldn't do that with Delilah.

Even if I wanted to.

"Look, I think you should practice that breathing technique while I drive away from here. Idling in a place like this—"

"We're not going anywhere without my sister." She shoved my hand off the gear.

The spark came from our contact that time. The same spark I got when I wanted to have someone submit to me.

Fuck.

"Delilah, you're like family to me, you know that. Izzy, too, but you know that Izzy has been in trouble for a long time. Opioid addiction–"

She cut me off as her voice cracked with emotion. "Don't start. Do not even start with putting up an excuse from her past to justify what you're about to do to her future. So what if she was addicted to something?" A new fire stirred in her eyes. "So what, Dante? I was there too. They don't know whether I did it or she did. We're both guilty. If I get out, she should too."

Her loyalty to her sister, the willingness to defend, made her a lot stronger to me in that moment.

"We both know you wouldn't do this," I said softly, trying

to lessen the blow. "I could only get you out for now, but—"

"Nope." She basically shouted the word, then her head shook back and forth before she pounded her miniscule fist on the dashboard. "No, Dante. Don't feed me bullshit and empty promises. We are not leaving her here alone. We leave this parking lot with her, or I go back in there to be with her."

"Jesus, Delilah. She's been incarcerated, she'll be fine." I winced at my words. To even my own ears they sounded callous.

"Oh my God. You know damn well this isn't the same." Before I could stop her, she flew out the door, jerking away from my reach. "There has to be something we can do."

Oh, fuck me.

I was chasing her down, my dick in the wrong place all over again as I looked at her backside. I scrambled to grab her around the waist to haul her back toward the car. We didn't have time to be bickering outside a correctional institution. It would cause unneeded attention.

She literally fought me the whole way. It was a forbidden feeling to hold a woman like that because I usually only indulged with those who wanted it. With Lilah, though, my dick was harder than a rock before I even made it to the car. I shouldn't have lusted after her, kicking and screaming like a little wild animal in my arms.

"She's getting out in a few weeks, woman. If she'd listened, I would have got her out today. She wants this. Not me. So stop fighting me before I do something about it," I whispered into the nape of her neck.

The fight left her as I set her down near the car door. She looked at me with questions flying around behind her eyes. "Did you say she wants—"

"Get in and I'll explain." I cleared my throat and rubbed my hand over my head once, trying to keep my thoughts straight. "Just listen."

"If you're lying, I'll find a way to make you pay."

"Even though I've told you time and time again that you're as small as a lamb, I believe that, Delilah, I really do."

CHAPTER 7: GO UNDERCOVER

Delilah

I yanked the car door from Dante's grip and slammed it shut before he had a chance to.

What the ever-loving fuck was going on?

My whole body vibrated with fury by the time he rounded the hood of the vehicle and went to sit in the driver's seat.

Dante and I weren't like family. He said we were, but he was so wrong. So fucking wrong. I'd had an idiotic crush on that stupid boy since middle school. And he had my v-card. His assessment was enraging along with the fact that I knew something definitely wasn't adding up about this whole situation.

He glanced at me as he put the car in drive, and I told myself not to be impressed by the veins on his forearm as he navigated us out of the parking lot.

Dante Reid somehow multiplied in muscles and height every time I saw him. I hated that he still smelled like sandalwood but dressed in freaking tailored pants and a snug T-shirt that showed me exactly how well he'd aged over the last few years.

"Talk," I commanded louder than I intended to, but it was a great start. I needed to hold onto that anger and make it known that he owed me an explanation.

He cleared his throat as if he was nervous. "First off, Little Lamb, let's calm down. I learned this Reiki technique—"

"If you call me Lamb again, I'll claw your eyes out," I spat. "I don't need old nicknames and consoling techniques right now. I need the truth."

He took a deep breath before he said, "Okay, let's get back to your place, then. Are you still at the same hotel you stayed at with Izzy?"

"Yes. I live there on a month-to-month basis. The hospital set it up when I took the nursing job." I typed it into my phone, and the navigation started.

He tsked before grumbling, "I know where this hotel is."

"Great." I blew off his comment because it wasn't important. All that mattered was that they'd planned some idiotic part of this. "Now, explain how not getting Izzy out is doing what she wants, apparently."

"It's a long story, Lilah," he said like he was all of a sudden too tired to tell it.

"The cobbled stones of Old San Juan, although beautiful, will make for a slow drive. So start explaining."

He scratched his eyebrow before he continued. "Some of it's classified. And some of it you and Izzy should discuss. She's your sister and you two need—"

"Oh, please don't start with trying to smooth the waters for me and my sister." God, was he trying to be the peacemaker here? "And classified information? Wow, well, you can forget about that because obviously I already know too much."

"Let's keep calm." His voice sounded the exact same way it had when I was younger and he was trying to keep me from freaking out. Too bad that technique had never worked for me then and definitely wouldn't work now.

He grumbled, "I'm not giving you all the details, because you don't need them. Information is classified so you're not in danger."

"You're not— You owe it to me to tell me what is going on here, Dante," I practically screeched.

His piercing green gaze narrowed on the road, and his muscles bunched as he gripped the wheel. Dante was harder, colder, fiercer than I remembered. "I owe you your safety, Lilah." He glanced at me as he stopped at a light. "I won't coddle you. You get what I give you. That's it."

"Izzy has been in jail with me for two days. A lot has been said, and none of it was that she wanted to stay holed up there," I snarled before he could continue.

He nodded and rubbed a hand over his buzz cut. I used to love when he did that, like he wasn't sure how to continue the conversation. Now, I hated that I knew all his stupid mannerisms. It just proved that I'd never had a chance at escaping him. Memories lasted a lifetime, whether you wanted them to or not.

Dante didn't have brothers and sisters, so we became like a second family to him. Mostly he, Izzy, and my older brothers would run around like lunatics, and I'd sneak glances at him from the table where I did my homework.

"When Izzy called me—" he started.

"Izzy called you? From jail? Why the hell would she do that?" My mind pieced it all together, and I hated how fast I came up with the most logical conclusion. "Are you fucking her still? I thought you guys broke up!" I wanted to punch him in his big bicep and then go cry about the fact that it still sent pangs through my gut to think they were together.

We'd only had a minute together, but it seemed to last a lifetime when you fell in love with someone. I'd done that with him. And I'd ended it to save us both.

We would never have worked. The man was so far out of my league that I'd done us both a favor by cutting things off, especially with what happened after. Plus, he'd been trapped. I'd put the burden of my virginity on him. I knew Dante. He was raised like a gentleman. He'd always made the extra effort to be cordial with me, but that's all it was.

We were never a real option, even if for a few weeks, I thought we could have been.

"Break up? We were never together," he replied quickly, then shook his head and closed his eyes as we stopped at a light. "I mean, sure, I contemplated it. That's not the point."

I crossed my arms over my chest. "What's the point then? Why is she calling you from jail instead of calling my parents or a fucking lawyer or something?"

"You swear like this all the time now?" he almost growled at me.

The audacity he had to call me out on how I talked was infuriating.

"Yes, I do." I didn't. I only swore when I was mad. "And fuck you for thinking I don't talk like this."

He sucked on his teeth. I knew that sound from him. Good. We could both be irritated.

"And let me guess, this is what you wear all the time now? Even to an airport," he grumbled.

If I throttled a military official, would I end up back in jail? "Is *what* what I wear all the time now?"

"That bra."

"It's not a bra. It's a crop top." What a jackass. I'd left my sweaters at home and embraced this casual look. I had maxi dresses, flowy skirts, and bright colors to wear for my stay here.

"Your tits and stomach are on display. It's a bra."

Jail didn't seem so bad at that point. I mean, I was willing to go back if it meant I could knock one of his teeth out. "We can agree to disagree."

"Your brothers would agree with me. They'd be pissed."

"Oh, you're concerned with my brothers being mad at how I dress now? Get real. You all hook up with girls dressed in half of what I wear all the time back home."

"You having someone keep an eye on who I'm hooking up with back home, Lilah? Because from what I know, you haven't been home in years." He smirked like he'd won a point. "Even if that's the case, I know your brothers wouldn't want their baby sister drawing unnecessary attention with hundreds of guys around."

"Well, I drew enough attention when the TSA officers took me away like a criminal. You can tell them I graduated from 'baby sister' to felon," I threw back, so frustrated with myself that my stomach dropped at him calling me their baby sister.

I should have been happy I was nothing else to him now, but the title still hurt, like it always had, coming out of his mouth.

He took a deep breath, and then I saw his hands tapping on the wheel while he murmured something to himself.

"Are you seriously meditating right now?" Like I was the one pissing him off.

"If I don't, I'm going to lose my shit on you," he said, his voice low.

"You're the one critiquing my outfit."

The light turned green, and he practically floored the gas as he snapped back, "You're the one dressing like you want a guy to lick you all the way from your pretty head down to those toes."

"Oh my God." I couldn't believe this was where the

conversation was going. "I'm so happy you haven't seen the rest of my wardrobe."

"If it's anything like what you're wearing, you'll be getting a new wardrobe."

I scoffed. "You're ridiculous." He'd always seen me as this young girl. And even after everything, he still wasn't veering from it. I was an adult now. I'd had my legs around his head, for God's sakes.

And yet when he talked to me like this, I was reminded that he was also the guy my mom asked to drive me to school when no one else could, because she trusted him that much. I'd gotten so ready for that day, knowing I'd be alone in the car with him. Then, even though the conversation in that car had been going so well, we'd been halfway to school when he said softly, "My mom told me you got your period for the first time yesterday. Let me know if you need anything."

Yep. That actually happened.

I'd literally wanted to die.

He'd meant well.

That was Dante, always caring, always present. Always there for every embarrassing story but not actually making fun of me. The guy would have gotten me tampons, I swear it.

It felt like, to him, I was a little girl he was taking care of as a family duty.

Our relationship was doomed from the very start.

Handing him my v-card had been a colossal mistake. One that grew in me for two-and-a-half months after.

I'd carried his baby.

I'd thought I'd have to raise a child on my own. I struggled with so much that first semester at college that I could barely bring myself to go to class.

And through it all, my twin sister was gone, the only one

who probably would have understood my pain. When she was released after a few months, I'd planned to tell her. But she'd continued to hang with other people and continued to ignore me, continued down the wrong road. We talked still, but it wasn't the same. Then, that next summer, she called, so happy to report that Dante was taking her on a date.

Somehow, Dante, the man I dreamt about was going out with my prettier, more rebellious sister, even if he'd given me the only orgasms I'd had that year.

Not that I could blame him. I'd pushed him away. I'd pushed everyone away after my miscarriage. I was depressed and had to seek so much help for it.

And even though Izzy told me nothing big happened between them, I knew they talked. I knew they were good friends. I knew Dante had accepted her like he'd never accepted me. As an equal. Not as a kid sister.

"Just so we're clear, my twin sister and your *friend* were probably dressed worse than me."

"Izzy's always dressed differently than you."

"You would know," I grumbled.

He sighed and pulled at his shirt collar before he continued. "Lilah, I don't want to frustrate you anymore than you already are, okay? This is awkward for both of us."

"Awkward because Izzy and you have some sort of relationship that you've been hiding?" As much as I hated to admit it, my voice sounded dejected.

Had they been sleeping together all this time?

Back when I'd heard he was taking her on a date, I almost called him to tell him off. But at that stage, I'd been trying hard to handle my emotions better. I was seeing a therapist for my miscarriage. I was discussing my downfalls, and I was growing. Sliding back to a place where I didn't feel good enough, or to a place where memories of my miscarriage would surface, wasn't healthy.

Dante wasn't healthy for me, period, back then. I'd built him up to superhero status and made him out to be my only safe zone. He'd been the one I told all my problems to before we hooked up, and then he'd been the only one I wanted to share my pregnancy with but also the one I knew I couldn't tell.

I wanted him so badly in those moments, even succumbed to him in a bathroom during our Christmas party, only to find that it drained me for the following week.

I wanted his comfort but knew I had to comfort myself.

And then the blow of him comforting her the following summer came.

"The relationship is a professional one," he ground out. "I'm not with your sister. She works for me now."

"Yeah, 'now,' he says," I mumbled because I was on a roll at this point. I'd never confronted him about dating my sister while I was off at the university trying to get over the miscarriage. I could barely bring myself to keep my grades up, let alone tell a guy who was my crush that I had deeper feelings for him.

"What are you insinuating, Delilah?"

I glared at him. I hated when he used my full name like I was in trouble. "Well, you were with her over a summer." Saying it out loud still had me sick to my stomach. I knew their relationship didn't last long. Izzy called and visited in the fall and told me she and Dante were just friends now, that she had enrolled in community college.

We'd celebrated. I was happy for her. I was happy to see her shine. Now, I thought she probably shined like that because she was having a secret relationship with him the whole time.

I didn't see her much after that. I just struggled to get through college where everything seemed tainted. The student hospital where I'd been told I was pregnant, the cafeteria where I'd had morning sickness, the library where I'd researched how to be a good mom.

I hauled ass when I graduated, telling my family I didn't want to walk in the graduation ceremony or have a party because of the opportunity in Puerto Rico. It seemed to be how I'd change my life. I was ecstatic, in a new place and ready to explore the world away from all the expectations back home.

And all that had been ripped away from me now.

Because of Dante and Izzy.

That thought alone had my gut twisting up in a way it shouldn't.

"So you guys used me as, what? Cover? Was I some decoy so Izzy could get through TSA?" The words came up like vomit out of me, the acid in them vile in my throat. It tasted of old times, of being overlooked, but now with the icing of my childhood crush and my sister using me for that exact reason. "Are you dealing drugs?"

"No." He pulled onto a small side street and killed the engine. He grabbed my chin so I would look him in the eyes. "Is that what you think of me? I'd never put Izzy in harm's way like that."

I should have been thankful, but my stomach twisted. "Well, lucky her," I whispered back.

He caught my pain, snatched from the passive-aggressive comment, and threw it back in my face like he was ready to confront everything head-on. "Lucky? As opposed to you, Lilah? I know you're not insinuating that I'd ever put you in harm's way either. You damn well know better. You were never a part of our plan. I know you're not made for ..." His voice tapered off after he realized his mistake.

"I'm not made for what exactly, Dante?"

He rubbed his forehead, and I saw his jaw moving up and down like he was deciding something. Then those light eyes snapped to mine, and they hardened to the color of a stone I wasn't privy to the name of. The Dante I knew was gone. "You're not made for this, for me, for a life of undercover work which—" He glared at me then, swallowing me up in his gaze and captivating me all over again with a stare that was meant to hold me hostage. "By the way, that's what this is. A government operation. I'm contracted and so is she. And obviously you're not."

My jaw dropped as my mind spiraled, trying to decipher fact from fiction. "You can't be serious?"

He shook his head, and we let the life in the streets of the town play out around us as I searched his eyes for a lie. Then he glanced out at an old building down the alley. "I am. It's too dangerous, and you're a lamb, Lilah."

"My sister and I are made up of the exact same genes, you know that, right?" I pointed out.

"Your sister—" He huffed and then grumbled low, "You know your sister is built different. You might be identical twins, but you played it safe. I'm guessing the only time you've done something out of line was with her."

"*My sister*, the one you dated?" Suddenly, I couldn't stop myself from feeling even more betrayed. My sister had continued to lie to me while we were behind bars. Dante had probably been lying to me with her all these years. Not that I really gave him a chance to talk to me. I was barely around, but that wasn't the point. "The girl you've been partnering with all this time? You two break up just for appearances? You still screwing, even while on the job?"

"Watch your mouth," he threw back like I was a child.

"Oh, are you that protective of your relationship with her

that I can't say you're screwing? Fine, making love? Sleeping together. God, you're both such assholes. And I'm the stupid, stupid—"

His hand snapped out to catch my neck and push me back against the headrest as he turned to glare at me. I gasped, not in fear, but at the spark that flew between us as his pupils dilated, as his hand squeezed at the body part pulling oxygen into my lungs. All his muscles tensed; his veins protruded under the sleeve of his tattoo. I bit my lip as he leaned in close to my ear and whispered against it, "Stop talking bad about yourself. Jesus, Lilah. I'm trying here. I'm not fucking your sister. I never did and never will because I had you first. I told you a long time ago I wouldn't forget, and I haven't, Delilah Hardy."

"What?" I stuttered over his declaration. "You dated one summer. She called me to tell me you guys made out."

His thumb rubbed up my jawline, and he took a second to drag his face across my neck as he took in a deep breath. I didn't know if he was trying to calm himself or if he meant something more, but I was embarrassed at how quickly my body reacted. The goosebumps popped up everywhere, and my pussy pulsed for a man I hadn't had in years.

"Lilah, your sister and I went on *one* date. She tried to kiss me, and that was the end of it. I didn't fuck her because she wasn't you. You're not replaceable."

I recoiled at his confession, how he threw it out like an accusation. My heart pounded while I searched his face, searched for something we still had but shouldn't. I felt the tension between us, thick with secrets and omissions, but also with want. I wanted to cry over the fact that I still longed to run my hand across his strong jaw, taste his soft lips, and have his tongue own every spot on my body.

I hated that I couldn't stop thinking about it even now. "I

highly doubt you're not hooking up with her because of me."

"Think what you want. I didn't sleep with her and I'm never going to. Our relationship is a professional one. One that needs to remain pristine for us to close this operation."

Their years' worth of lies was like ice water being thrown on me. I shoved his hand off my neck, and he let me. "Then do it. I'm not stopping you." I crossed my arms over my chest and glared out the window.

He pulled back onto the road and didn't elaborate for a while longer as he made calls to a few people. Someone named Cade was working on their operation and was going to get Izzy what she needed behind bars.

"She needs money on her card for food," I murmured to Dante as he was listing the items to Cade.

He nodded and added that to the list for Cade to work on.

Once he hung up, he disclosed, "She's fine. She's talked to Cade since you got out. Everything is on track. We get you home and get this finished up and she'll be fine."

"Get what finished up, exactly?"

"That's classified information, Delilah."

I rolled my eyes. I already knew half of the classified information. Izzy was undercover. "I'm not going home." I cleared my throat and spoke louder. "I want to stay here. I have a job here, and I'm more than capable of handling myself, Dante."

"Lilah, I know you can handle yourself ..." He hesitated for a moment and then finished it off, "in a much safer, calm environment."

"Oh, what the fuck ever."

His eyes narrowed, and his grip worked that wheel like he was trying to strangle the life out of it. Good. I'd show him I'd grown way up, even if, at that moment, my maturity level was probably that of a teenager's.

"Can you put aside your emotion for a second? I know you're hurt, and that's fair, but we have a government operation in play and a woman who is undercover in jail that looks just like you."

"I've been here this whole time. No one cares what I'm doing, Dante." I mean, I had to be right about that. Why was I all of a sudden a risk to their operation?

"Jesus, what happened to you just listening for the sake of your family?" he grumbled.

I could have told him my good girl rep wasn't following me here to Puerto Rico with my whole family. I'd come here specifically for the opposite. "What happened is I have a life here outside of them. And what about you two? What happened to being honest with family? God, Dante, she made me think she was still using in there, and I even went as far as ... My words to her were cruel. And she just let me say them all." Remembering it stung, and my heart ached over it. I waited a beat before I said, "It's official. I'm going to kill her."

Dante sighed as if he was processing it all, and then he chuckled. "I'll admit, it was a shitty thing for her to do. But in her defense, she's been working on this case for years."

I shook my head. "I'm not leaving. So you'd better inform me of what's going on."

He cracked his neck both ways before he continued. "If it was anyone else, Lilah, I'd drug them and put them on a plane back home."

He said it with so much honesty, like it was a normal thing to do. It should have shocked me, but I was just sad that this was his life. That the sweet guy I knew as a kid had been subjected to all this. It felt like a movie, like something out of a nightmare.

I cleared my throat. "Well, I guess I'm lucky to be me right now, then."

He sniffed and glanced out the window before he continued. "Your sister is undercover. She got out of juvie and was running in the right crowds for it. She was struggling and I gave her something to strive for. I like to think it kept her clean and focused."

"What? A job as an undercover agent where she was around drugs all the time, Dante?" I wanted to hit him.

"She's always liked a challenge." He shrugged. "Maybe it was the wrong move, but we were both green. I'd been honorably discharged from Delta Force, was given an opportunity for contract work, and recruited her under me. She's been clean ever since, so something worked. Now she's at a point where she's been working her way up the ranks within a drug smuggling operation so we could get intel on larger shipments. It brought her here for the weekend."

"So, her visiting me wasn't even real?" She'd called a week before saying she needed a break from it all, and I'd been so happy to hear from her that I'd agreed. Sure, I couldn't get off work and she'd just have to hang out, but I would still get to see her. "She lied about everything. And me going back home—"

"I'd like to think that was probably your family wanting you home and her thinking she could handle it. You can talk to her about that later. Right now, she'll do time behind bars, make connections, and get out when your parents or the dealers get her out. She can maybe pull off getting a shipment location and we're done. We got enough to arrest the main players and bring down the operation. This hopefully won't jeopardize anything."

"If I've been here the whole time, the only thing that would jeopardize it is if I leave now and don't come back," I pointed out. "You bailing me out of jail and forcing me home is what would call attention to your undercover work."

"Lilah." He shook his head because I think he knew I was right. "We'll figure something else out. It's not safe for you to stay. Izzy and I never wanted you to be a part of this."

"Dante, please shut up," I said, the vile taste in my mouth real at this point. We were nearing my hotel. "I need to get my bearings. How long will it take? Can you speed her bail process along?"

"No." He rolled his eyes like I was an imbecile.

"I'm asking questions to make sure I'm on the same page as you. Don't get irritated with me."

"There's no page for you, Delilah. You have to go home, where it's safe."

I shook my head. "I don't want safe!"

How could I tell him that my mental health had been in the gutter, that maintaining a 4.0 in college was exhausting, and even when I tried to make friends, that fell flat? That I'd never quite found myself because I was too tired and sad to do anything other than get through each day. That when I'd date, I could not find one man who'd live up to the expectations I'd set for them, or maybe the ones Dante had set for me.

That last one was the absolute worst.

"You don't understand anything," I whispered and pointed to a side street. Then I motioned to the building. Just as he parked alongside it, I opened the car door and puked into the gutter.

"Oh, damn," I heard him grumble, and then he was out of the car and around to my side instantly, like he cared. Cared about a sister that could be used as a tool, I guess.

I wondered if Izzy had thrown the idea of me as cover out to him before. Had he turned it down and they'd laughed over my clean image? Or had Izzy thought this all up on her own?

I couldn't stand how mad I was at her and how relieved at

the same time. Relieved that she wasn't using, but mad that she hadn't told me.

And to think I'd accused her of being an addict. I'd been the one who'd supported her this whole time and then threw it all in her face. The idea of our argument brought tears to my eyes, along with the fury running through my veins for her lying to my face again.

"I think I'm going to be sick," I murmured.

"You already were sick, Lilah," he whispered back.

It was then I started crying. Deep guttural cries of relief that my sister was truly clean, guilt that I'd accused her of using, and pain that they'd used me. Maybe one tear was for the fact that the guy I'd lusted over for years and years was the one to get me out of jail and now I'd have to deal with him too.

I mean, it was fair to cry over that, right?

I deserved a minute, or a month. I probably needed a year of therapy or more to get over all this, though.

"Do you know that I was the only one who stood up for her with my family time and time again? The last time we were home, my parents actually said she couldn't come inside. God, how I fought them. And my brothers are such assholes half the time, I swear they relish me getting worked up about something they think isn't a big deal. Dom even said he'd like to be banned from the house for a holiday."

Dante wasn't paying attention to me as I practically slid out of the car over my vomit and started toward my hotel building. He was assessing the location, I guess. He squinted those piercing eyes that I tried hard not to look at toward the building adjacent to us, and then he whipped his head back and forth, looking up and down the street.

I waved him after me and lifted my purse. "Let's get inside."

He nodded without saying much else. He was quiet most

of the time, and so I tried to think nothing of it.

We passed the lobby where I waved to the bellman. He stared past me at Dante with big eyes. Rightfully so. Dante drew attention everywhere, with his tattoos and large frame. I waved Dante toward the side lobby.

"You always take the stairs to your room?"

"Well, yeah. The elevator is always busy, and no one uses these stairs. These only go up to the third floor."

He hummed as we climbed each flight. By the time we got to my floor, I was out of breath. I didn't pride myself on working out, but I was less out of breath than when I'd started here two months ago. I spun to find him not even huffing a little.

Dumb military and secret missions kept him in shape, I guess.

"So, can you tell me what it is I can tell my family, because I need to know what to say to my mom and—"

"I'll tell you inside." He nodded as he stepped close to me, so close I could smell the sandalwood on him. Jesus, that smell I remembered. It dominated most of my dreams through high school. My hand shook as I put the key in the lock.

I heard the lock click, and then I turned the knob to let him into my place.

Which was a bit of a mess. Izzy and I had gone out the night before, and we'd packed quickly. I hurried to grab a bra off the floor and move the scattered toiletries off my bed.

The man always tried to be respectful. He turned toward the window to look out as I tidied up. It gave me enough space to calm myself.

While straightening the white sheets of the bed, I informed him, "I need to call my family and let them know everything is going to be okay. My mom is worried sick. As you know after her telling your mom—"

"Izzy called me, Delilah. Not your mom."

Right. That snippet of information continued to roll around in my head and knock every button of irritation in me. I tried to contain it, though. That was their life. They lived undercover. I had to be okay with it.

"Well, I called my mother, and she's worried sick. My story was obviously a lot harder on Izzy than it should have been. I need to clear that up with her and let her know everything is going to be okay."

"You can't let your mom know about the undercover work."

"What?" I whispered. That was impossible. I told my mother pretty much everything. I'd even divulged my crush on this man to her at one point, only to be told to wise up, that he went for women like Izzy.

It was true, but it still hurt to hear it from my own mother.

Over the years, I'd learned a thing or two about being a different woman. I knew what I wanted now, and I was going to put my foot down when it came to it. I was going to live a different life here.

And no one was going to stop me.

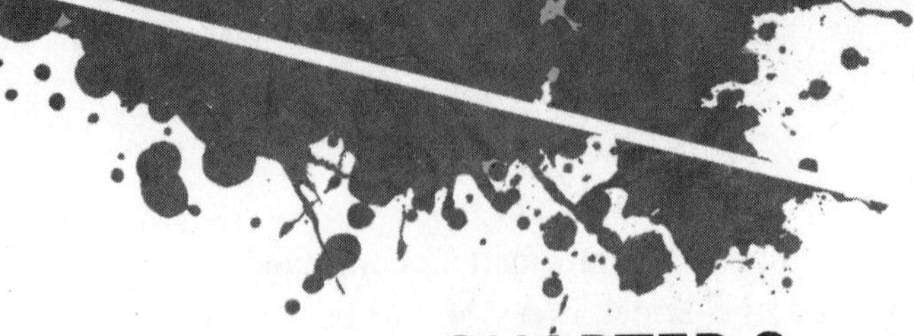

CHAPTER 8: MAKE THINGS DIFFICULT

Dante

It took me two seconds to make the decision that Delilah was going home. Whatever plan she had here was over and done with. She'd have to figure it out somewhere else.

I couldn't focus with her ass here, and I knew the mission was in jeopardy with her gallivanting around the island.

Plus, her hotel room was in no way, shape, or form safe for her now.

I knew she was used to seeing a side of me that appeased her, that went with the flow, but that wasn't an option anymore.

"Delilah, you're not telling your mom anything, and you're getting your ass on that plane."

She dropped the clothes she'd been putting away. "Excuse me?"

"You're not staying here. You need to go home to—"

"To what, Dante?" Her arm flew out with her shout. "There's nothing for me there. I'll get lost in ..." She drifted off and glanced away. She was keeping something from me; I just had to figure out what. "Boredom. I'm so bored, I would die back home. Do you think I enjoy being the forgettable sister? The one that people literally don't remember. I mean, my sister used me as a fucking decoy probably for that very reason."

"I don't think that's the case." Izzy wanted this as badly as I did, but I didn't think she would have done that to her sister.

"Why not? You think she was inviting me back home while smuggling drugs for funsies? She and I both know that she's prettier, louder, and crazier than me. No one ever forgets her. And I know I sound stupid and petty and bitter about it. I'm trying to grow from that and learn who I am *here*. That's fair, right?"

Why was there sudden pain in my chest? Was this girl about to cause me a heart attack? "This isn't about fair—"

"Maybe not for you. But for me, it's what I have to do. Because if I'm there, I'll just fall back into what I was and I can't. *I can't.* I wasn't happy, and I thought so much about— I just need to be away from that place. And let's be honest, no one misses me there. They have Izzy to worry about. I can go to the supermarket and literally five people stop to ask how she is, what she's up to, and when she's coming home. You dated *her* for God's sake, and I would have died to date you back then."

"Delilah," I started, trying not to get whiplash from her confession. She'd pushed me away long ago. She'd left me high and dry in that bathroom and told me not to call her. I took a breath, trying to leave the past in the past because we were spiraling out of control before we even figured out the next step in this operation. "If you want me to apologize for—"

"Oh, God. I don't care now." She shuddered like suddenly I was repulsive to her. Me, the guy who made her come when her mom was right outside her bathroom door. Me, the guy who'd taken her virginity and had her orgasming numerous times that same night. Me, the guy whom she'd promised a relationship to, only to snatch it back weeks later.

I couldn't stop the words that came from my mouth. "You don't care? Well, I still get to say my piece. You hopped off that counter at Christmas and told me we were better off family friends. You said you didn't want me, even while the taste of your pussy was in both our mouths. So if I fucked half the country—including your sister—since then, you definitely shouldn't care." There went all the meditation I'd done to get over her.

Her jaw dropped like she couldn't believe I'd go there. "The taste of my ... You cannot say things like that to me."

"I'll say whatever I want to you. I'm not sugarcoating anything with you anymore. We're adults." What Delilah didn't understand was that my go-with-the-flow attitude that charmed most of our small town was long gone. I'd been subjected to too much for too long since then. And I'd embraced the other side of myself.

"Oh. Well, I'm glad I graduated from kid sister to adult. In that case, I'll say that we obviously did the right thing by stopping our sexual relationship in that bathroom that night. We are very different people now. I, for one, would not lie to my family the way you both have. Nor do I ever want to be with someone who throws the taste of my pussy in my face."

I should have gone to my car and meditated or some shit. This woman had the ability to drive me to insanity within seconds. "You sure about that?" I stepped close to her, and her breath hitched. "I seem to remember you liking me talking dirty to you about it with your legs spread."

She licked her lips and fisted her hands. I saw her gaze drop to my mouth. It was fast, but it was there, right before she took a large step back. "Just because we fucked a few times, Dante, doesn't mean I enjoyed you any more than the others. I wanted to date you *before*. Not now."

Her confession gutted me. Didn't she know she had been it for me at one time? The thought deflated my anger. So I met her truth with my own. "I would have dated you then, Lilah. I tried."

"No, I'm not ..." She blushed and shook her head, like she didn't need my validation, but it still raised an emotion in her.

That I got any reaction almost had me smiling despite our arguing. This wasn't supposed to be what I was doing. I shouldn't have wanted to make her remember that we could have worked, but I had to know that she felt the same. If I had to remember her screaming my name and the taste of her pussy, she needed to remember too.

"I don't need you to say that, Dante. I don't want you to feel bad for me, okay? I hate that you do. I'm fully capable of handling myself." She shook her head fast, and her soft waves fanned out around her as she rubbed her eyes. Then she chuckled. "Why are we making this so complicated? I'm here to uncomplicate all my little complexes, to not worry about this anymore. I mean, do you know I screwed a guy from our hometown in college because he wanted to pretend I was Izzy? He basically did it as a favor to me—"

My eyes bulged at her confession, and she snapped her mouth shut like she hadn't realized what she was even saying. What type of men was she hanging out with? "What the fuck is his name?" I grabbed my phone out of my pocket to figure out his address as soon as she gave it to me. "I want his name right now."

She snapped her fingers in my face. "Dante! You're not focusing. I made that choice. I wanted to screw around. I wanted to be free to be a mess. I was so sick of being this perfect, innocent little bird to everyone."

"Innocent?" I spat. "I seem to recall us—"

She cut me off as her face heated. "Okay! That was one time. Please do not bring it up. Let's continue to successfully avoid it like we have for all these years."

"More than once, Lilah," I corrected. "And do you mean how you've 'successfully avoided' me in general? Because I never avoided you," I threw back. If we were going there, I was going all the way there.

"That's neither here nor there. We don't have to talk about any of this ever again."

"Okay." I dragged out the word. We needed to table things. We needed to reset and recenter. The more pressing issue I had was that she never told me nor reached out about any of this. "Still, why didn't you tell me you felt this way?"

"Seriously?" A laugh bubbled up from her like she was confused. Then she was doubling over and laughing like it was a big joke. "Dante, we weren't talking."

"You'd emailed me for years, Lilah, before ..." I stopped because I didn't know how to describe what we'd had. "I would have been there for you."

"I didn't want you there for me like that. I didn't know where I wanted you. I just knew we weren't friends."

I stumbled back like she'd physically hit me. "Of course we were." I'd tried to be everything to her back then. I might not have been close to her, but I thought I was her rock like she was my last glimpse of light. "I drove you to school. I brought you gifts from overseas. I went searching for hours for little shit you'd like. You think I just stumbled across a damn lamb carving? I hung out with you that night because I wanted to. Not because you were the last resort without Izzy and your brothers not being home. I definitely didn't—"

"Don't, Dante." She pursed her lips. I was pretty sure she was trying not to smile about the fact that I had been about to bring up fucking her again.

"Fine." I held up my hands. "But I wanted to be there for

you. I thought I was. The guys that followed you around, I made sure you weren't subjected to their bullshit."

She shook her head and let out a little huff that could have been a chuckle. "I'd have loved to be subjected to someone's bullshit, but honestly, I'm happy I subjected you to mine first."

"Lilah, what we had wasn't bullshit."

"Oh, God. Do you listen? Look, we're both better for it, okay?" Her lip trembled like she was holding in the world.

"Did I hurt you as much as you hurt me?" I had to know because the pain that overtook her eyes made me want to pull the information out of her any way I could.

She shook her head and closed her eyes so tight, I wanted to grab my question back. "I went through a lot. And I know that I probably owe you an explanation as to why there was so much avoidance after I went off to school, but I can't visit that now. I need to be here and be happy and be away from my life back home."

"You'll tell me why one day?" I ventured, trying not to push her.

"I think so." She nodded once and then glanced around her hotel room. "I love it here, okay? People know me here. They think I'm great, and for the first time in a long time, I think that about myself too. I'm not running back to Mom and Dad just because you two messed up something here. Figure it out and leave. I want to stay."

"Lilah, that's hard to do." I cracked my knuckles, trying not to be turned on by her new stubbornness. All of a sudden, I was nervous that I wouldn't be able to handle this situation as well as I had all the ones in the past. "I have to focus on the right way to get your sister out of jail, and then we have to finish up an operation that has been years in the making."

"Am I jeopardizing the operation?"

"Not necessarily." I tried to work through how I could protect her here, if I could make it work. For anyone else, I wouldn't even have contemplated it. Yet, Delilah didn't stick to her guns about anything. She'd always been the person everyone could rely on to go along with whatever made everyone else happy. Her not doing that told me she must really need this. I also knew from experience that I had a hard time not giving her exactly what she needed. "But this can put you in harm's way."

"I'm the good girl, Dante. No one has been worried about me, right? I hung out with Izzy the whole time she was here with no mishaps. Just leave and know that I'm fine."

"It would be easier if you went home."

"I'm staying here. Leaving doesn't actually help you two, anyway. It would look suspicious." She turned on her heel and waved me off. Like she could walk away from me.

My hand shot out and grabbed her elbow. The sparks between us, the ones I felt every time I touched her, singed my skin and ignited the fire in me for her. "You make things so difficult, you know that?"

"I definitely don't. I make things less difficult! I never put up a fight, and I don't normally do things for myself."

"Could have fooled me," I grumbled, and she spun around to stare me down. I didn't waver in my stance.

"What are you talking about?" she whispered, like she was daring me to bring it up just one more time.

No one had to dare me or coax me into that. I had it locked and loaded. "You know damn well what I'm talking about."

"I don't think I'd be held liable for decking you in the face at this point," she ground out. "But go ahead. If you're going to keep circling it, you might as well spell it out for me, Dante."

Aside from where her chest heaved, the color on her cheeks deepened just a little but not too much like when she was embarrassed. Her chin lifted to accentuate that thin, beautiful neck of hers.

It was a side of her that I was instantly addicted to.

"You think I wanted to be the one to fuck the virginity out of you?" I asked the question slowly and pointedly.

"Oh my God. That's how you're going to describe it?" Her voice carried disdain at my audacity.

She was going to learn I had a lot more where that came from. If she was staying here, she was going to get a whole new side of me.

CHAPTER 9: MAKE A LIST

Delilah

Focusing on his words rather than my own embarrassment was the only way I could come out of this situation with any pride intact. I wanted to crawl under a rock and never show my face to him again. Still, I stood my ground. I'd learned that it was the only way I could face things. If I didn't, they'd eat away at me for months and months. "You have some nerve throwing that in my face like your dick wasn't happy."

"Delilah." His gaze was fire now, his voice low. "My dick is always going to be happy when it's inside that pussy of yours."

I gasped at his words. I think I even took a step back because I wasn't expecting them at all. Dante used to be the sweet man who treated me like Dom's baby sister, and then I was this girl that he seemed to think had his heart. But his words were laced with lust and bite this time. I wasn't used to the sting of them. "I don't think this is the best time to discuss this."

"When would be a better time?"

"Well, probably never. It's not going anywhere. It already happened. We've both moved on from it." I shrugged.

"Did we move on, though?"

"What's that supposed to mean?" Was he insinuating that I was still hung up on him? If so, I could get over his huge ego and his huge everything else real quick.

Or at least, that's what I would tell him.

He sighed and pulled at his neck while looking at my ceiling. "I don't want to fight with you. I'm tired. You're tired. You probably haven't had a good shower since you've been in jail, and we need to make a plan for Izzy."

"Great. Good. Go do that. I'll be here."

"No." He shook his head slowly. "You won't be, sweetheart. You can't stay in this room. You shouldn't have been staying here in the first place."

"It's the best place for me to be."

"The street isn't patrolled enough, your locks on this level aren't great, and the lobby man is letting strange men walk in with you. Not to mention that staircase is so dark a man could kill you in it without security cameras picking up on it. We'll have to change that."

"I'm fine." Scratching my temple as I thought over his assessment and backed up toward my bathroom, I realized I should probably just give in and go home.

Yet, whatever little food I had in my stomach curdled in disgust at the thought.

"I'll agree to you staying in this hotel because you're right that anything else would cause attention, but I'll be talking to them about changing your accommodations and room number. You'll be moving to my level," Dante concluded.

"Your level? What are you talking about?" I was too tired to figure all this out. "You can't force me back to our hometown, Dante."

"I literally can and I will. I've done a lot more to people I don't care about. For you, I'd drag your ass across the ocean in a heartbeat if I thought it was necessary. I'll help you pack and move up to the twentieth floor where I'll stay too. Your choice."

On top of the small table in the room, I'd propped a clock against the wall. It had little birds on it that chirped every hour. It was a stupid reminder of home that I couldn't leave behind. We let the seconds tick loudly by, and a bird chirped.

"Six o'clock," Dante announced, not looking at the clock at all. "The robin says time for me to go home so you can all do your homework. That's what your mom would have said. Today, it's time for you to make a decision."

"Mom always listened to that clock, didn't she?" I tried not to smile at how well he remembered our childhood.

He nodded. "What's it going to be, Lamb? You coming with me or am I dragging you home?"

I took a breath and hoped I was doing what was right for my mental sanity. "If I go to your stupid floor, I'm doing what I want when I'm there. I'm doing *Eat Pray Love* type stuff here. This is my way of finding myself. I need this, Dante. I don't have anything else."

"You need to stay safe first. I'll allow for anything around that."

"I don't need you to take care of me." I ran a finger over the clock and tried not to look at him.

"Oh, believe me, I know. You've made that very clear over the years."

"Are *you* mad at *me*? After all you and Izzy did?" My gaze snapped to him then.

"I'm not taking the blame for what Izzy did. Maybe we should have disclosed our operation to you and maybe I would have, had we been closer. But we weren't. And yeah, I'm not happy about it. Haven't been for years. I don't really care one way or the other at this point, though."

Even though he suddenly sounded defeated, like we couldn't argue because it made no sense to do so, the words sliced through me. My heart wanted him to care, and maybe that was because I'd been so lost within my depression for so long.

Not that he knew. And not that I could blame him for getting over me. I'd wanted him to.

I sighed and told myself I had to be strong. I just had to accept what we were. And that was nothing.

"Well, I think it's better we don't bring it up, then," I told him. Because I couldn't tell him I did him a favor by not writing him back. That my life got so dark and twisted in college that he wouldn't have wanted to be around me.

"Just pack up so we can go, okay?" he grumbled.

"Fine." I matched his tone. "Remember what I said. I don't want a keeper while I'm here."

"Until you go back home, I'm your keeper, your bodyguard, and whatever the hell else, Lamb."

"What if I never go home? What if this is my home now, or what if I want to travel the world and never set foot in our godforsaken hometown again?"

"Mm." The rumble from his chest was low, guttural almost, and I wanted to bottle it up and have the sound for my late nights alone with my vibrator. I didn't know how he'd turned into the only man I lusted over, especially after the pain I went through after losing our baby. Yet, he was pretty much the only guy I thought about when I touched myself or was getting off. My body seemed to know that and responded instinctually to him all the time. "I think I'd have fun chasing you around the world."

Was there innuendo there? Had I caught a flash of something more?

Then he cleared his throat and blinked once, and every emotion I thought I saw there was gone. Dante was cool, calm, and collected around me. I was back to being friend-zoned. The little sister.

It was where I belonged. I knew that.

We'd swept that little stint of a relationship under the rug.

The bump wasn't too big, even if I tripped over it every single time I walked by it.

He dropped me and my bags off at a room on the twentieth floor after making a call to the front desk. I was sure it was the top one, and the room was luxurious enough that I made a mental note to ask him the cost in the morning.

He told me he had to figure out some room logistics before he left me there, putting his number in my phone.

I showered.

I changed into clean clothes.

I cried.

And cried.

And cried.

And then I fell asleep.

* * *

When I woke up, it was to a knock at the door the next morning. And I didn't think before opening up, forgetting to ask who it was.

"Lilah, did you check the peephole?" He glared at me.

"I'm ..." I stammered, not at his question but at seeing him standing there dressed in business wear that fit his wide shoulders just right, looking utterly delicious with a bag of what I figured was breakfast food. "I'm very tired."

I made a show of rubbing my eyes as he sighed and walked past me. He set down the bag on the counter of my hotel room because, yes, it came with a whole freaking kitchen and granite countertops. "You took in a lot of information yesterday, and we also got off on the wrong foot."

I nodded at whatever he was saying like I was paying attention to it, but I was actually paying attention to how nice he looked in slacks and a collared shirt. The white on his honey-colored skin made me want to tear it off and lick him, my body craving one more taste.

"You sleep well?" He turned and leaned on the counter to assess me.

"Of course. Seems this floor has a lot more luxuries." I waved my hand behind me. Then, I bit my nail as I assessed everything more. "I'm pretty sure my comforter is down, and my pillow might be made of clouds. My view up here is spectacular too. How much is this costing me?"

"It's costing you nothing," he grumbled and dug a food box from the bag and set it on the counter. When he opened it up, I saw a sweet breaded pastry with icing and eggs with chorizo. He then pulled out some fruit I'd never seen.

"What is all this?" I asked, my mouth watering.

He pointed to the pastry. "Pan de Mallorca. It's sweet and pairs well with their local fruit here: quenepa and guanabana."

My stomach growled. He smiled and stared at my midsection. "You hungry, Lamb?"

"I don't think I realized how hungry until this second."

He pointed to my bed. "Sit. Let me feed you."

I dragged a hand along the comforter before I sat. "The bed's much better than the one downstairs."

He hummed but didn't say anything.

"The access to this floor is exclusive, Dante."

He nodded, not giving me any indication as to why we were getting such special treatment.

"Does the government put all their officials up in places

like this?"

"I'm contracted, Lilah. It's technically private but for the government. Different from when I was in Delta."

I sat on the bed as he took the pastry with the ooey gooey icing from its container and placed it on a plate. "I didn't talk to you much when you were in Delta Force."

"You didn't talk to me at all," he retorted, an edge to his voice.

Sighing, I combed my hand through my hair, something we both knew I did when I was nervous.

"I'm giving you a hard time, Lilah. Don't pull your hair out over it." He glanced up and winked at me as he licked some of the icing from his fingers.

Snapping my gaze from his, I silently scolded my body for reacting. I felt my nipples puckering under my tank, and I knew I didn't have a bra on.

It wasn't my fault the man was as hot as he was or that I still remembered everything he excelled at in the bedroom.

I cleared my throat. "Thanks for bringing food." I tried to stare at that instead. I hadn't had a good meal in days. The hotel never served food like this, and obviously the food in jail was a joke. "Where did you get it?"

"Just downstairs."

I narrowed my eyes. "Dante, I've been to all these restaurants."

"But you haven't been *with me* to all these restaurants, have you?" He smiled big enough for that dimple to indent his cheek, and I rolled my eyes. My body was never not going to be attracted to him.

He brought it all over to me. Then he sat in the chair across from me, lifted one of his leather loafers onto the knee of his gray slacks, and stared at me as he leaned back.

"Um, what are you doing?" I waved my hand at the chair and table where he lounged.

"Watching you eat," he said matter-of-factly as he pulled at the collar of his tailored white shirt. "Put food in your mouth."

The smell of frosting was too good to pass up, even if he wasn't going to eat with me. I sliced a piece off the pastry and popped it into my mouth. "I'm not going to eat all this." I said around the food, and then I let it melt and enjoyed the sweet, savory taste all at once. I hummed and then said, "You should eat too."

"I worked out and ate already."

"You did all that? Are you down the hall? When did you wake up?"

He shrugged. "Before you."

"And you showered and got ready, obviously, because this"—I motioned with my fork—"is not the way I'm used to seeing you dress."

"Guess we both have to get used to one another's new wardrobes."

I rolled my eyes. "Mine is much more casual than yours."

"Yours is going to get us both in trouble."

I shook my head and ignored him. I wasn't going to indulge his big brother attitude. I could wear what I wanted, when I wanted to wear it. It was something I made sure to do here, along with a lot of other things. I deserved not to worry about what other people were thinking or what I should be doing after spending so much of my life doing the exact opposite.

He checked his phone while I ate in silence. I tried my best not to ask him a million questions, because it was better to start on the right foot.

"So, I should thank you for the room upgrade." I'd had a better night's rest than I thought I would. "Like I said, the bed is really soft, and today I'll probably end up jumping on it since I have more energy."

"Jump on it? Really, Lilah?" He shook his head at my idea of fun.

"Try it before you knock it."

"I don't jump on beds, Lamb," he said through a smile.

"Ever?"

"Ever."

"Well, why not? It's fun."

He quirked a brow at me. "There are other fun things to do on a bed."

I blew a raspberry and continued eating my food. I practically shoveled it into my mouth so I didn't have to respond.

When I'd cleared the plate, I glanced up to find him trying to hold back a grin. "You done avoiding my comment now?"

"Oh my God." I grabbed my plate and went to put it in the sink. "You could just drop it."

"Fine." He rubbed his head and got up, testing the softness of the bed by pressing his large hand against it. "Guess it has good bouncing power."

Maybe it was because I felt like we needed to kill the awkwardness between us, or maybe I needed to just lighten the mood, but instead of agreeing with him, I shoved him hard. He fell into the plush pillows. Or glided. I knew he'd let me because Dante was practically immovable when he wanted to be.

I jumped up on the bed and sprung up and down, with him lying there. He looked up at me as I said, "Soft, huh?"

"You look like you did when you were about twelve." He put both his hands behind his head as he lay there.

I plopped down next to him and stared at his big body taking up half the bed. Muscle on muscle on muscle. The tattoos on his neck peeked out from his collar. I didn't know what was farther down, on his chest. Never got a chance to really look since he got inked, but now my fingers itched to peel back the shirt and see.

I sighed and smoothed the sheets under me instead, busying myself with nonexistent wrinkles. "I don't feel twelve anymore. And I have a lot more responsibility. Like for this hotel. I'll pay you back somehow because this is ..."

Suddenly, my throat tightened up and relief washed over me. I had a full belly of good food, wasn't alone, and was free from jail. I hadn't figured out everything with my sister, but in this hotel, with Dante, I felt a lot safer. Going out on my own after being surrounded by family had been scarier than I'd ever expected.

I struggled not to burst into tears.

You don't realize how close to the edge you're living until someone pulls you away from it.

"I'm really, truly thankful," I whispered through the knot that had taken root in my throat.

"Lamb, pretty girl, what's wrong?"

I wrinkled my nose. "No sweet names, Dante. You'll make me believe them and cry."

"I only say what I mean."

Dante was too good a guy and had always been a charmer. Did he say *pretty girl* to most women? Did he believe that about all of them?

I breathed out a heavy sigh. "I think I'm just overwhelmed. I didn't realize until now. I've wanted so badly to do all this alone and have something of my own. It's been hard to adjust sometimes, though. And now, this. It feels like a blessing and a curse at the same time."

"Curse, why?" He frowned at me like he couldn't understand that anything could be wrong.

"Well, for one, jail. What am I supposed to say to everyone here? I'm supposed to be gone for days."

"Stay holed up here and be gone, then."

I nodded. It couldn't be that easy, though. I picked at my nails as I thought about it all. "I said such nasty things to Izzy, Dante. And now she's stuck in there."

"She'll forgive you," he said and pulled at a strand of my hair. "And she wants to be stuck. You forget how strong the Hardy girls are, huh? And remember, not only are you strong, but it's pretty much impossible not to forgive you."

His stare was on me, but it looked far away as he rubbed the tress between his thumb and a finger. He'd done the same exact thing the first night we'd shared together.

It made me want to throw all my cards on the table and address the elephant in the room so we could move on. "Do you forgive me for everything?"

He smirked at me and lifted a dark eyebrow. "What was it that you did that I need to forgive you for, Lilah?"

I shoved his shoulder and then fell back on the bed to stare at the ceiling. We both lay there, the chandelier above our heads shining crystal clear down at us. Someone definitely cleaned this room every day—and a lot more thoroughly than the one I'd been staying in.

I cleared my throat, hoping to clear the air between us too. "You know exactly what I did. I shouldn't have acted like we were just casually hooking up the first time, and I shouldn't have stopped responding to your emails. I'm sorry for that."

He nodded, like he was waiting for me to continue.

"In my defense, the first time ... Well, you would have said no if I'd texted you what I wanted."

"Damn right I would have said no."

His honesty stung. "Was it that bad?"

His jaw worked next to me. "Bad to be with you? No. Never. Bad to feel like there was something more? Maybe."

"There was more!" I said immediately. "Things changed in college. And I probably should have explained better, but what I wrote in the email was all I could say. At least I did say we could catch up when we got home."

He grunted. "We caught up all right."

"Dante," I warned.

When he met my gaze, his was hard, cold, and unrelenting. "I seem to remember you getting a pretty good Christmas present, but that's about all."

"Wow." My jaw dropped. "If you wanted an explanation so bad, maybe you should have stayed. You were gone after Christmas Eve. Then my brothers said you left the bar with a woman." I poked him in the shoulder and then sat up, furious at myself for letting my hurt show.

"Lilah, you didn't ask me to stay. You specifically said we were better off as friends. So I found someone who wanted to be more than that. You didn't, right?"

I chewed on my cheek so I didn't let my jealousy unfurl. "I didn't." I threw the words out fast. I couldn't let him know that I still thought about his hands on my skin or how his eyes traveled up and down my body with a heat I hadn't experienced since. I got off the bed fast, knowing that if I checked my panties right then and there, they'd be wet. "I don't want more. I'm just saying it wasn't as easy as me fluttering off to school where I was having so much fun."

"Why not?" he pried.

I bit my lower lip and glanced out the window at a different view of Puerto Rico to the one I was used to. It showed the beach and the sun and a life of beauty and freedom. I came here to be free of my obligations back home, to be free of what everybody thought I was—perfect ... when I wasn't.

"Because my life changed."

"Did I do something wrong?" He sat up and stared at me, really assessed everything about me in that moment.

"You couldn't do something wrong to me even if you tried," I whispered, and I felt it through my whole soul.

"So something happened that I don't know about," he concluded.

I did the stupid thing and ran my hand through my hair.

"You're nervous and about to lie." He pointed to my hand, which I dropped immediately. He sighed, and his jaw ticked. "Don't bother. Tell me when you're ready."

I went to the window and said, "This is much more complicated than it should be. Izzy was only supposed to be here for a few days, Dante, and this is supposed to be the place where I—"

"*Eat Pray Love*, I know. What's that mean, exactly?"

"It means I do things for myself. It's the ultimate self-exploration trip. My therapist ..." I hesitated on the word. It felt good to admit I had one, but I knew people often recoiled when they heard it. Dante didn't flinch or even lift a brow. "My therapist said I should make a list of things I want to do. Not worry about anyone else. So I did. And now I'm doing them."

"Where's the list?"

I pulled at a dark wave of my hair before I answered. "In my head."

"Want me to dig through your suitcases? You were valedictorian and are the most organized, driven person I know. Let me see it."

I couldn't remember all the stuff I had on it. Well, I could. And it was embarrassing. "It's not important."

He got off the bed and went toward my suitcase. "It's

important enough that last night you told me you had to do it."

I hustled up behind him and tried to get around him as he rummaged, but the man was fast and much better at finding hidden objects than I would ever have imagined. He checked the exact pocket I'd put the notebook in first and sidestepped me as I tried to grab it from him.

"This is a complete invasion of privacy," I whined.

Instead of responding, he read it out loud:

Lilah's *Eat Pray Love* List

1. Leave home

2. Do something crazy

3. Explore food here and EAT

4. Explore places here and PRAY

5. Explore men and LOVE

6. Find peace

"Care to elaborate on number five?" he grumbled and tilted his head, staring at me with those emerald eyes of his.

"No." I straightened my back.

"It's not safe to go dating people you don't know in a place you're not comfortable in. Your brothers would—"

"I'm an adult, Dante." I snatched my book from him and spun around to put it back in my bag. "My brothers sleep with women all the time."

"Your brothers can take care of themselves."

"As can I."

He growled at my statement and pointed my way. "This *Eat Pray Love* stuff is only you looking for trouble."

"You have to take risks to know your limits and yourself. I know you know that. You were in the army. Did you not take risks there?"

His strong jaw worked up and down, up and down. "You don't want my life."

"I want a better one than I have. I've done nothing but wallow in what everyone expects of me so far."

"That's a good life," he bellowed. "We expected great things."

I shook my head. No one understood. "Well, lower your expectations."

He pulled at his neck and stared at the ceiling. "Just remember not to get on your knees and eat, pray, and love with the wrong man."

"Did you just ... I'm not dignifying that with a response, Dante. I'm going to get dressed." With that, I hurried to my luggage and grabbed my swimsuit and a sundress.

I took seven breaths in the bathroom before I threw on some strawberry lip gloss and changed into a summer dress.

I could be around him and still find my way here. I simply had to get a handle on myself.

He'd said I was an adult, and I knew that was true. Still, I felt like a damn child sometimes. What way was right, what way was wrong? Did anyone in the world even know?

I spritzed on some body spray and came back to the room to find him lounging still.

"What is your plan for the day?" I asked, hoping he would be leaving me to my own devices.

"I have to work, but if you're going down to the beach or—"

"I think I need to decompress here today." I planned to get lost in a book or three. It was my only way to calm down. "And I need to call my family today or tomorrow."

"Well, Izzy wants you to make it clear this is all her fault."

My eyes widened. "Is she going to ever call me?"

"You know her phone time is limited."

That made me want to scream. I smoothed an imaginary wrinkle in my dress instead. "She can't seriously expect me to keep this secret."

"We do and you will."

I stomped over to the kitchen and grabbed a glass to fill with water. "I tell my mother everything."

"Well, you'll have to exercise restraint."

I took a sip. "She's already so mad at Izzy. We can't keep throwing her under the bus when—"

"I thought you were mad at her, anyway."

"Well, yeah, I am. But that doesn't mean everyone else gets to be mad at her."

Dante never understood sibling dynamics. The proof was in the way he squinted at me like I made no sense. "Okay. Well, I'll be working in my room. If you need to leave, call me."

"Hardly freedom when I have to tell you exactly where I go and what I do with my time. And is your room just across the hall from mine? That's ridiculous." My tone was pouty and immature, but he was ruining my whole traveling nurse gig.

He chuckled as he walked past me and handed me my list. "I'm happy to eat, pray, and love with you, Lamb, but I'm not letting you out of my sight for too long."

I breathed out a loud sound of frustration and stomped over to my books when the door closed behind him.

My freeing trip had just turned into what felt like witness protection.

* * *

I wasn't proud to admit that I stayed in my room the whole day reading.

The next morning, I almost called him to see if we could go over exactly what I'd say to my mother. I'd charged my phone all night and ignored the missed calls and emails waiting for me.

I'd been off the radar for a couple of days, anyway. The only person I needed to update was my mother. She'd spread the news to all who would listen in our town.

I bucked up and dialed her number. When she answered, I sighed at the fact that I was about to lie straight to her face.

Obviously, I knew it wasn't literally like that, but it felt like it as she cried over the phone. "I'm so happy you're safe. And Dante will get Izzy out too, right? Is he with you? Can I talk to him?"

"With me?" I repeated like the idea was ludicrous.

"Well, he came to get you out, didn't he? I don't know what that means, Lilah." She had the audacity to act affronted. "You certainly thanked the young man, I hope. And there's no better thank you than—"

"Mom!" I bellowed into the phone, my eyes widening.

"What?" I pictured her shrugging and pushing that dark hair that looked so much like mine out of her face. "You had a crush on him, no? Maybe it went further after he did such a nice thing for you. That's all I'm saying."

"I can't believe you right now."

"Well, I would approve if you did. That's all I will say." All of a sudden, she was whispering angrily at my father, and I knew he was chastising her too.

"Thank God that's all you'll say." I was floored by how

quickly she wanted me to put out.

"Oh, don't act like he's a stranger. You've known him your whole life, Delilah. He's practically your brother. He was with your siblings every second of every day."

"All the more reason for me to not do anything with him." I almost said *ever again* but I caught myself.

"Well, Dom is here, and he said Dante better not. So maybe it's a good thing you're the responsible one, huh? I don't want those boys fighting. I just want grandbabies, and can you imagine the little munchkins you two would have?"

"I cannot with you right now, Mom," I grouched. She had six kids and somehow wanted more, even though I knew my brothers were still running through her house half the time on vacation. "I'm going to lie low for a few days, okay? I'll call you when I'm back at work. Let's focus on getting Izzy out of jail."

"Well, maybe she needs to stay there for a few weeks," my mother grumbled, but I caught a hint of sadness as she said it.

"Let's not jump to any conclusions about what—"

"Lilah, don't make excuses and don't tell me to hope for the best with this one, okay? You could have been in danger. You still might be, right now," she huffed. "Has she even called you?"

Well, no. There was that too. I knew she was making calls to Dante's associate, Cade, and to Dante. She didn't think to call me to apologize, though. "I don't think she gets much call time, Mom."

"Well, she barely calls me anyways. I don't know where we went wrong with her."

That should have been the moment I told her. Speaking up was the right thing to do.

Yet, the government thought it wasn't.

I sighed. "She'll get better, Ma."

"You were always better about understanding her."

"She is my twin." I shrugged and tried to chase away the frustration by rubbing my eyes.

"Well, please make sure Dante stays with you for a few days, if possible. I think I'll call his mother."

My gut reaction was to tell her no. It would help with our story, though.

So instead, I appeased her. "I'm sure he'll be working around here for a while, Mom. I'll keep in touch with him. No need to worry, okay?"

"Of course I'll worry. Your father and brother are mumbling that they miss you. Come visit soon, okay?"

I got off the phone with her a minute after and went to shower. The water pressure deserved a massage award compared to where I had been staying. I tried to relax into it and not think about a thing for all of ten minutes.

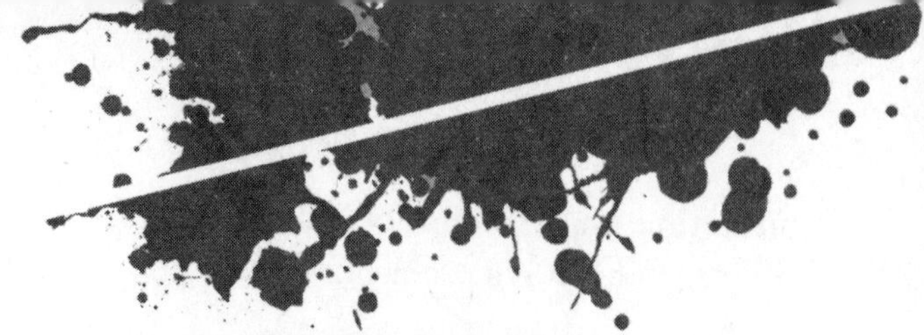

CHAPTER 10: LIE TO YOUR BEST FRIEND

Dante

We'd only been near one another for a few days, yet already the smell of her was fucking with my head.

I rubbed a temple as I got two guys stationed on staircases of the hotel that very next morning just in case.

I'd left her alone all night, which was more than enough leniency. In my mind, she should have been in witness protection. I wasn't putting Delilah in any unnecessary danger. I called Cade to watch the security cameras so no threat would go under the radar. "Make sure no one suspicious is down our hallway."

"I'm not watching a fucking camera for hours, man," he said it like it was above him.

"You watch a screen all day while you fiddle on computers. What's the difference?"

"Fuck off." He knew he didn't have to dignify my question with an answer. "I'm waiting on this cruise ship to set sail so I can see what guys leave on it. I got other shit to do. Call someone else."

"I don't trust anyone else," I griped into the phone as I heated some water on the stove.

"Man, unless this girl is your girl, I'm not spending this

much time on her. She's not Izzy. There's barely a threat—"

"Any threat is a problem." I wouldn't have Delilah exposed to anything I did, ever.

"Why? Izzy's threatened daily."

"Izzy signed up for this job, dumbass. She's trained. I'm not working unless I know she's safe."

"So, she's your girl, then?"

"Fuck off. She's my best friend's kid sister."

"She's a hot piece of ass, isn't she? She hotter than Izzy?"

"Say it again and I won't be working on torturing anyone but you."

He laughed like he enjoyed all this. Cade hid behind the screens and coding. He didn't let many people into his world, and most who knew him just a little thought he was a bit off. Yet, I knew he'd gone to great measures to make sure his now sister-in-law and brother ended up together. There was a soft spot for love in the man that he didn't want anyone to see.

"I'm going to enjoy seeing you get pussy-whipped, man," he said.

I didn't have time to argue with him, because my cell lit up with Dom's name flashing on the screen.

"Shit," I grumbled. Delilah was up. I'd heard her moving around and then talking with someone. It meant my best friend knew I was here, and I was going to have a hell of a time explaining why to him. "Do as I say, Cade. I'll talk to you later."

I switched over and didn't even start with a hello. "Before you say a word, you know I'm special ops here and your mom told my mom. It didn't take much else." I poured some of the hot water from the stove into the manual pour over coffee maker I'd bought. It was only right to drink Hacienda San Pedro coffee that way. It was some of the best in Puerto Rico. After the hurricanes there, I was happy to be able to find some.

"Before I say a word? What the hell do you think I'm going to say?"

That I was fucking around with his baby sister.

We sat in silence because I wasn't admitting that. Ever.

Then he sighed. "I'm calling to say *thank you.*" He emphasized the word, and it made me feel like a pile of shit right away. "I heard Ma talking to Lilah. Jesus, I almost flew down there today to try to work something out."

"We got it under control."

"She okay? She look shaken up or anything?"

"Nah. She'll be fine. I'm going to be here for a while, so I'll be able to check in on her." I didn't tell them I'd moved her right next to my hotel room. I wasn't even sure Delilah knew there was just a wall separating us.

Which was probably for the best.

"Alright. Good." I heard his breath of relief over the phone. "I'm happy you're looking out for her. She's more of a kid sister than Izzy, you know? And Izzy needs to be in jail long enough to realize the consequences of her actions."

"Izzy's probably just going through a rough time." God, they gave her hell, and she took the beatings in stride because she wanted this mission to play out.

"You always had a soft spot for her, Dante. Probably too soft."

"Fuck you," I grumbled. Dom was way too protective of both his sisters, and I'd already gotten one fist to the face after taking Izzy on a date.

"We can't keep giving her passes. She got Lilah locked up this time." I heard him sigh, and the turmoil in his voice was palpable.

I ignored it, though. My job was to ignore the pain and trek forward at any cost. "Delilah's fine."

"How long you there for? I'm going to fly down in a few weeks. Mom and Dad are working on bail money for Izzy but are researching rehab facilities first. I think she needs time there."

I winced at that, but it was what Izzy and I were banking on. She would build her name in prison, dig out more intel on the drugs being smuggled, and then we'd find enough evidence on the boats Cade was watching to hopefully bust a cruise ship or two.

"I'll be here."

"So, you and Lilah are good?" He asked the last question with a bit more caution. Izzy was one thing—I'd gotten a fist for that. I'd get him trying to kill me for Delilah.

With Delilah, no one was good enough.

"We're fine, man."

"Nothing going on there?" His voice was low like he wasn't sure he should have asked the question.

"What the hell does that mean?" I didn't have a right to be offended, but I still was.

"I got to ask. I know she's like family to you too, but she's still my little sister."

"What if there was?"

Silence stretched over the line before he ground out, "There better not be, asshole. You might be military, but I'll still kill you."

"You know I'd take care of her."

"Do I need to get on a plane right the fuck now? What the fuck are you talking about?"

I didn't know what I was talking about. Didn't know why I even pushed the idea. "Nothing. Nothing's going on." The lie slid out faster than I would have liked. Truth was, there was always something between me and Delilah, even before I slept with her. Maybe it was the fact that we all put her on a pedestal and, in the dark of the night where my thoughts ran wild, I wanted to drag her off it. Or maybe it was because she looked at me like she didn't want to be up there in the first place. She'd been locked up there for ages, always wanting to come down and explore. For far too long, I'd ignored it. Until she took the leap down from the pedestal herself.

Now, I'd had a taste and I couldn't seem to forget about it.

"Just keep it that way, Dante. You got a world full of women. My baby sister isn't one of them."

"You're on some shit today," I countered and then changed the subject. "Go out and have a drink. You got a world full of women too."

That had him laughing, and his concern was forgotten.

So easily was a mind distracted. I wished I could distract my own enough to not think about the woman on the other side of the wall. She may not have known that I was just a room over, but I'd made sure I was. I needed to keep her safe.

I went on to take a shower, one that was cold enough to freeze my balls off. Didn't stop me from gripping my cock and thinking about the blush that rose up over her tits and cheeks when I'd said that her pussy might still taste as good as I remembered.

"Fuck." I jacked my hand up and down, over and over again. I told myself she couldn't taste as good. I was putting her on that pedestal again where no woman belonged.

Still, she'd been sweet and salty and so wet for me. I remembered how the smell of her sex had mixed with that coconut oil she used as lotion and that floral shampoo of hers. She still smelled the same, and it made me wonder if her pussy did too. It'd been years, but I still wanted her. If only for the pure goal of proving she wasn't as delectable as I remembered.

Yet, as I fucked my hand harder, the head of my cock reddening as I got to the edge of reason, I pictured her dark hair and how it had grown out long in waves that curled around her curves in all the right places. How she'd gasped when I'd told her my dick was always happy in her pussy. How her lips had parted so wide that I could imagine them around my cock.

"Delilah," I groaned as I came harder than I had in a long time. Women weren't doing the trick the way Dom had said. Unfortunately, his baby sister was it for me.

I had all the women in the world, but the one I wanted was off-limits, and that just made me want to cross the line even more.

CHAPTER 11: BEACH FINDINGS

Delilah

The ocean breeze blew in and mixed with the coconut oil I'd put on after talking with my mom and then showering. It reminded me of the times I would rub oil on my belly in the hopes the pregnancy stretch marks wouldn't come.

I never got that far though. My tummy was unmarked, brutally pure in a way I realized I didn't want it to be.

I jumped when I heard a ping from my phone, and my hands flew from my stomach.

I grabbed the device from the counter and wrapped a towel around my body.

Dante: You staying in your room today?

Me: How'd you get my number?

Dante: That's classified. Now, tell me what you're doing today.

Me: Do I have to stay in my room?

Dante: At least stay at the resort. Go

swim if you want, but don't leave. The buffet isn't open to the public, so you can eat there. Otherwise, let me know what food you want and I'll bring it to you.

Me: This is only until tomorrow when I'm technically back in town, right?

Dante: As long as the threat to you doesn't change.

I sighed because that wasn't the answer I wanted.

Me: I guess I'll swim or maybe go to the beach. I read theirs is private.

Dante: I'll go with.

Me: Don't you have to work?

Dante: You're now part of my job, Lilah. Get used to it.

I jumped again when I heard the knock at my door, my body so wired from him being near.

I glared at the door. He damn well knew no one could be ready that fast. So I yelled, "One minute."

Quickly surveying the room, I threw on a white swimsuit I'd just bought a week ago off some inexpensive website and added my flowy yellow skirt and matching crop top over it. The color made my skin look tanned and I needed all the help I could get when it came to looking good in front of my childhood crush.

As I walked across the white tile of my hotel room, I shoved a few pieces of clothing in my suitcase and opened the door.

Dante in beach shorts and a white linen top probably should have been illegal.

"Hey." I waved him in as I combed a hand through my wet hair. "You don't have to follow me around. I'll be fine hanging out here."

"I know," he replied and plopped his butt right on my bed. "I'm just trying to figure out how I'm going to check things off your list with you."

I huffed and plugged in my blow dryer. "Those are my plans, Dante. Not yours. And tomorrow I go back to work and can do all those things on my own. Don't you have a job to be doing?"

He started to say, "It's my job to keep you—"

I held up my hand. "Not following me around. I can get a cop to do that if it makes you feel better."

His brows slammed down. "That's not happening. I have guys I trust guarding the hotel when I'm out. Otherwise, it'll be me. No one else."

"You have guys guarding us?" I squeaked. "What for?"

"As a precaution."

I tried not to let him see my hand shaking. "That's so over the top. Izzy was trying to do these men a favor by carrying drugs back to Florida, right?"

He narrowed his eyes like he wasn't going to answer.

"If that's the case, she got caught with me, but I didn't do anything. I was out in a day or two because of my family friend, right? No one knows you or me here. We're fine." I waited a beat and then said again, "Right?"

"Maybe." He shrugged. "Maybe not. It's class—"

I turned the hair dryer on. I didn't want to hear that word again.

When I smirked at him, he shook his head and got up from the bed to stalk toward me. My body still reacted the same to him after all these years. My adrenaline, the jitters in my belly, and my core tightening all happened at the same time. The logical side of me told me to back away from him.

I wasn't looking for logical and safe here, though. I wanted to live.

So I stood my ground as he came closer and closer. When he leaned in and stared at me, inches from my face, I was reminded that he was a whole head taller than me. I couldn't stop myself from looking at his pillowy lips with him this close. I didn't know if only a second went by or a whole minute.

Suddenly, the sound of my hair dryer cut off. He held up the cord end as he took one step back.

Unplugging something: that was the reason he'd come so close.

Not to kiss me or tell me how much me being his best friend's kid sister didn't matter. Or anything like that.

"Let's go have breakfast and go to the beach, huh?"

I shrugged and grabbed my purse. "I'm going either way. If you want to come, that's fine, but I don't want to be a burden. Go work if you have to."

Dante just smiled and opened my hotel door for me.

I followed him as he walked me through the hotel. I pointed out the bird sanctuary where I'd seen peacocks on my first day and also told him that there were all sorts of lizards running around. "It's such a beautiful hotel."

"It is. Probably one that should have better security for the first few floors, though."

I rolled my eyes. "My room wasn't that bad."

Before he could argue, I pointed out a swan on the water and murmured an 'aw' when another swan came to nestle into the other bird's neck.

"They're monogamous for life," Dante told me.

"I wonder if those two are."

"Probably." He shrugged and kept walking like he knew the way to the restaurant.

"Have you stayed here before?"

"Once or twice," he admitted, and I sighed. No wonder he had breakfast connections.

I didn't pester him about not disclosing that information. He'd been all around the world, so I couldn't expect him to share everything. Plus, the weather was a balmy eighty degrees and there wasn't a cloud in the sky. My day at the beach would be perfect.

"I might try snorkeling today," I said. "It could be one of the things I love enough to pray to."

He squinted. "So praying is just being grateful for new hobbies?"

"Sure." We got to the restaurant that overlooked part of the beach and the pools that sparkled in the sunlight and were seated immediately. "I figure my mom already raised me with church every Sunday, and I don't know. I don't have things I know I like to do other than read and study."

"You like studying?" He lifted a dark brow.

"Well, I like doing well in school and in my career. I like learning new things."

He chuckled. "What's your work schedule going to be? I can teach you a hobby or two that doesn't involve studying."

The waiter came by to take our order, then I rambled off my weekly schedule. "I work twelve hour shifts three days a week because the ER has long hours. I leave a bit early to catch Ubers, though."

"I can get you a driver."

"The government will do that?" I asked, not understanding that type of perk. Then I shook my head. It was confidential and he wasn't going to tell me more. "It's fine. The hospital reimburses me because I was supposed to have a place closer to them, but it filled up."

He nodded, but it was like he wasn't listening. "A driver would be best."

"Dante—"

"Lilah, we follow my rules for protecting you and your bucket list gets done, okay?"

Our bickering was cut off by our food arriving and me trying a quesito. It was a fluffy pastry wrapped around cheese, and I almost fell on the table in delight as I savored it. "Okay, I should have tried these way sooner."

Dante sipped his water and winked at me. "I think we might have found your favorite food here."

I smirked, and the butterflies that had long been dormant with other men fluttered to life. Avoiding his charm was near impossible when my heart knew him so well and my body longed for him. So I embraced the good meal with good company and relaxed. When I finished, I grabbed my sunglasses out of my beach bag, along with my Kindle.

He asked, "What are you reading?"

"Would you believe me if I said a self-help book?" It was a lie. My kindle was filled with hot men on covers and spice so hot that I was sure my face was on fire.

"Lamb, when you blush like that, it's motivation for me to steal the thing from you to read myself. Self-help doesn't do that to you."

"Well, it could be a different sort of self-help." I shrugged, and my cheeks heated even more. Was I flirting with him now?

"Okay." He narrowed his eyes in challenge. "What's the self-help you're reading today?"

I bit my lip. "Well, the guy in this one explores temperature play with the main character."

I saw how his eyes widened just a fraction, and I tried my best not to glance away.

"Anyway," I announced fast while I pointed at the lounge chairs out on the sand, "Time for me to go read."

"I'm thinking I might enjoy reading with you," he mumbled it so quietly, I wasn't sure he wanted me to hear him. Then he cleared his throat. "I'll go for a swim and grab a few towels."

I waved him off, my heart beating fast from just our little bit of flirting. I needed to get away from him, try to relax, and enjoy what I had come here to do in the first place.

Explore the world, Delilah. And maybe explore some men, my therapist had told me. As I spread out on one of the lounge chairs, I remembered that she'd also said to bring my romance novels to Puerto Rico and take a page out of one or two of them. She said I deserved to be happy.

Happiness was fickle, though, and I'd been chasing it for a long time. Through grades, through the approval of others, and through doing what I thought was the right thing.

I found my eyes drifting to the one thing I wasn't supposed to indulge in that seemed to bring me all the happiness.

Dante.

He stood there in all his glory, smiling at a beautiful towel girl who flipped her hair dramatically in front of him.

When he laughed at something she said, I blew a raspberry. I was far enough away and the waves crashed loud enough that he wouldn't hear.

That view of him with another woman was exactly why I needed this place to myself. My body needed to stop lusting over a man who didn't lust over me anymore. I needed to get over my trauma and move on.

And that need had me scrolling my Tinder account and swiping left and right for what felt like an hour. It was draining trying to figure out if any of those men would even be compatible.

I started messaging a guy who I thought was really good-looking and figured I could work through the texts I'd gotten during the time I'd been in jail.

I'd avoided them until now, thinking it would be too much to lie to everyone.

Thankfully, there weren't many, but my brothers were being dicks on the family group chat now that they knew I'd been in jail.

Dom: Did you make sure not to drop soap in there?

Dimitri: Man, that's a joke for men in jail, idiot.

Declan: Yeah, they don't put men and women together in jail. Do they?

Dom: They better not have. Lilah? You weren't with men in there, were you?

Me: Can you all please do something else with your time? I'm trying to lay low before I start work. I actually

have to focus when I'm there. Lives are on the line.

Dom: Not like Declan's work where he just tackles people for no reason.

I laughed at that because we constantly teased Declan, who was in the NFL. My other brothers made good livings in tech and engineering. Collectively, we'd made our mother and father proud.

I ignored the group chat after that so I could go through the rest of my texts. One in particular I had been avoiding was my work friend, Allan. He was a resident to become a doctor, and I was sure he was into me.

I thought I was into him too. Enough that I'd maybe indulge in some fun with him.

Still, my fingers hovered over his text message inviting me out for drinks once I was back in town. We'd already been out twice. And he was everything I thought I wanted.

Except that Dante was back here.

Swimming in the ocean right in front of me, making it hard to concentrate on anything else.

But beautiful towel girl made her move, running to give him a towel as he came striding, soaking wet of course, out of the beautiful blue water. When he idled near her, drying off, I had the reminder I needed.

There was nothing between us. Dante and I may have bickered, and he may have teased me with a few lines here and there, but he probably had women around the world waiting for him. I needed to have my fun here.

Eat. Pray. And freaking Love. That meant putting myself first and moving forward instead of back.

I texted Allan that drinks would be great. And hopefully, things would progress to mind-blowing sex so I could forget about Dante's muscles dripping with ocean water.

I grabbed my belongings and hurried back up to the room without him. I glared at my reflection in the mirror, my hair windblown and most of my makeup gone from sweating in the sun. I threw my clothes off and stared at the new lingerie I'd purchased in my suitcase for this trip.

I slid into the red lace and took a peek at myself again. This time, my cheeks were flushed, my hair wild but maybe sexy.

I nodded.

I was just as good as any girl on that beach and Allan, at least, would see that. I jumped when I heard a knock at the door and raced to throw on a night shirt and shorts over my lingerie.

I sighed as I opened it. "I'm just lying low the rest of the day, Dante."

"Delilah, ask who it is before you open the door." His voice was low like he wanted me to really listen this time. "When you leave the beach, you need to tell me."

"I didn't leave the resort." I crossed my arms over my chest to hide how my heart had started to pound out of my chest from him standing directly in front of me in wet swim trunks with no shirt on. I couldn't make out all the tattoos without staring but the ones across his chest and ribs looked intriguing.

He lifted a brown bag. "Got you some food since you forgot to eat and it's almost dinnertime."

I didn't invite him in. He was half naked and my body had gone off the deep end imagining what it would feel like if I rubbed my hands over him.

"I even got a *quesito* in here. Let me in." He tilted his chin at the door I was holding half-closed.

I shook my head and opened the door wide. "You may

enter."

He patted my shoulder and walked on by to set the food on the counter. "You didn't snorkel today."

Glancing out the window at my ocean view, I didn't confess that I had to get out of there before I clawed the towel girl's eyes out for staring. Plus, there was another reason. "I think I'm scared of it."

"Scared? Little Lamb, what for?" He smiled softly at me like he genuinely wanted to know.

"You know, that nickname is demeaning."

He blew a raspberry and pulled out a box of food that smelled delicious. "It's not. It means you're cute and—"

"—innocent and pure and probably naïve. I don't want to be any of those things."

"But those things make you close to perfect," he murmured.

I blew past him, ignoring how smooth he was. "Your charm only works on women who don't know you use it on every one of them."

I probably shouldn't have said it, but I was remembering the long blond hair of the towel girl and couldn't stop myself.

"I don't use my charm on everyone, and I only say what I honestly mean." He handed me a box of food with a look of question in his eyes.

"I believe you really mean everything you say, Dante." I shrugged before I took the carton and went to sit at the table near my bed. "You just view the world beautifully and make everyone feel beautiful in it."

"You forget I've seen a lot of uglier things than most, hence why I appreciate the beauty."

"Fair." I opened my carton and stared at the food that smelled so sweet and glorious. There was nothing to say other than, "What is this? It smells like I died and woke up in heaven."

"*Mofongo.* It's plantains and garlic and olive oil, with a few hidden ingredients, fried and mashed together. If done right, it's the best thing in Puerto Rico."

"I think I can officially check off my favorite food here, and I haven't even explored good food outside of this hotel."

"We will." He stood leaning against the counter while he watched me eat.

"Do you want some?"

"Already ate."

"Well, you can't keep feeding me and not eating, Dante. It's weird to have you watch me eat every single time."

"I'll make a note of that," he murmured. "Anyway, I just came by to give you food and let you know I won't be around much tomorrow."

"That's fine. I have work and ..." I physically had to stop myself from combing a hand through my hair. Was it weird that I didn't want to tell him about my scheduled date too? "So, I guess we won't see each other much for the next few days." I wrung my hands around and around at the thought.

Dante immediately caught me doing it and slid a hand into mine. I glanced up at him in confusion, but he didn't let go. "What's worrying you? You wring your hands when you're nervous."

"Well, do I tell everyone at work what happened?" I squeaked out. Jesus, what would I say? *Sorry, on my few days off, I got arrested for carrying drugs, but it's fine. I wasn't actually guilty. Just my sister.*

"No." Dante took my chin in his big hand and turned me to look at him. "You tell no one. Got it? You did nothing wrong in the eyes of the law. To everyone, on paper, it was a complete misunderstanding. In three weeks or so, Izzy will be out too and we'll finish things up and be gone. If you're going to stay here longer than that, you just go about your business like nothing happened."

"Okay," I whispered, but my brain wasn't catching up. I tried to tell myself this was all right, but it felt all wrong. How could I go back and work in the ER with sick patients and act like I was an upstanding citizen when I'd been in jail this last week? I sighed and grabbed a plastic fork from the bag to dig into the food.

He leaned against the counter and watched me eat. When I moaned around the food, he chuckled.

"One day, I'll learn to cook this." I pointed to the food. "You sure you don't want any?"

His eyes twinkled as he shook his head and kept smiling at me. "I'm not going to take your happiness from you."

"It is seriously pure joy. Good food and good books are probably my favorite things. And I need them right now because I'm about to go to work and have to speak a second language while worrying about whether or not they think I'm a criminal."

Dante knocked his knuckles on the counter, grabbing my attention. "Focus on your job, Lilah. Don't worry, okay? I'm going to have to teach you new tricks to calm that overwhelming anxiety of yours, aren't I?"

"It won't help. This is a serious situation, Dante."

He stepped toward me like we'd been in each other's personal space a million times before. I leaned back because we hadn't. Not for years. "If you say so, I guess I'll believe you. Actually, in all my time in the military and working for the government, I haven't been thrown in jail."

"Yeah, well, you have credentials. I don't. What if my supervisors find out I lied? They did a background check. I take care of people for a living, and they can't have a criminal working among them. What if they sue me or something? I don't want to go broke and be thrown back in jail. Or worse, lose my license."

He shook his head and chuckled before covering my rapid-fire mouth with one large hand while putting the other behind my head to hold me in place. "Stop talking, Lilah."

"But ..." It came out garbled, and his hand tightened to keep me quiet.

"Listen to the silence."

I squinted at him and, after being silent for a second, threw my hands up. I shoved his hand off my mouth. "What are you talking about? That doesn't work."

"It does. The silence tells you to calm down and realize there's a world around you still moving, still making noise. There's no real silence because your little catastrophe didn't end the world."

"This isn't little!" I screeched and stood up, moving away from my food. I took a breath. God, would he make fun of me if I started counting? I spun away from him. "And on top of all this, I have a date tomorrow after work with Allan."

"A date?" He narrowed his eyes. "A date? You think that's smart right now?"

"I've been putting it off. We already went on two, and he knows I'm supposed to be back in town by then. I can't stand him up."

He hummed but didn't share his opinion. He just stared at me, his piercing green gaze assessing. His jaw flexed, and the tattoos on his neck seemed to grow bigger and bigger. "Fuck it," he grumbled before he said, "You're tense. Let's try something to relieve some of that, huh? I'll go get it."

I was about to respond, but he turned slowly, pointedly not heading back toward the hallway. Instead, he walked past my plush bed, past the nightstand, and right to the wall.

I blinked.

One, two, three times.

Then my mouth dropped open.

"What the hell is that?" I gawked at a small straight crack I saw in the wall near my bed.

"It's our adjoining room door." He faced me and smiled as he said it so matter-of-factly that I wanted to smack him. He then took a key ever so slowly from his back pocket and swiped it behind him into what looked like the edge of the wallpaper and crown molding.

The stupid wall buzzed, and he opened it.

"No." My voice came out low and angry, my heart beating fast. He wasn't on the other side of the hallway or just down the hall. The man was a wall over, literally a door away, easily accessible, especially for him. I shook my head, pacing up to him, and then reached around him to try to close the door. When he stood in my way, his arms crossed, I shoved him. He didn't grunt or move an inch.

Growling, I spun toward the hotel's phone. "Have you been there the whole time? I'm not sharing a room with you, Dante."

"It's not exactly sharing. Plus, I need to make sure you're safe, Little Lamb," he whispered, waiting a beat before finishing, "from anyone and everyone."

I threw a withering gaze his way. "Where is my privacy? What if I have someone over? I don't need you listening ..."

"Listening to what?" he goaded me. He knew exactly what I was trying to say.

I didn't answer him. Instead, I continued on my mission. He chuckled at my stomping and leaned on the doorframe like he had all the time in the world to watch me throw a tantrum.

He'd see how he liked the tantrum when the hotel traded

my room. I dialed the service desk and listened to the man greet me. "Yes, my evening actually isn't going well at all. It seems my room is adjoined to another man's and he has the key."

"Oh, my goodness. I'm so sorry about that, Ms. ...?

"Ms. Hardy. Twentieth floor. I'll need a room—"

"Oh, Ms. Hardy. Of course!" He cleared his throat. "We can't provide you with a room change. Mr. Armanelli requested that you be next to his room."

"What?" I whispered as the name he announced over the phone traveled through my mind. "No, Dante booked my room. Dante Reid."

"No, miss. Dante Armanelli checked you in. And we so appreciate—"

Dante ripped the receiver from my hand to finish the call. "This is Dante. I'll take care of the misunderstanding." He hung up the phone, and I stepped back, confused.

"You took the pseudonym of a mob family here?" My voice was high as I asked him.

"I took the name I was given by my father here," he said it calmly and quietly like he was trying to soothe my nerves.

My hands shook, though. And my heart felt like it'd moved to my throat to beat furiously. I glanced up at him. "You're telling me ..."

"Go on." He waved his big hand in front of him, urging me on. "Ask the question."

I considered throwing the phone on the nightstand at him.

"You're related to them?" I whispered.

His beautiful face moved up and then down. Once and then twice. He was nodding, confirming what I said, and keeping his gaze on me like I might run.

"You can't be." I shook my head and tried to suck in air, although it seemed all of it had been stolen from the room.

The Armanellis were cold-blooded killers. Since the '60s, they'd been in the news for drug trafficking, money laundering, and murder. They were the biggest and most infamous crime family in America. Even now, their name was tied to rigging elections and controlling the government and nuclear bombs, having enough money to rule the country.

"You aren't one of them," I murmured. "There's no way."

"Why? Because my mom is mixed?" He scratched the side of his face. "Lilah, my dad is Italian. Directly related to Mario Armanelli. Cade and Bastian Armanelli are my second cousins. We tell most people we're friends if they see us together and I try my best not to be seen with them now when I'm undercover. Still, we're family."

I knew my eyes widened. Everyone was aware of those names. They were infamous. We saw pictures of them in news articles and read about the crazy stories of them controlling billions of dollars within the country. I tried to understand what he was saying. "But I've never seen you in the news."

"We go to great lengths to control the media, Lilah. And my mother doesn't share my family background with many. I went into the military knowing I'd need training beyond what we did quietly for me at home growing up. They also provided me with other skills while I was in. I've worked with the mafia most of my adult life."

"No." I sat down, trying to process the news articles we'd seen over the years. Dante was good. He was safe. He wasn't them. "They're murderers."

"I've always been that too."

"No." I shot up off the bed and rounded it to point at him. "Don't you ever say that being in the military is killing. That's being a patriot. A war hero."

"And I've done what I had to do for my country as a war

hero and as part of the Armanelli family. I came to terms with that a long time ago." He took in a breath that I knew was measured, the type he took when he was trying to calm himself. "What I do for the government and for the family is one and the same. We're not all bad. We've done a lot of good recently."

"You mean to say—"

"I'm telling you everything is intertwined, and you're smart. You know this. You watch the news."

"So I'm living with the mob now?" I bellowed.

"Well, I live a door over. I can move in here if you'd like to make your statement a fact."

"You have the audacity to make a joke right now?" Fisting my hands, I spun away from him and then thought better of that. Don't turn your back on a killer, right?

The smile that whipped across his face was devastating. "Little Lamb, are you suddenly scared of me?"

"Don't be a jackass, Dante," I sneered and combed a hand through my hair.

"You fiddle with your hair when you're nervous. Want to breathe?"

"No. I don't want to breathe with you!" I wanted to punch him instead. "You've been lying to me. About everything. Izzy! Yourself—which, by the way, is an epic betrayal on so many levels, and about your own freaking name."

"Lying?" He paused. Then something broke in him and he yelled, "Lying? You haven't talked to me in years, Lilah."

"I can't with you right now." I pushed at my temples and waved him away. "Just go."

"Or what?" he whispered, and the menace in it was real, tangible, almost sadistic. My heart leapt at the same time as my pussy clenched.

"Or I'll make you, Dante," I snapped back because I didn't

want to be the one who appeased him anymore.

He hummed. "I like this new fight in you, Little Lamb. I have half a mind to make you really show it to me."

I hated that my whole body lit up and blushed at his statement, that I licked my lips automatically and he watched me do it. Still, I wasn't backing down. He'd pushed me over the line into losing common sense. I met his lies with taunting and anger, ready to throw accusations in too. "And how exactly would you do that? Torture me? Kill me? What is it, exactly, that you do for the mob, Dante Armanelli?"

One small flash of hurt was all I saw before he spun away. "Enjoy your book, Lilah," he murmured. Then he slammed the stupid adjoining door shut behind him.

CHAPTER 12: A MASSAGE TO REMEMBER

Delilah

I slumped onto the kitchen's little barstool and tried to move all the puzzle pieces of my life around. After about ten minutes, I sighed. They didn't fit the way they were supposed to anymore, and I knew our lives were creating a whole new picture.

Even if I wanted to go after Dante, I needed a second to comprehend all the omissions, all the lies.

One breath, or maybe seven, and I could focus again.

One. He was the mob.

Two. He was still Dante.

Three. He'd gotten me out of jail.

Four. His name wasn't what I'd thought it was, and I'd screamed that name countless times with my vibrator.

Five—

"I got some stones." His deep voice from behind me made me jump.

"Dante!" When I spun to find him standing in that adjoining doorway again, my jaw dropped, and I tried my best not to look like I was salivating. He stood there like the Dante I remembered, in sweatpants and a T-shirt that fit snugly over his massive chest. His biceps bulged against the fabric, and I licked my lips as my gaze trailed down the veins of his arm to where he held a dark bag.

"I was going to read and go to sleep," I said.

"No, you weren't. You were going to be mad and stew. You need to relax. So let's try something else." He lifted some stones and then oil out of the bag to place on the nightstand. "A massage."

"Um, I don't like massages." I clammed up immediately, my shoulders tensing and my back going ramrod straight. The idea of someone's hands on me like that made my skin crawl.

"Who doesn't like a massage, Lilah?"

"Me. I never relax. I feel like a stranger is poking and prodding me in all the wrong ways."

"Well, I'm not a stranger, Lilah," he said quietly, a look of something like determination on his face.

No. He was worse than a stranger. I'd only breathed to four, but that four was a good reminder of why this man could not give me a massage. He was the guy I'd lusted over far too many times to have him rubbing me in a non-sexual way. Then he was the guy I'd cried over because I'd lost something he never even knew was partially his. Now, he was someone I didn't even know.

"Sometimes, you look at me with such sadness, Little Lamb." He moved the stones into a line on my nightstand like I'd agreed to this. When I didn't respond because I knew I couldn't, he blew out a breath. "Lie on the bed and tell me why you can't stand the sight of me. You had that sad look long before you knew my real last name."

"You're not giving me a massage, Dante." I threw my hands up and paced the tile between the kitchen and TV.

"Delilah, I don't issue commands for people not to follow them." There was that voice again, the one that sounded so different from the boy I knew and grew up with. Here, he was dark, ruthless, unrelenting.

And it made me stop pacing immediately. I froze and stared at him as I chewed on my lip. "I'm not sure I know who you are at all. You've omitted the truth about your name, about my room, about everything. Maybe you are a stranger, Dante Armanelli."

"I can be if you want me to," he said, holding my gaze like he was asking permission. There was some line there, one we'd never crossed, and maybe I wanted to toe it, see if it burned me to be on that edge. There was a part of Dante I'd never seen, and even after all these years, I wanted to be greedy with him.

Even more, I wanted us to coexist here, and I wanted to be able to stand on my own without getting lost in this man. That might have meant seeing what I could handle with him, seeing what I was capable of.

Or maybe I was indulging in not doing what was expected. I wasn't quite sure. Still, after a beat, I slumped onto the bed, sighing out, "Fine."

"Shirt off," he commanded.

I couldn't help my eyes widening. "Seriously?"

"I'm giving you a massage. That requires oil. You want it on your clothes?"

I rolled my eyes. "Turn around, then."

He lifted a brow as if I was being ridiculous. "We're not past that? I've already seen you naked."

He was practically saying he wasn't attracted to me, I swear. He smirked like this was all so easy for him, and that made a dimple pop in his beautiful cheek. I had to stop myself from literally getting up and licking it. The fact that my body reacted to him that quickly—but he didn't react at all—had me wanting to show him otherwise. If he was past it, I suddenly wanted him to prove it.

I narrowed my eyes, and just as he was about to turn around, I pulled my shirt over my head.

It was his turn to look shocked. "Fuuuuck," he dragged out and stared down at me. His pupils dilated, and I felt the wave of his hunger as he licked his lips.

"Dante." I leaned back as I placed my hands behind me on the bed and let my breasts hang out on display within my red lace bra. I was so happy I'd bought some lingerie before I'd come to Puerto Rico. "I can put the shirt back on if you aren't past seeing me without one."

He cleared his throat, and I saw his Adam's apple bob once before his intense gaze was back on mine. "Lie down, tease."

"Me?" I giggled as I turned to lie on the bed and face the TV. "I didn't even want my shirt off. I thought it would be weird."

"Sure," he grumbled like he regretted his decision. He walked past me to grab my ice bucket and filled it with ice from my fridge in the kitchen area.

"What do you need that for?" I pondered out loud.

"It'll cool the rocks." He didn't elaborate much as he walked back to the nightstand.

"Okay. Well, are you going to turn the TV on or something while we do this?"

"No." The rummaging behind me had me glancing over my shoulder. He had poured some sort of oil that smelled like peppermint onto his hands and was rubbing them together, slowly, methodically, rhythmically.

I was doomed.

"Head down and relax," he murmured. "This is to get some of your stress out. You can't do that with the television on."

"TV always makes me relax."

"Sure, but it doesn't make you work through whatever

issues you're having."

Suddenly both of his big hands were on my back, rubbing warm oil into it, and all I could respond with was a hiss. Dante's skin on mine was like gasoline to fire. I sparked and blew up every time. My whole body tightened under him. My nipples, my pussy, my ass, everything. I would be surprised if he couldn't feel my skin going taut.

"They aren't issues," I grit out. "They are real life concerns. You're not who you said you were. After all these years ... Does my family know?"

"You think they all know and kept it only from you?" he inquired.

"You know, I'm the older sister—even if it's only by three minutes—but everyone still treats me like ..."

"Like a baby and their prized possession?" He chuckled. "Because you are that. You've made all of them proud."

"Not sure why. I'm an adult, not a baby, and we all have good jobs."

"You're the one who didn't do much wrong."

"True. I worked hard to become a nurse."

He hummed, and I felt it right down to my toes. "I know. You always tried hard at school."

His hands slowly dragged all the way up my back, fingers feeling each vertebra and pushing into the divots of my spine like he knew exactly which points needed his pressure. I moaned when he got to my neck, and I didn't know whether to relax into his kneading or jerk off the bed. My body warred with itself, desiring more but knowing I couldn't give much of anything.

"I should have tried harder," I said, "and we both know it." The fact that I hadn't become a doctor was always a point of contention with my parents, and I'm sure my mother shared it with Dante's mom.

They didn't know, though, that I had just been trying to stay afloat. Getting good grades had been harder than ever before. I'd been drowning in self-loathing, and my therapist kept saying I had to give myself time to heal, to relax, and to be less than perfect.

"Try harder for who?" he pried as he kneaded at a knot. "You seem happy being a nurse. What good is a job if you're not happy?"

Dante always tapped into the journey of being human and made it sound so simple. "Maybe I like being a nurse and maybe I like the idea of climbing to the top and being a doctor. I just wasn't sure I was good enough to do it," I confessed. It was something I never said out loud but the words tumbled out like I'd been holding them in for a long time.

"You can be whatever you want, Lilah."

He said it with enough conviction that my throat clogged before I replied, "Sometimes, I wish we'd continued to talk through my college years."

"Are you admitting that your issues with me stopped you from reaching out?" He asked the question barely above a whisper, and I contemplated acting like I hadn't heard him.

Instead, I opted for lying. "I don't have issues with you, Dante."

"Is that so?" He pushed his thumb into a tight spot on my neck and then rolled a stone into it.

"Jesus!" I tensed under the pressure and tried to move away from him touching that spot. He didn't let up. Instead, his body pushed harder into mine, making it so I couldn't wiggle away.

"Relax," he commanded, the rock still pushing into that area, but I tried to listen to him and let out a breath. As I did, he dug in harder, and I hissed at feeling my muscles being worked out of a knot they'd probably been in for months. I practically orgasmed from the feeling. Somehow, it was painful pleasure; the line you walk between agony and pure bliss.

"Dante, that feels amazing," I moaned as he continued working. "I should be embarrassed by the sounds you're pulling out of me."

He rolled the stone over me again, and I gasped and wheezed. This time, his hands were lower on my back, and I knew I couldn't ignore what I was starting to feel. My pussy had been wet from the start, and now I knew for a fact I would end up orgasming and making a fool of myself if we kept this up. I knew it was wrong, that he didn't want me that way, but my body still reacted to him like we'd slept together, like it was desperate for him, and like I'd masturbated to thoughts of him more than once.

My body didn't lie.

I willed myself to bring my hands up toward my shoulders so that I could try to lift myself from the bed. "I don't think this is a good idea, Da–"

He shoved me back down. "Delilah, you need this. Your muscles are rigid. You'll go crazy with the amount of anxiety and pain you're bottling up here."

"I bottle a lot up." Most specifically, my sexual desire for him. "That's beside the point. I can go to a masseuse."

"They won't do it right." He sounded irritated.

I hummed. His hands were like magic, and they hadn't stopped. "They'll do it just fine. Plus, this is bordering on the limit of what my body can take."

He chuckled. "Really? I seem to remember your body taking a lot more than you thought it was truly capable of."

I narrowed my eyes and looked over my shoulder at him. "If that's a joke about that night—"

"What night? The one where I fucked you over and over again?"

"When did you start thinking it was okay to bring this up all the time?"

"Since the moment it happened. You just never give me a chance. You haven't been to a block party or a Christmas that I've been to in years, Lilah. And if I see you, you're hiding some turmoil I can't understand."

I counted up all the times I'd gone home, and most of them had been around holidays. "I don't think it's been that long, and I'm not in turmoil around you."

"You think lying to a guy who pulls lies from people for a living is a good idea when I'm on top of you with my hands near your neck?"

He wrapped one hand around the column of my neck, and the other worked a shoulder muscle. My core was responding like I couldn't believe. I knew my panties were drenched at that point, and I was having a hard time not rolling my hips into the bed to try to relieve some of the desire that had built up. He worked my shoulder until I melted like butter in a hot pan.

Instead of responding, I tried my best to focus on anything else.

The traffic outside and the waves from the nearby ocean filled the air. They were the only things that could be heard other than Dante's hands rubbing over my back.

I wondered if silence made him antsy or if it was something he used in his work. As a nurse, we were told to get used to it, to utilize it as a tool when we needed a patient to communicate.

Humans, by nature, didn't function well without communication, and I think as we evolved, our attention spans got worse. So silence acts as a tool to pry information and communication from even the quietest person.

Were we both so stubborn and well-trained in that quiet technique that neither of us would break?

I hoped so until I felt Dante's breath near my ear as he chuckled. "You're better at this than I thought you'd be."

"Better at what?" I grabbed for the change in subject instantly.

"Avoiding the elephant in the room."

"What elephant?"

His thumb dug into another tender spot he'd been working on. I swear he used it to his advantage to punish me for me not cooperating. I hissed, but he kept on. "The elephant that kept you from me all these years, from the moment you sent me that Dear John email. This elephant is going to keep bothering us like this little knot in your back here until we work out the kinks. You and I both know that."

"Sometimes those knots are pretty big, Dante."

He'd talked of my pain, but it was a devastation that had rooted itself deep within me and made me cold to the world for a long time. I'm sure he felt my muscles bunch under his hands as I thought about it. Devastation had a way of seeping out and showing itself, even if you didn't want it to.

"Sometimes it's best to let them work themselves out over time," I said.

"Right." Suddenly his hands left my back and landed on either side of me as he lifted himself up and over my body to straddle me. His legs encased my hips, and the pressure when his hands returned to my back was a whole new level. "Guess we're going to have to approach this a new way. Settle in for something a little more intense."

His hands rolled the stones over kinks in a more aggressive way, slowly but with angles that dug in and under those knots. I wiggled beneath him as I tensed at the pain that felt so good.

Every knot he undid, I moaned in relaxation.

"You still don't know what your body needs the way I do, Lamb," he whispered behind me.

I almost cried as another knot unraveled. How could he work every part of my body right? How did he know the spots that needed help?

Something in me shifted, and after the last few days of having him near me, I couldn't really blame my body for wanting him the way it did. I tried my best not to roll my hips under him, but the next knot that released caused a reaction in me I couldn't stop. I ground my pussy down into the bed, and with him straddling me, I knew he'd felt it.

"Or maybe I'm wrong. Maybe you know exactly what you need now. Tell me," he rasped out into my ear, and my eyes shot open to stare over my shoulder into his.

I bit my lip, not sure of what to say, not sure we could cross that line. Was that what he was asking? Did I care?

This was supposed to be the place I jumped in, where I went for it without hesitation.

I couldn't say the words, but a whimper and a nod were all he needed from me.

He dragged a finger down my jawline and then pulled my lip from my mouth. "Use your words, Lamb. You're more experienced than last time we were here, right?"

I gulped in a shaky breath, my heart pounding so loud, I'm sure we both heard it. "Yes."

He growled at my confession, like he hadn't really wanted me to admit it. "Then tell me. What do you want me to do? You need a massage on your back or ..." He lifted himself from me and then flipped me over, parting my legs for his body to be in between them. His hand dragged across my belly and up to my chest. "Or is it here? So experienced that you know what you need now?"

I gasped as he gripped one breast and rolled it around. The lace against my nipple had me wanting to cry out, but I wanted things harder, faster, rougher. I gripped his wrist and pushed his palm into my chest as I arched into it.

I knew what I wanted and here, with his hands on me in Puerto Rico, I was going to take it.

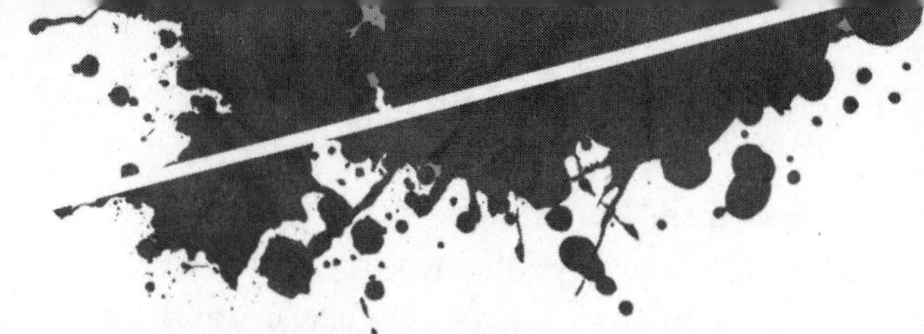

CHAPTER 13: TEMPERATURE PLAY

Dante

She'd been so wrapped up in a name that, for a second, she couldn't see who I was, who I'd been and who I'd always be to her.

Armanelli.

That name had been bound to come out during all this anyway, and she needed to know who she was dealing with. Still, the way she looked at me when she found out my true last name, like I could hurt her, like I was capable of that shit.

It had me storming back into her room to put us in our rightful places. And when her shirt came off, I knew I wasn't leaving until I had my hands where they belonged.

"See, Little Lamb. I know what you need because I know you and you know me." I pinched her nipple, and she practically purred as she ground her pussy against me.

"I don't know anything." She shook her head and squeezed her eyes shut but kept rocking her body back and forth as if she couldn't get the release she wanted.

My hand slid up her thigh as her breaths came faster. "What do you need to know?"

"I don't know, Dante. This isn't the time," she ground out, and her eyes shot open to glare at me. Gold and green and brown and beautiful, all mixed with fire.

"You're beautiful when you're angry, Lamb." I slid my thumb so slowly it must have been painful over her slit, pushing just hard enough that her panties caused some friction.

Through clenched teeth, she said, "Stop playing with me, Dante. This is basically—"

"Torture?" I nodded, keeping my eyes on the way her face blushed, how the swell of her tits was now stained with the same pinkish hue. "I'm aware. There's a ton of ways to torture a human."

"And that's what you intend to do?"

Her hands gripped my wrist, but I freed myself to take two small stones I'd put on ice near her bedside. I maneuvered one so it was between my thumb and forefinger, the other between my middle finger and pointer. When I moved my other hand to her clit and pushed one rock against her slit, she hissed. "I intend to make you see that my torture for you is seduction, my punishment is pleasure, and you'll only fear how much your body can take."

She moaned as her hips rocked over the stone, trying for more leverage, but my hand was big enough to rub her clit and hold her pelvis in place. This little lamb was mine.

"Look at your arousal, shining so fucking pretty on this stone through your panties and shorts. You ride everything like this, Lamb?" I asked her. "You make it so wet, it could slide into you for you to warm it up."

"Oh, God. Please do it. Please." She begged because she knew I was right. I knew her pussy wanted anything in it at this point.

Lilah had always been greedy when it came to her sexuality with me. We'd been greedy with each other, and it was only right that I reminded her of it before she brought another guy into the mix.

Damn, the idea that another man would even get remotely close to my little lamb had me wanting to turn into a wolf—a wolf that would protect its prey.

I slid her shorts and panties to the side so I could tease her entrance and feel how wet she was. I dipped my head just enough to breathe in her pussy. "Smells as good as I remember, Lamb."

She whimpered, "This can't be happening."

"It is. You knew it would too. You still look at me with that same fire in your eyes. I'm not going to forget that look, even if it's from a lifetime ago."

"I just want ..." She drifted off, too lost in her pleasure to finish her sentence.

I needed to hear it, though. Her begging was my addiction, one that roared back to life the moment she started. "Lilah, words."

"I just want to get off, Dante. Please just let me get off. You know how to do it, you know what I need."

Smiling, I placed one rock at her ass, and she gasped at the cool feeling against her virgin hole. "Still protective of some places, I see."

Without giving her time to tell me any different, I placed the other cool rock at her glistening, pink entrance, and she bucked in response.

"Careful," I growled. "I need you relaxed. So put those hands on your pretty tits for me, baby. Roll your nipples between your fingers. Just like that. Good girl. Such a good little lamb."

I swear her clit pulsed at my praise. Then I slid the rock inside her fast. I wanted the temperature so cold that her pussy tightened instantly around it. With just the right amount of her arousal coating it, I got the exact response I wanted. She contracted around that rock and my finger like she needed it to breathe her last breath.

"Dante, holy shit," she mewled as she arched off the bed. Her hands worked her breasts while I scissored my fingers inside her. "I'm going to come," she panted, and I was pleased to see her nipples standing erect, her head thrown back, and her hair messed up around her face like she'd lost all her inhibitions.

This was the Delilah I'd fucking yearned for over the years.

This was the one I knew still existed because we didn't get to turn off the passion between us, even if something else got in the way.

I knew my cock couldn't take much more of seeing her like this before it would seek out its rightful place. So I pinched her clit in rhythm with her riding my hand.

"I can't ... This is ..." Delilah couldn't articulate what she needed. It was how I wanted her. I wanted her to realize I was the only man who could push her to the brink.

Right when she was about to hit her orgasm, I stopped everything to command, "Eyes on the stranger who knows your body better than you know yourself."

They whipped open and sliced through me, fury and pleasure and desire and need all in one gaze. "Don't you dare stop, Dante."

"One breath." I pushed my thumb hard into her clit, and she hissed.

"Two breaths." I lowered my head to lick it better, and she moaned. "Count for me, Lilah."

"Three," she whispered as I took a bite of her thigh.

"Four," she whimpered as I slid a third finger into her.

"Five." I barely heard her as I sucked her clit and then let my tongue explore down to her center.

"Six and seven is heaven, Lamb," I murmured as I stared

up at her and pushed the rock into her G-spot.

She screamed out *heaven* over and over as she orgasmed like it was her first time ever getting there.

Delilah Hardy coming around my hand literally could have kept a dying soldier alive. That girl rode an orgasm right, like she'd studied it, and she was fucking valedictorian of it too. The way she let her whole body feel it, the way her pussy pulled me in, the way her hips moved like water, trying to lap up the world.

She might have been screaming *heaven* like I'd delivered her there, but she didn't know she *was* heaven.

She was my heaven wrapped up in a tiny lamb.

I slid the rock out and removed the one near her ass as she came down from her high.

"What are you doing? Leaving?" Her voice came out a murmur, like she wasn't sure what planet she was on but was too groggy to work it out.

"You're relaxed enough to sleep, and you seem to know I'm not going to torture you in a way you won't like now."

"So, you just did all this to change my mind about you?" Her brow furrowed, like she couldn't understand that I'd do basically anything for her.

I guess I'd have to show her. "You said you were reading about temperature play today, right?"

Her eyes narrowed and then widened as her mouth formed an O.

"When you practice what you read, you get a real good understanding of it, huh?"

"You can't just do that to me and then leave. We didn't ... You didn't—" She peered down at my hard cock. It was more than visible under the sweatpants since it practically pulsed to get into her.

I hated that she thought she needed to return the favor, like her getting off from me wasn't enough. I sighed. "Your list said explore men, Lilah."

"Okay?" She dragged out the word.

"I slide home into you, you'll only be exploring one for the rest of your life. I won't share you."

"You can't be serious. You know I'm trying to be casual here. We can't ... We don't even know each other anymore."

I dragged my eyes down to her pussy, which was still glistening. "Seems I know you well enough."

She slammed her legs shut and pulled a sheet tight around her body as she tsked at me. I noted how quickly she built her walls back up. I wasn't used to exercising much patience with a woman. Normally I could force what I wanted out of most people. It was my job to do so.

Instead, I gathered all the rocks off her nightstand back into my bag, ready to go back to my room.

"I can clean those," she murmured as she pushed her wavy hair out of her face, attempting to appear like she wasn't thoroughly satiated.

When she started to sit up, the rope around my control pulled taut. I glared at her. "Move from that bed and I'll fuck you back down onto it, Little Lamb. I try not to be the wolf around you, but there's only so much restraint in me."

"Dante," she chastised.

I took one small rock that'd been deep inside her and put it in my mouth, sucked the taste off it, and moaned as I stared at her before dropping it back into the bag. "You still taste like I remember. Like you're mine, Little Lamb. But let's have some fun. Go back to work. Bring your date over here. See what happens. If you want three weeks of casually crossing things off your list while I'm here, you get them. But I can guarantee you will beg me to be at the end of that list. Your body already wants that."

Her eyes flared as she tied the sheet around herself and scoffed at me. "You don't know that, Dante."

I chuckled. "How many men got you off at that college you went to, huh?" I narrowed my gaze.

Her tits rose and fell faster under the fabric. "This is not a conversation I'm having with you." She slammed her hand down on the bed, and her anger told me all I needed to know.

"Is the answer zero?" I asked.

"I had fun with lots of guys," she said, and her hand twitched to fix her hair.

"That's a lie. Something else happened on that campus, but it wasn't that." She froze at my assessment, and the fight left her. Damn, I wanted to pry that information from her, but I knew I couldn't. I had to back away. "I'm not going to ask what, Lilah. We'll be good enough friends one day that you'll tell me. I promise you that."

Her lips rolled between her teeth, and she glanced away from me. "Yes, well, as this is the start of our friendship, you'll have to understand that sometimes I need to be free to go out and have fun here, to go through my list."

That stupid list.

I wanted to tear it apart or cross number five off myself.

My jaw worked up and down, and my voice was strained as I said, "You have my number?"

"Of course. We'll be at a restaurant down the street. I end my shift at nine, so we'll be back here soon after."

"*We'll*?"

"Maybe just me." She sighed and slumped. "Maybe not."

"Be careful with your choices, Delilah," I warned. Fuck, if I didn't leave, I was going to rip that sheet off her. Still, I needed to touch her one last time. I stalked up to her, and my fingers trailed up her arm as she held her sheet in place. Goosebumps popped up everywhere on her skin, and when I reached her shoulder, I dragged one finger—slow, deliberate, powerful—along her collarbone. She sucked in a breath as I wrapped my hand around her neck and squeezed. "You're so small. Someone could break you before they decide to eat you alive."

She narrowed her eyes at me. "And what would be so bad about being eaten, Dante?"

I growled at her boldness and my cock twitched. She was baiting me when she knew damn well I wouldn't let her go after I had her. "Make sure you're careful with what's ultimately going to be mine."

I didn't give her a chance to respond. I spun and swiped my key through the slot to go through our adjoining door.

I let it slam shut.

For now, I'd leash the wolf.

But not for long.

CHAPTER 14: SEXT YOUR ALMOST EX

Delilah

"We'll be good enough *friends*," he'd said.

That's all my brain heard, really, because Dante might have been talking of owning me one minute, but I knew his mind wanted to place me firmly in the friend category for the rest of time.

And then what would I do with my mediocre life? I'd lost his baby, wallowed in misery until I needed a shrink, and now I was trying to live a life that wouldn't leave me spiraling.

I got ready for work, putting on my blue scrubs and tying my hair up. I'd dress for my night with Allan in one of the locker rooms—we both had crazy work schedules and had already been on a few dates, so we didn't expect much primping from each other. I packed my makeup bag and a form fitting black dress. Simple and sexy was what I needed tonight.

A text came through that a black SUV would be waiting out front for me. When I got to the lobby, Leonardo ushered me right to it, like Dante had updated them all on my new mode of transportation.

I sighed and typed out a thank you to Dante before my shift started.

The man knew how to make me feel safe, that was for sure.

He knew how to make me feel a lot of things. My heart was already starting a war with itself over whether I could take things further with him, even though I knew it wasn't an option.

At work, we had an emergency C-section, a broken leg from a car accident, a man having a heart attack whom we lost, and another heart attack victim whom we saved.

By nine, my mind couldn't focus on much. Although I'd majored in Spanish in college, it was still difficult to speak it fluently during emergencies. Thinking of my relationship with Dante, or lack thereof, should have been the furthest thing from my mind.

He was mob. I was a nurse. He was my older brother's best friend. I was the kid sister. He was my heart, while our lost baby was my heartbreak.

I pulled my black dress on and sighed at how simple it looked. Simple like this date with Allan would be.

Simple like Allan in his jeans and gray button-down standing at the doors of the locker room, offering me his arm.

Simple like my steady heartbeat not jumping out of rhythm to sync with his as it did with Dante.

"You look great, Delilah," Allan whispered to me as we made our way to his car. "I'm excited for this little restaurant we're going to. I hear the mojitos are great."

I nodded as he opened his Honda's black door for me. "Have you been there before?"

"No. The guys at work were talking about it, and I figured before we're back home, we have to go."

I nodded. Allan and I were both from the Midwest, and he'd come to do his residency here. I guess we'd bonded over the fact that we weren't locals, that we could explore Puerto Rico together rather than by ourselves.

Except now I had Dante.

I shook my head and stared out the window at the colorful buildings we passed. A man played the guitar on the corner of a cobblestone street, and a few families stood around listening. I murmured, "San Juan has so many things I want to see."

"It's heaven, right?" He smiled and his straight white teeth that were most likely bleached showed a little too much.

I nodded but didn't comment, because heaven had set off something in me that I didn't need my body remembering right then. Dante and I shared that place, shared our own paradise away from the world. I hated how he'd done that to me, how I'd never share that place with anyone else.

We had to walk through a store to get to the restaurant. The figurines displayed on the counter had jewels molded into them. Just like the ones Dante would bring me from overseas.

I sighed, and Allan asked me if everything was okay as we sat down.

"Of course. Of course. I just had a long shift."

"Right. I heard about the emergency C-section. Good work saving the mom and the baby."

I chewed on my lip before the waiter came over to offer us drinks. "I'll take a shot of rum and a mojito."

Allan's eyes widened. "A shot? Wow, make that two."

When the waiter left, I shrugged and said, "We have to enjoy the nights we're given, right?"

"Absolutely." He nodded vigorously like he couldn't agree more.

When our drinks came, we ordered food, and gradually, Allan's easygoing personality loosened me up. Allan was always nice to look at with his dark hair and dark eyes. He had a great face and was a bit taller than me too. I'd been attracted to him before Dante showed up.

Now, with a little alcohol to relax me, I found myself

enjoying his face just fine. Plus, he wasn't my brother's best friend, he didn't work with my sister, and we had no history together. I laughed at one of his jokes, and then Allan excused himself to go to the bathroom. As soon as he did, my phone dinged with a text.

Dante: You didn't take your ride.

Me: Wow. Leonardo really updates you about everything. Anyway, telling my date that I need to be chauffeured around would probably be a red flag.

Dante: You're making things difficult again.

Me: Not difficult. I'm on a date. Please stop texting me.

Dante: Your date's in the bathroom sniffing coke. So the sooner you end the date the better.

His text had me jerking my gaze up and whipping it around the room. The restaurant was so small that I would have seen Dante if he were there.

Me: Are you watching me?!

Dante: So what if I am?

Me: That's a complete invasion of

privacy. How am I supposed to be casual and free to do what I want here with you doing this?!

Dante: I told you you're free as long as you're safe.

Me: Stop watching me.

Dante. Fine. Stop drinking.

Me: Are you kidding me right now? I'll do whatever I want.

Dante: Don't make more trouble, Lilah.

Me: Don't tell me what to do.

Dante: Why not? You listened so well last night.

I looked around for security cameras and saw a red light blinking in the upper dark corner of the restaurant. He probably wasn't watching live but I still flipped it off in anger. I threw my phone into my purse when I saw Allan coming back to the table.

He looked completely normal, except that his finger tapped the table very fast and suddenly he wanted another drink and then to leave.

Our date went in fast-forward for the next five minutes. Allan downed a shot and offered me one, which I took as I glared at the camera. Then he was paying the bill and ushering me to his car.

That should have been the moment I told him I could take an Uber alone, that I didn't want him back at the hotel. Instead, I told him the Uber would be better for both of us. "We shouldn't drink and drive, right?"

"Of course, of course," he mumbled.

Texts from Dante were blowing up my phone, and before I could even get my app to work, Leonardo pulled up and lowered the car's window. "You Delilah for an Uber?"

I stared at him for a second as Allan went to open the car door for me, but Leonardo just winked. I sighed and folded into the car as I read Dante's text.

Dante: You want to play games, Lamb, you'll lose. Drinking when you're out with a strange man isn't smart. You know better.

Me: Maybe I don't.

Dante: End the date.

He had some nerve.

Me: I'm not ending the date! I'm having a great time.

Dante: I could show you a better time back here. You want dinner and your pussy licked, I'll do both.

Me: I don't want to have dinner with a friend. And I don't want my pussy licked by you.

That was very clear. He couldn't cockblock me after saying we'd be friends. He had me on some pedestal, and I was about to jump off right into the arms of another man. I was ready for it. Except ... I was texting him instead of making out with my date.

Dante: Now, that's a lie. Bet it's wet just thinking about me.

I scoffed out loud as I texted him back, and Allan shifted next to me. "Everything all right, Delilah?"

"Oh, yeah. Sorry. Just a bit of family drama." I shrugged.

"No worries. I have to get back to the new doc on rotation, anyway."

Dante: You bringing him here won't end well. All he wants is ass while he's high.

Me: Oh, so to him I'm just a piece of ass?

Dante: Yeah, you're too good for him.

Me: I don't want to be good.

Dante: End the date, Lilah. Or I'll end it for you.

Oh, God. I knew Dante was going to ruin this for me. How could I get over him when all I was thinking about was getting under him? It wasn't fair. He'd practically helped mold my sexuality in the first place.

And as I stared at Allan, I couldn't stop looking for a

stronger jaw, bigger muscles, and tattoos on his arms that I knew weren't there.

It was stupid, it was wrong, and it was everything I knew I shouldn't be doing, but I grabbed Allan and kissed him hard, trying to search for any spark. He kissed me back rapidly, like he couldn't bring himself to slow down.

When the car stopped in front of my hotel, I invited him up.

Not because we had chemistry, not because the kiss was so good, and not because his hands knew what they were doing under my skirt—they didn't. I did it solely to piss off the man who *did* know how to do everything under my clothes.

He'd breached my trust with this whole stupid date night, and I was going to breach his.

Allan and I practically fell out of the car from the alcohol running through us both, and I invited him into the hotel.

"Ms. Hardy, are you sure you'd like this gentleman up on your floor?" Leonardo asked, standing near us by the bell station. Leonardo was obviously very loyal to Dante, or to the Armanellis or something, since his hotel job extended to chauffeur when needed.

I rolled my eyes at him. "Yes, Allan is allowed up any time he wants."

We made out in the elevator and all the way down the hall to my room. I was going to go all the way with him just to prove a point ... even if I had to imagine Dante between my legs to make it happen.

This was my story. This was my *Eat Pray Love*.

I was seizing the moment.

I would have done just that if I hadn't fallen backwards as my own hotel door swung open from behind me. I toppled right into strong tattooed arms that immediately sent stupid sparks through my whole body.

"This not your room, baby?" Allan stared at Dante, confused. "Sorry, man. If we were loud—"

"Quite frankly, she wasn't loud enough. Considering I know exactly how she sounds when she wants someone to fuck her."

My jaw dropped along with Allan's. Dante didn't seem at all fazed as he righted me so I could stand.

I shimmied my black dress back down to just above my knees and turned to glare at Dante. "Excuse my brother's best friend here, Allan. He's a little overprotective and a lot crude."

"Your brother's best friend?" Allan squeaked. "Why is he talking about how you sound when—"

"Because I know her very well. I'm not *just* her brother's best friend. I'm also the guy taking over your date. So thanks for getting her home safe. Next time you take a girl out, don't do blow in the bathroom. Then you'll know whether or not this is dream. Now, leave."

"What the ... ?" Allan was already backing away, his eyes so wide I now believed he might actually have been doing drugs in the bathroom.

"I'm so sorry, Allan," I whispered, but he was already tripping over himself like he'd been caught doing something illegal and didn't want to go to jail.

When Dante yanked me all the way into my room, I spun on him immediately. "You ruined my date."

"The date would have been done had you not wanted to prove a point."

"I can't believe you." I ripped my elbow from his grasp.

"Me? You're the one fucking around all of San Juan causing me a heart attack with your antics."

"A week ago, you were barely aware of my existence! We

were different people on opposite sides of the world, living our own lives."

"And now we're tied together again." He crossed his arms over his ginormous chest and scowled at me.

"Well, I don't want to be tied to you. You think I'm some good girl who shouldn't do shit, and I want to do everything. I deserve it after college and ..."

"And what?"

"Oh my God. It's none of your business," I shouted and shoved at his chest. "I don't want you here. I don't want Izzy here. I just want to cross things off my list."

"You can't cross things off that list like it's a damn exam, Lilah. It won't make you happy."

I tossed off my shoes and screamed, "Just get out of my room. I need to shower. And I need you to leave me alone."

He threw his hands up like he didn't want anything to do with me at that moment either. He paced toward the adjoining room door and then froze, turned, and stalked back to stand chest to chest with me. Without my heels, I had to glare up at him.

His hand went to the base of my neck and gripped a handful of my hair. He pulled my head further back so my neck was exposed as we glared at one another. Then his green eyes dilated right before he lowered his head and dragged his nose across my skin. "I don't like another man's mouth on you. I don't like that I smell him here when I know it's one of the most sensitive parts of your body."

The breath I took in shook my whole body. His whispers against my skin caused my nipples to tighten, my pussy to clench, my brain to short-circuit.

"I'm being patient because being your friend *first* matters." Then he stepped back and let go of my hair. I took one giant step away from him too. He spun and was gone in an instant.

He left me shaking with need, my hands quivering as they combed through my hair, as I tried to take in enough breaths to clear my head.

I counted to seven ... seven times.

I tried my best to ignore what I was feeling, but my pussy couldn't stand another moment without being taken care of.

I hurried to my nightstand and grabbed my little vibrator, waterproof and a godsend. I hurried to the shower and turned it up so high I knew it would scorch my skin. I wanted the pain with the pleasure, to burn away Allan's touch.

I thought of Dante's rough hands all over my thighs, skimming up to my pussy where I slid the vibrator inside and turned it on.

I gasped at the feeling, knowing Dante knew exactly what I needed. I rubbed a finger over my clit again and again, letting myself get lost in an addiction that I knew I'd never really gotten rid of.

I screamed his name, happy the walls of my bedroom seemed thick enough to keep the sound of him on my lips a secret.

When I got out, my body was finally relaxed, finally unwound, and finally satiated. I wrapped a plush white towel around myself and left the bathroom for clothes.

I almost lost hold of the terry cloth when I saw Dante at my nightstand putting Advil and water on it.

He smirked to himself without looking up and murmured, "Allan didn't have the means to get you off, I see."

Why couldn't I get ahold of my temper with this man? "Dante, you can't come into my bedroom uninvited."

"Why not? I have the key."

"I could have been naked," I pointed out.

"Aren't you naked under that towel of yours?" His eyes trailed up my damp legs and then hovered on my thighs. His perusal all the way up to my face had my whole body shivering in a way I wasn't used to.

"That's my point. A second earlier and my towel could have been off."

"Nothing I haven't seen before, remember, Lilah?" He lifted a brow.

"Oh, shut up." I spun and walked to the other side of my bed. I needed to find a way to get my vibrator out of my hand because it was turning my cheeks redder and redder just thinking about him catching me holding it.

I wondered if he'd heard me in the shower. I always got a little carried away when I was doing it to myself.

Instead of him giving me any personal space, though, he followed me like he needed to be next to me.

"Lilah." His voice was so close to my neck that I had to turn and see if he was where I imagined him. He was. We were so close I could smell his aftershave. "That vibrator of yours must work wonders if you're using it as a substitute for me."

"You want to discuss that right now?" My jaw almost dropped. "This is so inappropriate. You wouldn't even know about this little device had you not come into my space without my permission. You want me storming in on you? What if you were with a woman?"

"If I was with a woman, you'd have heard her screaming." It came out a whisper, but his words rocked through me and settled boldly at my core.

That confession of his had me wet and jealous at the same time. I wanted to be the one to scream his name again, even though I knew that wasn't being offered here. "Well, good for her."

He hummed as he eyed my vibrator in my hand. "You know, that thing can be used in a lot of different ways. Maybe if you invited me into the shower to use it with you, screaming my name would be much more rewarding."

"I ..." My brain was short-circuiting as Dante brought his hand up to the device and snatched it from me. It was just a pink little egg, but when you pushed the button, it vibrated enough to shake your whole body. "Wh-what are you doing?"

"Taking this with me." He slid it into his pocket. He raised an eyebrow. "Unless you plan on retrieving it from me."

"You can't take my—"

"I can and I will. Next time you need help from this and want to use me as a fantasy, knock on my door for the real thing, Lilah."

I stomped my foot. "You just told me last night I had to be done with other men if I wanted—"

"Oh, you're done with other men."

"I'm not." I lifted my head boldly. Screw him. I would sleep with the whole island just to prove a point. "I want to enjoy myself here! I need to. Don't you get it? That was the point of me taking this job!"

"Is enjoying yourself spreading your legs for every dumbass that comes near them?"

My eyes widened as if I'd heard him wrong, but he hadn't stuttered. "Fuck you!" I shoved him, but he didn't move even an inch. "You can't talk to me like that. These are my goals. I need to accomplish them. I need to make sure I do it right or ..."

"Or what?" he asked, crossing his arms over his chest.

I stammered at his question, not sure why the list was so important, only that it was. "I need this."

"Have you told your brothers and sister about this list?"

"My brothers and sister? Is that a joke? This list is for me!"

Maybe I was too tired and tipsy to have this conversation, or maybe I'd taken the list too seriously and was only just realizing it, but suddenly I felt childish needing it to be done. "You don't get to come here and change all my plans. You and Izzy are ... I don't want any of you in this part of my life. It's supposed to be for me."

"Do it with me, then." He shrugged like his idea wasn't totally and completely ludicrous.

He didn't understand that half the reason I was here trying to find myself was because I lost myself to him and the baby in the first place.

"My family ... my brothers would kill you."

He glared at me, and then suddenly his mouth broke into a smile so big it put a dimple in his cheek that made my knees ache to buckle. "You think I'm afraid of your brothers, Lilah?"

"Well, no. There's nothing to be afraid of. We aren't doing anything. If we did, though, they'd give you hell."

Suddenly, Dante's gaze was dragging up and down my body, so slow I swear I could feel his touch somehow on my hips, my waist, my tits, and my neck.

He paused at my lips and then met my eyes before he said, "So you're not done playing with men on the island?"

"What?" I whispered. My mind tried to keep up, and it almost responded with a yes just to get him close to me, but I mentally grabbed my answer fast, stomped it out, and then stammered, "No ... I'm meeting Troy in a few days and ..."

"When you're done, just know that if that pussy still tastes as good as last night, hell, I intend to take a whole goddamn inferno from your brothers when the time is right." He shook his head and said, "Lock your door, Lilah."

And then he slammed it shut.

CHAPTER 15: SHARE YOUR SECRET

Delilah

I didn't see Dante for two days after that. I worked and so did he. Or so I thought. He made himself scarce.

It was for the best. Us bickering over my date wasn't what should have been happening. We should have been acting cordial until Izzy was out and they were gone.

I told myself that over and over during those two days. When I passed him in the hall on the third morning in my scrubs, my heart almost stuttered to a stop. My body instantly lit up, and I found myself holding back too much emotion, like I needed to see him, like I'd missed him.

I needed to get more sleep. The long night shifts were making me crazy, especially on not much food and after having to avoid Allan all night.

"Hey, Lamb," he leaned against the hallway wall instead of sliding his key card into his room slot like he'd been about to do. "Blue looks good on you."

I rolled my eyes. My scrubs were nothing to write home about.

"And you look good in slacks," I added.

"You going to breakfast?" He nodded toward the purse I'd slung over my shoulder.

"Just a quick one. I had a long night." I pointed in the direction of the hotel restaurant.

He hummed. "I heard you get in about an hour ago. Your shift usually ends three hours earlier."

"Emergency with a big pile-up on the highway." His eyes scanned my scrubs for evidence. "I showered and changed at work."

He nodded. "I'll join you for breakfast, if that's okay."

I pursed my lips and waved him on. We walked in silence together down the hallway. This was the Dante I remembered, the quiet appeasing man who smiled and nodded at about five other guests who walked by. He murmured hellos and a thank you to a man who opened the restaurant door for us. Then he put his hand on my lower back, like we were comfortable with each other's touch but just in a friendly manner.

My body wasn't. I felt the heat immediately, my nipples tightened, and I gasped. His light eyes met mine, but he didn't call attention to the spark between us.

That was for the best.

The buffet wasn't very busy, but families buzzed around with kids, and a couple of pilots ate in the corner, probably only here for a day or two before they had to jet out again. I went to grab some fruit, and two little girls dressed in red-striped pajamas pointed at my scrubs. When I caught them looking, I did a little twirl and they glanced up to find me smiling.

We all giggled, and one tilted her head to the side and said, "I want to be a doctor when I grow up."

"I like your red pajamas." I nodded to them both, not correcting them and telling them I was a nurse.

"We're twins!" They grabbed each other's hands.

Their mother arrived and put her hands on their shoulders, smiling at me. "Sorry."

"No worries." I waved her off. "We're just admiring one another's clothing, and I have to tell them, I have a twin too."

Their eyes lit up. "Really?"

"Yep."

"Is she pretty like you?" asked the one who hadn't talked yet. She reminded me of myself, standing back while Izzy shined.

"Well, we're both pretty in our own ways. Just like you both are amazing in your own ways."

They giggled, and the mom shooed them away. The love in the way they looked at one another must have drained all the happiness out of my stare.

"You want kids," Dante said from behind me, and I jumped, my plate of food slipping from my hands.

The reflexes on the man would have rivaled a superhero's because he caught my plate before it hit the ground without dropping a single morsel of food.

"Jesus, you scared me," I murmured as he pushed the plate back into my hands. "Thank you."

"No worries." Then his hand was on the small of my back again, leading me to our table. This time, he hovered closer, so close I could feel his warmth. Like we were together. Like we knew each other intimately. And my heart couldn't help but race toward the idea.

He pulled the seat out for me, then rounded the table.

I bit my lip and tried not to focus on how accommodating he was. Yet, considering how my body was reacting to a single touch from him, I wondered if I needed to set clear boundaries or keep avoiding him.

He smiled, all cool, calm, and collected, as he sat down across from me and continued his questioning like we were old friends. "Your mom would love you bringing home a bunch of babies with a nice man."

"Why are we talking about this?" I grumbled and grabbed my fork to eat.

"Because you looked at those little girls like you wanted them about as bad as you wanted your own car in high school."

I groaned, knowing where this was going. "I deserved a car, okay? My brothers were hellions, and they ruined that car before it ever got to me and Izzy."

We got the hand-me-down station wagon that barely ran, and Izzy always took it everywhere. I was stuck catching rides with whoever I could.

Dante waved me off. "At least it gave us time to catch up when I was home on leave." He caught my stare, and I shifted uncomfortably. I'd treasured those car rides but wasn't sure he had too.

I took a bite of the pineapple I'd grabbed and sought neutral ground. "They were nice."

"They were more than nice, Lilah. I was cooped up with men for three to four months at a time overseas, and then when I was home, I got you in my car for twenty minutes here and there, smelling like strawberries and coconuts and sweet as hell."

I wrinkled up my nose. "I didn't smell."

"You do. Best smell ever. Well, except for when I've got your legs spread—"

"Nope." I cut him off and waved the fork in front of him. "Are you kidding right now?"

He chuckled and leaned back. "For someone who wants to have fun around the island, you're being pretty uptight."

"Can we just not?" I asked.

He shrugged and then frowned before he cleared his throat. "Joking aside, I'm sorry about the other night."

I breathed out a sigh of relief. "Me too. I just want to do what I came here to do and that's it. So I'm sorry if it jeopardizes the safety of your mission or if I'm skewing your view of me or—"

"It's fine, Lilah. I get it. You want to have fun."

"It's not just about fun," I tried to explain as I pushed a piece of pineapple around on my plate. "I was so engrossed with getting straight As in high school. Then in college, when things ... when I couldn't, I didn't know who I was. If I didn't have perfect grades, I had nothing."

He hummed and seemed to search my face, like he was cataloging my expression or something. Then he said, "Go on."

"Well, there's not much else to tell. I didn't fit in without my brothers and sister around. I struggled to get good grades and ..." I cleared my throat. "I was really depressed." I met his gaze, waiting for the recoil or the pity or the shock. He stared back at me, accepting all my words without any judgment.

Then he said, "Would you like me to teach you self-defense?"

"What?" I sputtered. It was so off topic from what we were talking about that I was sure I'd heard him wrong.

"Self-defense." He pointed his fork at me before he looked down at his food to stab a piece of it. "You're small. You've probably walked around here at night alone. Every woman, unfortunately, will always have to deal with concerns for their well-being. I figure it's good to equip you with some escape techniques in case you're ever in a bad situation."

"Did you hear anything I just said about college?"

"I did." He shrugged like my confession was nothing. "Working out and building confidence in your body can help with depression too."

"Aren't you more concerned that I suffer from bouts of

depression? I was practically depressed throughout all of college." At first, I'd been waiting for him to react negatively, and now I was pissed he hadn't reacted at all.

"Lilah, you were bound to suffer something with all the pressure you put on yourself. Now, we'll figure out ways to deal with it. Self-defense and exercise should be a good start."

"I was bound to ... ?" I trailed off. "Are you saying I did this to myself? I'll have you know that ten percent of women who've lost a—" My mouth snapped shut as his eyes shot up and narrowed.

"Lost a what, Lilah?"

Shit.

* * *

The white tile on the seventh floor of this building was so white it made me wonder if it had ever needed a cleaning. So pure. So pristine. So sterile.

It mocked me as I sat there for my twelve-week appointment.

Such good grades. Such a solid life ahead of her. Such a damn disappointment she got pregnant.

I could hear my little town running wild with the accusations. I could picture my mother's face, my father's anger, and my brothers' desire to seek revenge.

It was going to be hell. There wasn't an easy way out.

I told myself I deserved my choice, that it was mine to make either way, and that I wasn't going to let expectations of society creep in. I scrambled for that control even when my world was spiraling out of it.

I didn't make any decision the first time I went to the doctor's office. I heard the heartbeat. Fast, strong, and maybe a little rapid because it was scared just like me.

The fear was crippling, like I was standing in the middle of an island all on my own with no roadmap to anything I knew. How could I take care of a baby when I didn't even know if I could care for myself? What foods would it eat, how would I hold it? Would it sleep in my arms or only in a crib?

Should I have been calling the baby "it"? Or "he" or "she" now? Where was the line?

I'd been reading parenting books like crazy the past three weeks and knew I would never know enough.

I knew how to get a hundred on a test. I could look up my score and know exactly how I'd done. If I got a ninety, I'd try harder the next time. Never did I give up when it came to any subject. I aced AP Trigonometry, outscored every other student in the school on my ACT testing, and could speak two languages fluently.

With a baby, though, I'd never get a grade. No one would ever tell me if I was doing it all right, and even if they did, it was completely and utterly subjective.

I took a deep breath. If I had the child, I would be barreling into the unknown and wasn't sure if the barrel was going to roll the right way.

I wanted babies, eventually. I knew that. I wanted little beautiful babies that called me Momma and some guy Dadda. I couldn't put that on Dante, though.

Even now, I hadn't told him. I had to be sure.

I smiled at the thought of kids with his green eyes. He'd be a perfect dad, even if I didn't know crap about being a mom.

"Delilah Hardy?" The nurse waved me in for the twelve-week appointment and went through all her questions. Everything was fast in that this was a routine check-up for them, even though it was brand new and life-changing for me.

She squirted gel onto a wand and rubbed it over my belly.

"Let's grab that heartbeat really quick, and then we'll have Dr. Pally come in to go over any questions you have."

"Okay," I breathed.

She rubbed that wand over my belly again and again.

Over and over.

That fast little heartbeat I'd heard the first time was pure silence this time.

The look on her face grew more and more concerned. "Sometimes I'm not great at catching the little guys. Let me grab the doc."

A doctor came in, then another. Searching now transvaginally for that heartbeat again and again as my own heartbeat grew faster and faster.

"Is something wrong?" I asked. How was I so concerned when I wasn't even sure I wanted a baby?

"We're just checking some things." Dr. Pally patted my shoulder.

They switched tactics as my mind shifted to worst-case scenarios.

"You lost the baby, Ms. Hardy. I'm so sorry."

It only took three months for my body to prove to me I couldn't do everything right and that I couldn't do the most basic biological thing that women were designed to do well.

"I lost the baby?" I stared down at my stomach, confused.

My heart beat loud.

Too loud.

And all by itself now, no little one to accompany it like it had for weeks.

"But how? I didn't do anything wrong," I whispered. I'd eaten all the right foods. I'd done all the right things. I hardly even moved, I was so scared to hurt her or him.

See, I was even using pronouns.

"Sometimes this just happens. It's not your fault. Let's run some tests and ..."

Nothing they said to me mattered after that. She'd said it wasn't my fault as if there was room for it to be. My mind scoured over everything I'd eaten that week, everything I'd done, how I'd slept. Had I slept on my stomach and hurt the baby? Was that possible?

My baby had stopped growing at ten weeks, and that meant my body had missed expelling it. I had to have a procedure. I had to utilize medical technology to do something my body should have been able to do naturally.

I'd failed at pregnancy, and now I'd failed at miscarrying. I'd failed myself, my baby, and maybe Dante, although he'd never know.

No one would know, I told myself. I couldn't bear to let them know of my failure.

Depression crept in, bleeding like black ink over the colorful world minute by minute, hour by hour. The bleed might have been slow or it might have been fast, but once it took over, it consumed me. Everything was dark. The weight of my worries and the negative parts of the world buried me so deep down in my soul that it seemed impossible to move.

When I miscarried that baby, I suffocated under the weight of that blackness. I hadn't been aware of that type of pain until my own trauma.

But it halted my life, changed my path, made me into a completely different person. I didn't take anyone's calls. I didn't go out when my roommate asked me to, and I didn't reply to messages from Dante or my siblings.

Maybe I should have told them, but my family had been dealing with Izzy in juvie. Maybe I could have shared it with Dante, but he'd been fighting a war overseas. Who was I to not tell him about our baby in the first place, then burden him with my grief?

I didn't have energy to do anything but keep breathing.

That, in and of itself, was almost too much.

CHAPTER 16: EXTRACT THE INFORMATION

Dante

There it was. That look of anguish across her face. The one I'd seen whenever we'd encountered one another back home after I took her virginity, except this time, she'd started to tell me why, and I wasn't stopping until I found out the answer.

"Lost what, Delilah Hardy?" I ground out.

She took a breath and bit her lip, looking around. "This isn't the place to talk about it."

"The place is here and now. Answer me."

"Let's go somewhere more private." She wrung her hands like she knew it was going to be bad.

It was. Because I could only imagine one thing she might have lost that would cause that much depression, and I was about to lose what little control I possessed around her. "Leonardo," I barked over my shoulder to the host who'd directed us to our table, "clear the restaurant."

He jumped into action, mumbling an, "Of course, Mr. Armanelli."

I wasn't paying attention to what he was doing, though. I was watching the woman across from me, how her eyes widened at my last name, how she watched the host and his employees buzz around at my one command.

Lilah didn't understand my power, but she was about to.

"Dante," she whispered, "you can't ... People are leaving. We can't ruin people's meals. Why are they listening to you?"

"Because I'm an Armanelli, Delilah. And people listen to Armanellis."

"This is ludicrous." She shook her head and started to stand up from her chair. "You can't just go around commanding people."

Leaving me without an explanation wasn't an option anymore.

She had to know that, especially when I already knew what the answer was going to be. She needed to say it out loud, though; she needed to make it true so that I could be sure.

"Sit. Down," the voice from deep within me bellowed.

A couple rushing past jumped at the sound.

Delilah, to her credit, didn't jerk back, but her body instantly knew who was in charge. She plopped right back down into her seat.

"Don't yell at me, Dante." She mustered a scolding although she knew she had no right. "And that party trick you just pulled with all these people—it's disrespectful."

I chuckled at her trying to put me in my place and rubbed my jaw. That attitude would have gotten anybody else the beating of a lifetime. With her, I somehow kept it all bottled up. The rage was rattling, though, and I knew if we didn't settle this, I was bound to pop off. "What did you fucking lose, Delilah? It's the last time I'll ask you."

She shut her eyes and tucked her chin into her neck before she exhaled slowly. One breath in, one breath out. Seven times.

I counted while I breathed with her.

"Seven to heaven, right?" she said to me as she opened her eyes. They glistened with a rainbow of color—hazel and gold, brown and green—as she murmured, "Our baby went to heaven too. I lost her or him twelve weeks after we slept together."

Silence was supposed to be my ally, the thing that brought me back from any emotion that barreled through me. It became my enemy as I sat across from her and she stared at me without another word.

"My baby?" I whispered.

It wasn't possible.

She'd been on the pill.

Every woman I'd ever slept with other than her I'd been adamant about protection. I made sure no part of me was going to grow in another human unless I planned for it.

I'd always been careful. And I'd always protected her.

Except when I hadn't.

Just one time.

"You were on the pill."

"It wasn't effective, I guess," she whispered, one tear falling over the rim of her lashes and down that smooth cheek of hers.

"You had my baby in your belly and you didn't tell me?" It shouldn't have come out as an accusation, but it was one.

She recoiled at my words like I'd whipped her. "Dante, I was trying to do the right thing. I'd already trapped you into taking my virginity."

"Trapped? Oh, now you trapped me. I thought I shouldn't complain because my dick was happy."

"Jesus." She combed her hand through her hair. "I know this is a lot, and I'm sorry, okay?"

"No." She wasn't going to get off that easy. "No, Delilah, you and your need to be perfect and do all the right shit doesn't have a place here. Your sorry isn't good enough."

"Well, what would be good enough?" She threw her hands out, then winced at how loud she was. "Me emailing you while you were overseas to say that I had a positive pregnancy test? That I was sure the pill was ninety-nine percent effective, but somehow we'd messed it up? I was supposed to be the one good girl you slept with, and then I'd done it all wrong. And on top of that, I carried the baby wrong too. I couldn't even bring them to life or know when they were dead inside me and ..." She choked on her own sobs and sucked in air as tears fell from her pretty eyes.

She curled into herself as if the pain was too much to endure on her own. And her sobs had me in anguish along with her.

"Lamb, nothing you did was wrong. You're taking responsibility for something you can't control," I said to her immediately.

She dropped her face in her hands, and her shoulders shook with her crying. My reaction to her pain was immediate. My hand shot out to the leg of her chair and gripped it. Then, I dragged it and her around the table so she was close enough for me to grab her by the waist and pull her to me.

"What are you doing, Dante?" she murmured as she wiped her eyes.

"Taking care of you," I said into her neck as I made her legs straddle me. Then I wrapped my arms around her and pulled at her hair so she had to look up and meet my eyes. "I was always here to take care of you. I'm your family. I picked you up off the cement when you hurt your ankle, drove you to school, and even knocked more than a few heads together when they looked at you the wrong way. Me. I'm supposed to be your guy, huh? The guy who takes care of you, Lilah. You didn't let me."

"I didn't know what I was going to do, Dante." She frowned at me. "I thought about getting rid of him or her."

When she hung her head in remorse, I tipped her chin

back up. "You were eighteen. You had every right to consider every option. No one should judge you for that."

She sniffled and searched my eyes for a lie. She wouldn't find one. She cleared her throat. "Well, my body made the choice for me. I just honestly didn't want you to hate me and so I didn't tell you. I never wanted any of my family to hate me. I couldn't let any of you down," she whispered. The fear I saw when she shivered at the thought was enough for me to at least try to let go of my anger.

Try.

It wasn't gone.

"Hate? No. But I'm fucking furious with you, Lamb," I said, as her tears fell into my neck and her pain poured out in waves. I was her shoulder to cry on, and I had to be that before anything else.

She nodded into my neck like she couldn't bear to lift her head. I wouldn't have let her, anyway. My hands were in her hair, soothing, petting, massaging. It was like we were finally one again and I was checking my other half for permanent damage.

She had internal bumps and bruises, sure, but we could fix all that.

This had to be fixable.

"You owe me all the answers, but I'll let you give them to me slowly."

"I probably deserve to have you torture them out of me fast," she mumbled.

"Yeah, there's about a million different forms of torture and punishment that I shouldn't be thinking about inflicting on you, but I am."

That finally got her to lift her head, and she squinted at me. "You are?"

"I'm always thinking about how to make a person submit to me, Lilah. It's in my nature."

She bit her lip at my words, and I knew this was headed in the wrong direction fast. I couldn't have this woman sitting on my dick and hold a serious conversation with her.

I gripped her hips, about to lift her off, but her hand shot out to grab my wrist. "Wait. What do you mean, *submit*? And what type of punishment?"

"Lilah," I warned in a low voice. "Now's not the time."

"I'm here because of my mental health, Dante. I'm here because I can't get over the thing I can't do, which is make a baby. I suffered for four years in college. I cried through most of it. I hooked up with men thinking it would change me. I mean, I couldn't even get off until Christmas in that bathroom with you—"

"What?" Her confession had me halting her. "Were you ... Did I hurt you?" Suddenly, my mind was trying to calculate whether I could have hurt her, if she would have been in physical pain, and I almost heaved up my fucking breakfast.

She slapped my chest. "No. Of course you didn't. You never hurt me. I don't think you're capable."

"I don't think you know what I'm capable of." She hadn't seen what I did behind closed doors for the mafia, how I'd broken bones for the government, sniped men off rooftops, studied every technique of torture there was so we could get the intel we needed for our country, for our family, for our power.

"You made me feel better than I ever thought I could again. I'd tried for a whole month to get myself off after the miscarriage, and nothing worked. I thought I was broken." I took a deep breath, and she took one with me, then wiped under her eyes. "I need this job, I need this life, and I need to get over this thing I created between us all those years ago. I lost our baby, but I shouldn't have lost me too." Her voice shook like she was trying to be strong, like a scared puppy facing down a wolf.

"Okay, Lilah." I nodded like I could work with it, like I could help her get over us when I still wasn't. "Okay."

She let out a shaky breath and whispered, "Count to seven."

I replied, "All the way to heaven, Lamb."

We breathed together, and I swore I'd try to help her.

Deep down, I knew, though. Lilah was still mine. We were going to be together ... even if it meant I had to go through the hell of her ridiculous *Eat Pray Love* agenda.

I carried her back to my hotel room. She'd never been in it before, but it looked exactly like hers. I set her down on the bed and went to get a big t-shirt of mine for her. Then I nodded toward her shirt. She didn't even hesitate. This wasn't about sex. It was about comfort. I needed her comfortable, and she trusted me to give her that.

She raised her arms and I slid the t-shirt over her head before undoing the drawstring of her pants. She lifted her hips slow, those hazel eyes on me the whole time. Then she murmured, "Thank you."

"Any time, Lamb. Now, get some sleep."

I would have stared at her the rest of the night had I not gotten a call.

CHAPTER 17: WATCH HIM WATCH YOU

Delilah

I don't know how long I was asleep in his room before I came to. ER shifts drained me, and dropping the bomb of the century depleted any of the energy and emotion I had left.

The weight I'd carried had been lifted, and I'd fallen into my first deep rest in years.

Now, Dante knew.

He knew why we weren't compatible, why I was broken, why I wasn't as perfect as everyone made me out to be.

I stirred in his bed, half thinking I might find him lying beside me. When I cracked one eye open, though, I found the room dark, so I checked my phone.

It was ten at night already; he'd let me sleep all day. I glanced around the bedroom and heard the shower running.

Heat crept through my body, even though I knew we were past that. Dante had held me as a friend, desperate and broken in his arms, just hours before. The moments came rushing back like a tidal wave, trying to push me down and drag me out to sea.

Some would probably say I was mourning something I never had, but what they didn't understand about the miscarriage was that my brain had started planning even if I didn't know whether I'd keep the baby or not. I still dreamt about them. I'd researched the baby's growth and stressed over her or him. My future shifted as I pictured my life with them in my arms.

Then something in my body I couldn't control ripped it away. Maybe I'd done something wrong ... but whatever it was, I couldn't get my baby back.

Dante hadn't looked at me like I was crazy. He'd held me, told me he wanted to protect me, that I was like family to him.

The word *family* crushed my heart, though, because to him that meant I was the kid sister, I was another person he wanted to protect. But I reminded myself that's all we could be, close family friends. My mental health was too fragile, and he was too much of everything I wanted.

If I lost something like that again, I wouldn't survive.

Even so, hearing the water on the opposite side of one door, knowing he was washing himself, picturing the soap sliding over each of his muscles and down his smooth skin, my body reacted. It always did when it came to him, especially after he'd let me sleep all day. He'd taken care of me. I knew I was safe here with him.

I sat up in bed, willing myself to leave without looking around. Yet, I was a product of a big household that was extremely nosy. My mom and dad read our diaries, they taught us to look inside everything, and we pretty much dug through each other's business like there was gold at the bottom of it.

I didn't have to even scan much of the room to see what I saw, though. His clothes were bundled in the corner, full of mud and a dark red stain that could only be blood.

As I tiptoed over to his clothing, I heard a crash in the bathroom and a groan. It didn't take me more than a second to run to that door. What if he was hurt? What if he'd gone and done something and was gravely injured? He was an Armanelli doing undercover work.

My mind took me to that typical scene in a James Bond movie. I was the girl who was going to help our country's spy survive.

I swung open the door, practically crying out, "Dante, are you o—"

As my eyes whipped to the shower stall, my question died on my lips. I saw a white towel stained pink and red and a needle that was definitely intended to sew something shut. I was a nurse. I knew medical grade materials when I saw them.

None of it mattered when my eyes found Dante, though. I stared at the god of a man in the shower. One muscular arm was braced against the tile, tattoos wrapping around it and mingling with the large veins on his skin. I knew his gaze was on me, but he didn't move or attempt to hide himself.

Instead, he stood there in all his glory, muscles taut as he held his huge rock-solid cock in his fisted hand.

The tip glinted under the light, and my eyes bulged when I saw dark metal glistening from beneath water droplets. Visible on either side of the tip of his cock were three balls of steel. They looked just big enough to rub the walls of my pussy exactly the way I'd want.

Those hadn't been there years ago.

I couldn't look away. I mean, I told myself to. I willed myself to back out of that bathroom, but my mind short-circuited as I stared at him. Every part of him was better than I remembered, better than what I'd dreamed about for over half a decade.

That cock—how the head swelled in his hand, how it looked as solid and hard as the metal pierced through it—it was the same but different. Familiar and brand new.

My whole body shivered as I tried to form an apology and

pull my gaze from what I knew was the best dick I'd ever had with added hardware. "I heard a crash ... I thought you were hurt. I'm so sorry for barging in." I started to back away, but his stare pinned me where I stood.

"Lilah, if you're going to apologize, might be a good idea to take your eyes off my cock."

I nodded without really listening because I was still staring, but the words registered, and my gaze snapped up fast. "I'm sorry. It's just that ... well ..."

"Lamb, I'm in the middle of something here. You going to join in or say what you need to say and leave?"

"You weren't pierced before," I blurted. Why I had to make that announcement, I didn't know.

"And?"

"Well, I ... I didn't expect that."

He smirked and turned the shower off, keeping one hand on his cock. "You expected something from my dick, Lamb?"

I shook my head and felt the blush rise to my cheeks. "No. Of course not. But I don't know." I shrugged. "It must have hurt. Why do it?"

"I like to perfect what I do, Lilah." He stepped out of the shower and moved toward me. "That includes fucking women."

I gulped at his words and how he said them while he slowly pumped his length once. I focused only on his face then, not taking time to scan his body at all.

"I'm really sorry," I mumbled. "I thought I heard a bang and that you might be hurt. I'll go."

I was almost out the door when I heard his voice come low and feral. "You walk out that door now, I'm going to have to chase you, Lamb. And I will catch you."

"What?"

"Sit your ass on that counter and watch like you want to."

Maybe it was a dream I could wake up from. I knew I would die of embarrassment later. But it would be much later. Because right now, instead of hightailing it out of there to lick my embarrassed wounds, my body listened.

I bit my lip and did just what he said, keeping my eyes on him while I pushed myself up onto the counter. I'd always done what I was told, so he had that advantage over me right then and there. Dante was the wolf. I was the lamb.

He was the predator; I was the prey. I wanted to submit to him, and he knew it.

Or maybe I knew that Dante and I were going to combust one way or the other, that we could run as fast as we wanted in opposite directions for years and still find ourselves face to face someday.

My breath hitched as he moved between my thighs. It was then my gaze skittered up and down his body again, taking in bumps and bruises with all of his tattoos. I zeroed in on a gash near his collarbone, naked with beads of water sliding down into the blood.

"Jesus, you're hurt," I murmured. "You need stitches or glue for that, Dante."

"I know. Just give me a minute." He leaned in to smell my neck, and then his forehead dropped to it as he whispered, "After nights at work, I have to get rid of the adrenaline."

I nodded, not sure what to say but my hands made their own way to his back where I rubbed softly, trying to soothe him.

"You being here ... It's messing with my head. I tortured a man tonight and came back to you asleep in my bed. You. The most innocent thing in my damn world, and I needed a release," he whispered.

It was Dante's turn to confess his demons, and I'd known

they'd been lurking. They had to be. He was too perfect, too charming, too put together to not have something clawing at him to get out.

"It's okay," I told him as I massaged him.

He hummed at the pressure from my fingers and stroked his cock right next to my pussy. It was wrong that I rolled my hips on the counter, that one of his hands went into my panties and tested how wet I was for him already.

"It's not okay," he said. "You're struggling with losing our baby and I wasn't there for you then. Now, I'm still not sure I can be. I'm not who you thought I was. I'm an Armanelli."

I bit my lip as my pussy responded to his words, the danger in them, the desire I suddenly had to be taken by him, knowing he could cause destruction. My body had always wanted him when he was the hometown Army hero, but I wanted the gritty, forbidden part of him too, the one everyone would shun .... because it was the part I'd always needed to connect to. "You're still you."

He growled, pushing his cock directly into the spot of my panties that he'd been rubbing. It was soaked with my arousal, and I saw how his dick swelled like it was close to where it needed to be.

"Yeah, I'm me with blood on my body and hands, Lilah. Can you handle that? I know." He placed his left hand on the mirror behind me so that he could lean in and stare at the gash right in front of me. It was about an inch wide, just large enough to potentially be a stab wound.

"That trapezius muscle is going to hurt for a long time." The wound was right in it. "Did someone do this? What happened?"

"I did a lot worse to them. And it's classified, Lilah. Or I'd tell you." He stared down at me, waiting for me to move, to leave him, to say what he did wasn't right.

I did none of those things. Instead, I held his shoulder still and tried to ignore the sparks flying around between us. "I'm glad to hear it. I'm guessing you're not going to a hospital."

"No." He shook his head slow.

"I can't talk you into it?"

One side of his mouth pulled up. "No."

I sighed. "Then, let me clean you up."

"You going to take care of me, Lilah?"

"Someone has to," I grumbled.

He searched my face for something, maybe fear or disgust. None of the things he would find there. I just wanted him, more than I ever had before.

His jaw worked up and down, up and down. "You're staying?"

I studied him then. This man had blood coming from his body, scars marking him, and pain seeping from his gaze on me. When I scanned over his chest again to make sure there weren't any other wounds, my eyes landed on one of his tattoos: a small lamb in a pasture.

I gasped and instantly traced it with my fingers. "A lamb, Dante?"

He pointed to a wolf on the side, on his rib, looking on at that lamb eating grass. "And the wolf that watches it."

I bit my lip. With all the other art, I'd never seen it before. Yet, now that I had, I couldn't stop myself from asking, "Is that for us?"

"No one else it would be for." He shrugged and pulled at a strand of my hair. "Now, I got to get myself cleaned up so you should go—"

"I'm staying." I nodded once, determination in my gaze. I wasn't leaving him now, probably not ever if he had me tattooed on his chest the way he did.

"The needle's there,." He pointed to the counter next to me before returning his hand to his cock. My pussy clenched at the sight. "Stitch me up while I fuck my hand to you doing it."

My throat went dry listening to his words come out dirty, low, and raw. It was like he was daring me, trying to push my limits, trying to spook me to see if I'd go.

I gulped and grabbed the needle. "It'll look bad if you move."

In response, he bit my neck and I hissed. "Do as you're told, Lamb. I want to feel you work."

He pumped his cock slowly. I felt his eyes on me as I wiped alcohol over my hands, tied the knot of the sterile thread, and pushed the edges of the cut together to create a line I would sew together. "This might hurt a little."

He hummed. "I intend to mix pleasure with pain."

I bit my lip and focused on his injury. "It should only take six or seven stitches."

He smiled at me with a sparkle in his eye as he said, "Let's make it seven, huh?"

I shrugged and tried not to feel the butterflies in my stomach as I dabbed alcohol on the wound, smirking when he hissed. "Try to focus on your pleasure, Dante, and keep still."

He narrowed his eyes at my cheeky comment, and just as I put the first stitch through, he sucked on my neck and his hand left the mirror to slide under my panties.

"Jesus, Dante." I hissed, but he was working us both now, stroking his cock and my pussy at the same time. And my hand started to shake with how turned on I was getting.

"Be a good nurse, Lilah. I know you studied hard to be one."

I whimpered and announced, "One stitch done. Six more to go. You should have done this before the shower. You were losing blood and could have—"

His thumb put pressure on my clit, and instantly I bucked, my hand jerking the thread of the needle, pulling his skin. He hissed and then smiled at me like he enjoyed making me lose my concentration even at the expense of his comfort.

"I'm going to fuck up, Dante." I glared at him.

He chuckled. "Delilah, you only swear when you're mad. You told me when I picked you up it was all the time." He licked my neck.

"Two stitches done. And honestly, that's what we're talking about right now?"

He slid another finger into me and scissored them back and forth to the slow rhythm of him pumping his cock. "I like knowing everything about you. You made it seem like I didn't."

"I can't ... can we just focus here?"

"Oh, I'm focused, Lilah."

I pushed another two stitches through, harder than I should have. He enjoyed me writhing underneath him while I tried to do the job I'd gone four years to school for, which was to make a patient comfortable even while they were in pain.

The scruff of his face brushed against my ear as he nipped it and whispered, "I like the pain, Lilah. Make sure you make your mark with those stitches. I want to know they're yours and will be on me forever."

"I take pride in my work, Dante," I told him through clenched teeth, trying my best not to drop the needle and jump on his dick. "I probably won't even leave a scar."

His teeth bit down hard on my neck this time, and he slid his fingers out of me fast so that he could slap my clit. I was on my seventh stitch, and I almost jumped off the counter with my gasp. His chest slammed into mine as he wrapped one arm around my waist and devoured my lips. He sucked my tongue into his mouth like he was starved for it, like suddenly I was all he needed to live. "Tie it so I can get to heaven, Lilah. If I don't fuck you now, I'm going to turn into an animal."

I fumbled over my knot. It should have been so easy, but I couldn't focus on anything except his cock near my pussy, my body against his, his mouth skimming over my skin and down my collarbone toward my breasts.

Then he smirked at me. "Done?"

I bit my lip, knowing that this was us crossing the line. "If we do this, Dante—"

"I know. You still want to *Eat Pray Love*." He swore under his breath. "I thought about this throughout the day and, damn, I want to, but I can't give you what you want, Lilah," he murmured, his forehead on mine.

I nodded into him, like I agreed, like my heart didn't fracture at his words, like just him shutting down the idea of us shouldn't hurt. But it did. It smashed hope that had somehow leaked in past the walls I'd built up. And even with the pieces of my hopeful heart shattered on the ground, I pursued the stupid road we were going down.

It was my hand that slid between us and pushed my panties to the side. "I'm still clean and on birth control."

"Shit, I don't think it'd matter to me at this point," he ground out like he was waiting for me to give him the go-ahead.

"Make me see stars in heaven, Dante Armanelli."

He didn't even hesitate. His cock was already at my entrance, and he thrust in deep, the cool metal of his piercing rubbing the soft flesh of my walls as his gaze, the color of evergreens deep in a forest, jumped to my neck. He caught my every movement, and I hated that he probably knew what they all meant. His hands gripped my hips as I arched. His dick pulsed into just the right spot within me, and I clung to him for every ounce of ecstasy I could get.

"Don't you get that you're the heaven, Lamb? You're the heaven." He whispered it in my ear over and over as he thrust in and out. The metal on his cock was too much, the feel of him in me after all these years was like finally being full after being empty, finally being found after being lost, finally being healed after being broken.

Our pieces, whatever we thought was ruined, somehow fit together to make something beautiful.

I felt my pussy tightening, and as his hand rolled over my nipple, he murmured, "You better look at the man who makes you come, Lilah."

Staring into his vivid eyes, I lost myself and screamed his name over and over as his cock pumped hard into me.

Keeping my legs around him, I took every last second of us connected, trying to savor and hold on to the moment, because I knew when he bent to kiss me that it was a goodbye to this part of us. I knew he didn't think our relationship was going any further.

To him, we'd met the animal urge and now we needed to walk away, be responsible, be what everyone always wanted us to be.

I hated the thought.

His muscles went taut, and I ran my hands over his abs, his biceps, and his back as he thrust one last time, emptying himself into me.

We stared at one another, panting heavily. Then my forehead fell to his shoulder as he slowly withdrew from me.

"Jesus," I breathed out as I felt each of his piercings against my sensitive flesh. "Those could be dangerously addictive."

He hummed. "Only with the right guy." Then he glanced up and winked at me. His cock slid the rest of the way out of me, and he stood there, completely exposed, my arousal glistening on him and his seeping out of me.

I moved to close my legs, but his hand shot out to hold them open there on the counter.

"You right here are a fucking fantasy, Lamb. Don't move. I get the honor of cleaning my mess off you."

I stared down at myself as he grabbed a white hand towel from the shelf near the mirror and tested the water before he put the cloth under it. My breasts felt heavy and swollen from what we'd done; his hands had rubbed them so hard that the red marks would be staying for a few hours. My body glistened with a sheen of sweat, and my pussy was bare and open for anyone to see the milky evidence he'd left behind.

He stepped between my legs and looked down too as he licked his lips. "I swear I belong in you forever. Nothing looks this good unless it's meant to be."

"I don't think I could fathom losing someone I care about more than once, Dante," I whispered because I needed him to know he meant something, that this meant something, and that I was scared to have it mean more than it already did.

He sighed. Then he placed the warm towel on my thighs and slid it up to my core. I shivered at the feeling of being treasured enough that he would clean me up. He always had treasured me, but it wasn't something I'd ever expected from him.

I kept my stare on him and saw something change in his eyes as he looked at me. "What?"

"You're broken because of something I can't fix, Lamb."

I sighed. "I'm fixing it myself. I'm the only one who can. It might take some therapy and a lot more than a list, but it's a start, right?"

He nodded, his forehead falling to mine as he threw the

now dirtied towel into a basket. "Maybe I'm just as broken with my need for you."

I stared into his eyes and tried my best not to look desperate. "My body aches for you constantly, Dante."

"Yet, we're not compatible." He glanced over at his wound. "Both of us know we're not compatible. Damn, I mean, my life isn't the one you want. I can tell you that right now."

"Is it the one you want, though?"

"It's the one I have." His jaw worked up and down. "I killed a man tonight."

I gasped at his confession, and he nodded as he let it settle around us.

"I'd do it again if I had to. You know me as your protector. But I'm also the one who can cause your destruction."

"I don't believe that." I shook my head, but he was shutting down inside. He was pulling away. And suddenly I was scared to lose him, to lose anything we had between us.

He put his lips to mine with gentle nips and a soft touch. He was tucking back the Armanelli in him and giving me the Dante I'd always known.

"You need to go to bed," he grumbled.

I didn't fight him on it.

I went willingly, trying to sift through all my emotions, trying to make sense of us.

On my way out, he murmured, "Lilah, I'll still cross that list off with you. If you have any time off in the next couple days, I'll take you through Old San Juan. You'll find everything you love there."

Dante Armanelli, what a man he was, giving me everything I wanted but nothing I needed.

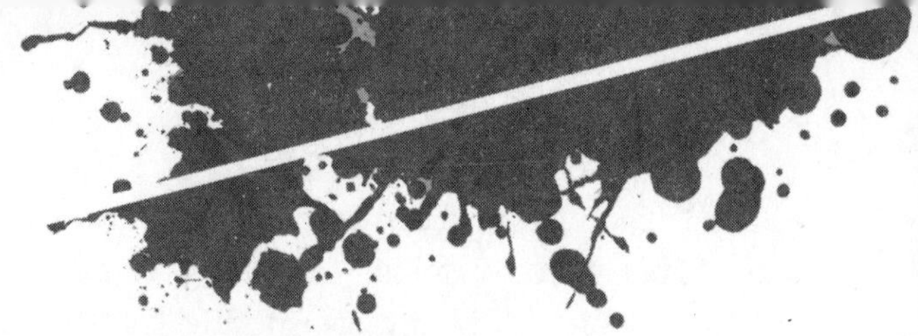

CHAPTER 18: EXPLORE HER

Dante

I kissed her slowly that night because I wanted to relish my heart beating fast. Had she felt it too? Our hearts galloped toward something they wanted so badly, they'd pump blood through us faster with need. She was the only one who could cause that unsettling feeling in me. Delilah had essentially found a way to release everything I thought I'd locked down.

I was ready to give that girl anything she wanted, even if it meant I'd suffer through the whole damn thing.

"You know we got at least a thousand kilos about to be shipped back to Florida, right?" Cade sounded giddy as he lifted the barbell up, his tattooed hands gripping the metal tight.

I nodded as I stood over him in case he needed a spot. Cade had come to use the hotel gym for the morning before I took Delilah sightseeing. She had the day off already and so we were going. "I'm not working today. I got stabbed last night."

"So what? Remember when you got shot in Syria? You went home two days later."

I had, but that was only because it had been Christmas and I'd thought I might catch a glimpse of Delilah. She hadn't come home that Christmas, though. Or the Christmas after.

Now, I had her here, wanting to cause havoc everywhere.

"I'm going to Old San Juan to keep an eye on her."

"That all you're doing?" He waggled his eyebrows.

"Fuck off," I said, my jaw working. Cade knew how to rile even the calmest horse in the stable, and unfortunately, I wasn't anywhere near relaxed when it came to her.

"She's Izzy's sister. I have to know what I'm in for when that girl comes flying out of jail. You know she's going to have her ass going twenty times the normal speed."

"We'll be ready," I said as he let the metal bar drop into its cradle so I could switch spots with him.

Most days when I fucked a woman, sleep came easily, but I knew the woman I wanted for more than just a one-night stand was on the other side of the wall, and I had half a mind to drag her from her bed and into mine.

So I'd tossed and turned, wondering if she was doing the same. Early morning meditation hadn't helped much, then I ran an extra two miles along the ocean before I told Cade to come lift with me. I needed to drain my body of its desire for her. The only way to do that was fatigue. Or so I thought. Nothing worked.

My lust and care for her had been embedded in my bones for a long time. It was part of the blood my body made, part of what pumped through my heart.

And it was going to be hell detoxing from her, absolute hell to filter her out of my blood.

"We might be ready, but is Delilah ready? She know what's going on or not? Because I'm confused as to why she's even still here."

"She needed to stay." I pushed over 250 pounds up and down, knowing I needed more weight if I was going to tire out.

"What for?"

"It would have jeopardized the mission to have her up and

leave." I gave my sorry excuse and then told him, "Get more weight. You're getting too weak for me to even work out with."

He chuckled, and instead of grabbing weights, he leaned on the barbell as he smiled at me like he enjoyed seeing me struggle to push against his body weight. "We both know that's not true. Izzy could have wormed her way around that story with these guys. They ain't that bright, Dante."

Cade was right. I'd seen the crew operating the shipments of drugs here. They were underpaid, probably using the drugs they were shipping, and weren't that smart. Their boss wanted idiots risking their lives, not his main guys.

"Wasn't worth the hiccups," I breathed and then lifted him and the weight so that my arms were fully extended. "That would have been one. We've had too many already."

"If you're keeping her here, you'd better break your damn contract and let her know the situation."

"Don't you have some computer to be staring at?" I lowered the barbell again.

Cade smirked at my biceps starting to shake. "Your girl's in her hotel. Nothing worth looking at now."

"If you're looking at her like that ..." I growled and shoved the weight all the way back up so fast that Cade had to step back from the momentum.

He shook his head. "You've got it bad, man. I'm not staring at her. And you didn't correct me, so I'm assuming she's basically an Untouchable at this point."

It was a coveted title to have among the mob—a woman who was married into the family, or at least seen as a person other families couldn't touch. It would be the same as touching the boss himself. Bastian Armanelli was the head of our family, and he didn't take kindly to anyone disrespecting us. He'd murdered two men for even contemplating hurting his girlfriend at one point in time.

"She's the one," I admitted out loud for the first time.

He sucked loudly on his teeth. "When's the wedding?"

"There isn't going to be one. We're not going to be together. She'll be protected always, though."

He hummed like he disagreed. "Izzy know?"

"It's not about Izzy or anyone else. It's about keeping her safe. Other than that, it's nobody's business."

"Damn. You've known this family most of your life, man. You can't hide whatever relationship you have with her. I saw you going into each other's rooms enough times to know. I know you're fucking her, and if Izzy finds out—"

"Stop watching my goddamn room."

"You told me to watch that hallway, dumbass. I have an alert for motion."

I wanted to punch the wall. We were already having a hard time hiding our relationship, and it wasn't even one. "I gotta go."

"Tell your Untouchable that we're about to bring down a large drug operation, and she'd better not fuck it up."

"Delilah doesn't fuck anything up."

"Yeah, neither do you. Except last night you got stabbed by a guy who can't even hide his face from hotel cameras."

I sighed and rubbed a hand over the scruff on my beard. The man had been idling by Delilah's old room, then had waited in the staircase for hours for her to come home from work.

Cade let me know he was in the same cartel that Izzy was undercover with. They were scoping out Izzy's sister. It had me on edge, so I went to confront him in the stairway, and when he lied to me about what he was doing there, I should have left him to it.

Leonardo would have had him removed quickly enough,

and there would have been no issue. We would have gotten better security and made sure Delilah was protected.

All the training I'd had, how I'd always prided myself on my restraint, all of it seemed to be for nothing when I threw him up against the cement wall of that staircase and demanded he tell me why he was there.

His eyes widened in fear. "You're not just some guy Izzy's sister's fucking. They're rats, aren't they? You're a fucking cop or something."

I slammed him into the wall again, and he got one good stab in my trap before I broke his arm and disarmed his weapon.

"I'm going to kill those girls. Kill them. But first, I'm going to torture them. You won't catch us. We're too big. Too—"

When I put more pressure on his injured appendage, he screamed. Then he swore and taunted me with the idea that he and his boys were going to take good care of Izzy and Delilah.

So I took good care of him instead, and the information died with him. I couldn't let him go back to the cartel and tell them that we had eyes on Delilah everywhere, that Izzy wasn't really a part of their crew.

"A knife wound is barely something to write home about."

"You were distracted," Cade pointed out, following me to the corner of the gym to get my bag. I was done working out for the day because Cade was right. Delilah's news had distracted me, torn me apart, and made me want more than I had all at the same time. Suddenly, being a man in control, a man who had access to all the world and knew how to extract information from anyone, wasn't enough.

Nothing would be enough when I didn't have her, and I knew I never could. I was able to kill a man with my bare hands and walk back to my room to fuck a girl who was so sweet she should be given a ticket to heaven without hesitation.

I didn't deserve that, and she didn't deserve me sticking around to remind her of the pain we caused one another.

I got to have her for another week or two and that was it.

"I'm going to go enjoy Old San Juan, Cade. Make sure that no men come near us," I grumbled.

Cade had been watching us long enough for me to know we were safe exploring, especially when most everyone thought we weren't tied to Izzy's operation.

I got ready and texted Delilah.

Me: It's hot out and we're walking the roads. Wear something comfortable.

Delilah: I have the perfect thing.

Me: Giving you five minutes to be ready to go. I worked out. You should have come with.

Delilah: You didn't invite me.

I didn't invite her because I would have fucked her in the gym. My cold shower put me on my best behavior to knock on her adjoining room door, though.

"Coming," she announced and whipped the door open with a bright smile on her face. Her hazel eyes twinkled with mischief, and when I looked down, I knew exactly why.

"Delilah Hardy ..." I murmured as my eyes tracked down her body. She wore what looked like one yellow strap which wrapped around her neck, crisscrossed so that one side covered each breast, and then I guessed it tied in the back.

No bra.

No coverage of her midsection.

Her skirt was long and flowy and yellow and so thin I knew her ass would jiggle just right under it when she walked.

"You like it?" She spun in the doorway, and her dress flared out around her. "I bought it at a shop downstairs and thought it was something I'd never wear back home, something no one would expect me to wear. When I tried it on, the cashier said I looked beautiful." When I didn't say anything, her face started to change. "Is it too much?" she asked, her hands wringing in front of her bare stomach like she had anything to worry about.

Would it have been wrong for me to tell her it was too much for the world?

Being a friend and doing this *Eat Pray Love* shit was going to kill me. I already knew it.

"You look beautiful, Lilah. If you see me glaring at a man today, I'm just keåeping them in line, okay?"

She beamed and waved me in. "This isn't going to be weird, is it? We probably shouldn't have slept together."

I smirked at how she let the words tumble out of her as she packed up her purse to head out.

"You nervous we can't be friends after we shared our secrets and I licked your—"

"Dante, that's not allowed," she cut me off.

"I joke with my friends."

"You friends with all the girls you've slept with?" she inquired, her cheeks flushing.

"If you're jealous, the answer is yes."

She rolled her eyes and asked what was on the agenda first. I guided her through the hotel and told her we would go shopping. She needed to see the little places I'd shopped while searching for her trinkets over the years.

The girl I'd lusted over was finally shopping with me

for things I had to guess she'd like when I was overseas. She stopped at every little knickknack to ooh and aah over it, but she surprised me when she picked up a small gold wolf with green eyes.

"It's you," she murmured and proceeded to turn to the cashier and haggle over the price.

The piece was inexpensive to begin with, but she got it down to what she wanted by smiling and telling the guy this was the only thing she'd wanted to find today and he had it, that his shop was exactly what she'd been looking for.

The shop played Puerto Rican music and connected to a little restaurant in the back that smelled like sweet plantains and olive oil. At one point, a girl about the cashier's age came to the front to smile at us both and offer us a lemonade drink, one that was more sour and authentic than the sweet lemonades back home. Of course, Delilah had no problem paying full price for that.

When we left with our drinks, she squealed, "I always wanted to do that. It's so rude."

"What's rude?" We walked down the cobblestone street, and she stopped to pet a stray cat.

"To haggle. I left a big tip for our drinks, so I'm hoping that made up for it."

"You left a ... You got your wolf fair and square, Lilah."

"Even so, I wanted the experience." She smiled and walked on.

It was that part of her that made her better than anyone I'd ever known. She wanted to be good to everyone and wanted to be her best self always—even when no one was looking.

"Anyone ever told you that you might be too sweet?"

She hummed and then shrugged. "Anyone ever tell you that you might be too charming?"

I smirked and pointed down the road. Homes colored green, pink, light blue, and yellow lined the street. "Maybe a time or two. I've been called just about everything with the life I've lived."

She nodded and stared down the road. "I'm jealous that you've had so much experience in just one life."

"Sometimes it feels like I'm living about ten in one."

"Can I ask why?" She stopped to look at me, and her hazel eyes peered up at me like she wanted to know every secret I had, like I could tell her anything. "Why did you hide your name from me all these years?"

I stopped and chewed my cheek, not sure if I should burden her with my shit and let her know what I didn't tell anyone. Not even her brothers knew what she did about me.

"My name isn't one you throw around. My dad was revered by some but hated by most."

When she let the silence grow between us, I smiled. "You use that silence to your advantage as well as I do."

She shrugged. "Some of my work with patients has taught me that people will disclose a lot if you keep quiet and let them."

"Silence is a technique with a lot of men I've worked with." I nodded, thinking about how I could quietly clean a tool behind a tied-up man and he would start talking faster than an auctioneer.

"Do you get tired of all the lives you live and all the men you've had to work with?" She'd known exactly what I was talking about when I used the word technique, and I sighed, pulling her over to a bench where we could let time pass as we talked.

A cat immediately ambled over to Lilah, who took no time at all to pet its orange fur.

"You know they aren't all that friendly."

"Of course they are." She rolled her eyes. Lilah always had a knack for animals even back on my mother's family farm back home. "They just need love."

I hummed and took my time mulling over her question. To Lilah and her brothers and our whole town, I was someone very different. I'd always been reliable, always been sweet instead of vicious, and I always did the right thing when it came to her and that town. My mother made sure of it. She used to tell me a mixed little boy running around the suburbs was bound to run into trouble if he didn't act right, and that an Armanelli man was just a walking, talking target without his family beside him.

So we'd hid my name and I'd channeled anything bad in me into the military and mob.

There were only a few men in the military who could get answers the way I got them, and there was only one guy like me as an Armanelli. I was trained in torture, in extracting answers, and I did it with finesse. That took control, patience, and restraint.

I tried to have those traits in every life I lived now, but Delilah was seeing my work and my personal life get all jumbled together in a way I didn't want her to. She was seeing me lose control and restraint with her time and time again.

"I'm not tired of who I am. I'm proud most of the time. Normally, I enjoy the work I do. It's for the people I care about."

"The Armanellis?"

"They're my family, yes. They take care of most of this country, Lilah. It's not all bad. What we do is the lesser of two evils." I waited a beat. "And it's difficult, dangerous, and takes a shit ton of training. I meditate, I work out, and I keep my mind clear most of the time to make sure I don't mess up."

She nodded and let the cat curl up on her lap as she continued to pet it. "I hope you know I'm still as proud of you now as I was when you told us you were going into the military."

I knocked my shoulder with hers. "And I'm still as proud of you for being a nurse and getting through college. Prouder now that I know what you went through alone."

She rolled her lips between her teeth and nodded. "I'm sorry I didn't tell you."

"Don't be sorry, Lilah. Just be sure it never happens again."

She blinked once, then twice, then whipped her head toward me with wide eyes. "Of course it won't happen again. I'm not ... We're not doing that again."

I smiled at her and grabbed her hand to take her to the next place I wanted to show her.

Our day was filled with all the things she'd wanted to do but hadn't yet. I took her picture under colorful hanging umbrellas down the Calle de la Fortaleza, got her gelato, and fed her until her stomach was full.

My lamb was happy, bright-eyed, and bushy-tailed for all the world to see.

It was a perfect day between friends.

Or lovers.

I don't think either of us knew which.

CHAPTER 19: WATER PLAY

Delilah

It was our third day of exploring the city. We'd eaten gelato again, played a bit of soccer with the locals, and fallen into this weird friendship.

It'd been days of him stopping by to see if I needed food or wanted to work out. I always answered no to that one. Then, he would offer a massage after I got home from work and we'd plan the next day to explore. Maybe this was healing, because I couldn't stop smiling or laughing or floating, quite frankly, around the whole island.

I had talked with my mom that very morning, and she told me I sounded happier than she'd heard in a long time. Sure, I kept out the part about me sleeping with Dante, but I told her it was nice to have a friend to explore the island with.

Friend.

It still tasted a little sour in my mouth, but I would fake it 'til I made it.

And he'd been great. He even had me take out my list and add things to it that I'd read about. I wanted to see the fort. We went. I wanted to eat more gelato, so we did. I wanted to get drunk on mojitos at the bar. He rolled his eyes at that one and said he'd think about it.

My list was helping me heal.

Helping me be happy.

Or maybe helping me fall in love.

The man I laid down with on the grass after going through San Juan's fort was the guy I was supposed to be getting over. He was the one I couldn't lose again, not after what I went through with the miscarriage. I knew it, and still each day, I went exploring with him. It wasn't something that I'd forgotten. It was just something I avoided.

I had him as a friend now.

That would be good enough.

It had to be.

"You can't be seriously contemplating a date with that man." He pointed to my phone screen.

I dove back into completing number five again, even though Dante avoided it. I couldn't work around it forever. Izzy had to be getting out soon, and that meant we would be back to our regularly scheduled programming.

Dante and I had just walked through the fort and gotten gelato. I was sure it was the best tasting thing here next to the mojitos and *mofongo*. We laid on the grass in a big field and watched kites fly above us.

"What is the alternative, Dante? I can't ... You're the only guy who makes me feel anything. That's like some twisted trauma I'm holding on to." I'd become a freaking open book with the guy over the past week. He massaged my back, he brought me my favorite foods, and he stayed up late talking with me until I told him to get back over to his room before he fell asleep in my bed.

If that happens, I won't sleep and neither will you, he'd responded, and I'd practically spread my legs for him right there.

Still, we'd kept everything PG like we thought was best.

"You're kidding me, right?" He rolled onto his side and propped himself up on his elbow, staring at me. "It's just that the men you get with are fucking shit shows."

"You haven't met any of them."

"Well, I know Allan didn't do his job with you right. And I still need the number of that guy who wanted to fuck Izzy instead of you."

"You went on a date with Izzy too," I tossed back, and he instantly recoiled.

"I already told you I would never have slept with her. Not when I wanted you. Damn, Lilah. I'd been training overseas and was doing so much shit for the family that I ..."

"You don't have to share it with me."

"I can't. It'll go to the grave with me, but my mind wasn't always as settled as it is now. It took a lot of time and healing to get where I am."

I probably shouldn't have, but I grabbed his hand in the grass and turned to look at him. "And where you are is amazing. I should probably still be mad at you and Izzy, but I'm not. You're both doing a lot. And I know your hearts. Or at least, I think I do ..."

"You know it better than probably anybody," he murmured.

We'd spent all these moments in this beautiful place together, and as the kites flew over us in that field, I couldn't have stopped what happened next if I'd tried. I don't know if his lips met mine or my lips met his, but we fell into one another to steal each other's hearts, if only for a second.

I got lost in the way he tasted, the way he coaxed my tongue to submit to his, and the way he pulled me up on his body to straddle him in that grass. I felt all of him below me, and I didn't know if I could stop myself.

I gripped his jaw as I consumed him, and his hands ran over my back and ass.

Had his phone not rang, I think we both would have fucked each other in broad daylight right there.

I straightened and glanced at it lying next to us. The screen showed the county jail calling, and it was like a bucket of ice thrown on me. "It's Izzy."

"Lilah—"

"You should answer," I said, climbing off him, not sure what I was feeling but knowing we were too intertwined to take what we were doing any further.

He sighed and took the call, getting up from the grass and walking away to discuss whatever he needed to with her. When he stalked back, I couldn't stop myself from blurting out, "It's crazy that she hasn't called me even once."

"She wants to talk to you after, I know she does."

"Are you saying that, or is she?"

"She's hung up on the case, Lilah."

"She calls you a lot, right?" My question sounded like an accusation, even if I hadn't meant it to.

"I'm her boss. She'd better call me if she has information. I—"

"Calling her family once in a while might be nice too."

"She can't talk to you in there, Lilah. It would jeopardize—"

"You don't need to explain, Dante. She's my twin. She can explain once she's out."

He sighed and pointed toward our driver. "Sun's going to set."

"Then I should be getting ready for my date."

He groaned but didn't try to stop me again. Izzy's phone call had created the wedge we both needed to realize this was as far as our relationship went.

And on the ride back to the hotel, he took another call from a woman in another country who I could hear begging to come see him or fly him out to see her.

It reminded me that Dante was a man of the world, and I was a woman in her own *Eat Pray Love* fairy tale. I needed to conquer number five more than ever.

If I couldn't, my whole time here would be ruined.

I mumbled a thank-you to him and slammed my door before he could say anything else. I was happy I'd kept the dating app, even though I hadn't responded to any of the messages until last night. That was when I'd decided Troy might be able to at least get me out of the hotel to go have a few drinks at a bar.

I could get drunk on mojitos and explore guys tonight. It was a win-win.

I dressed in the yellow two-piece outfit I'd worn out with Dante just the other day. His eyes had been glued to me from the moment I'd put it on, and it made me feel attractive.

When I opened my hotel door, Dante stood there in the hallway. His eyes ate up my whole body as he looked me up and down, burning every part of my exposed skin with the heat we shared between us. "Fuck, Delilah, not that dress."

"Jesus, Dante. Why are you outside my door?" I let it slam shut behind me.

"I should have burned that thing the first time you wore it," he grated out, his eyes still stuck on the material.

"You seemed to like it. You stared at it then like you're doing now."

Those piercing jade eyes sliced up my body to meet my gaze, and they burned bright with emotion. "I like it enough to know I'm going to ruin it later. And if your date touches my friend in it, I'll probably ruin him too."

I breathed in and out, chewed on my cheek, and then bit

my lip as our standoff in that hallway went down. "If we're friends, we won't ruin each other's things. I didn't ruin your call with that woman on the way back to the hotel tonight, did I?"

"Did you want to?" he asked and tipped his head.

He caught me combing my hand through my hair angrily as I said, "No, of course not."

He smiled. "Go on your date. Bring him back to meet me, huh? Let's see if he can make you forget the way your pussy feels with my cock in it."

My jaw dropped at his words, and he brushed past me as if he could talk like that and get away with it.

I should have smacked him across the face, but he was gone before I picked my jaw up off the floor.

I stewed all the way down to the lobby and stomped to the stupid black SUV with Leonardo in it.

Of course Dante had set up my ride.

My date was tall with dark hair and dark eyes and had a way of smooth-talking that didn't exactly feel slimy. Not that I was paying that much attention.

Instead, I was downing my drinks and glaring at my phone, willing Dante to text me to say he was watching me through Leonardo. I even danced to a couple of songs with Troy in the hopes that it would push Dante to text.

When the third song turned fast and pushed the bass and tempo to new levels, I rolled my hips into Troy's and felt his hands slide over my midsection.

I held my phone in my hand the whole time I was out on that dance floor, and when it vibrated, I practically preened because I was being an immature teenager still wanting her first crush to get jealous over her.

I excused myself to hurry to the bathroom and see what the text said.

Dante: I'm coming to get you. Tell me the name of the bar.

Jesus, typing to him after I'd had four mojitos wasn't the easiest.

Me: I'm having a good time. Let your friend have a good time with her date.

Dante: Your date is a handsy fuckboy. What bar?

Me: Like you can't get the name from Leonardo

Dante: Fuckers won't give it to me. I even called Cade. Don't make me go to every one to find you.

Me: Troy and I are coming back to the hotel soon. Go to bed, friend. I'll be doing number five.

Me: Lol doooing ... get it?

I was going to regret drinking and texting in the morning.

Dante: How many drinks have you had?

Me: Two or three ... or ...

Me: Seven brings heaven, right?

Dante: You bring him back here and I'll remove every part of his body he's placed on you.

Me: Not very military of you.

Dante: I'm not military anymore. I'm an Armanelli. Get your ass back to the hotel. Now. Or I'll find you and drag you back myself.

He couldn't tell me what to do. But suddenly, Leonardo was knocking on the bathroom door and shaking his head at me. "We have to go. I can't lose my job over this."

And the fact that Dante had threatened his job made me want to teach him a lesson.

Troy hopped in the car with us and Leonardo shook his head the whole way to the hotel. We rounded it to go straight for the resort's lit up pools.

I was getting over Dante tonight. I shucked off my skirt and smiled at Troy as I pulled him into the pool half naked with me. He'd make me feel good. How could he not with the ocean breeze and the glowing pool in the middle of a beautiful island? I was drunk on mojitos and trying to find paradise without the man I thought was paradise.

Troy was supposed to be making me feel something in this pool. The water lapped around us, and the night air was damp and warm. I should have been loving his lips on mine, his hands roving over my body.

Instead, I wanted to cringe away.

Dinner had been nice, dessert had been nice, dancing had been nice, and his hard dick against my stomach felt nice too.

Except my mind drifted to Dante's hands on my back, how he worked all the right spots, how he knew just which part of me needed attention.

I moaned at the thought, and Troy took it as encouragement. "God, I want to fuck you in this pool," he groaned and pushed his dick harder into my stomach. It wasn't even that big.

I shouldn't have been comparing, but as it turned out, I wouldn't be checking much more than getting drunk off my *Eat Pray Love* list tonight.

I let our kiss linger and tried a last-ditch effort to hold on to his hair as I deepened it.

The sound of the waves just feet away from the infinity pool were relaxing, and the smell of sea salt and tobacco loosened me up, but—

I froze at the smell.

Tobacco. Not just the type from cigarettes either. I'd know that cigar smell anywhere.

He'd only smoked it one time around me, but I'd fallen asleep to that smell, I'd reveled in it and cataloged it as a comfort.

I jerked away from Troy and sobered up fast, not even sure what I was thinking in the first place with the lesson I'd wanted to teach Dante. He wouldn't be okay with this.

Not even if I were only his friend. Or simply his best friend's little sister.

I was breaking hotel rules, I was sure. I was making out with a stranger in the middle of the night. I was being reckless. Stupid. And drunk.

The alcohol tasted sour in my mouth as I searched for him. My gaze flew everywhere, only to find his dark silhouette lounging comfortably on a small white hotel chair near some shrubbery. He seemed to take up the whole area, to swallow the chair, and his legs in just swim trunks spread out to own the space around him. When he lifted the cigar's glowing cherry, it illuminated his tattooed chest and how his lips sucked on the other end, his cheeks hollowed, and his brows lowered.

Our gazes caught in the darkness, and he took a long drag as he stared like he was trying to curb the emotion he felt. Like the cigar might soothe him a little.

His green eyes burned bright, though, and the emotion didn't dim at all.

I bit my lip and murmured to my date, my eyes still on Dante. "So, I don't think this is going any further tonight."

"What?" Disbelief sounded from Troy's mouth, like I was being a cock-tease. A Tinder hookup gone wrong wasn't that hard to understand, though. Things like this happened all the time. He glanced behind him to see the dark figure and scoffed. "Is it because of that creep watching us? So what? Let's give him a show."

Troy grabbed my waist, a little rougher than I anticipated. I tried my best not to make a scene as I shoved his arm. If I did, I had a feeling Dante would break it.

"Look, I know I probably led you on—" I gripped Troy's arm and glared at him to get my point across.

"Led me on?" His eyes widened and then narrowed in malice. His hand on my waist tightened.

I glanced at the chair where Dante had been, but the glowing red cherry was gone. No sign of him anywhere.

"Led me on, Delilah?" he sneered this time. "You practically spread your legs—"

"Careful." Low and vicious in warning, Dante's voice was right beside us. "You're talking to the one person in the world I refuse to have hurt."

"Dante, it's fine." I turned to see him close to us in the water. His muscles glowed against the light, his abs rippled, his neck flexed. I gulped as I saw how the veins wormed over his forearm like they were struggling to contain the strength that lay beneath them.

His green eyes didn't even flick my way. They were on the guy's arm where he still held me.

Troy didn't take the hint. "Look, asshole, you've been watching us like a creep for the past five minutes. You want a show, I'll give you one. I just need a minute with her to get her on the same page as—"

He must have seen the way Troy's elbow bent to pull me in because suddenly I was free, water was splashing, Troy cried out, and then there was silence.

Silence except for the waves in the distance.

I squinted and found that Dante held that man's arm in a very awkward position and small bubbles floated up to the surface of the water.

"Dante—"

"How long do you think he was holding you against your will?" he asked just loud enough for me to hear.

"You're drowning him," I stammered as I glanced around to see if anyone was going to stop him. The only person I saw was Leonardo, who stood completely stoic except for a hand that went to a button. Suddenly, all the lights around us, already dim, went out.

Well, that would be aiding and abetting in court, I was sure. "You can't—"

"I can do whatever I want." His words were pointed and meant to make me see the man I was really dealing with. An Armanelli.

A wolf.

A vicious protector.

"When a man pushes himself on a woman, more

specifically my woman, I intend to teach him manners or have him die learning."

"Dante ..." I murmured as I stared at the bubbles getting smaller and smaller. "He's learned."

His jaw worked for seconds that felt like hours. The tendons in his neck strained like they couldn't hold the fury in this man's head much longer. Then he took a long, deep breath. His eyes closed, and his whole body—except that hand holding Troy—relaxed. Then he said, "Only for you, Lilah," before yanking Troy up by his elbow.

Choking and gasping, Troy floundered as Dante shoved him away.

Troy didn't even try to fight as he used the momentum of the push to scramble away from us. "I'm sorry. I'm sorry. Jesus, you could have killed me. I—"

"If you see her on a dating app again, swipe the other way, Troy. Or I will find you, and I *will* kill you."

The dim lights turned back on, and Leonardo, suave as he was, told Troy to have a good night as he rushed past, leaving his towel behind.

"Now ..." Dante inhaled air deeply and slowly let it out while water droplets cascaded down his chest. He took his time wiping some of the water from his face before stalking toward me. "Let me check you."

"Check me?" I sputtered and started to back up. I couldn't have Dante near me all wet and slick and half naked if I wanted to keep my options open, if I wanted to stick to the plan. Plus, he'd nearly just killed a man.

He smiled as he approached and I retreated. His teeth glowed, and his eyes sparkled in the night like he was enjoying every second of this.

"Want to run and see if I can catch you, Lamb?" His

eyebrow quirked.

My heart jumped, and my adrenaline spiked. I'd actually enjoy the chase. Still, I shook my head no. "You don't need to check me."

He pursed his lips. "A man's hands were just on you, Lilah. Without your consent, might I add."

"Well, I consented at first," I pointed out. I was nearing the stairs of the pool, but with each of my steps, he took two. He closed the distance between us, and I wasn't sure what was about to happen when he met me chest to chest.

"Don't you ever justify or minimize a man putting his hands on what's mine without your consent." Then his hands were on my waist, running over it as his eyes checked for whether or not Troy had left marks. He hadn't. Dante had gotten there too fast, and even if he hadn't, I would have kicked Troy hard enough in the balls to run.

"Yours?" I questioned.

"Yes, Lilah. I don't know why we've been ignoring the inevitable. You're my lamb. I'm your wolf. It's about time I stop letting others play with my food."

"Food? Really?"

"Well, I'm going to eat that pussy, aren't I?"

I shook my head. "You said you'd help me check off the seven boxes. I can't find the right guys to have fun with if—"

"I'm the right guy to have fun with, Lilah." Then his hands were on my hips, lifting me onto the first step of the pool. He spread my legs so he could kneel in between, so that our bodies were aligned. His cold chest pressed against my breasts, his breath cascaded against my lips, and his pierced cock, even through the fabric of my panties and his swim trunks, pushed against my pussy. "Let me make you feel good, huh? You and I both know I'm the only one who can."

I bit my lip to keep from agreeing with him and shook my head.

He chuckled into my neck, and I shivered at the vibration. "You want me to show you, Lilah? You didn't moan for Allan the way you moan for me. And it took Troy about a minute for you to write him off. That kiss was going nowhere. You and I both know it."

"You can't keep making me feel good, Dante," I whispered, but already my hips wiggled closer to him, and my hands found their way to his back.

He smirked like he knew he had me, like he knew my cunt submitted to him every time he got near it. "But I can make you feel good right here, right now, on this island. You want to satisfy some kink and explore some fantasies with guys, we got water play right here."

His arm wrapped around my waist so he could grind his cock into me, and I moaned.

Then, his strong, calloused hand, cold and wet from the water, slid up my thigh. With both of my feet on the second step, the water lapped right below my ass, and Dante spread his cold touch over my hot skin, causing my core to clench, my pussy to tighten, and my insides to scream for him to touch me anywhere and everywhere at the same time.

We both watched as he leaned away from me so the cool air drifted over my wet skin. My nipples pebbled as his hand moved to my slit, neither of us saying a thing. My breathing came too fast, my mind suddenly focused on how the water moved back and forth under my ass, just barely touching my entrance.

When his thumb got close enough, he dropped it into the water and then slid it under my bottoms to rub against my clit. "Jesus," I hissed as I bucked on the step, but his opposite hand went to my other thigh to hold me there as he rolled my clit to a cooler temperature.

He smiled as my elbows flew back onto the wall of the pool and I used the leverage to relax into his touch. "Want me to warm you up now, Lilah?"

There was no hesitation anymore. I'd have to find a way back from Dante tomorrow or the next day or whenever he decided to let me go. For now, my body was his—and it submitted to him always.

The risk came with a great reward, anyway. My mind's frustrations of the day, my worries, my anxieties, the way I drifted toward pain ... they all seemed to disappear. I was doing what I wanted *finally* and not what anyone else expected me to do. This was it. This was what embracing life was. "Please, Dante."

He lowered his head but kept his vivid green eyes on me. We watched one another as he pushed my panty bottom to the side and his tongue dragged low enough to dip in the water, bringing the chill up between my folds. I shivered, my head fell back, and I moaned as his tongue went deep. He took his time before moving his hand from my clit to my hips so he could suck my bundle of nerves instead.

His hands held me there while he took me to the brink of orgasm fast, nipping at me and then sucking me better, like he knew exactly what I needed.

"I'm so close, Dante," I whispered and wrapped one of my legs around his neck. My breathing had gotten louder as my muscles tightened everywhere, and my vision tunneled.

But a gasp and a light turning on a couple of stories up in our hotel building had me freezing. Dante raised his head to smile at me. "You nervous someone's going to catch you, Lamb?"

I lowered my leg from his neck and bit my lip before moving my arm from behind me to comb it through my wet hair. "We should probably go back to the room."

Instead of agreeing, he tilted his head like he was questioning me. "Exploring your kinks also means the ones that make you nervous too."

"Dante, this is illegal," I pointed out.

He raised himself up and pulled my ass from the step so he could push two of his fingers inside me. My pussy practically sucked them in with how wet and wanting it was. "Not illegal when half of this hotel is mine. I do what I want in my pool."

"Oh, fuck." I dragged out the word because my hips were already rolling on his hand, my body a complete whore for this man.

"Little Lilah, I wonder how good a girl you'd be if we made someone really watch me get you off. And maybe we need to teach other lessons tonight too."

I tried to keep from moaning and coming all over the man's hand. I wasn't listening to anything he said. I just nodded, hoping his thumb would find its way back to my clit.

"Leonardo, come over here," Dante said loudly, and I practically jerked back onto the steps, but his hand followed me and pinched my clit into submission.

"What are you doing?" I said through clenched teeth, though it came out half moan.

"You want a safe word before we go further, Lilah? Because when we're exploring kinks, I'm in charge. You submit until you can't anymore."

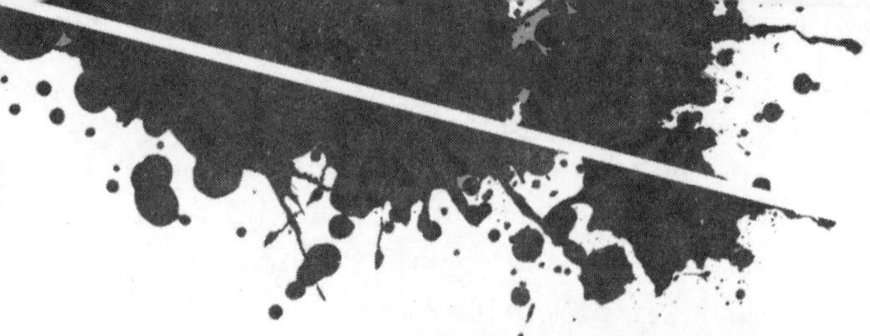

CHAPTER 20: VOYEURISM

Dante

"Elephant is my safe word," she whispered.

Her soft breath on mine and the way her eyes changed from heated to full of mirth in an instant had me knowing it'd be mine too. "Why? Because we can't have an elephant in the room and enjoy ourselves?"

"Exactly." She nodded.

I kissed her then, soft and gentle, the way I needed to right then. My mind was tumbling down the same rabbit hole of connecting with her, of wanting her, of falling in love with her. I swirled my tongue around her mouth, tasted her sweet lip gloss, and held her neck as my other hand worked her pussy. Her nails dug into my shoulders.

By the time Leonardo walked over, I'd pushed her legs apart so she was spread eagle on the first step. Then my hand inched up her stomach to her neck and pushed it down onto the curve of the cement.

"Tell Leonardo who you belong to."

"You. Dante. I belong to you."

"And tell him what your ass was thinking bringing another man into my hotel and into my pool." She whimpered as I pinched her clit. "Go on, Lilah. Tell him what you could have possibly been thinking." When I slowed my movements, she clawed at my wrist. I knew I'd have marks in the morning and smiled down at her. "You don't answer, you don't get to come."

Her eyes narrowed, and she rolled her hips as she gave in to me. "Fine. I was thinking I wanted someone to fuck because I shouldn't have been thinking about fucking you. God, I'm a slut for your hand, your cock, everything. I want you always."

"Mm," I hummed low. "That's right. Such a good little slut for me, though. Look at you riding my hand like it's the best thing you've had in your pussy. But we both know that's not right, huh?"

"Oh, God," she moaned when I curled my fingers into her G-spot.

I lowered my mouth to her clit. I wanted to taste how wet she was. She drenched my face right above the water and bucked off the step as I sucked. Sweet as strawberries, and a little salty too. Her hands went to her own tits and rolled them around. Her whole body arched when I slid another finger in and let my last one probe her ass.

She couldn't have held on to her orgasm if she tried. The picture of her hitting her high was that of a phoenix catching fire. She screamed and burst in beauty and flames for both Leonardo and me to see, soaking my face with her come. It dripped down my chin and tasted sweeter than heaven.

As her muscles relaxed, I stared up at her. She was about to shrink back; I felt her putting her walls back up immediately.

Grabbing her waist when she was so pliant made flipping her over fairly easy. I walked us deeper and deeper into the pool, until the water lapped at the middle of her waist. That would be perfect. Without saying anything, I turned her hips and then lifted her up so that they aligned right at the edge of the pool. "Bend and hold yourself over that edge, Lamb."

She listened so well. Immediately, her ass was out for me to see, her legs and feet dangling in the water while she propped her upper half up on her elbows. I didn't want her to have any leverage against me.

I'd take her hanging off the edge of this pool.

"Dante, I don't think I can take anymore," She said over her shoulder.

"Is that so?" I gripped her ass with one hand and then slid my other hand up her back so that I could push her down further onto the cement. She moved her elbows and hissed as the cool surface hit her stomach and tits. I gripped her hair and positioned myself just behind her, my chest against her back. "You want to stop, you use that word."

My dick was already nestled against her ass, and she pushed back into me. I pulled it from my shorts and dragged it against her slit under the water. She shuddered and moaned.

"Tell me you want it. Tell Leo you want him to watch and enjoy." I felt her nodding under the grip I had in her hair. "Use your words, Lilah."

"Jesus." Her breaths came fast. "Fuck me, okay? And Leo better enjoy the show."

Leo's eyes met mine in question, and I growled because I knew what he was asking silently. I was going to give Lilah everything tonight, even if it meant letting another man see me fucking her. I nodded to him but grunted out, "Step back."

He did so as he unbuttoned his trousers. His hand was on his dick in front of her then, far enough away that I knew he wouldn't be able to touch her, that he was only witnessing me own her and her own me.

She murmured a string of curses as she realized what was going on. Her head had turned to watch him pumping himself slowly in front of her.

"You like knowing we can bring someone to the brink while I bring you there too?" I'd have to break her of that nodding. "Words," I commanded.

"Yes, I like seeing what we do to him. I love it." She dragged out the word and then rolled her hips on my cock. "Please, Dante."

My girl was ready to take more than I ever bargained for.

"I'm going to fuck you, Lilah, until you scream my name loud enough for this whole damn hotel to hear."

This time, my thrust was straight into her. I slid into that tight, soft flesh all the way to my balls. I held myself in her, savoring the feeling, and my whole body seemed to unwind like it'd just found its place in the world. That girl's pussy was my heaven, and I never wanted to leave.

"Dante, I need you to move. I need you to fill me up over and over. Please. Please. Please." Her voice drifted off as she repeated the begging over and over.

"Love those words. Love how you beg, baby. Such a good girl." I moved my fingers to her lips and said, "Suck."

She did as she was told, swirling her tongue around them. I brought my hand back and pushed a finger against her other virgin hole. Probing it, I kept thrusting, and with each hit, I ground out, "Good girl ... good girl. This is where you belong. Bent over for me. This is why I've always wanted the good girl in you. Be proud of what you are."

Her head turned so she could gaze at me, and I let her. I wanted her to know. She'd followed the rules, she'd been safe, and her innocence, to me, was one of the most beautiful things in the world.

"Proud?" she murmured.

I slowed my pace, letting her feel every inch of my dick. "It takes strength to do right and not give in to pressure. You're strong, Lilah. So say it and own it."

She bit her lip, so this time I smacked her ass, and she gasped.

"Say 'I'm good and strong and proud of it.'"

"I'm good." I thrust in. "I'm strong," she wheezed as I rolled her ass cheek in my hand. "And I'm proud of it."

"That's it, pretty girl," I growled close to her ear.

Everyone was close. I felt Delilah's center start to twitch around my cock, and Leo's movements had become erratic.

"Now tell Leo, baby, what should he do if you ever bring another man into this hotel again?"

She shook her head like she didn't know the answer.

"Leo should inform me so I can kill him. And I will. I'll kill anyone who touches you from this point on. Say this pussy is mine," I commanded as I thrust in hard and pushed my finger up her ass, knowing my dick was surrendering to what really owned us all: her. "Matter of fact, scream it loud."

She did as she was told. Just like the good girl she was.

When I picked her up off the side of the pool and Leonardo went back to his station, I made sure to whisper in her ear as I carried her back to our hotel, "We can add and cross off voyeurism and water play from your list. If you want, you can put a heart next to them. Seems that you like them both."

CHAPTER 21: NEW LIST

Delilah

The next morning, I woke up to Dante gone from his bed. He'd left me the updated list, though. His handwriting was basically a scribble, and I squinted as I read the new bullet points:

* * *

~~Lilah's *Eat Pray Love* List~~

Seven to Lilah's Heaven

1. Leave home (*done*)

2. Do something crazy (*you went to jail, Lamb*)

3. Explore food here and EAT (*you like gelato,* quesitos, *mofongo, and mojitos ... too much*)

4. Explore places here and PRAY (*you read at the beach, saw the fort, the streets, the stores, any other places?*)

5. Explore men and LOVE

**explored voyeurism*

**explored water play*

**What else, Lamb?*

6. Find peace (*I can search with you forever*)

7. Find heaven (*you with me*)

* * *

Love sneaks up and snatches a heart from its owner so fast they might not know it's gone for days, weeks, sometimes months. I think Dante had my heart all along. Even when I tried to protect it from the disaster that could happen between us, I never really had a chance.

The wolf gets what he wants, and I was just the lamb, too overpowered by who he was to do anything else.

He came back to the room not much later with all my favorite foods, dressed in sweats and a T-shirt like he didn't have anywhere else to be.

"A new list?" I held it up, a small smile on my face.

"Sure. You needed some help." He shrugged, completely unfazed. The man didn't embarrass easily, didn't think he overstepped, and definitely didn't question himself.

I loved it all.

"I have a whole phone full of ideas to help me. I even bought a book to read on it."

"Should we read it together?" He handed a *quesito* over to me, and a smirk teased my lips at the way he catered to me.

"No, Dante. I have to go to work, and I have to do these things on my own." I sighed around the food as I took a bite. The flakiness of the pastry rivaled some of the best things in the world.

"Without sharing the experience, the joy is lost," he murmured.

"Who told you that?"

"Just a switch up of the *Into the Wild* story."

"What was that story?"

"He went searching for meaning in the wild and found that 'happiness is only real when shared.'"

Dante sat next to me and took a big bite out of his own *quesito* while we mulled over the quote. I wiped my mouth as I stared at his, hypnotized by how his lips wrapped around each piece of food.

"Maybe I'm being selfish with my happiness, and you should come along for some."

"Maybe." He nodded, but he didn't push me.

"Well, I want to see bioluminescent water. Have you heard of it? The water lights up this magnificent blue."

"Blue?"

"Yes, but you have to ferry out to a small island. Oh, and there's a sculpture that my book said I have to visit before I'm done here."

He grabbed the list from where it was lying on the bed and started to scribble notes. Then he pocketed it.

"You're keeping the list you made me?"

"I made the list for us."

My heart fluttered at just that one word, and I bit my lip, glancing away from him and trying my best not to feel more than I already did for my childhood crush.

"When do you plan to be done here, Lamb?"

"With my food?"

"No." He chuckled. "With your trip. With Puerto Rico."

I hesitated with my answer, knowing exactly when my contract with the hospital ended but not at all sure if I would be ready to go home by then. "My contract was for three months."

"That wasn't my question." He popped the rest of the

pastry into his mouth and wiped his hands on his sweats before rising to stand right over me. Then he placed both hands on either side of my hips on the bed. "When do you plan to settle down, Lilah? When does my lamb turn into a sheep?"

I wrinkled my nose. "I don't think I ever want to be a sheep."

He hummed and dragged his nose across my neck. "You ever want to settle? To be happy with the good girl you are?"

I bit my lip as he nipped at my collarbone. "I don't know. I feel different here. Happy." I took a deep breath. "I'm scared to go back to feeling ... not that. And I'm scared my happiness might be tied to you."

"Why are you so scared you need me, Lilah?" He cupped my cheeks. "Why not share your happiness with me?"

"I don't want my happiness to *depend* on you." I took a shaky breath, and his lips descended on mine. He coaxed me to open up to him. Then he took my love, happiness, and desire for him. I knew he tasted it all—I felt the smile on his lips like he had me.

And he did.

He had all of me, and my heart beat fast with the idea that he could continue to massage and nurture and cater to all my needs.

Except, if happiness only existed when it was shared, what happened when the person you shared it with had to go? What happened if you couldn't give them what they wanted? Or if you couldn't make what you wanted together?

Would our families accept this? Would I be able to accept this between us, knowing that we'd lost the one thing a family was supposed to make? For some reason, my body didn't carry a child of ours well. He could have that with someone else. He could have a totally uncomplicated relationship with a stranger, one outside of our families, one where my brothers wouldn't grill him, where my mother wouldn't insist on grandkids, where my sister wasn't his colleague.

I pulled away. "I need to get ready for work."

His jade eyes squinted at me, trying to cut through the wall he could probably see me building. His jaw worked before he pushed away and nodded. "I need to work too."

"What exactly do you work on?" I sat forward in the bed and winced from the ravaging of the night before.

"You're sore," he murmured, immediately back in my face, staring me down, running his gaze slowly over me. He sat next to me on the bed, his big hands searching my hips and stomach and all parts of my skin for marks. When he came across a reddened mark, I saw the way his jaw worked. "I'm proud and appalled at the same time, Lamb."

The realization of love must have made everything shine brighter and everything become clearer for me. "It's not appalling." I chewed on my cheek before I let go of the words I was holding in. "I'm happy, Dante. Happy in a way that makes me scared it's all just a dream—that I'll blink, and all this will be gone."

"Lilah, I've always been here. I'm not going anywhere."

"You weren't always here." I chuckled at him as I watched him lean over to his nightstand and open a drawer. He grabbed a small vial of oil before he closed it back up, but not before I saw the pink color of my vibrator. "Also, I need that back."

"If you were fucking your vibrator to my name, I must have been there in your mind. Always. Right?" He motioned for me to turn my back to him on the bed.

I scoffed but did as he wanted because my body was already yearning for his hands to migrate back to it, to smooth out any of my kinks. I was getting used to us bound together by touch, and I wasn't sure if I was ever going to be able to extricate myself from him when the time came.

I could smell when he opened the glass container and dropped a few beads of a minty scent on his fingers. He smoothed it over a particularly sore spot on my hip.

"Maybe it wasn't always to your name." I bit my lip as his hands started working around the sore area and up my back, massaging, kneading, and pinpointing my body in the way only he knew how. My muscles shifted under the pressure of his strong fingers, and I moaned when he turned me to face him and laid me down on the bed.

"I should be getting dressed for work, Dante," I groaned when he dripped a bit of oil onto my stomach and smoothed it over my skin.

"This should help. I was too rough with you."

"If you were too rough, I would have used the safe word."

"You don't know what's too much for you, Lamb."

"Or maybe I know exactly what's enough." I winked at him and scooted up and off the bed quickly. "Now, work. I have to get ready."

I made my statement clear and giggled when he tried to grab me. "You ever play hooky and not go to work? Should we add that to your new list?"

"You can't keep changing the list."

"Of course we can. That's life. Change, adjust, find what you love. Plus, I know this island better than you. You need help navigating it."

"Is voyeurism part of the island?" I popped a hip and lifted a brow.

Dante's laugh boomed through the room, so big and bright that it infected me—and the whole atmosphere—with joy.

My heart swelled with it too. I clung to it and hurried to

get ready for work.

The night should have gone off without a hitch. We had three great nurses working our floor, and the rest of the team was great.

A gunshot wound victim rolled in screaming, but we'd seen a ton of them before. We operated quick, but blood was everywhere. Our doc was yelling for more when the man's hand shot out to grip mine. The red of it smeared all over my rubber gloves, and I tried to yank it back since I needed to be able to handle tools for the physician operating on him.

He didn't let me go. His grip was tight, and as I caught his gaze to tell him he had to settle down, he stared at me with dark eyes.

"You're Izzy's sister. You're that girl with the boyfriend who got her out."

I shook my head immediately.

"You look just like her. I knew she was bad news. And you. You're worse. Your boyfriend did this. I saw him. I saw him!"

My eyes widened. I yelled, "Necesitamos intubar ahora." His oxygen saturation was dropping, and I needed him to shut up.

One of the nurses nodded and agreed with me, but Allan froze and stared like he'd seen a ghost. He stood staring so long that the head physician screamed at him.

More blood poured from the victim. His oxygen kept dropping.

We couldn't get it to stop.

His life ran away from him just like my joy fled from me at his words.

For the rest of the night, I tried to remember the joy Dante and I shared. I tried to relish it. Then, as the cases got worse and my mind kept concocting ideas of what he was doing out there,

I fought to hold on to it.

A mother lost her baby at eight months that same night. She held my hand as she cried and cried, then she stared up at me and said, "I wish I'd never even tried."

I watched the joy flee from me. Fear and sadness and loathing crept in. So many hours at the therapist's office, so many checkmarks on a list, so many smiles and bouts of laughter hadn't stopped the darkness from inking over it.

It never would.

Depression wasn't an emotion to stop, my therapist had always said. I couldn't ace my way through it or navigate around it or avoid it. Sometimes, I had to accept the piece of me I didn't want, and as I left the hospital that night, the thing I feared most was whether or not Dante could accept that part of me too.

So instead of processing it with him, I tried to go without him.

He had to work too, I figured. Maybe he wouldn't be home.

Only about ten minutes into me getting a massage from the spa downstairs, I got a text.

Dante: Where are you?

Me: I'll be back in the room soon.

Dante: Don't make me ask you again.

Me: I'm getting a massage.

Dante: I give you massages. What the hell are you going to get one for?

Me: I had a gift card from a patient,

and the reviews on the website were good.

Also, I was practically addicted to his massages but needed to be self-sufficient sometimes. The man had done practically everything for me in the past week, other than accompanying me to work and putting on the nursing uniform to do my job. I figured I'd give him a break.

Dante: Mine are better. Mine are the only ones you should ever be getting.

Me: Oh, please. This guy has strong hands too. It's only a twenty-minute one. I'll be back soon.

Dante: A guy?

Me: Yes.

Dante: Where are you?

Me: I'll be back soon.

Dante: Where. Are. You?

I rolled my eyes and let the young man finish what he'd been doing. I'd received a gift card from coworkers as a welcome gift at the hospital. It'd paid for a way to relax, where I could digest my thoughts. It was a smart thing to do, I thought.

My mind whispered that I was avoiding what I was terrified of, though.

As the young man turned on the lights in the room, there

was a knock at the door. "One minute," he called out. "We're just finishing up in here."

The door swung open, and there stood my overprotective superhero, breathing hard and looking ready to cause havoc. "You're done now."

The young man's eyes widened. "Mr. Armanelli, I'm sorry. I didn't realize—"

"Ms. Hardy is not to have any massages here unless they're approved through me."

"Of course." He nodded once and didn't even glance my way before rushing out.

Dante prowled toward me, his green eyes as bright as I imagined the aurora borealis to be against the dark sky. Both bright and dark, his pupils dilated like he was about to devour me. "Why were another man's hands on you?"

I grabbed the sheet from my butt and pulled it to myself as I sat up. "Are you kidding me right now? You can't barge into another person's massage."

"*Another person*? You're not some other person, Lilah. You're mine. Even if you're avoiding the hell out of me right now."

"I'm not—" My eyes darted everywhere around the room because I couldn't look at him and straight-up lie.

"Lie down," he commanded.

"What?" I whispered.

"Lie down, Lilah. Now." There was no room for objections. "Back on the table and lose the sheet."

"Dante, we can go to your room."

"We're staying here. This hotel seems to not understand how close we are, even after I made that clear to Leonardo. He should have spread the news to the spa staff also."

"They were very accommodating and—"

"Lie down." His voice was sharp and cut through the calm ambience of the room. I jumped and did as I was told this time.

I stared up at him as he walked toward me. I bit my lip at how good he looked in his work attire. His loafers, slacks, and white-collared shirt tucked into his leather belt appeared so businesslike, I wouldn't ever have guessed that underneath were stitched-up wounds, tattoos, and a man who delivered all forms of torture to men who deserved it. The only giveaway were those loafers, so clean and shiny with that brown leather, but one drop of red stained them.

One drop.

Was it the man's from the hospital?

"Where were you tonight?"

He quirked his head at me. "At work."

I raked my teeth over my lips and asked, "When you go to do the work that had you bleeding out in your shower, do you always feel this way after?"

"What way?"

"You're not you," I mumbled as I rearranged the sheet over my body and smoothed it so everything was covered as I stared up at him.

"Who am I then?" He leaned over me and set his hands against the massage table, on either side of my hips.

"A man who looks like he's just done something crazy. A man whose job winds him up and shoots adrenaline through him when all I know of him is a man who can soothe a wild-eyed horse."

"Well, you grew up down the street from my mom's farm. So that's the man you know me as."

"Is there someone else I should know you as, though? Because you have blood on your shoe, Dante."

I didn't tell him about the man at work, didn't tell him

someone had accused him of murder. I wanted the easy excuse. I wanted him to give me an irrefutable explanation and for that to be the end of it.

My mind wanted to ignore it while my body was occupied with him right in front of me. The spiral around that dark, dark drain was starting to swirl, and I was going to cling to anything outside of it, even if it meant avoiding the real problems between us.

"I'm going to keep you safe, Lilah. You and your family and my family. That's it. Everyone else and what they think of me doesn't matter. Tonight, I protected my family, and the blood on my shoe is proof of that. Now, I'm here protecting you from another man's hands."

The knots in my stomach unraveled. I found the excuse and ignored that valedictorian brain of mine. "That's what has you all wound up? The hotel staff seems to know you make the rules."

"Well, they will very soon," he growled as he glared at the door like they might appear.

"What? You intend to have them hear me moan your name?"

"Is that what you want, Lilah?" he asked. His gaze flew back to mine, and he moved his hand to hover over the sheet on my stomach. We both watched it, and I swear I felt the heat of it spreading through my body, up to my breasts that tingled and down to my core that clenched with need immediately. I licked my lips as his hand moved up and then down, parallel to my body but never touching it.

I may have been struggling internally with what our future held, but the present always led to my body overpowering my thoughts.

He curled his fingers into a tight fist, and my body tensed

with it, my soul somehow connected to his movements, wanting only what he showed—tension, heat, or both, I wasn't sure.

He growled before he said, "You're fighting me and building up walls I want to tear down."

"You've never used force to get to me before, Dante," I murmured, mesmerized by how we connected, how my body felt his energy, how he must have felt mine too.

His fingers danced over my collarbone before settling on my neck. "Some force, torture, or punishment could be classified as something else." He breathed in deep and glanced at the smoke curling up from the candle that was still lit on the table across from us. "Remember your safe word, Lilah."

Why my cunt instantly got wet when he said those words, I wasn't sure, but I nodded before he squeezed my windpipe, and then I gasped as his other hand went to the sheet to rip it from my breasts. It all happened at the same time his lips flew to mine and tore them apart with ferocious lust.

A moan escaped from deep down inside me as his hands worked my breasts, kneading and squeezing them to the rhythm of his tongue.

"That's the sound I want everyone to hear," he said, his voice a whisper on my lips as he rubbed his nose back and forth over mine. "I've perfected the job I do, Delilah. You know that right? Do you think I do it just because it's the job I was given in the military, because it's my family name?"

His hand left my breasts to skim down to my center folds, and he didn't waste time testing if I was ready for him. I stuttered out a response, not even sure I could string together a sentence with his fingers so close to the bundle of nerves I knew he could work into oblivion. "I guess that's what I thought. Of course. I mean, most people do that. I fell into nursing. It's fine—"

"Don't downplay that job. You love nursing."

"Of course, but I heal people."

He rolled his thumb over my clit, and I hissed. "And I do what, Lilah?"

Biting my lip, I didn't answer. His question was meant to goad me, to push me to say what we hadn't discussed properly.

He tsked when I didn't answer, and suddenly his hands were gone from my neck and pussy. He turned around while I fumbled with my protest.

"What are you doing? Are we not ... ? I mean, should I—"

Right when I started to sit up and saw him fiddling with his phone, he commanded, "Stay where you are."

The music in the spa's room changed to a darker instrumental. "Is this ... from *Bridgerton*?"

"It's the music I play when I work. Keeps me and my victims focused."

"Focused on what?" I whispered.

"On whatever I want. What I want them to tell me. They say if you play music, your mind can only process a certain number of things. You surrender to the ones you need to focus on. Ready to surrender to what I want you to?"

The music built, but I felt a million and ten things just looking at him there in those slacks. Like I wanted him but couldn't have him and needed him all the same. I took a shaky breath, "We should go back to the room."

"You should tell me what it is I do." He moved back to hover over me and placed both his hands on my shoulders. Then he slid them up to hold my cheeks in his hands. We stared at one another, his green eyes pulling me in, losing me in that deep forest of his.

"You do the opposite of me, Dante. You hurt while I heal. I enjoy healing, but how can you possibly enjoy coming home wound up like this or enjoy ..." My words drifted off because it wasn't that I was scared of what he did exactly.

I was scared that we couldn't fit together.

That I would lose him.

He may hurt others, but he always, always healed me.

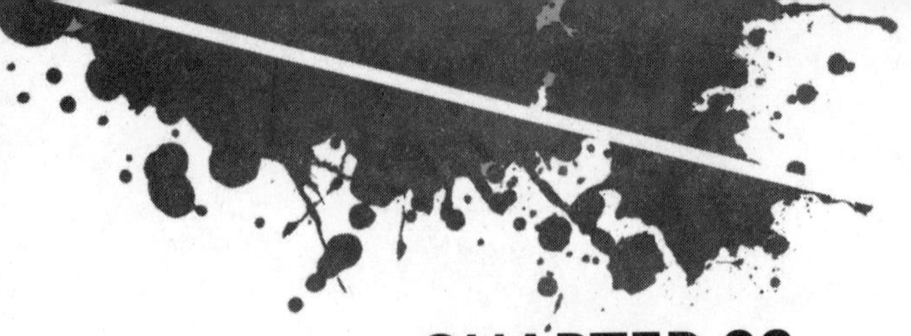

CHAPTER 22: WAX PLAY

Dante

"Inflicting pain on another human being?" I asked Delilah because I needed her to finish what she'd started. We needed to rid ourselves of whatever was infecting her views of this relationship.

She recoiled at the idea, and my instinct was already on high alert. I wanted to tower over her, make her cower in the corner, and make her beg for mercy from me.

I would have done it with anyone else.

I was bred to acquire information. I was the predator to her prey.

I leaned forward, and she sucked in a breath like she was about to lean back, like she wanted to run. Retreat looked good on her.

"That I enjoy seeing someone squirm in fear?" I asked. "That I like to earn a scream or a gasp or a moan?"

Her breath came faster, and I saw the goose bumps scattered across her soft skin. When those wide eyes dilated at my last word, I knew we were on the same page, even if she didn't yet.

Still, she cleared her throat, trying to appear unaffected. "Yes, how is that possible? I can't ... I can't imagine it."

"Well, you'd better start, Lilah, because I've wanted to drag every one of those sounds out of you. I intend to earn them. One by one."

"You think we can go that far? We've had fun, but you think I'm made for this? For you?" She shook her head. It was the fear talking, the fact that we'd been childhood friends and she didn't want to change the course of our relationship. "Izzy is the wild one, not me."

I quirked my head. "Would you classify a rabbit as wild? Or the hawk that hunts it? Do you think that a rabbit zigzagging through the forest, away from a predator, is any less than the animal that chases it?"

She stuttered. "A bu-bunny?"

"A lamb. A mouse. Prey is as wild as its predator, Lilah. You're as wild as me, and you want this as much as I do."

She shook her head, her hazel eyes wide as saucers. She pushed my hands off her and got up from the table. She grabbed her clothes, and her hand was on the handle of the door to go change when I slammed my palm above her head, holding the door closed.

She yelped and spun around, clothes clutched to her chest. All I saw was the flesh above her hand moving up and down, the swell of her breasts rapidly pulling in those breaths.

"Safe word, Lilah. Use it."

Her stare was suddenly determined, and the little fist at her chest squeezed tight as she tilted her head and uttered the only word I needed to hear. "No."

Fuck.

The wolf in me let loose and snatched the clothing from her hands and body viciously. Then my grasp was back around her neck, shoving her hard into the door even as she tried to open it.

"You want to run from me naked, woman? I'd punish you painfully for that," I growled in her ear before biting it hard.

My hand on her neck tilted her jaw so I could ravage her shoulders, the swell of those breasts, every unmarked part of her body.

I wanted me everywhere on her. "The next man that has his hands on you loses those hands, Lamb. Got it?"

She shook her head, eyes squeezed shut like she was trying to keep me out. Yet she held on to my head like she'd crumble if she let go. "This won't last. We can't. We just can't."

"We'll last forever. You'll be mine forever. No massages. No other men. Nothing. This body is mine." I picked her up, wrapped her legs around my waist, pulled her close so I could keep her. Keep her forever. That's all I wanted. I pinned her against the door, our bodies molded to one another by force.

My hands dug into her hips as I sucked hard on that sensitive part of her neck, breathed in her scent, and tried my very best to hold on to the person I couldn't lose again, even if she couldn't figure out how to stay.

Because I felt it.

I felt her slipping.

Our unhappily ever after crept in, and I didn't know how to fix it. She was right. I was a man of destruction, but she knew me as one of healing, and I didn't know how to heal us when we weren't even broken yet.

Her heart actively worked to shut me out even as her body let me in. She searched for the what-ifs and the darkness and the pain in her mind to wedge between us, and I couldn't control it except when I had her like this.

And this only lasted so long.

I spun her and laid her back on the massage table. Her dark waves cascaded over her shoulder and over the table's edge as she turned her head to look at me. I let myself take her in for just a moment as she lay there breathing heavily. Took in the way that skin stained pink for me when I touched her, the way she bent her knees and her hands went between her legs as she bit her lip, like she couldn't stop herself from touching the sensitive parts of her body while she waited for me to do it. Her muscles moved fluidly to a secret rhythm that mesmerized me. The spectrum of color in those hazel eyes hypnotized me, and I found myself grabbing the candle from behind me and moving to stand right above her, holding it out over her stomach.

I opened my mouth to remind her.

She beat me to it. "I know the safe word, Dante."

"If I lose you, Lilah, you know I'm going to make sure you remember me," I said before I poured the hot wax from a foot above her stomach, knowing it wouldn't burn too much from that height. Still, I wanted her to remember, wanted her to experiment with her pain and let me redden her unmarked skin so I could replace the pain with pleasure.

A tear escaped and trickled down her face as she nodded, and I tried my best not to fall to my knees and beg her forgiveness.

Instead, the gasp that came from her as I slid my finger up her pussy at the same moment the wax hit her stomach made my cock so hard I knew I'd need to be inside her soon. "That sound is mine. Will always be mine, Lilah."

She nodded as we watched the wax harden, and her hips rolled against my fingers.

I tilted the candle again, dripping a path of wax up to her breasts, over them, around her nipples. "The next sound is going to be you screaming."

"I don't scream in public places, Dante," she whispered.

"You're about to. Spread your legs like a good girl." She

whimpered like she couldn't do it, like she was above it, but her body submitted to me immediately. "Such a pretty little lamb. And look at that pretty pink pussy. The color I see in all my dreams. Fuck, you deserve everything I'm about to give you. Always have, always will. You're *my* good girl, *my* very best girl ... *Mine*."

And then the wax was teetering over the edge of the candle and falling fast onto her clit.

The sound from her was pain and pleasure mixed together, loud enough for the whole hotel to hear as I curled my fingers into her G-spot. Her pussy pulsed around me, and her orgasm dripped from my fingers to my wrist and down my forearm.

"This is only the start of me taking those sounds from you," I told her as her body relaxed.

The image of her on that table should have been in a damn museum, the Museum of Perfection, and access would only belong to me. I would buy the whole building, too, so I could stare at that art for eternity.

I unbuckled my slacks and nudged my cock's barbell against the wax on her clit.

"Oh, Jesus, it's too much, Dante."

"Never am I too much for you," I told her, but I was on the brink; it was all too much for me too.

We were giving in to each other's lust for one another instead of fighting for the love.

Thinking I might not always have her made me want to brand the shit out of her, made me want to hear my name on her lips over and over. I flipped her so her stomach was against the table and pushed her flat. Then I thrust into her, hard, fast, and raw.

My control had snapped at this point. I grabbed a fistful of her hair and yanked it toward me. Her body arched as I fucked her, her ass reverberating with my motion. My other hand snaked up to her tits, pinching the nipples covered in hardened wax and rolling them until it fell away so she felt only my fingers on her skin.

"Dante ... I'm scared," she panted as she met me thrust for thrust.

I smacked her ass to correct her. "You're strong, Lilah. Not scared. You better overcome your fear of me. We got this. I got you."

She bit her lip, and then her gaze shot up. I saw her reflection in a decorative mirror, those hazel eyes vivid, determined, but sparkling with unshed tears of fear.

"Seven, baby. Keep those eyes on me."

"Seven to heaven." She took a deep breath, and I escaped into the rainbow of gold and sage and misty gray of her eyes as we breathed together. Seven breaths. Seven moments. We breathed each other in. Then we let each other go. I fucked her like it was the last time, hoping it would be one of the first.

We got to heaven together.

But who knew it would be just seven days before I experienced the hell that was losing her.

* * *

She fell asleep in my arms as I carried her across the hotel to her room. In the damn spa's sheet.

Everyone was getting a raise when I left here.

Which had to be soon.

Our bubble, the one I'd kept her pretty much captive in, was about to pop. Our glass house was about to shatter. The freedom, even if it was fractured, that I'd given her was about to become complete lockdown.

I let her sleep for a couple of hours and took a call from Cade that afternoon.

"If Izzy's out, why isn't she here yet?" I almost yelled into the phone at Cade.

"You know I'm just watching security cameras. I'm guessing her guy got her out."

"What guy?"

"Iago, man. He's here. That means Albanian families are definitely involved. Bastian's pissed."

Bastian was the head of the Armanelli family. It meant things were getting out of hand and that we needed to end this now or a war would rain down on us all.

"Iago's been dealing with Izzy for a year or so in Miami. He knows her. If he's here, he wants this shit to go off without a hitch. She told me, once she's out, she'll try to get to your hotel under the radar. She'll call Delilah, right? Because that wouldn't raise a red flag. Make sure Lilah has her phone, that you guys—"

"I'm not a fucking idiot, Cade. You sound nervous. She's been doing this shit for years. We got this. We got her. They're not going to—"

"I'm missing something underground on the dark web. If something happens to Izzy—"

"Izzy?" I said, completely shocked. "What the fuck do you care if something happens to her? You've been calling her an addict since the day you met her."

"She is one," he growled. "If something happens to her, I'm going to have to hear about it from my brother, okay? His wife likes Izzy. They met, so now I'll be on the hook if—"

Cade, the crazy hacker of a brother to the head of the mob. He didn't give a shit about anything, not even Bastian being pissed. "You don't care if you're on the hook for anything, Cade."

"This I do. I'm not having her blood on my hands, even if I hate her."

Fair enough. None of us wanted blood on our hands anymore. Bastian had started a new reign. We were done with the bullshit our fathers had done before. We wanted a clean family, legal business, and a government we worked with, not against.

"Nothing's going to happen."

I hung up on him and told myself that same thing over and over again the next day. We were waiting now. Waiting like sitting ducks until we heard from Izzy.

I didn't tell Delilah. We didn't mention the spa or anything we'd talked about there, but we enjoyed one another's company. I catalogued the day like I was heading to fucking jail the next, like I was being shipped overseas and I'd lose her all over again.

I knew our train wasn't heading in the right direction. It was veering, careening off course, away from a happily ever after into a fiery explosion down below.

It was my job to read people's emotions. I had to know what was pushing them and what wasn't in order to find their weaknesses and strengths.

In my line of work, I'd perfected it, but in my personal life, it was the opposite.

In those seven days after the spa, I saw her retreat into the darkness of whatever shell she thought she needed to hide inside, and I couldn't fix her. Her light disappeared, and whatever she was thinking dragged her down, drowned her in her sadness. It felt like not even I could breathe around her.

"Want to talk about it, Lilah?" I asked as I gave her a massage that night, knowing she'd still turn over and let me fuck her into satiation until the sun came up. Her body still wanted me, even if her mind was far away.

She let me work her muscles and shrugged like she couldn't do much else. No words or smiles came to reassure me that she was okay.

"My momma used to tell me I couldn't make everyone happy. Did you know that?"

"You made plenty of us happy all the time," she mumbled. "I just sometimes can't be happy, no matter how much I try."

I should have taken it as an indicator of something more serious, I should have been more on the ball, but her phone rang, and we both stared at it as an odd number flashed on the screen.

"Izzy?" I asked, and Lilah lunged for the phone like she'd been waiting for the call her whole life.

"Hello?" Lilah waited, and her eyes narrowed. "You're here? Our room numbers?" She shoved me off her and moved faster than I'd seen her do all week. She threw on the bra she claimed was a crop top and slipped back into her black shorts. "Sure, we're on the twentieth floor, rooms 2001 and 2002."

She stared at the phone for one beat, and I stared at her. She was ready to bolt and formulate a plan to smooth out the situation.

Her hands wrung together. "Let's just say I was grabbing food here."

I glanced around my room. Her things were everywhere. Her makeup on my bathroom counter, her toothbrush at the sink, her clothes over the chair. Two pairs of her shoes were right by the door. And my stuff was all over hers. We'd spread out so much there was no way of hiding it. "Why would I lie, Lilah?"

"Because it will complicate things and I don't want her to—"

"Fly off the rails? I can assure you Izzy has been clean for years. This won't cause a setback."

"It's not what I want," she blurted out.

"*What* isn't what you want?"

"This." She motioned between us. "I can't give you what you want. So I don't want this."

"What is it that you can't give me?" I whispered. Her words cut my organs, like she was trying to rip me apart fast and clean but doing a bad job.

"Oh my God! Everything. I'm lost. I'm scared of whatever we have. And what if it's real? What if we really have it, the love and the life, and then we want a kid, Dante? I can't give you a kid. Or a family." Her hand flew over her mouth as though she couldn't believe what she'd said. "I know. We've only been sleeping together for two weeks. This is probably just casual—"

"It's not," I answered for her. "This is forever. It always was, Lilah."

"And that's why it can't be. If it's forever, our genes don't work in me, or no genes do, I don't know." Tears formed in her pretty eyes. "We can't talk about this right now. I can't beat whatever happened in that miscarriage, Dante. This is done. Leave it. Don't even tell her."

"Little Lamb." She was ready to dart, and I could only whisper the words and hope she wouldn't. "I don't want children if it's not with you. We either have them or we don't."

"No." She almost yelped the word and then pointed her finger at me. "You're not suffering because I'm suffering. You have a way out."

"I don't want one." I shrugged because she had to understand what she was saying was nonsense. "I don't want 'a way out' from you ever. I could have told you that the first time you tricked me into taking your virginity, the time I carried you home with your broken ankle. Hell, the time I asked what you needed for your first period in my car. I wasn't going anywhere without you. I'm still not. I'll wait forever for a baby with you, or we'll be happy without one."

"What if you're not happy, though? What if I can't be happy? What if I'm depressed all the time?" Tears streamed from her eyes.

"We got a million tools in the toolbox for that. I've perfected a few things in my lifetime, Lamb. I'm not afraid to perfect making you happy and aiding you in your mental health."

"I don't want you to have to fix me. I don't want to be broken all the time. Do you enjoy putting me back together?" she shrieked like I was insane.

I was when it came to her.

"I do. I enjoy every part of you. Even the dark parts. Even the ones you're scared of. I might tear people apart, but I enjoy putting you back together. I want to do that for the rest of my life."

She shook her head. "You'll change your mind."

The knock on my door sounded and her eyes widened. Then she wiped her face while swearing and moving toward the door all at the same time.

CHAPTER 23: FEEL YOUR HEART BREAK

Delilah

I held the handle and took seven deep breaths. Seven. I could pull together a million lies and bury a million emotions in seven breaths.

Just seven. It was all I needed.

I swung open Dante's door. I might have hesitated, taking one extra breath before my world crumbled. This was it. They were going to complete this operation, and that meant things were going to change.

They had to.

Twins, even just siblings, are always on one another's radar. We might live our lives separately, but there's always a tiny worry or thought of what the other is doing. We are each other's responsibilities. We are family and intertwined—sometimes in ways we don't want to be.

I didn't want to worry about Izzy.

Still, seeing her standing there reminded me that I had been. Tears were already in my eyes when I opened the door, but they poured out on seeing her there, even if I was furious with her, even if she was furious with me. I held open my arms, and her brow furrowed before she sighed and rushed into them.

At first, our muscles were taut, stiff, and uncomfortable.

Our relationship hadn't been nurtured or watered lately, and we'd already broken a ton of branches from our tree before she got out of jail.

Yet, I squeezed the girl with my same genetics so tight, as if I could consume her. Three minutes apart in age. Just three minutes. Somehow, we'd grown miles apart, but it didn't matter.

We might have been very different, but all the moments we'd shared rushed back as I held her. We'd lost the same teeth within the same month, failed the same test questions in middle school, and hated the same freckles that popped up on our noses in the summer. We both cried when our mom put us in separate rooms because our sleepovers were out of control. We both giggled when we snuck into the other's room late at night. I'd been the only one to defend her sobriety, but I was ashamed as I pushed her back to arm's length to stare into her hazel eyes, just a bit browner than mine.

"Sober as a fucking judge, Izzy," I whispered. "I knew you were, and then I questioned it."

She wrinkled her nose and then smiled. I swear the sun shined brighter, flowers bloomed, birds chirped, and society perked up. Her hair was a bit longer than mine, her curves a bit sharper, her eyes a bit bigger. We looked the same, but she stole the attention from everyone in the world with that smile.

"I won't apologize, Lilah."

I sighed and shook my head. "You should."

"Fine." She shrugged and looked over my shoulder at Dante, winking at him before saying to me, "I'm sorry you were in jail for two whole days."

"That was a long time for me." I sounded appalled as my eyes darted back to Dante and then to her. "And that's not what I mean. You could have told me or called me once!" My voice broke as I said it. I rolled my lips between my teeth, trying not to let the emotions through.

"I couldn't. You know I couldn't."

"You hid so much." It was an accusation, and we all heard the pain in my voice.

She nodded. "I get that. I do. I have to live with it, and I'm sorry for that too. I won't be sorry for doing it though. It saved me." She said the words softly. Then she dragged in a breath, looked past me again, and said, "He saved me."

She walked around me to get to him, but I stood there frozen.

Her voice. The hitch in it, the tone of it, the way it shook. I knew that voice. I knew it because it was my own when I whispered it softly at night ... the scariest thing I'd ever felt: my love for him.

I loved Dante.

And my beautiful twin did too.

It felt like my heart had bottomed out in my stomach, like my mind swooped around and stuttered to a halt as it short-circuited over the revelation.

I placed both hands on my stomach; I took the breaths; I tried to channel that calm that Dante always seemed to find.

Still, I didn't turn to face them as they talked. I couldn't make out their words as my world dimmed, tilting horrendously off its axis. The tunnel was speeding toward me full force, not going toward the light but toward the dark.

Izzy.

My sister. Clean and free and brilliant.

I turned slowly so I wouldn't be walloped by the image I was about to see.

Her smiling at him with that twinkle in her eye so clear and full of hope.

Him smiling back at her.

She pulled him in for a hug, and her whole body flew into his—chest to chest, hips to hips, feet to feet. I saw how she looked at him, and I knew that look because her face was the exact same as mine.

When I stared at myself in the mirror, I saw my cheeks flushed, my eyes sparkling, all the wrinkles of worry disappeared from my face. Dante brought love out of me, just the way he brought it out of Izzy.

She turned to me, and her gaze dimmed. "What's wrong?"

I nodded and gulped twice before I stammered, "I-I just need ... a minute, I think. I need a-a minute."

"Okay." She scanned my face in question, then her gaze darted around the room. "I got a room here for a night—301. Come down and talk to me when you're ready. Today, though. I'm staying one night and then ..." She trailed off and glanced at Dante, probably considering how much she could tell me.

I nodded quickly, my emotions welling up in my throat too fast to think of anything other than getting out of that room.

I rushed to the adjoining door and pushed through it as I heard Dante call after me.

I didn't stop in my bedroom at all. I beelined to the shower and peeled my clothes off as I turned on the water, cranking it as hot as it would go.

Scalding off my love for him was the only way I could think of to rid myself of it. If my sister loved him, I couldn't.

His happy ending could be here in an instant, and they would fit together like yin and yang.

To me, it all made sense.

I cried and watched my tears mix with the water drops for as long as the water was hot. I let it wash over my shoulders after it turned cold too, cooling the heat on my skin and in my soul.

I grabbed a bright-red crop top and shorts, ones I'd been

so comfortable in a week ago, and winced when they reminded me somewhat of Izzy's style. Maybe Dante had seen a new me here that wasn't really me at all ... and maybe she was what he really wanted. He could love her.

I jumped when I heard the knock at my adjoining door.

"Jesus," I whispered, and then I was up against it immediately, ready to barricade it if I needed to. "I need to talk to her first, Dante. I can't see you right now."

I heard a sigh.

Then my cell pinged, and when I saw his name, my fists clenched. I wasn't sure I could take any of his words. Still, I grabbed the phone like it was my last bubble of oxygen down in the deep ocean.

Dante: Lilah, why do you think I knocked instead of barging in. I'm hanging by a thread though.

Me: I need some time.

Dante: I should barge in there and fuck you until you understand.

Me: I'll understand once I talk to her. Once this is over.

Dante: As long as it doesn't mean we're over.

I didn't answer him. The fear of that was real, tangible, and what hurt most was that it was also probably best.

I went to her room shortly after. I'd heard her leave Dante's room after listening as best I could through the thick walls. The murmurs between them told me they worked comfortably together, that they had things to talk about, that their relationship was already prepped for more. When I heard his door swing shut, I knew she'd left.

I'd known that always, but to see it on her face, to see how she looked at him now ... that was the blow that I hadn't seen coming.

Still, I walked to her room, ready to confess everything because Izzy wasn't stupid. I'd watched how she'd absorbed what she saw in Dante's room.

My belongings were there, scattered around like the pieces of my heart. What was left of it.

I knocked on her door twice, and she opened before I hit the third time.

She waved me in with no words. Her room was smaller than mine and bare. She plopped herself down at the tiny oak table, and I joined her.

"So?" Her hands were folded in front of her. "Seems we have a lot of catching up to do."

I nodded and combed my hands through my hair. "Not much on my end other than working and living here, waiting for you two to tie up whatever it is you're doing."

"Dante said he told you just about everything. You know I'm undercover trying to bust a big drug operation. Iago should let me know when soon, then I'll be able to get him." Her stare was far-off for a second. "Finally. Him and his boss, Lilah. We're fucking close. The jail—"

"Was shitty." I stopped her because I needed her to know she wasn't off the hook. "You used me."

"In my defense, Mom really did want to see you, and us traveling together attracted less attention. I didn't know we were going to get caught, but it was the best thing that could have happened. I made some connections in there, and now we'll get him. They don't suspect a damn thing. I mean, some of them did ... but Dante and Cade were able to clean up a few loose ends."

"*Ends* or people?" I whispered as I lifted a brow at her. It hurt that he was probably sharing all this with her and not me, that I was in love with a man who shared more of his life with my sister than he did with me.

"You realize that's Dante's job, right?" She chewed on her cheek before facing the issue head-on—not like she would have done in the past when she was using. She would have avoided it for weeks and weeks. "If you're sleeping with him, you should know that, Lilah."

"I don't want to talk about that right now. First, you." I pointed at her. "Mom and Dad and our brothers, Izzy. They're all so scared for you. I was scared for you. And all this time, you embraced that lie for a job."

"For my life, Lilah. There's a difference." She sat back like she couldn't believe me not understanding. "If I can't do *this*, what good am I? Don't you get that?"

"But you were gone. Our family's hurting. I'm hurting, trying to defend your fake lifestyle and your sobriety."

She picked at a nonexistent chip in the table and didn't look at me when she said, "You were always the strong one, Lilah. You were strong enough to deal with my shit even when I wasn't. You figured out how to get over my addiction and then believed in me right when I got out of juvie. Even when I didn't believe in myself. You were strong enough to deal with this too."

"Strong enough?" The question bellowed out of me. The words still tasted like rancid filth in my mouth. "*Strong enough*? I could barely open my eyes in the morning, let alone get out of bed back in college. I wanted to die."

That thought and the fact that my family probably wouldn't miss me made it all the simpler for it to fester and grow. And grow it had, until it was such a weight that there was no way to move out from under it.

"You fell into drugs, and I lost a baby. A baby, Izzy."

"A ... what?" Her gaze snapped to mine. "When? What are you talking about?"

I bit my lip, and then the story flew out of me. "All cards on the table," I murmured and shrugged at the end of it. "And I think the baby would have loved me more than anyone. More than people loved you because I truly was so scared that no one could. Mom and Dad and Dom and Dex and Declan and Dimitri ... and Dante! God, all of them loved you. They couldn't stop talking about you. And I know that's terrible," I choked out, tears streaming down my face now. "But, Jesus, you'd think with a twin I'd never be lonely, and yet, I felt lonelier in those moments than I could have ever fathomed. And it's embarrassing. I was supposed to be strong enough for you. I was supposed to be able to shoulder your pain, but I couldn't because I was going through my own."

I took a breath, gasping for it, giving her an opening, but she didn't say a word. She waved for me to carry on.

I did. It was like the words wouldn't stop. "And who knew depression is like a drug, too? It eats away at your happiness, it makes you not the person you want to be, and it guilts you into thinking you can never resurface from it. God, the guilt. And the fear that I'll fall back into it."

"Lilah, you're so strong."

"So are you! You struggle with your addiction."

She tried to deny it.

I cut her off, though. "Don't feed me the bull. You put those opioids right in front of you to tempt fate with that job. You must have. You went into the industry where they'd be in your face daily. I get it. You want to make sure you're strong enough to deny yourself. *That's* strength, but I'm so scared of falling back into depression that I'm avoiding anything that will even make me happy."

"Like Dante?"

"Izzy, no." I shook my head and stood from the chair so fast it flew over.

"You love him."

"I don't." I shook my head fiercely. I was scared I'd push her to the edge or that I'd fall over it too. I didn't need her concerned that I'd fallen for the man she most likely loved.

"Are you scared I can't handle it if you love him? If he loves you back?" she whispered, her eyes searching my face.

I threw my hands up to shield her from any emotions I might have been showing. We were twins, able to read one another even if we didn't want the other one to see what we were feeling. I couldn't let her see this. I didn't even want to witness it myself.

"What will it take for this family to think I can handle something?" she asked me. "Do you think I'll drown my heartbreak in drugs?"

"Your heart will be broken? Because you love him?" I asked even though I didn't need her answer.

"Of course I love him." She spat the words out like she hated the taste of them. "I've loved him forever. He's always been there. We're a team, we work well together, and he's always believed in me the way—"

Our eyes met, and the pain she felt hit me like a freight train, hard and heavy enough to knock the wind out of me.

I whispered, "I don't know what to do here."

"Well"—she stood up tall and wiped a hand over her face

like she was wiping away emotions—"you'd better figure it out, Lilah."

"What do you mean?"

"I've tried my best to be straight to the point these days."

I nodded. "I see that. You seem to face things head-on now."

"You've always been the one who knew exactly what to do, right? You got the grades, you got into college. You took care of a miscarriage, for God's sake—all on your own. You handled it all. So you'd better figure it out now. I'm going for a walk to clear my head. *Figure it out*, Lilah, because if you don't love him enough to fight for him, then he deserves me ... because I will."

"I don't know if I love him." I shook my head repeatedly. I couldn't feel that for him. Not after what we'd been through, not after I'd lost his baby. I couldn't go through that again, not with him. "I shouldn't because I won't survive loving him."

"You will," she said and walked past me with tears in her eyes. "You're strong enough."

"I just don't know. It's only been a few weeks. How could I know?"

"Because *I* know." My sister's voice was pleading. With that, the door shut behind her, and she left me in her small, empty hotel room.

Silence was either an enemy or a friend. It calmed you or left you alone with the worst of your thoughts.

Dante had taught me there was never really any silence, because the world was always talking. The sounds I heard now were my tears falling one by one on that table. I had a choice. Or so I thought. Love never *really* gives you a choice. I thought I would have to choose between breaking my sister's heart or my heart, or maybe even Dante's.

There wasn't an easy answer.

There was no right answer.

And I always searched for the right one.

I'd only ever known how to do the right thing.

When the knock at the door came, I found myself wanting to be anyone else at that point. I wanted to save everyone and not ruin one more thing.

CHAPTER 24: STEAL AN IDENTITY

Delilah

"Izzy, I know you're in there." He banged on the door after I looked through the peephole and didn't answer.

I didn't know the tall lanky man outside my door, but I knew he must have been a part of Izzy's undercover work. She didn't know anyone else here and had only been on the island a few days before she ended up in jail. I'd never seen her with anyone like this.

I took a deep breath. It was answer or throw a wrench in everything.

I did the dumb thing.

I told myself I was smart enough to act like Izzy for as long as we needed.

I swung open the door.

"Hey, sorry. I was in the bathroom." I cleared my throat and tried not to shrivel when he stepped up to me and then narrowed his eyes.

His pupils were dilated, his breath smelled of alcohol, and the way his body twitched told me it wasn't the only thing affecting him. "You ready?"

"Um, ready for what?" I tried to hold the door closed to indicate I didn't want him inside, but he shoved past me and glanced around my room.

"We're going to the ship now. Fucking agents are onto us. We got word someone's sniffing around. Probably from you fucking up by getting thrown in jail."

"I don't think—"

"No. You don't think at all." He turned around, and his words rumbled out so fast that spit flew from his mouth. He pointed a long bony finger at me. "You're lucky Iago wants to fuck you six ways to Sunday, because otherwise you wouldn't even be on this boat with us. We got a car out back. Let's go."

I didn't have time to grab anything, and my heart beat so fast that I couldn't stop the adrenaline from rushing through my veins. I tried to stall. "I need to shower."

"Shower on the boat." He smiled, his eyes roving over my body like the slimy scum he was, and he sucked on his yellowed teeth. "We'll enjoy the show. We have in the past, right?"

He winked at me, like I wanted his advances, like I was into it.

My sister never would have been into this.

And what I had to do became crystal clear at that moment. The shaky ground settled, the quiver in my hand stopped, and my blood ran cold.

Ice cold.

"Let's go to Iago." I brushed past him, and he hurried after me like he suddenly couldn't keep up.

"Remember, I make the rules, Izzy." He narrowed his beady eyes at me in the elevator. "Iago may want your ass, but it isn't going to interfere with me getting my cut of that thousand kilos."

I shrugged. "If you say so."

The man was fast, so fast I didn't feel my head ricochet off the side of the elevator wall from his punch to my temple until five seconds later. Maybe I blacked out; maybe I wasn't exactly used to being hit in the face. Either way, I took my time before responding. And I tried my best to be strategic.

What would an agent do? What would Dante do?

I pointed to one of the cameras. Someone who wasn't on drugs may not have looked where I was pointing, but this man did. He looked right up at them, and then I murmured, "There's security at the hotel. Don't make a scene."

He nodded, and his brow furrowed as he mumbled, "Good idea. Good idea. Shit, I forgot. Okay, let's get out of here."

As the elevator doors opened, I pointed to the back exit. "Less cameras."

And less Leonardo.

He would be able to tell the difference between me and Izzy and would alert Dante.

I didn't want anyone alerted. Not until everyone was on that boat with police raiding it, then my sister would be safe.

Safe from whatever Iago had done to her.

Safe from these men.

Because I saw from the look in this man's eyes, something had happened between her and Iago. It wouldn't happen again.

I was strong enough. Izzy was right about that.

I let the silence descend and didn't say a word as I folded myself into the black SUV. I took my phone out of my back pocket in front of the idiot of a man, and when he stammered out, "What are you doing?" I lied like I would have if I had been late to a test, to a job, to anything that I knew meant something to my family. This meant the world to Izzy, and I'd always put her and the rest of my family first.

"I'm texting my sister to tell her I'm going out so she doesn't worry."

"Your fucking sister," he mumbled. "She almost cost us

this whole damn shipment. They thought her boyfriend was an agent for a minute." He chuckled like the idea was stupid. "Turns out that guy fucked her more than a few times. We got real nervous when we had someone go check the first time and he turned up dead, but it was a deal gone bad."

I tried to tune him out as I turned my phone away from him and texted Dante.

Me: Track me. Shipment's happening tonight. Don't call. They mistook me for Izzy. We're going to the cruise ships.

There were three dots. Then they stopped. Then they started again.

"You writing a novel over there?" he sneered. "Let me see that phone."

My heart was in my throat as I responded, "Fuck off," and slid it into my pants.

I had to hope my demeanor matched my sister's. I'd lived with her. I knew how she'd been when she hung with groups like this. But I didn't know how she was with him.

There was a beat of silence before he chuckled. "Maybe that's why Iago likes you so much. That fire in you is a turn-on."

"Want me to tell him you said so?"

His eyes cut to mine as we drove slowly down the darkened cobblestone streets of Old San Juan.

Men and women laughed beyond the car windows, danced right outside the club, enjoying the beautiful night air and the beat of the music that poured from the bar onto the street.

In this car, though, there was nothing beautiful. The push and pull of power, the coiled, unhinged anger in this man, was unpredictable.

"I should fuck you and see if you tell him," he muttered.

"What? You think I'd like it and just not tell Iago? I haven't slept with him either." I hoped that was true.

"Yeah, well according to him, you're saving it for after this shipment, huh? You think your pussy is that good?"

I rolled my eyes and scoffed, but my palms were sweating, my pulse was going a mile a minute, and the bile rose in my throat. Jesus, these men had been near her all this time. She'd subjected herself to—at the very least—so much sexual harassment in the past years that I couldn't imagine what secrets she held on to.

He flicked a piece of lint off the dark slacks that were much too baggy for him. He probably used to have more weight on him, but drugs would do that to a person. "Maybe to him. You ain't worth the work to me. I don't like the fight like he does. You do put up a good one, though." He smacked his knee and laughed like he was recalling a specific time. "Damn, when you got Iago in the balls after he grabbed your ass and tried to get your shirt off that one time ..." He cackled and cackled as I turned my face toward the window to try to hide how my throat seemed to close, how pulling in air felt impossible.

What Izzy and I had squabbled over just hours before felt so small. Heartbreak, miscarriages, jail time ... None of it seemed relevant if my sister was a shell of a human because a man was planning to assault her or had been trying to for years.

Unwanted attention could wreck a soul just like drugs.

She had to know that.

She had to know she couldn't keep going undercover if this was what the work entailed.

When he sobered from his laughing fit, he pulled a pipe from his pocket, held a lighter to the bowl, and sucked in the smoke. "Want a hit?"

The driver, who had a dark beard and round face, turned around, "Fuck, man, we're almost there. You show up high, smelling like that, and we're all going to be in trouble. We got to be on the ball with this one. It's the biggest one we've done in a year."

"Oh, fuck off. I'm just as Albanian as any of them. They couldn't get rid of me if they tried. Plus, we got this in the bag. It's supposed to start raining in a minute, and we'll be hidden from cameras too."

I tried to keep breathing in and out. Seven breaths, seven times, over and over.

I'd count to seven seven million times if it kept me calm enough to live through this.

As the rain started to fall on the SUV, the driver turned our headlights off, and we crept down an alley, the vehicle rising and falling over each cobblestone. "Ship's just down the street. We ditch the car here."

We filed out, and it seemed silently agreed upon that we'd walk quietly down the street. Neither of the men made eye contact with anyone, and we swerved around a couple talking animatedly on the sidewalk. She held her partner's hand and rejoiced over the deal she'd got at the store up the street.

They looked as happy as I had a few days ago with Dante, and I found myself holding back tears, holding back fear.

Would I die in a crop top and shorts that I now knew had probably contributed to this guy thinking I was Izzy?

Would Izzy and Dante get here in time? Would they know how to find me?

The cruise ship was larger than life. I'd seen them out on the water from the beach and knew they were grand, magnificent in the way they seemed to glide over the waves.

This ship was no less magnificent inside. Chandeliers hung from the lobby ceiling, sparkling and greeting us like we were on vacation.

The two men I was with nodded to the captain and concierge. No greetings were exchanged, no questioning of our identities or tickets. This was a planned operation.

"I want to get down to see that everything's there."

The driver shook his head and kept walking toward an elevator. "We go to Iago's room. We stick to the plan."

"Fuck the plan," he grumbled but followed us.

One foot in front of the other. I didn't scream out to the other passengers, didn't even look at them. I walked to what would be my death or my sister's salvation.

I'd find a way to make that man pay, and then I'd drag her out of this profession kicking and screaming.

She'd done this to prove a point, and maybe I'd done the same. Maybe I'd flown to Puerto Rico and made a stupid list to prove the point to myself that I could be happy, that I could live outside the expectations everybody had set for me.

Izzy was doing that too in her own way. We wanted out of the box everyone put us in.

But we'd climb out of it together and we'd move on together.

And it wouldn't be by dangling drugs in her face. Hard times would no longer push her to her limits. I wouldn't avoid everything I loved in the hopes of never experiencing loss again.

The door to Iago's room was oak with a gold door knocker and beautiful carvings swirling toward the handle.

"Do the honors, Izzy." The man next to me smiled, and his yellow teeth glowed. It was like he knew this was the end. He didn't realize it wasn't the end he'd hoped for, though.

The man who swung open the door met us with a smile.

He had blue eyes and dark, dark wavy hair. His face was soft, no real hard lines, but he was big enough to throw someone around, even if his muscles looked as soft as his face. He towered over us, and the smile on his face dropped off as he stared at me. "What the fuck is going on? Why would you bring Izzy's sister here?"

"I brought ..." The man stuttered before his head whipped around to stare at me.

All of their eyes widened as I stood there without denying that I was Izzy's sister. They were hoping for a correction, one I was sure I no longer needed to give them. My phone was still in my back pocket, and I could only hope Dante and my sister were coming in hot with a fucking cavalry.

"Well, should I say surprise?" I quirked a brow as I said it, feeling the fear leave my body and the anger washing in as Iago advanced on me.

Good, I thought to myself. *Let him come. Better me than my sister.*

His large, meaty hands grabbed my hair and my neck, and he threw me into the wall. He wanted to cause pain as he said, "I was so excited to tell your sister that we finally had all night for me to fuck her. That she wouldn't be able to fight me off. That we'd finally done it together. And we would be together forever. You know, I think I'll do all that to you instead. Will you fight as well as she does?"

I clawed at his face. I went for his eyes, and I screamed as much as I could before he squeezed my windpipe shut, all while holding a ball of my hair at the top of my scalp. Over and over again, I hit that wall.

I didn't shut my eyes, though. I stared at him long enough to spit right in his face.

That got him to let my neck go so he could rear back and

punch me square in the cheek.

I really wished I'd taken Dante up on those self-defense classes, because my world went black so fast.

The last thing I remember thinking was we were going to have one hell of a story to tell if I got out of this alive.

CHAPTER 25: TAKE A CRUISE

Dante

"Cade, how did you miss the fucker coming to her room? And how did we have the wrong ship?" I tried to control the rage. I tried to bottle what I knew had been in me all these years but had never let out.

He rolled his eyes. "I look away one second and see them walking out. I'm staring at twins. I thought it was Izzy leaving too. You were all there. I got other shit to watch." He sounded pissed.

Losing the one person in my life who kept me sane, though, had me more pissed. It would cause me to unravel and unleash everything I kept bottled. "If Delilah Hardy has one fucking hair out of place on her head, I'll kill them all."

Cade had called in his brother, Bastian, and he was on the car speakerphone as Leonardo navigated the side streets to get us there as soon as possible. We'd also called the authorities, but they had protocol to get through. They needed to get approval. Goddamn red tape. This was a big bust. They had to do things right. But they also had other intelligence that said it was the next ship over.

Fuck them.

We'd seen Delilah's phone location.

"I shouldn't have left her," Izzy whispered, looking out her window.

Damn right she shouldn't have. And I shouldn't have let her leave the room without telling her I loved her. Without telling her we'd get through the shit and get to the other side.

"I'm getting the authorities' clearance right now, Dante," Bastian said over the car's speakers.

Cade chuckled as he looked at me. "Not going to help, Bastian. Dante's killing them before anyone gets there."

"We need to keep it clean."

"You keep it clean and legal when your wife was in danger?" My question was met with about two seconds of silence.

Then, his wife's voice came over the phone. "He still hasn't forgiven Cade for not protecting me diligently even though the guy only held me at gunpoint for less than a minute."

"That's beside the point. You and I were married. The disrespect—"

"Lilah's as much a fucking Untouchable as your wife, Bastian. She's mine. My Untouchable. My whole goddamn future. I will tear this island apart, I promise you." I clenched my fists. I put them over my stomach, but the energy that flowed into them burned hot and monstrous.

"Hey." Izzy turned to me and grabbed one of my hands, quickly threading her fingers through mine. "I know my sister. She'll be fine. She'll stall, okay? She was smart enough to get that text off. We'll get there in time."

Her hand shook, and it reminded me Lilah wasn't just mine. She was my best friend's family's kid. Little Lilah who at twelve had come home with fucking pigtails and a huge smile on her face because she'd won the spelling bee.

Lilah who'd tried not to smirk when her parents praised yet another straight A report card on the refrigerator, or the girl who'd taken her five siblings to feed a lamb because the mother hadn't made it. She'd refilled the milk over and over again and let each of them give it to the lamb first.

A fucking giver.

And then she'd given me her virginity, and I'd never been the same.

I'd never be the same.

I wouldn't lose her again. Not this time.

We pulled up to her phone's location, and I was out of the car before it stopped moving, rushing past everyone, rain falling on my collared shirt and tailored slacks. I splashed through the puddles, raced across the sidewalk, dodging pedestrians, and then flew like a crazy motherfucker through the security entrance. Cade was behind me making amends wherever necessary.

And it only took me two seconds to scan the lobby of that ship to find the perpetrators. They saw me, and their eyes widened. Maybe things clicked into place for them.

Their friend who'd gone missing after looking into Lilah and me on that staircase, how they'd tracked my whereabouts, the man who'd listened in on our hotel room romp and been gunned down by me later that night.

As the police raided that boat, I turned to the officer and said, "Iago's room is mine. Don't come in until we give the signal. Cade"—I met his eyes, and he rubbed those knuckles tattooed with *chaos* across his cheek as he smiled wide at me—"let's go."

We let the police take the men who'd tried to rush away quietly with eyes as big as saucers. Except for the one at the front desk. I approached and asked quietly, "Iago's room or you die." I laid my gun on the counter.

The man didn't hesitate. He knew he'd lost it all already.

The Albanians didn't scare their associates well enough if their men folded this easily.

Cade and I ran to the stairs because I knew I could beat the elevator at the speed I was going.

Cade laughed behind me the whole time, throwing out, "Man, we haven't fucked someone up this bad in a long time. They're going to wish they'd never taken the wrong sister."

He needed therapy.

"You need some help." I was surprised to hear Izzy behind us.

Had I been a better man, not scared of losing another second, I would have told her to stay back. I would have argued that the scene may not be one she wanted to see.

Yet, Izzy and I had worked together long enough for her to know that.

When I didn't hesitate for one second to kick in the door, Cade and Izzy flew in, guns already pulled. Thankfully, we'd been smart enough to wear bulletproof vests, because the bullets sprayed immediately.

With only three of them and three of us, we may have been even in numbers, but they were outmatched in skill tenfold. Cade was hit once in the chest, and I heard the wind get knocked out of him as I dropped the shooter, then Izzy ducked past a wall as we scanned for the other two men. One had barricaded himself in the bathroom, and the other stood with a gun pointed directly at the floor.

At Delilah.

"You guys make one more move and I shoot her."

Izzy and I looked at each other, then she shot his leg while I shot his arm. Hesitation was for cowards, and we weren't either of those things.

Cade whooped and went skipping to the damn bathroom

like a lunatic about to find his calling.

"Iago, you're going to pay before I kill you," Izzy whispered over him as he screamed, but then she went to Delilah and checked vitals.

She fell over her sister, slid Lilah's limp body up into her arms, and curled around her. "She's okay, Dante," she whispered, tears streaming down her eyes. "She's okay. Just knocked out."

The assessment had me snapping my neck and stalking over to Iago, who tried his best to wiggle across the floor, the blood from his wounds smearing beneath him.

Cade jiggled the bathroom door lock, then stopped to grab a roll of duct tape from his suit pocket. "Brought this just in case," he sing-songed. He threw that and a lighter my way, waggling his eyebrows.

I didn't wait to grab Iago and drag him to a chair.

The man was going to admit everything before he died. And he was going to suffer while he did it.

CHAPTER 26: BLACK OUT

Delilah

"Dante," I whispered, rubbing my forehead and opening my eyes to see him standing before me.

I jumped to claw at whoever's hands were around me, but their arms gripped mine and then my sister's voice was in my ear. "It's me. It's just me. You're okay. Everything's okay."

I winced as I touched my hand to my head. I felt a bump as large as an egg. "Wow, ow."

Izzy smoothed my matted hair. Her legs were around me; she had me cradled on the floor where I must have fallen when Iago hit me. "Yeah, you're gonna have a pretty good shiner from that one."

I nodded but didn't answer her. I took in the man before me as he stared down at my abuser. Dante's hands clenched and unclenched. His whole body seemed three times bigger as he stared down at a bloodied Iago. He wasn't just a wolf here, he was a werewolf, ready to kill, ready to rip apart a man.

I saw him now, for the first time ever, as the man he truly was. A ferocious beast ready to protect, breathing in and out.

In and out.

I breathed with him as his eyes met mine, and the wild in them calmed for just those seven breaths. His piercing emerald eyes closed for a second like he was settling his soul, and then he opened them again and they landed directly on me.

"Cade, get the knife." His gaze cut back to Iago, and I watched Cade smile as if the ideas flying through his head were lollipops floating by and he was a hungry kid with a sweet tooth. He walked to the kitchen counter and pulled a large knife from a wood block.

I hadn't had a chance to take in the room—the plush carpeting, the granite countertops, the lights twinkling above us in a low-hanging crystal chandelier. This room on a cruise ship probably cost a fortune.

It would be expensive to ruin too, I thought to myself as I stared at the blood seeping into the carpet below Iago's chair. It dripped from his pant leg.

Cade handed the knife to Dante as he continued looking on, lost in a reverie we couldn't pull him from.

Cade said softly, "One of the guys on the police force can get us more essentials if you need them."

Iago wriggled in the dining room chair. The motion was the equivalent of a mouse in a trap. Nothing worked. The duct tape dug into his wrists; a large hole in his arm looked like it had been cauterized closed. His eyes pleaded with mine as he tried to mumble something against the tape over his mouth.

"Did they touch you?" Dante asked softly without looking at me. His voice was full of pain, like he'd wronged me somehow.

"Touch me?" I asked, my mind probably a bit too fuzzy for questions. I shook it. "It's fine. I'm fine."

"Besides the bruising on your face, Lilah, did he put a hand or weapon near you?"

Running a hand through my hair and glancing away, I lied. They'd hit me in the elevator, choked me, and beaten me too. I didn't lie, though, to spare the man's life but only to soothe my wolf's soul. "No. They were just angry about the twin swap."

He growled and stalked toward me. Then he leaned down to whisper in my ear, "Lilah, do you know that I know your body better than you know it yourself?" He touched my hair. "You lie, and still I love that I get to find the lie you're telling me, just by one movement. I've learned them all over the years. It's how I know they've hurt you, how I know I'm going to now make them wish they were dead."

His warning should have scared me. "Dante, you don't have to do anything for me."

"Lamb." It was a plea, heavy in emotion and from deep in his gut. "Don't ever do something like this again, you understand?"

My eyes filled with tears as I nodded at him. I whispered, "You don't have to do this."

"Do you want me to stop?"

I chewed on my cheek and glanced back at my sister. Her chest was still at my back, her arms still wrapped tight around me, like she wouldn't let me go, like she was protecting me.

My sister.

The one Iago had tried to hurt.

I looked past Dante at the man whose eyes begged for his life.

I'd tried so hard most of my life not to make a mess in other people's. I'd tried to be perfect. I'd tried not to share my true emotion, my true pain, everything.

"Had it only been me you touched, Iago, I would have told Dante that you could rot in jail." I tilted my chin as I said the next words. "I would have shown you mercy."

This was me embracing the mess, embracing that I was capable and entitled to causing destruction. I wanted it here and I wanted the man who could do that with me. Dante accepted me for who I was, and I accepted him too.

Dante nodded, his jaw working up and down as he got up from kneeling before Izzy and me. When his hand left my face, I immediately missed his touch on my chin. "Tell me, Lilah. What happened? And then I want you to watch what happens to them. It'll be a lesson for you to never risk the life of my love again. These are the consequences of your actions as much as theirs. And these men, for the time they are still breathing on this earth, need to know what happens when you mess with an Armanelli's Untouchable."

Iago's eyes widened. He shook his head fiercely. I squinted at what he meant, whether he was talking about Izzy or me or maybe himself.

The other guy tried to argue through the duct tape, and he kept saying in a muffled tone, "You? You're an Armanelli? Well, we didn't know she was yours. We didn't know. We didn't know." He started to cry then and looked to me for help.

"You know, it would be one thing to take a shot at the person undercover working against you. It's another to take an innocent bystander and cause her pain. Did they know you were innocent, Delilah?" Dante asked, but we'd lost him. His voice was monotone as he twirled the knife in his hand.

I bit my lip, my brows furrowing. I nodded yes.

The sound that came from him was animalistic as he stopped the knife from spinning and drove it down into the man's hand.

Flesh being stabbed sounds a lot like meat being thwacked with a mallet. It has that wet, squishy sound, like you're ridding it of blood.

Iago's scream must have been heard throughout the cruise ship. Both Izzy and I jumped, but I didn't shut my eyes. They were on him.

Glued to him.

Mesmerized by him.

Before I knew what I was doing, I'd grabbed the phone from my back pocket and found the soundtrack Dante had played for me during my massage. Dante stopped for a split second to whip his head around and stare at my phone. His brow furrowed, and a small smile teased his lips. "Lilah," he murmured, and I thought I caught what I felt for him in those green eyes of his.

Love.

Hope.

Comfort.

Then he turned and stabbed the second guy.

The music mingled with the screams and whimpers.

"Damn, this is going to be bloody," Izzy murmured.

I shrugged. "You need to report Iago's assault on you, Izzy."

I felt her body tense, and I didn't ask for more information. She'd share when she was ready.

All she said now was, "There will be nothing to report on a man who's gone, Lilah."

I chewed my cheek, not sure what to make of it all. For some reason, my body didn't reject what was happening in front of me. I knew the man I loved planned more torture. I knew as he sucked in air nice and slow like it was feeding his soul that he was going to truly enjoy what he was about to do.

I knew it all.

And it made me love him more.

He hummed as he bent down to glare at both the men at their eye level, just inches from their faces. "Did you think the Armanellis would let you get away with drug smuggling in our territory when we cleaned this up years ago?"

He ripped off the duct tape from Iago's mouth. The man

had long since stopped talking; his groaning was all that could be heard, just louder now without the barrier of the tape.

"Now," Dante snarled, and I found my body reacting in a way it shouldn't have to all this.

My mind swirled at seeing my wolf take his territory back; all of my insides tingled with a newfound kink completely unlocked.

"I should ask Lilah and Izzy what part of you they want as a gift, but I can't bring myself to let any part of you remain. So instead, Cade, call the police. I need acid for Iago."

"Wait!" he cried. "I know where the drugs are. Only half are on this boat. Please!"

Cade stopped him. "Police already found both locations. We got it all."

Dante chuckled.

It sounded so far away, though.

The tingling didn't seem very pleasurable anymore, either. It was like I was losing the feeling of myself, like my mind was running away and I couldn't catch it.

"I don't feel right," I murmured to Izzy.

I heard her mumble *shit* and something about the back of my head bleeding, but I lost that running mind.

It got away.

And everything went black.

* * *

I'd handled brain traumas in my nursing career. I knew what they were, knew they could affect speech and cause paralysis, comas, death.

I knew all that.

I just hadn't expected to experience it myself.

Snapshots of what I thought was reality pushed through my subconscious to the all-encompassing black abyss I kept falling into.

I knew the hospital was in the United States—I heard English from the doctor, and I heard my mother crying and asking if I would be okay.

I focused long enough to tell them my age, my name, and what I thought had happened. I believe I answered all the questions. I was just too tired to answer more.

Blackness found me, and I went under again.

When I came to, I heard my sister's voice. She was crying now too.

Everyone was always crying.

Had a week passed, a day, just an hour?

She wasn't alone with me though.

"She's going to be okay, Izzy," Dante said. His voice was the one I needed to hear.

My muscles relaxed, my body stopped tensing, the pain in my head seemed to vanish.

But then I heard the strain in his voice, the little quiver. "Izzy, don't cry. She'll be just fine, huh? And then we'll be back to work. You and me, right?"

That sounded odd.

Wrong.

Him and her.

"She has to be," Izzy whispered. Then I heard footsteps pacing back and forth. "Thank you for staying with me and her tonight. I don't think I could be alone."

"I wouldn't leave." Dante's voice was firm, solid, like he wanted to comfort her.

Not me.

A soft breath was taken before she whispered, "I know.

I'm ... You always take care of me, Dante. Jesus, when no one else did, you took care of me."

"And I always will, Izzy. You're my girl, you know that?"

I heard rustling, and it was enough to make my eyes open to see what I needed to see.

Izzy was in Dante's arms, her lips on the lips I thought were mine.

He didn't fight her off.

He wasn't even pushing her away. His hands were on her shoulders.

He'd said she was his girl.

And then the hospital did what hospitals do. It recorded my heart beat—how it picked up, how suddenly it started going a million times a minute—as I stared at them, eyes wide.

Immediately, Dante's hands pushed her back like he could hide what I'd just seen. He rushed toward me, but my mind ran away.

I whispered, "You let her kiss you."

And I was gone again.

CHAPTER 27: FIGHT FOR THE ONE YOU LOVE

Dante

There's a moment when a person knows they're in love because they find themselves wondering what can be done to make the other person happy, even if it causes their own pain.

They find themselves doing things that are completely against their own logic.

Iago probably could have fed us more information. He probably could have been an asset in one way or the other. The authorities didn't need unnecessary clean-up either.

Yet, I found his demise necessary. I contemplated ripping him apart limb by limb in front of her. I was blind in my love for her, too furious to see any other way.

Love for her would breed that emotion in me always. It was the only thing that could rip me from my calm. It made it clear that Lilah would have been better off without me. She needed a stable person in her life, someone to comfort her and be a steady rock when life got hard.

But I could protect her.

She was my lamb. And I was her wolf.

And no one, not a single soul, would protect her better than me. And if I was going to bring her pain or torture, feast on that prey like a predator, I would do it in the best way possible because I knew her. I breathed with her, molded to her, and was within her. We were one entity, and no one was going to tear us apart.

When she passed out on that cabin floor, I had been ready to meet her in heaven or hell had we not gotten her vitals stable. We called in medics and doctors to check her, and her brain injury was monitored as we flew her home.

I was by her side every moment I could be. I fielded questions and answered calls. I don't think any of the family thought to ask anything because it was technically part of a drug bust. Izzy explained our undercover work to her parents. She admitted it because she'd finally accomplished the job. Case closed. Her brothers weren't home yet, but I saw how her parents looked at me. Her mother's brow furrowed, and she rubbed her forehead like she wasn't sure whether to thank me or smack me.

"Mrs. Hardy—" I started.

"Oh, don't smooth the waters now, Dante. I'll probably want to thank you later. I just need a minute to take it all in." She waved off any explanation I could offer and hugged me in the hospital's waiting room.

Izzy and Delilah's father never said much, but he patted my arm as he walked by. "I would have killed you if you hadn't brought them both home. I'll let you deal with my boys now, though."

That was all he needed to say. I saw their family structure shifting, building a fort around Delilah and making sure I couldn't infiltrate unless they wanted me to.

Delilah's brothers were on their way, and I'd avoided them long enough. Dom had been blowing up my phone since Izzy's confession. Mrs. Hardy's words traveled fast. I turned the phone on silent as texts started coming through.

This wasn't going to be an uphill battle for me; it was going to be a war.

I was prepared for that with her brothers.

But I hadn't expected Izzy to throw an additional wrench in the mix.

That night, after her parents had left, after she'd told me her brothers wouldn't be here until tomorrow, her kiss came fast. Any other day, I would have caught it. Yet, my mind was more exhausted than it had ever been. Love will drag down anyone, and it spares no one's anxieties. I could live through war, live through being tortured, beaten, shot at—anything.

I couldn't live without Lilah, though.

Izzy was my partner, my friend, and someone I trusted more than most. I should have seen her feelings growing past friendship long ago, but I hadn't been focused on that. I chose to be laser-focused on our mission, not our relationship.

I started to push her away gently, ready to let her down easy. Somehow I'd need to make her see that she was wonderful, but for me, there was only Lilah.

Delilah Hardy.

The girl who'd always had my heart.

The one whose heart beat faster now as she stared at her sister in my arms.

That look she gave me was lucid, more awake than I'd seen her in days, and full of devastation.

The words she whispered cut through my soul so fast I didn't even think to call the nurses as I lost her again.

Her eyes closed as I rushed to her side to hold her hand, to put it against my face, to feel her touch on mine. The spark was there, but it was dimmer. It was missing her signature spirit.

I growled out for Izzy to call the nurses and the doctors, and then we stared at one another.

Her chin trembled as her eyes ping-ponged between us. "She doesn't think she's strong enough to be with you."

"She is," I ground out, even though I wasn't so sure I was strong enough to let her. I wanted her to have everything. The beautiful home, the beautiful life filled with crossing off a million lists, and the beautiful kids she deserved.

"I know. I didn't want to know, though. She's it for you, then?" she whispered. "You can't see yourself with me instead? Not after all we've been through?"

"Izzy." I looked down at the love of my life, then back up at her sister. They were so much of the same and yet so different. "She's the slice of good to my bad. She's the heaven to my hell. She's always been it. She always will be."

Izzy looked toward the ceiling as her unshed tears threatened to pour over. "You look at her like I wish you'd look at me."

"You and I are too much the same, Izzy. You gotta see that, right?" I sighed. "And I've helped you more than most men, but it hasn't ever been there for us. The chemistry ..."

She shrugged. "I don't need chemistry. I needed someone to believe in me, and you did more than anyone in my life. Addicts normally don't get that."

"You will."

"You're so sure of it?" She tilted her head and pulled roughly on her hair, a gesture so much like her sister's but completely different at the same time. "I'm not, but I am sure I want what you have with her. I want a man who can face anything for me, and you'll do that for her. It kills me that you can't do that for me."

She curled her arms around herself then, tears overflowing. Izzy was as much a little sister to me as a real one could be, and I pulled her in for a hug to comfort her.

Nurses and doctors filed in. Vitals were taken. We straightened up to answer the questions about witnessing Lilah wake up.

Things looked better. They knew she was on her way to getting there. The brain trauma caused these bouts, and she'd be good as new soon.

I still stayed the night.

Izzy went home, and the next morning I left to fetch breakfast.

Lilah woke up while I was gone, and her brothers came to her side.

It happened fast. Dimitri stood outside her room. He, along with his other brothers, was a spitting guy image of his sisters with dark hair and hazel eyes too. Except his held a death glare filled with rage I didn't want to meet. I lifted the breakfast bag and tried for the easy route. "Brought us all some fuel."

He reared back and swung fast but not fast enough. I dodged his first punch before he came at me again, right hook, then left. He missed both times.

The fact that I had him in a headlock while still holding our food was a pretty good indicator that he wasn't going to win this fight. He wriggled in my choke hold and mumbled, "You're a fucking asshole."

"Agreed, but let's not do this here."

"Oh, fuck off," he wheezed because he couldn't breathe. He was the youngest of the brothers. His fighting showed it.

I let him go, and he fell to his knees, gasping for air.

"I'm here just as concerned as any of you."

"As any of us? You put both our sisters in danger. And it's Delilah!" he shouted, disbelief in his voice. "She could have died."

"You think I don't know that?" I walked up to him and

kneeled down, setting the breakfast food right next to him. "You think I don't know we could have lost her?"

We stared at one another a long time after that. The look in his eyes was foreign and filled with a fury I never wanted to witness again. The Hardy family had taken me in as one of their own, but now that one of their own was hurt, I was the outsider.

I'd known it was coming, but the impact still felt like a bomb blowing up in my face, the shrapnel cutting deep into the insecurities I already had.

I was the only child of an Armanelli, and I was trying to prove to a nice, upstanding family that I was good enough for their daughter. My best friend's little sister.

I heard Dom's voice in her room, heard her whispering back to him. I stared past Dimitri as he said, "She doesn't want to see you."

"What?" I growled, my whole body rebelling at the news.

"She actually winced when Dom brought you up. She said if you come here, she doesn't want to see you. And she wants to rest. She doesn't want anyone here."

"She's not thinking straight," I told him, although I knew that wasn't true. The woman was shutting everyone out fast and quick, ready to barricade the room so she could hurt on her own. She'd done it before, but I wouldn't let her do it again. "Give me her physical update."

"What for?" he sneered and sat back on the floor as he rubbed his neck. "You're not going to come around, Dante. Go back to your job and leave our sisters out of it."

"Look, I know you're coming to terms with what happened but—"

Dom walked out of the room and stood over both of us. He narrowed his eyes at me and said, "I've come to terms with it in the last five minutes listening to my little sister recount the bullshit you put her through. You need to leave."

"Dom—"

"Did you come to apologize to her or to us? Because we can tell her sorry for you, but you know we're not going to accept shit from you right now. My kid sister's in a hospital bed for God's sake. And you and Izzy knew what the hell you were doing. You should have got her out of there that day."

"It was complicated," I said calmly and folded my arms across my chest as I stood to meet him eye to eye. Dom was as big as me and he glared at me with a rage that might have matched my training. He'd put up a good fight. "It's not always black-and-white."

He stared at me, assessing everything I was saying. "What wasn't black-and-white about getting her out of danger?"

I think he knew right then that there was something more between us. I don't think Delilah had admitted it outright, but Dom knew because we'd been best friends for a long time. We knew one another well enough to recognize when one of us was chasing a girl. His gaze flicked to the breakfast bag and then back to me as I stood there quietly, not answering his question.

"You want to give me a few days before you admit the real shit? Or give her a few days? Because she really doesn't want to see you ... or anyone for that matter."

Dimitri shook his head at the ground, looking like he might cry, and Dom shook with fury. I stood there, making it worse rather than better.

I had to change the wolf in me that wanted to see her. I had to do what was right rather than indulge in a side of me they didn't know.

"I'm giving you all until she's home. You get me?"

Dom nodded, Dimitri sighed.

I backed away, pointing to the food. "Give her the quesito

in there."

And then I was gone.

For days, I didn't see her, even though I knew she was awake. For days, I sent texts and made calls that went unanswered.

I told myself it was all just a lot, that we'd make things right when she got back home. I worked. Or pretended to. Paperwork had never been my thing. I did what I had to do and left the paperwork for the government and official personnel to figure out.

Izzy was the first who called the day Delilah got released. "You don't have to call, Izzy."

"I told her our kiss was nothing, that she saw it wrong. She thought you engaged with me when obviously you pushed me away. I told her how you feel. She's just not really responding. And I know I don't have to call you. Quite frankly, giving the guy I thought I might love updates on the girl he loves isn't my idea of fun, but it's for her. She's got to get through this. She's not trying right now. She's talking herself into something terrible, Dante. I can feel her retreating, can feel my sister not moving forward but backward, and it's freaking painful. I can't stop it, so I'm calling you to tell you that you need to."

"I should give her space."

"Get your ass here. My family babies the shit out of her, and when she said she didn't want to talk to anyone, they listened and practically barricaded the door for her. My mom is scared she's back to college days, and honestly, she might be right. It's that bad."

It'd been three days. The minutes felt like hours. And then the hours felt like days.

"Has she gotten my flowers?"

"She doesn't read the notes. She barely looks at the flowers."

I took a deep breath. "Get ready for me to rip apart your

family."

"You'll make it stronger, but it might hurt a little first."

"No shit," I muttered, but I was already heading toward my car as I hung up the phone.

* * *

"Dude, you sent a shit ton of flowers already. She doesn't need fucking bouquets from you." My best friend stood in the doorway, not asking me to come in or opening the door any farther.

"I'm coming in one way or another, Dom." I ticked my head toward the door.

"You got a lot of nerve showing up here after we've asked you to stay away. She's healing, and shit, I'm healing from your fuckup too. You put my kid sisters in danger, man."

"I'll apologize. We'll get over it. I know it's a lot, Dom."

His jaw worked, and his fist closed and opened. I waited for a swing or a lunge, but he sighed and opened the door instead. "Mom, Dad. Dante's here. Should we grill his ass some more?"

My friend crossed his arms and glared at me. Izzy and I had hidden a secret for a long time. We'd broken a lot of people's trust.

Their dad ambled in, a big round teddy bear with his button-up flannels and worn jeans. He'd worked for a beer company most of his life and retired when the kids had all graduated. "Dante, she's not going to want to see you. She doesn't want to see anyone. She wants to sleep." He rubbed his large belly, a normal gesture, though it was usually one he did with a smile.

Her mom, with her wavy dark hair, came in and wrung her hands in front of her maxi dress, just the way Lilah did. "I think she's tired. Or I don't know. We need her to stop all this nonsense of traveling the world after this. Can you believe she was even nursing away from home?"

"Oh, she was just bored, honey," Mr. Hardy replied.

"She shouldn't be bored. She should be going back to medical school, for God's sake. And if she had, she wouldn't ever have had this happen."

"Not true, Mom." Izzy walked in and bit into an apple as she plopped down on their leather sofa by the TV. She clicked the remote and shrugged at me while she lifted a brow. "Dante and I sort of threw her into the mix."

"That one's on you, Izzy," I grumbled, not really wanting to take all the responsibility.

"How chivalrous of you," she shot back.

Dom didn't find any of our jokes funny, though. He stared at us both like we were enemies, menaces, monsters. "Want to explain exactly what the hell you're both doing for the government, anyway?"

"Confidential," we both said in unison.

Or so we wanted it to be, until another knock landed on the door. Dom had left it open, so I could already see the visitor. When I turned, my eyes bugged out, and I almost shut the door in his face.

"Surprise." Cade quirked his head and shot a fucking shark smile at me. It was calculating and intended to cause havoc. "News from the underground. Seems like our job isn't quite done. Iago's boss is Albanian, and he just went missing. So he's probably plotting against us, and that means we need to plot faster than him."

"What the fuck are you doing here?" I growled.

Izzy jumped up and told her parents that maybe they could go get us some lemonade while Dom stepped up to my side and said, “Who the fuck are you?”

“I’m Cade Armanelli, brother to Bastian Armanelli and cousin to Dante Armanelli, the man standing next to you.”

“What in the actual fuck, Cade?” I murmured.

Dom’s stare widened, his muscles bunched, and his head cranked slowly my way. “What did he just say?”

“Dom ...” I started, “take a breath.”

“You better not feed me that bullshit, Dante. What did he just say?”

I pinched the bridge of my nose. It was all going to come out anyway. “You heard what he said.”

Izzy and her mother were walking back in with a tray of drinks, and their father was just taking a seat in his recliner when Dom cranked his arm back and punched me square in the face.

I probably could have ducked, but I figured I deserved one, maybe two good ones.

“Dom!” Izzy dropped the tray. Her mom screamed, Mr. Hardy started to chuckle, and Cade laughed his ass off.

I rubbed my jaw and bent over. “Damn. Your right hook still don’t play. Dimitri didn’t even connect.”

“Dimitri swung at you?” Izzy asked, disbelief in her tone.

“I’m calling Dex and Declan. They’re going to hit your ass too,” Dom grumbled, turning to look for his phone.

I rubbed my jaw. “I’ll give you that one, Dom. No one else gets any more.”

“*You’ll give me that one*? You fucking lied to me about your name! You brought my sister into the mob with you!”

“Now, Dominic, lower your voice. They have their reasons for hiding their name.” Mrs. Hardy set her tray of drinks down on the dining room table to the right of the living room and bent to help Izzy clean up the glass she’d broken.

"Mom, you knew?" Izzy whispered.

"Of course I knew. Dante's mother and I are best friends."

"Oh my God." Izzy scoffed. "You *would* know and not tell us."

"You didn't tell me about being sober and working undercover as an addict, Izzy," her mom threw back, her brow furrowed like she was hurt by it all.

Jesus, this was a clusterfuck.

Mr. Hardy leaned over to grab the remote like nothing going on was a surprise. "Darcy, Izzy can make her own choices. She's a grown woman."

"Don't involve yourself in our mother-daughter relationship," Mrs. Hardy threw back, but she had a small smile on her face. She looked back at her daughter. "I'm just glad you're okay."

Izzy nodded but didn't really meet anyone's eye.

Cade's laughter trailed off as he took in the situation. "We should go, Dante."

That's when Izzy's head shot up. "Dante? I'm part of this too."

"No. You're done with this." Suddenly Cade's voice was firm as he and Izzy stared at each other.

"Izzy, you're not going anywhere with them," snarled Dom. "And they're leaving our house. We don't need the damn mob here."

Cade cracked his neck once as he stared at my best friend. "I'm not the mob, Dominic Joseph Hardy. I'm a *businessman*. Dante"—he glared at Izzy—"and only Dante, get back to Chicago soon."

With that, Cade walked out, and Izzy scoffed before stomping off.

"You can go right now," Dom spat.

"Knock it off, Dom," Mrs. Hardy chastised. "You two can't bicker when your sister is sick in there. I'm worried something is wrong."

"Nothing's wrong other than that she's mad at me." As I said it, her door opened.

The commotion must have brought her out to us.

And it died with her standing there. We all stared at Delilah Hardy. She looked like she'd lost weight in the baggy sweatshirt that basically swallowed her up. The bright colors she'd worn in Puerto Rico were gone, replaced by plain white, and her socks were long and black, coming up her calves.

She looked gorgeous. But closed off.

Her hazel eyes didn't hold much emotion at all, like she was tired of everything.

"That's not what shut her down," Dom sneered because he didn't get it. He didn't get that Delilah and I were more than friends. "She's traumatized from being held at gunpoint. You were the reason she was in danger, whether you wanted to be or not. You endangered my baby sisters and—"

"I'm not mad about that, Dom," Delilah said loud and clear. The entire room looked her way because, according to Izzy, she hadn't said a word for days. "Dante's right. I'm mad at him."

"Of course you are," Dom croaked. His eyes ping-ponged between us. "You should be mad at him for what he put you through."

She cleared her throat, but I stopped her. "She's mad because she thinks I kissed Izzy. That wasn't what that was, Lilah. You know I wouldn't let another woman's mouth on my lips willingly. Not when you're the girl I love."

Mr. Hardy muted the television for this one.

Not that he had to. The sound faded away as I looked

into my girl's eyes—hazel sparkling under wet tears. Her chin trembled, and her hands shook. "If you love me, then you'll know what I'm about to say is the truth." She took a deep breath. "I think you should try to date Izzy."

Izzy guffawed and tried to cut her off.

Lilah held up her hand and kept going. "Or someone else. Anyone but me. I can't be with you."

"Damn right," Dom bellowed and then he shoved me. I glared at him but stepped back.

Lilah's mom tried to jump in. "Oh goodness, Dom. Don't fight! And, Delilah. You need rest, and then we can look at colleges. This is for the best—"

"Enough." My voice cut through all the bullshit because that's what this was. "Enough."

Even Dom jumped when I said it that time.

"I'm only going to say this once because it's not in my nature to repeat myself. I'm an Armanelli. I've named your daughter my Untouchable. What that means is no one will harm her or disrespect her unless they want to deal with the wrath of my whole family. It means I take care of her now. It means you all respect our wishes. Respectfully, Mrs. Hardy, she's not going back to school unless she decides that's what she wants."

Her mother didn't even argue. She was smiling at me like I was going to make her dreams come true. Mrs. Hardy wasn't a dumb woman. She knew I would give her the grandbabies she'd always wanted. I only had to convince her daughter that it would be happening.

Dom's face had turned red, and his fists were getting ready to swing again. "You can't come in here and demand—"

"I love you, man. I love you like you're my only brother, but I've already put a man in a bucket of acid for harming your sister."

His eyes widened and his jaw dropped.

"It'll take some getting used to. You can start digesting the information now." I shrugged and continued, "But if you think because she's your baby sister I'm going to let you keep her from me, you got another thing coming."

"You *were* my best friend."

"I still *am* your best friend. You're just going to have to get used to me being your brother-in-law too."

"None of this is happening!" Delilah screeched. Her hands flew out beside her, and she stomped up to me to point in my face. "You don't get to make these decisions, and I don't want to be with you. I can't fathom being with you! I want you out of this house this instant. You need to leave."

"Little Lamb," I murmured as I set down the flowers on the table near the couch and took my time looking around the family room. "You're right. I do need to leave."

With that, I picked her up and threw her over my shoulder. Dom stepped forward as Delilah yelled.

"You come near me, I promise you'll regret it. And you know I'm good on my word." We stared each other down. "You need to trust me. I'm your best friend."

He pulled at his hair and sighed. "Nothing is fixed. And I won't forgive your ass for a long time."

"You've got to be kidding me!" Delilah said over my shoulder. "You're letting him kidnap me."

Mr. Hardy turned the TV back on. "Hardly kidnapping when you know you want to go."

With that, I took her to my car.

CHAPTER 28: GET A RIDING LESSON

Delilah

"I want to go home." I had more fire in my blood and emotion pulsing through me than I'd had in days. I'd felt myself slipping, felt the guilt and the pain and the anxiety enveloping me even before the cruise ship.

It was like I could watch the weight of all my stupid problems pour in on me but couldn't stop it, couldn't patch the holes. They filled my boat and pulled me down, ready to sink me.

I tried avoiding them, tried patching them, and tried filling them with happiness. But the worry overpowered all my efforts, spurting through and shooting my happiness straight out of the boat.

I was sinking now, drowning in fear at being with someone who could hurt me as much as seeing him kiss Izzy had. Then there was guilt at feeling that fear, at feeling the depression when I really didn't have such a bad life.

That one practically suffocated me, the guilt so intense I could barely breathe even when I had oxygen everywhere around me. Just like I had everything I wanted around me too. A good family. Friends. A man who really loved me. A twin sister willing to fight for us even though she was in love with him too.

She'd apologized for kissing him and cried. I'd held her hand while she did because that's what sisters do.

I knew her pain. Losing Dante wasn't for the faint of heart.

Even with the knowledge that they were never going to be together, that she couldn't love a man who didn't love her like she thought he loved me, I wasn't sure I would be able to commit to him.

The pain that shot through me at seeing another woman's lips on his was enough to let me know I couldn't handle it if I really did lose him. I wouldn't be able to move on. I'd be lost at sea, no one there to save me, because I didn't know how to save myself from that heartbreak.

Except my wolf was going to cross a fucking ocean of my worries and depression before he'd let me go that easy.

"Your home is right here with me," he grumbled as he started driving out to his family's farm.

When I was younger, and even in college, I hadn't questioned why his mother had all that land. "Did your dad buy your mom this farm?"

"Sure." He shrugged as he stared out at it. "Or maybe he stole it from someone or made them sign it over. Never really looked into it."

"Have you ever looked into him or wanted to get to know more about him?"

"Not anymore. I got his name, and that's about all I need from him. The rest is dead and gone. No point in dwelling on what can't be."

I nodded. His words held more meaning than he probably realized. "You've come to terms with that. Can you come to terms with what can't be between us?"

"Lilah." His voice was a hoarse whisper. "I almost lost you.

I held your hand, and the fire between us was so damn small—you know what that feels like? To have someone you love almost dead in your grasp, no way to bring them back?"

I pictured him on a battlefield because his eyes were far away as he said the words. I knew there were things he'd never tell me, war stories, mob stories, heart-wrenching ones. "I'm sorry I put you through that, especially since you've had to go through it before."

He slammed his hand on the wheel. "Shit, I put you through it *and* myself. Your brother is right. I should never have dragged either of you into this."

I shrugged and stared out at the sunset over the hills. "You wouldn't have been able to make me leave."

"Beautiful, smart, and stubborn," he grumbled as we turned toward the big red barn. "You remind me of one of my mom's horses, even though you'll always be my little lamb."

We pulled into his driveway and followed it around to the back of the house, out about another acre. The land was lush with green grass and rolling hills. A couple of horses gathered near a hay bale, and the gravel crunched under the tires, making a few cows *moo*.

He turned toward the big red barn we used to go to when an animal was in distress.

"Is she sick? The horse?" I asked.

"Sort of."

Dante turned off the ignition, and we sat there for a minute before leaving the car. He breathed in deep, and his hand was on his abs for about two seconds before he dragged his gaze up to mine. Pain and hunger and determination swam in his eyes. "I'm going to show you Autumn in that stable, and we're going to work out what is between us in there too."

"I don't think we can have anything between us. Not after

what we've been through. Not after seeing you let another woman kiss you, and not after how my heart felt about it." It was anger and pain and regret all mixed in my tone.

"Lamb, don't even try to do that today. I'm not in the mood." He opened his door and slammed it. I watched him stare up at the sky, pull on his neck, and swear once or twice before he rounded the hood of the car and came to open my door.

"Do you need me to carry you?" His green eyes trailed up and down my body and then stalled at my head, like he was trying to figure out if the brain trauma had healed.

"Carry me? What for?" I tried to push past him and get out of the car myself, but his hands were at my waist immediately, then around my back to aid me in walking like I was a porcelain doll. "Dante, I've been resting for a week. It was a minor brain trauma."

"It wasn't minor. You were in a coma."

"From the pressure against my skull, and it's completely subsided. It's not ... I'm fine." I chuckled at how ridiculous he was being.

He took a step and pivoted in front of me, never letting go of my body. My chest was to his, my stomach against his abs, and other things touching other things. Of course my body reacted immediately, but what I didn't expect was for the look of anguish in his eyes to affect me most.

His hand trailed up my back to my neck where he wove his fingers through my hair. His forehead fell to mine.

"One." He breathed in, and my body immediately relaxed into him. "Two." He sighed, and I closed my eyes.

He counted the rest of the way to seven. And then his eyes opened with a sparkle of unshed tears beneath a furrowed brow as his thumb rubbed a sensitive spot just below my jaw. "I almost lost you. And it's my fault for letting you run around on that island in the first place. It was reckless, and I'll have to live with that the rest of my life."

Even though my body longed to stay in his arms, I pulled back from him, stepped out of his reach, and shook my head. "Not true. I made the decision to stay there myself."

His lips thinned into a disapproving line before he slid his hands into the pockets of his slacks and began walking on the dirt path toward the barn. It was a sight to see, a man so beautiful in business attire, dirtying his loafers to walk to a stable. "You can say that, Lilah, but I should have forced you to come home rather than letting you run wild over there."

"Wild?" I trotted up to him to poke him in the arm. "I had a job. I was a responsible adult. And you know I didn't go there to get wild."

He hummed. "Can you admit why you went?" Dante peered over at me before he opened the barn door. It was one of two large wooden doors, the handles black metal with a large drop bar latch across them. He paused, like he was waiting for me to admit and accept everything in my life.

Maybe I needed to. Maybe we both needed to hear I was healing.

But I wasn't healed yet. "I went there to be free of myself."

"Free of yourself?" he whispered like he couldn't believe I'd said it.

"Yes, from this stupid idea that I'm perfect here, when really I'd lost a baby, when really I'm struggling with depression, with expectations, with who I am."

"You'll never be free of those things, Lamb," he murmured.

"Yes, I can be. I was getting there."

His hand flexed on the handle of the door. "No, you were forgetting and suppressing, but that doesn't work. You can't be free of it because it lives with you ... forever."

"That isn't freedom. This isn't a life if I have to live with that, Dante." Why did I feel like I was pleading with him, with the world, in that moment?

"That's all life is, Lilah. You know that. It's work and pain and suffering for the beauty of living. You think I tortured all those men and killed some in hopes I would forget? No, I took the ugly, and it chained me down, but the beauty of you and this world set me free. It's not a complete freedom. It's fractured and broken and wrecked."

He opened the door to the barn stalls. I'd been there before, years ago, but they'd since redone everything with sleek treated oak. They had ten individual horse stalls, five on each side of the barn. In the middle was a lunging ring, an open area where they ran horses round and round. There was a high-end fan above us that cooled everything down without displacing even a straw of hay.

I didn't respond to his viewpoint on life because my jaw had dropped at all the renovations. I walked over to one of the stalls. The beautiful wood was stained and treated so it was smooth to the touch. I ran my hand over it and gripped the gate where the wood ended and the iron began. It took me getting on my tiptoes to peer between the iron bars and to see into the horse stall.

"When did this happen?" I asked.

"We redid some things a few years ago so that animals in distress could feel more comfortable. My mom and the workers will bring them in here if they're pregnant, suffering from some ailment, or if it gets too hot out."

I was already searching to see if there were any in here now, ready to comfort them. "I used to love coming over to see the animals with Dom."

Dante smirked at me. “Woman, you didn’t only come with Dom. You were here every couple days, tending to a horse or a cow or a lamb.”

“Well, they needed someone,” I murmured, and then I saw a reddish horse in the corner stall. She shook her head and huffed a little as I walked toward her. “She’s hurt?”

“Physically?” He crossed his arms where he stood. “No. Emotionally, I think she might be dying of a broken heart. She lost her foal a week ago.”

I held out my hand for her to smell before running it along her neck. Staring into her kind eyes, rimmed with giant lashes, I smoothed the hair on the large bulge of her jaw. “Just a week ago?”

He nodded. “My mom’s kept me updated. Emmy hasn’t eaten since, and we had the vet come in to see if we should move her, but they think she should heal here for a month or so.”

“How did it happen?”

“It was stillborn. She was laboring, and they were sure it was alive, but the delivery didn’t go as planned, according to my mother.”

“Does Emmy pasture with the other horses?”

“She used to when I visited.”

I hummed. It felt safe here. Perfect temperature, perfect lighting, food right in front of her. Haystacks upon haystacks, and expectations upon expectations. Everyone expected her to heal perfectly here since the conditions were ideal. I faced Dante with determination. “She needs to go outside.”

He searched my eyes for answers. I knew he’d brought me here to see what this horse needed to heal and probably what I needed to heal too.

“You’re sure?” he asked. “Because it’s probably going to be painful out there for her.”

"She needs to feel free, even if she's not, and she needs to do it on her own, even if it's painful. She couldn't have the baby on her own. So"—I went to the lock on her stall and wiggled it as I said the words I knew weren't about the horse anymore—"let her do this on her own."

He nodded and went to get the keys for the lock at the opposite side of the barn.

I whispered to her as I pet her soft mane. "It gets better. And worse. And I think you can live with it like maybe I'm living with it. What doesn't kill us makes us stronger, except we'll have more scars, right? And that's not such a bad thing."

Dante came up behind me and let me do the honors of unlocking the stall door. Then he placed a halter on her.

Together, we led her to the back of the barn where large sliding doors opened into a fenced-in pasture. As he removed the halter once more, I swear she stood taller, held her head higher, and her trot had more bounce.

I smiled when she didn't even hesitate to take off galloping into the open field, the wind flying through her mane as she shook it.

With her went some of my pain, some of the failure, and some of the guilt. Other mommas went through what I had and made it out the other side, maybe broken, but probably wise enough to know themselves better. Our freedom may have been fractured, tainted by our pain and our growth, but we still had it. I could have it too. "We've all got to be okay in some way, right?"

"Of course," his low voice rumbled from behind me. "Let's give her all the time she wants."

I followed him inside, and we let the breeze blow through the doors as we went back to her stall.

Dante straightened it up without saying much. He hung

her halter on a large hook right outside the stall, then turned to stare at me in the middle of it. "You looked at that horse like you believed she could overcome it."

I nodded, frozen in place by his penetrating stare.

"You think you can't, though?"

"I thought that at first."

"And now?" He didn't move toward me, but I saw him ready to close in. He didn't have to circle me or take a step in my direction for me to know that he was about to pounce, that he was about to be the wolf to my lamb and that I would crumble beneath him.

"Now I know I did overcome it." I shrugged. "I'm just not sure I want to risk going through it again."

He growled and cracked his knuckles. "You're not sure you want to risk it *with me*?"

I glanced at the halter. What a representation of both freedom and prison. "I can't imagine losing you and living through it. I felt the pain of seeing you with Izzy—"

"That wasn't anything and you know it."

"You let her kiss you." I was still furious that he'd allowed anyone near his lips. "And I know you didn't want it, but the fury that licked through me probably made me pass out. To think what would happen to me if you actually wanted someone else—"

"Never going to happen, Lamb." He paced toward me on a mission.

"It could, considering I've decided to move on."

"You do have to move on," he concluded. But him agreeing with me almost brought me to my knees.

I gasped as he said it, sure I'd heard him wrong. "Right." I pushed my wavy hair back and tried not to give in to my heart breaking in front of him. This would have to happen anyway.

It was good he was on board. Even if it hurt like hell. "Well, I think the best way to do it is to remain friends for the family and try to forget all that's happened between us. I'm happy we had what we did—"

"You'll be even happier when you figure out that we're going to have more than we ever did before." He took a step forward, and I narrowed my eyes. "Together. Not apart, Lamb." He narrowed his eyes back at me. "Why can't you see we're better together?"

"You kissed my sister, Dante," I tried to explain, "and I almost died. That's an indicator we won't work. Also, my brothers—"

"You think I'm afraid of your brothers?"

"Dom is going to be livid."

"He's already livid. He'll just have to punch me a few more times."

"I have a disorder. I can't be happy half the time."

"Sure, but everyone has a disorder if you dig hard enough, and I'm willing to find your way back to happiness every time."

"I can't have kids with you!" I screamed at him, tears in my eyes.

"Little Lamb." He was in front of my face now, holding my cheeks like he could hold me together. I leaned into his touch because I think my body believed he could. "Do you know my mom's moving?"

"She's ..." His hands were in my hair, feeling my skull. "Are you checking my head?"

"Just have to be sure. Does anywhere hurt when I press?"

"No. Are you serious?" I stuttered. "I'm a nurse. I know when it's fine."

He pressed on my temples and then my skull and neck. "Pressure points matter, Lilah. It's an acupuncture technique.

This is good," he murmured and kissed my temple. "Real good."

"Your mom's selling her farm?" Why did that make the tears spill over immediately. "Who will take care of the animals? And Emmy? And my lamb is—"

"You'll take care of them," he said like it was just another sentence to throw out, not monumental at all.

"Me?" I whispered, but it sounded strangled, completely confused as I pointed to myself. "I'm not ... I don't have the means to—"

He shoved a note in my hand. It was wrinkled and worn like he'd been carrying it for days. I unfolded it slowly, my hands shaking, my heart beating fast.

Seven to Lilah's Heaven

~~Lilah's Eat Pray Love List~~

1. Leave home (*done*)

2. Do something crazy (*you went to jail, Lamb*)

3. Explore food here and EAT (*you like gelato,* quesitos, *mofongo, and mojitos ... too much*)

4. Explore places here and PRAY (*you read at the beach, saw the fort, the streets, the stores, any other places?*) - the bioluminescent water, a statue

5. Explore men and LOVE

**explored voyeurism*

**explored water play*

**What else, Lamb? (wax play)*

6. Find peace (*I can search with you forever*)

7. Find heaven (*with me*)

**buy the farm*

**accept a proposal*

**marry the wolf*

"I bought the farm at double her asking price. For us."

"You what?" I screeched.

Dante whispered, "I'm going to marry you, Little Lamb, and we're going to have babies here. Right where you think expectations are too burdensome and people are always thinking you're the absolute best. And instead, you're going to get dirty on this farm with me and prove them all wrong."

"Are you insane?"

He went down on one knee, and he smiled bigger than I'd ever seen him smile. "I asked your dad for your hand earlier this week. I don't think he gives a shit that your brothers are going to beat the piss out of me. I don't either. I'll let them have a couple good punches, then I'll make sure we're all on the same page."

"What page?"

He pulled a ring out of his slacks' pocket. No box around it. Just a big, beautiful teardrop diamond set on a band with three diamonds on either side. He held it out in front of me. "I was going to try to get every color in your eyes on the gemstones, but it would have been impossible. So instead, seven diamonds to get us to heaven, Lamb. You know I'm not letting you go. I'll spend the rest of my life trying to make you happy, and I'll rip apart anyone who makes you sad. Literally. I got a taste of losing you, and I know I should let you go so you can have a normal life, but I want to try for a future with you. It's what we both deserve."

"Dante, no one expects you or me to—"

"We're crushing people's expectations, Lilah. It's not about them. It's about you and me. What's going to make you happy?"

"I ..." There was a large part of me that was scared to say yes. Scared of what could happen. Scared I couldn't see the future, couldn't predict the pain or the failures. But none of that mattered as much. "I just want you."

"You got me, baby. For the rest of your life. Say yes. Marry me."

"We're going to have to be engaged a long time. Until we figure out the new family dynamic, Dante."

He nodded like he was willing to say yes to anything in that moment.

I took a breath.

"Don't make me count to seven with you right now."

"Yes," I blurted, smiling as tears streamed down my face.

"Thank fuck," he grumbled and slowly slid the ring onto my finger. We both admired how it fit snugly, perfectly, like he'd measured it exactly right.

His attention to details in regards to me always had been perfect.

He stood and, instead of kissing me, backed up to the stall door and shut it. It latched in place with a loud click.

The breeze blew from the fan above us, but my heartbeat escalated, my palms started to sweat, my breath hitched as my vision tunneled straight to Dante, staring at his eyes that hungrily roamed over my body.

He growled, and this time he really did circle me, once, twice, and then he kneeled before me.

"What are you doing?" I asked. He'd already proposed.

And now his slacks were in the dirt for a second time.

His piercing green gaze held mine as he grumbled out low and rough, grinding into all the right places of my mind, "I'm about to grovel, Lamb. I need you to forgive me."

I was about to ask for what, but my question was lost when he removed both my shorts and panties in one swift movement, then closed his mouth around my clit so fast that I didn't have time.

I fell forward, catching myself on his shoulders as I dug my nails in and gasped. I'd missed his touch on me, and my body practically bucked on his face right away, so wound up and ready for him that I knew the tears in my eyes would overflow.

Part of the emotion was from getting what I wanted. Dante was it. And I was jumping into what could be heaven or hell on earth, but I wanted to believe in love. It might not have added up most of the time, and it might not have been an easy study, but it was full of hope, and I could rely on that.

His hands were on my ass, kneading and caressing it to the same rhythm as his tongue. I clawed at his hair, trying to get closer to him, trying to have him consume me. I had this man's ring on my finger, and my body wanted the same symbolism acted out between us.

"Dante, oh my God, you're forgiven. Can we please go somewhere so I can have you? I need you in me. I need you. I need you. I need you." I whimpered it as if it would come true if I said it over and over.

He slid his thumb inside me and then pulled an ass cheek taut enough that his middle finger could graze my asshole. "Baby, I have to get you good and ready for me first."

"No, I'm ready," I cried. "I'm so ready."

He chuckled and grabbed my thigh to put it over his shoulder. He looked up at me then and commanded, "Show me how ready. Hop up, baby. Ride my face like the good girl you are."

"You're so crude sometimes," I said. Yet, I was already crawling up him and rearranging myself so both my legs were on his shoulders, and he turned me around so that my back was against the stall's gate.

"Ride, baby," he said, and I rolled my hips into his face as his tongue went to my pussy. With his finger probing my asshole and his thumb pumping me between my folds, I knew I wasn't going to last. I'd been without him for days, and I got off from just his touch alone.

Being back where we'd started and making it our own was enough to push me over the edge. Still, he played with my pussy like he wanted to drag things out. His tongue darted in and out, lapping at my wetness but not taking it to the next level. He sucked my clit and swirled it in his mouth, treating me like a languid hobby.

"Please, Dante. Faster. Please," I begged.

"Dante!"

I froze on his shoulders when I heard his mother's voice outside the barn doors. "Someone's here? Are you crazy?" I tried to wiggle off him, but his hands dug into my ass and held me there. "Don't you dare—" I warned.

Mrs. Reid called out, "Do you have Lilah with you?"

"Get rid of her and keep riding my face like a good girl, Lamb." His tongue doubled the pace. His hands were everywhere. It was everything my body wanted, and I felt myself approaching the freaking orgasm of a lifetime, the one that wasn't just fireworks but a nuclear explosion of epic proportions.

"I'm with him, Mrs. Reid. We're um—" I gasped when his finger dipped into my ass and curled. "He's giving me a riding lesson. We need a minute."

"Oh, totally understandable." She peeked her head in and I waved over the gate like a crazy person, trying to make sure she didn't come any closer. "Oh, goodness. Is he proposing right now? I'm ruining it."

I nodded frantically and then for a second thought that was rude, so I tried to shake my head *no*, but when he sucked hard on my clit, I waved her away. "Just give us a minute, please."

She shrugged. "Sounds good." I heard her footsteps retreating as she called out, "Dante, remember to tell her to keep her legs tight when she's riding. We don't want her falling off."

I felt the man smile against my pussy.

"You're an asshole. I deserve the best orgasm of my life now," I whisper-yelled at him.

"You'll get seven to heaven, baby, I promise. When has your wolf ever let you down?"

"Never," I screamed as the first one hit.

EPILOGUE: TWO YEARS LATER

Delilah

The crackling of the bonfire outside my window almost had me smiling. I breathed in summer, letting the smell of fresh-cut grass, charcoal grills, and the lilacs that lined my front porch fill my lungs. Dante had planted them last year after I sighed on a walkway lined with them, delighting in the smell.

He'd said he owed me flowers for the rest of my life after letting another woman touch his lips.

He was right.

Embracing that possessive jealousy inside me had balanced a large part of my mind, centered me, and made me understand that no emotion was truly bad. I needed the raw ones full of anger and sadness and jealousy so I could appreciate pure joy and happiness and calm when they were present.

"You going to go over there and help our mothers do whatever you all do in the kitchen while your brothers argue with me over the grill and the food?"

I rolled my eyes. "We literally make every dish except the shrimp and fish you're grilling, and we have to season that too. You all just stand around drinking out there," I said, not moving from the bed yet.

I felt the mattress dip behind me and knew he was sitting

close, trying to take in my energy.

"Let's go give your family hell, and then I'm taking you to see that blue water."

"The blue ... what?"

"You were reading about it in Puerto Rico. We never went. It was on your list. So I'm taking you there after this."

I turned over in his arms. "You planned all that for me?"

"I'd do just about anything to see you smile again, pretty girl," he murmured and laid down next to me, wrapping one of his tattooed arms around my waist and pulling me close.

I cried in his arms before he finally got me out of bed. He carried me to our big bathtub and ran the water, pouring some oil in and then bubbles that smelled like lilacs. I stood watching him, observing how meticulously he checked the temperature and then turned to me with quiet determination and undid the buttons of my sleep shirt.

"I can do this myself, Dante," I sighed, not really sure I could.

"Let me take care of you," he whispered as he pushed my mess of wavy hair from my face and continued to whisper sweet nothings in my ear, his strong arms holding me up.

I'd been resting for days, basically living in a pampered oasis. After Dante proposed, I'd quit my job, unwilling to do long distance with him. It took me about a day to realize that. And it had been a hell of a day. He'd fucked me in the stables before marching back to tell my brothers he was marrying me.

Dom had probably only half-forgiven him at this point.

Still, he'd faced my brother and my family, so I could face my demons too. I told everyone my struggle. Izzy hugged me while my mom cried and dad patted my shoulder.

We'd all sat around a bonfire that night, hashing out everything. With their support, therapy, and the man I loved, I was able to face a lot more. I embraced the idea of going back to college after months of therapy—both with and without Dante. I'd been diagnosed with high-functioning depression and a lot of anxiety, most likely brought on by my need to overachieve. I was highly critical of myself and overthought a lot.

We worked on it daily. I hadn't made my decision to go back to medical school lightly. I wanted to become a doctor, but I worked very hard to balance the demands of school with maintaining a healthy mental state. I'd been well into medical school, that beautiful ring on my finger after getting married on the farm, and I was pregnant. I wanted that baby more than anything, and the devastation of losing another baby hit me like a bull running at a target full speed.

Dante had tried to soften the blow. Every day he did. He let me go out to the animals on the farm where I cried in the stables with the young ones. I swear the mothers in that stable knew my pain. Our big red horse stayed by me always. Sometimes, I climbed up on her back and just laid on her mane, and she let me. We mourned our losses together.

Dante did too. Even now, he handled me like I was fragile, like I was about to break. Even though I'd seen firsthand how he'd ripped apart a man for me, his touch was the softest, most delicate thing I'd ever experienced. Dante knew people, though. He studied their weaknesses and their strengths. He could break you or put you back together better than you could yourself. Maybe he knew I was about to self-destruct, that the ticking time bomb of being perfect had already exploded, and now he didn't want the nuclear bomb in me to go off too.

He was doing everything perfectly, exactly by the book, and still, I couldn't climb from the darkness to tell him. The way he touched me, the way he softly kissed my neck, it all felt like sympathy. Like sadness.

I stepped into the tub, sat down, and let him wash my body. The silence between us was so loud with pain that I couldn't handle the heartbreak. When he shampooed my hair, he massaged my scalp and stared at me staring at him. Our gazes were locked on one another, and I searched his eyes for anything other than agony.

The man who normally looked at me with unrestrained heat and desire was leashing it, and suddenly I wanted to see it. He held the pain of losing our baby too, and yet he tamped it all down.

For me.

Dante did it all for me.

And I wanted to do the same for him.

I grabbed his wrist and slid his hand from my hair to my neck and then down to my breast.

He jerked it away. "I'm taking care of you, Lilah."

I stared at his hand where he'd fisted it and saw the veins pop in his forearm.

"I want you to take care of me in a different way now."

"I don't think we're ready for that. You've been through a lot," he said. I knew he meant it, but his eyes raking over my body told me differently.

"Get in the tub with me." I stared at him as he stood up from kneeling, a frown on his face.

"We have to get over to your parents'."

"They can wait. I want you, Dante." I pronounced each word slowly so he could take them all in. "Remember how you always tell me to use my words? I'm using them. I want my husband between my legs."

When he didn't answer right away, I glanced down at his sweat shorts and saw the massive tent that told me his cock wanted me, even if he was trying to talk himself out of it.

I sat up from the bath, bubbles and water cascading down my breasts, and shoved down his shorts. He let me do it, glaring at me now. I didn't care, though. I was taking in the way he stood there, completely naked, chiseled like a Greek god with a pierced cock big enough for me to choke on. I loved how it stood to attention just for me, how the dark metal glinted in the light like it wanted to show off.

He shook his head as I crooked a finger and moved to the side of the tub that was against the wall. "This isn't a way to solve our problems."

"Our problem is that you're babying and pampering me, and I'm moping."

"It's not moping, it's coping. We've been over this, and you're allowed to have ups and downs, Lamb."

I nodded. I knew he was right. I knew that my depression would hit, and I wouldn't be able to smile sometimes. Today, though, I felt strong enough. I knew we'd get through anything, and I wanted to make sure he knew that too. "So are you. You can't be my savior every single time."

He rubbed the back of his neck. I could tell he was frustrated, trying to tamp down on his pain to deal with mine. "It's not about me. You need to be loved—"

I shook my head. "You would baby me for the rest of my life, Dante. I swear it—"

"I wouldn't regret a single moment of it either." He shrugged, turning toward the mirror and vanity behind him rather than stepping into the tub with me.

"If you don't get in here and fuck me without a look of sadness on your face, Dante, I swear I'll scream and cry all night." There. That was using all the words I wanted to.

The man did as he was told. He couldn't deny me even if he tried. We worked through my emotion that day in the way

I loved best. He fucked me like a man on a mission in that tub.

After, I stepped out of it smiling at him. He reached for me, and I jumped away. "Stop. Now, we really have to get ready."

The man's green gaze held mine for a second longer before he murmured, "I love you, Delilah Armanelli. I love your smile, your hair when it looks like I've fucked you into oblivion, and the blush on your tits when I say things like what I just said. I love how hard you tried before you tried hard not to try. I fucking love you. I know this has been challenging, but I wouldn't want easy with anyone else. I think you know all that, but I wanted to remind you."

Dante's vows had been just like this, so deep from his soul that I think everyone in the farm fields of our home, where we had the ceremony, had been crying.

"I love that you love me at my worst but enjoy me at my best, and I love that I can sometimes catch a glimpse of the worst in you, even if you've practically found a way to control every part of you and the world. We might be living through a hard part of life together right now, but I'm an overachiever, so we're going to get to easy if it's the last thing I do."

The smile that whipped across his face held me up on a cloud next to heaven for the rest of the night.

* * *

We grilled up the shrimp and fish before sitting around the bonfire. My mom, Mrs. Reid, Izzy, and I were going over updates on everyone while the guys argued over what was happening in the news.

"I'm sure they'll be closing down the mall this year," Mrs. Reid sighed as our conversations merged over the fire.

"Retail is dead." My brother, Dex, shrugged before he took

a sip of his beer.

"It is not!" My mother looked affronted. "I need to try on clothes before I buy them."

"I'm sure there will be small boutiques that stay open, Mom." Dom patted her shoulder. "Or I'll bring in a shopper for you, okay? Don't worry."

Dimitri mumbled that Dom was a momma's boy.

Dom stood up and chuckled. "I'm not just a momma's boy. I'd do the same for any of the Hardy girls. Izzy and Mom and ... well, Delilah. I guess Dante and I can fight over you some more with regard to your last name."

Everyone around the fire groaned. Dom had been pissed that I had even contemplated taking the Armanelli last name.

"She took my name, bro. It's done."

"We can undo that shit in a minute," Dom grumbled, glaring at my husband.

"Dom, are we really going to fight about this? It's been over a year." I rolled my eyes at the same time Izzy did.

Our gazes met, and she giggled. "Can you imagine? In twenty years, he's still going to be whining about it. Stop being a freaking baby, Dom. So your best friend married your sister. If not Delilah, I would have begged him to marry me."

I choked on my drink and laughed even harder as she fell on my shoulder and laughed with me. After a few late nights at a bar days after Dante proposed, where the bartenders poured us alcohol and we poured out our hearts to each other, our sister bond was stronger than that vibranium in *Black Panther.*

Izzy had shared that she needed me as much as I needed her. She'd been a constant, by my side nonstop the past two years, even moving into a condo down the street. She'd continued working for the government but had switched into data analysis and coding instead of undercover work.

"Just so we're clear, I would never have let my husband marry you." We kept laughing at our ongoing joke.

"You guys have had enough to drink," Dom grumbled.

"Not possible," Izzy sing-songed.

"Totally possible," Dante agreed with Dom.

"Even so," Izzy continued, "I think I'm right when I say you've always been a part of the family, Dante, and now we can officially say we're a part of each other's."

My dad, who always seemed like he was half-listening, raised his beer bottle and said, "Here, here."

Everyone raised their bottles and drank—except Dom, who glared at all of us. "Y'all are forgetting Dante omitted a lot of truths over the years."

"Not forgetting that at all." I pointed my bottle at him and spoke up before anyone else could. "I remember it daily, considering I went to jail and was basically kidnapped because of these two brats."

"But it got us here, right?" Izzy's hazel eyes sparkled just like mine when they were on the verge of happy tears. "And *here* is pretty damn close to perfection, Dom. So like I said before, stop being a baby. You already fought him more than once about it."

"I only got two good punches in."

"Can't help it if you can't fight, man," Dante grumbled, and his hand squeezed my thigh.

"Exactly." Izzy leaned forward in her Adirondack chair and narrowed her eyes at our brother. "You're not mad about them being together or him lying. You're mad about your pride being hurt by your best friend. Suck it up. At least you didn't shoot your shot with him and kiss him only for him to let you down easy!"

We were all laughing at Izzy giving Dom hell because we

knew she was over it, having moved on, and was back to dating again.

In the darkness behind us, I didn't expect a cold and vicious question to come out of nowhere. "You kissed him?" Cade hissed from the side of the house.

Izzy, who'd had her head on my shoulder, jumped about a mile out of her chair and whipped her head around.

Cade stalked over and glared down at her, his features brilliant in the night.

"Jesus, where did you come from? Were you watching us?" my sister whispered, like she couldn't believe he was there.

"I'm always watching, Izzy."

The fire snapped, and I swear the tension between them burned and crackled just as bright.

Cade didn't take his eyes off her as he murmured, "Dante, Delilah. Jet's ready to go."

"Tonight?" My gaze ping-ponged between Izzy and Cade before I lifted a brow at my husband. "I didn't pack."

"Maybe we should go pack, then." Dante smirked like he didn't care about anything else but crossing off the last thing on my list. I squealed and didn't think twice about the fact that I was leaving my family. This was for me and my husband. And I'd learned my family wanted what was best for us anyway.

We helped bring in some food, and Izzy followed me to the kitchen with some empty glasses while Dante cleaned the grill with Dom.

"I can't believe Cade just shows up at our bonfire like this." She stomped behind me.

"I think Dante probably called him," I pointed out.

She was on her own tangent. "And he's deliberately acting like my babysitter lately just because I'm still working for the government. Like I'm not good enough to take care of myself."

"Well, he probably wants to make sure you're safe, considering you're friends."

"Colleagues. Definitely not friends," she almost shouted at me, her eyes narrowed like she was ready to fight me about it.

"Noted," I grumbled as I set the food down.

I would also be noting that she seemed extremely emotionally charged when it came to Cade. That was for damn sure.

When I saw Cade quietly step in from the porch, I pointed behind me, said, "Gotta go to the bathroom, Izzy," and beelined it out of there.

Of course, as soon as I closed the door, I put my ear against it. I was a nosy twin sister and didn't care at all.

I heard the whisper-yelling start immediately from Izzy. "Don't sneak up on me in my parents' house, Cade."

"Hardly sneaking considering I stepped right in front of you."

"Whatever. This is a family party. You shouldn't even be here."

"Technically, Dante's family. Want to go as far as to say we're related too?"

"Oh my God. You're so annoying."

"If you think I'm annoying, quit the damn job and start working in corporate America."

"Those guys aren't done. You and I both know it. The drugs are a fucking cover for nuclear warfare, and I'm helping to bring them down."

"You're digging where you shouldn't be. And you're not half as good at it as you think. I've tracked every fucking hack you've done."

"Fuck off." My sister sounded seething mad.

"If you get kidnapped, I'm leaving your ass with them."

"Great. They'll probably be better company than you anyway."

"Say that again and try to mean it this time," he growled.

Jesus, they hated each other on a whole other level. Or wanted each other on that same level. I wasn't sure if they could decipher the blurry line anymore.

I flushed the toilet, and when I reentered, they were both gone and my husband stood there smiling. "Ready, Lamb?"

I took his hand and nodded.

We took a private jet owned by the Armanellis straight to Puerto Rico where we then hopped on a private ferry to an island where the bioluminescent water supposedly showed up the brightest.

Dante paddled us out in a transparent kayak, just the two of us. Even with the night so dark it could almost suffocate you in blackness, the water lit up and shined an awe-inspiring blue, sparkling to the point that it seemed to light up the whole sea. It was that eerie darkness, so heavy with the unknown that could scare so many, that made the brilliant light possible.

I looked at my husband at the front of that boat and said, "We get the darkness and the pain before we get the light of our heaven, huh?"

"That baby is coming, Lilah. You can count on it."

He was right.

Ten months later, I held our baby girl in our arms. She had her daddy's eyes and my hair. We didn't sleep for probably her whole first year with the way she screamed for me at night.

Dante had the audacity to sit up smiling with me as I breastfed and said, "Well, the nights are hell so we can have heaven with her all day."

My wolf was right about that too.

***

THE END

***

For additional content, including bonus scenes, sign up for Shain Rose's newsletter: shainrose.com/newsletter

CORRUPTED
CHAOS
USA TODAY BESTSELLING AUTHOR
SHAIN ROSE

My enemy doesn't make the rules behind closed doors ...
Even if he's my boss.

Cade Armanelli might be an infamous hacker with billionaire status who operates better alone, but I earned my spot working alongside him...
Whether he likes it or not.

It's precisely why I'm on the first plane to an undisclosed location for our cybersecurity team retreat. I'm ready to prove to our company that I can handle anything ...
Except sharing a cabin and a bed with my meticulous, elusive boss.

He's antisocial.
Ruthless.
Enemy number one.

Unfortunately, he's also number one in tatted, dark, and dangerous. I quickly come to find that not only are his hacking skills perfection, but so is his performance in the bedroom.

Not that it matters. I have a job to keep, a heart to protect, and our nation's data to secure.
Cade can't help me with any of that.
He's a distraction. One I have to avoid ...

Even if it means I'm spray painting a red line down our bed and keeping my boss on his side.

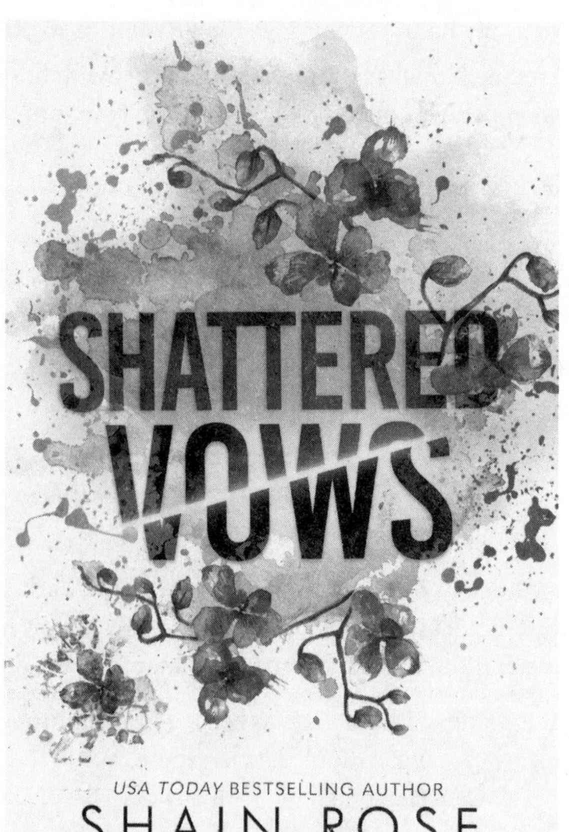
SHATTERED
VOWS
USA TODAY BESTSELLING AUTHOR
SHAIN ROSE